an experienced
g read."
—*...iver Life Magazine*

...pine, and a strong
—*...nd Times-Dispatch*

"...Adams makes Storyton Hall come to life . . . Readers will relish the way Ellery Adams weaves together books, mystery, and fantasy." —*Fresh Fiction*

"Book lovers are going to come for a visit and never want to leave . . . One fabulous story."
—*Escape with Dollycas into a Good Book*

"Adams has a new hit series on her hands . . . If you love cozy mysteries and books, this is the perfect series for you."
—*Girl Lost in a Book*

"Adams has skillfully crafted a fantastical world for bibliophiles, as well as a puzzling cozy mystery . . . [A] fabulous start to a new series." —*Book of Secrets*

D0035117

continued . . .

M1322AS0514

From *New York Times* bestselling author
Ellery Adams

MURDER *in the* MYSTERY SUITE

A Book Retreat Mystery

❦

Tucked away in the rolling hills of rural western Virginia is Storyton Hall, a resort catering to book lovers who want to get away from it all. To increase her number of bookings, resort manager Jane Steward has decided to host a Murder and Mayhem Week, where mystery lovers can indulge in some role-playing and fantasy crime-solving. But when the winner of the scavenger hunt, Felix Hampden, is found dead in the Mystery Suite, Jane realizes one of her guests is an actual murderer...

PRAISE FOR THE NOVELS OF ELLERY ADAMS

"Enchanting."
—Jenn McKinlay, *New York Times* bestselling author

"In one word—AMAZING!"
—*The Best Reviews*

elleryadamsmysteries.com
facebook.com/TheCrimeSceneBooks
penguin.com

M1509T0614

MURDER *in the* PAPERBACK PARLOR

Ellery Adams

BERKLEY PRIME CRIME, NEW YORK

BERKLEY
PRIME
CRIME

An imprint of Penguin Random House LLC
375 Hudson Street, New York, New York 10014

MURDER IN THE PAPERBACK PARLOR

A Berkley Prime Crime Book / published by arrangement with the author

ISBN: 978-0-425-26560-4

PUBLISHING HISTORY
Berkley Prime Crime mass-market edition / August 2015

PRINTED IN THE UNITED STATES OF AMERICA

10 9 8 7 6 5 4 3 2

Cover illustration by Shane Rebenshied.
Cover design by Diana Kolsky.
Interior map: © 2015 CW Designs by Carol Wilmot Sullivan. All rights reserved.
Interior text design by Tiffany Estreicher.

Penguin
Random
House

For my friends Maggie Tuckley and Beth Buckbee:

"It is more fun to talk with someone who doesn't use long, difficult words but rather short, easy words like "What about lunch?"—A.A. Milne, Winnie-the-Pooh

I declare after all there is no enjoyment like reading!
How much sooner one tires of any thing than of a book!

—JANE AUSTEN

WELCOME TO STORYTON HALL

Our staff is here to serve you

Resort Manager—Jane Steward
Butler—Mr. Butterworth
Head Librarian—Mr. Sinclair
Head Chauffeur—Mr. Sterling
Head of Recreation—Mr. Lachlan
Head of Housekeeping—Mrs. Pimpernel
Head Chef—Mrs. Hubbard

Select Merchants of Storyton Village

Run for Cover Bookshop—Eloise Alcott
Daily Bread Café—Edwin Alcott
Cheshire Cat Pub—Bob and Betty Carmichael
The Canvas Creamery—Phoebe Doyle
La Grande Dame Clothing Boutique—Mabel Wimberly
Tresses Hair Salon—Violet Osborne
The Pickled Pig Market—the Hogg brothers
Geppetto's Toy Shop—Barnaby Nicholas
The Potter's Shed—Tom Green

ONE

"You expect me to break that with my bare hand?"
Jane Steward, manager of Storyton Hall and mother of six-year-old twin boys, pointed at a piece of wood in disbelief.

"I certainly do," replied Sinclair, Storyton's head librarian. He was looking at Jane with the fixed stare he reserved for guests who made too much noise in one of the resort's reading rooms or had mishandled a book.

Storyton Hall had thousands of books, and Sinclair knew the location and condition of every volume. He cared for the books as though they were priceless treasures. And to those who worked and visited Storyton, that's exactly what they were. People came from across the globe to spend a few days in the stately manor house tucked away in an isolated valley in western Virginia. Surrounded by blue hills and pristine forests, Storyton Hall was heaven on earth for bibliophiles.

Jane glanced around and for a moment, nearly forgot that she was standing directly beneath the carriage house in a room that didn't appear on the official blueprints. In fact, only a few people knew of its existence. Like Sinclair, they used the practice space to hone their martial arts skills. Butterworth, the butler, was particularly fond of attacking the seventy-pound weighted bags hanging from the ceiling. Sterling, the head chauffeur, preferred to spar with nunchucks, and Sinclair's weapon of choice was a set of throwing knives he kept hidden inside a hollowed-out copy of *The Art of War*.

Not too long ago, Jane would have found the idea of practicing roundhouse kicks utterly ridiculous, but now, as she caught a glimpse of herself in the wall-length mirror, she knew that there was nothing amusing about her situation. It was also clear from Sinclair's expression that he expected her to break the board with her bare hand, and he expected her to do so without delay.

"It's easy, Mom! Fitz and I did it on our first try."

Displeased by the idea of being shown up by her sons, Jane frowned. "All right, I'm ready."

Sinclair held the rectangular piece of pine by its sides and braced himself for impact. "Check your stance," he ordered. "The power comes from your body. Whip your trunk around and you'll break the board without injuring your hand. Focus on a spot in the center of the board. See your hand going through the wood and continuing to move forward. Don't stop. If you think about stopping, you won't succeed. Lead with your palm, not your pinkie finger."

"Got it." Taking a deep breath, Jane trained her eyes on the board. She saw the grains in the wood and visualized the exact location she intended to strike. Raising her right arm, she pivoted her entire right side toward the back wall. Concentrating on whipping her hip and shoulder around as quickly as possible, she drove her hand, palm facing the ceiling, into the board. It parted with a satisfying crack, and a large splinter of wood flew past Jane's cheek and landed on the floor mat near Hem's feet.

He picked it up, tested its sharpness with his index finger, and promptly jabbed it into his brother's side.

"Ow!" Fitz howled and immediately retaliated by administering a front snap kick to his brother's wrist. The splinter came dislodged from Hem's hand and was snatched midair by Sinclair.

"What have I told you gentlemen about martial arts?" he asked, his voice steely with disapproval.

Hem dropped his gaze and tried to appear penitent. "We should only use it for self-defense."

"Or if our safety is . . . threatened," Fitz added, looking smug over having remembered the second half of the creed Sinclair recited at the end of every class. Too late, Fitz realized that he should have adopted a contrite expression as well.

"Next class, you two will drill the entire time while your mother learns a new kick." Sinclair turned to Butterworth, who'd just finished pummeling a practice bag. It was still jerking on the end of its chain as though it had been electrocuted. "Mr. Butterworth? Would you be so kind as to demonstrate a spinning hook kick?"

"Certainly," said Butterworth. He leaned forward, shifting his weight to his left leg. In a flash, he whipped his right leg around in a sweeping, one-hundred-and-eighty-degree arc. When he struck the bag with the ball of his foot, Jane was sure he'd knock it clean off its chain.

"You need to train until that kick is second nature," Sinclair said.

"Perhaps that kick should wait until after the Romancing the Reader week," Jane said. "I don't want to pull a muscle before the Regency Fashion Show. I'd be a poor representative of La Grande Dame if I limped down the catwalk in the gown Mabel toiled over for months."

Amusement glinted in Sinclair's eyes. "Ah, the fashion show. I'd nearly forgotten about that particular event— probably because every female under our roof can speak of only two subjects: the male cover model competition and the habits, interests, and whereabouts of Mr. Lachlan."

Taking the broken pieces of wood from Sinclair, Jane laughed. "Weeks before Lachlan first stepped foot on our property, you predicted that many ladies would fall in love with him."

Sinclair sighed. "Indeed I did. I also assumed that after two months, his allure would have dimmed somewhat. Obviously, I underestimated Mr. Lachlan's appeal." He shot her a sly glance. "How do you find him?"

Jane made a shooing gesture at her sons. "Run home and

change. If you get your chores done in time, I'll hand over your allowance before we drive to the village. A little bird told me that the Hogg brothers are hosting an indoor picnic lunch and special contest for all kids twelve-years-old and under. The winner will receive a new bicycle from Spokes and a gift certificate from the Pickled Pig."

The twins exchanged wide-eyed looks and raced off. Butterworth followed at a more dignified pace, his spine straight and his shoulders squared. Jane recognized that Butterworth was leaving his role of combat expert behind in favor of his butler persona and wondered if such a marked change came over her when she finished one of her training sessions.

I doubt it, she thought. *I'm still getting used to living a double life. Sinclair, Butterworth, and Sterling have been doing it for decades. And now, Lachlan has joined our secret circle.*

Once the sound of the boys' shouts and jostles faded, Jane finally answered Sinclair's question. "I find Lachlan a bit of an enigma. He's hardworking, courteous, and organized. He's also a master salesman. For such a quiet person, I'm amazed by his ability to talk people into sleigh rides and cross-country skiing ventures. Usually, wintertime means less business at the recreation desk, but not since Lachlan's arrival. He's certainly increasing our revenue."

"I'd hazard a guess that our female guests would happily risk losing the feeling in their extremities if it meant spending time with Mr. Lachlan." Sinclair flicked a switch on the wall and the practice bags began to rise to the ceiling. "Are you immune to that shy smile, that roughish hair, or those striking blue eyes?"

"He's quite attractive," Jane admitted. "But I have no real sense of him. He doesn't volunteer an ounce of personal information and he'd rather traipse through the woods than socialize with the rest of the staff. I know he's an outdoorsman, but I hadn't realized he'd be so . . . hermitlike."

Together, she and Sinclair walked to the door where they'd left their shoes and socks. Once their bare feet were covered and they'd bundled up in wool coats, Sinclair locked the door behind them. "Mr. Lachlan was an army ranger. He served on covert missions in both Iraq and Afghanistan. I was aware of his history before casting my vote in favor of hiring him. I don't think his past will impede his performance as head of recreation, and he's an excellent asset when it comes to guarding you and your family."

Sinclair hurried up the stairs, checked to see that the coast was clear, and waved for Jane to step through the narrow gap behind a workbench. After she was through, he pushed a button obscured by a rusty saw blade and the workbench swung back against the wall.

Jane had only learned about the surprising number of hidden rooms and passageways located around Storyton Hall and its outbuildings during the past few months. Until last October, she'd been completely ignorant of the fact that certain people she'd known her entire life were a part of a group called the Fins. These men had pledged to protect the members of the Steward Family with their lives. And since Jane had been born into a family that had been guarding a secret library and its treasures for centuries, she and her sons were also under the Fins' protection.

The first time Sinclair had led Jane to the attic turret and pushed open the door to the fireproof and temperature-controlled vault, Jane had nearly fainted. It wasn't every day that one discovered the existence of unpublished Shakespeare plays, gilt-covered Gutenberg Bibles, or the endings of famous, but incomplete novels. Treasures entrusted to the Stewards for all sorts of reasons—to keep them from being stolen, damaged during wartime, or sold on the black market.

There were also books deliberately kept from the public eye—radical works filled with disturbing and dangerous ideas. Jane had read a few lines from one of them and was shocked and angered by the author's proposition that women were vastly inferior to men. The author went on to encourage mass sterilization of any female lacking a genius IQ. Considering the book had been written by a prominent English scientist during the first stirrings of the women's emancipation movement, its publication could have crippled an entire gender.

After that unpleasant read, Jane had stuck to perusing the

secret library's incredible selection of rare fiction. A voracious reader since early childhood, it galled Jane that she didn't have enough free time to delve more deeply into the astounding collection stored in airtight containers in a nearly inaccessible room hundreds of feet from the ground.

It had taken Jane several weeks to reconcile herself to the fact that it was more important that she protect the library's contents than examine them. After all, to a lifelong book lover, the library was the Eighth Wonder of the World, and Jane referred to it as such when speaking to her great-aunt and -uncle or to the Fins.

Suddenly, the thought of her aunt made Jane start. She glanced at her watch and let loose a small cry. "I'm going to be late! Aunt Octavia will be furious if she doesn't get the best seat in the house for Edwin Alcott's soft grand opening."

Jane jogged around the building that had once served as the estate's hunting lodge. The lodge was so spacious that Jane's uncle had divided it into two residences. Sterling, the head chauffeur, lived in the front half while Jane and her sons inhabited the back. Jane loved the privacy this arrangement afforded her little family. She loved her side door entrance that led into her bright, cheery kitchen. She loved the open living room with its comfy sofas and book-lined walls. She loved her herb and flower gardens, which were protected from prying eyes by a tall hedge. Most of all, she loved how the house had seemed to open its arms to her after her husband's tragic death. A pregnant widow, Jane had returned to Storyton Hall in search of comfort and a fresh start. She'd found both within its walls and in the hearts of its people.

Now, bursting into her cheerful, yellow kitchen, Jane cast a longing glance at the coffeemaker and then bounded upstairs to change.

"Boys!" she hollered as she ascended. "I hope you're dressed. I also hope your beds are made. If that room's a mess, you'll get a smaller allowance."

Indignant cries came from behind the twins' closed door, and Jane knew they'd opted to put off their chores and were now regretting that decision.

"And I *will* be checking under your beds," she added for good measure as she hurried through her bathroom and into her small walk-in closet. "What to wear? What to wear?"

After selecting a pencil skirt in gray wool, a cowl-necked sweater, and a pair of riding boots, Jane fastened her strawberry blond hair into a loose chignon, added a pair of hoop earrings, and then dabbed on gardenia-scented perfume. Satisfied by what she saw in the mirror, she exited the bathroom and yelled, "Fitzgerald and Hemingway! Prepare for inspection!"

There was a crashing sound from the boys' room and when Jane pushed open the door, her twins cast guilty looks at the closet.

"We're ready, Mom!" Hem said, throwing his arms around her neck. "You smell nice."

"And you look pretty," Fitz chimed in.

Jane knew perfectly well that should she peek inside the closet, a cascade of toys, books, and dirty clothes would tumble out, but she was running too late to do anything about it. Glancing down at her sons, she tousled their hair and said, "I will delay the inspection until this afternoon in exchange for a kiss."

Because the twins were in the "girls have cooties" phase, Jane knew she was asking for a significant boon. After a brief hesitation, her sons gave her a quick peck on the cheek and then immediately held out their hands.

"Can we have our allowance now?" Hem asked. "Please?"

"I don't keep dollar bills in my boots. I'm not a—" Jane stopped herself before the word "stripper" rolled off her tongue.

Fitz cocked his head. "Not a what?"

"A walking bank," Jane said and ushered the boys downstairs.

Five minutes later, the trio arrived, red-cheeked and panting, in Storyton Hall's main lobby.

Aunt Octavia was already there, of course, looking regal in an indigo coat with a fur-trimmed collar, cuffs, and hem. She made a big show of examining her watch and then glanced across the room at the grandfather clock and muttered, "'I wasted time and now time doth waste me.'"

"I hope Mr. Alcott's café is a salubrious establishment," Butterworth said to Aunt Octavia as he held open the front door for their little party. "Mrs. Hubbard is most concerned that your healthy eating plan will be compromised."

Aunt Octavia glowered at the butler. "This has nothing to do with my diabetes. Mrs. Hubbard is just put out because she wasn't invited. She's a fine woman, but all she wants to do is gossip about the event to anyone passing through the kitchens of Storyton Hall."

Butterworth was smart enough to drop the subject. Instead, he informed them that their car was ready and wished them a pleasant lunch. No one would have guessed that the butler, impeccably dressed in his blue-and-gold Storyton livery with his hair neatly combed and his shoes polished to a high shine, had been mercilessly pummeling a practice bag earlier that morning.

The twins jumped into the back of a vintage Rolls-Royce Silver Shadow while Jane settled Aunt Octavia in the passenger seat. Behind them, Sterling was helping an elderly couple out of his favorite Rolls, a Silver Cloud II. He tipped his cap at Jane. She waved and then drove down the resort's long, tree-lined driveway.

At the end of the driveway, Jane slowed as the car approached the massive wrought-iron gates bearing the Steward crest—an owl clutching a scroll in its talons. The family motto, which could also be found on the guest room key fobs, had been inscribed in an arch-shaped banner over the owl's head.

Aunt Octavia pointed at the crest. "Let me hear our motto, boys."

"De Nobis Fabula Narratur," the twins replied, doing their best to pronounce the Latin words correctly. *"Their Story Is Our Story."*

Aunt Octavia smiled. "Excellent. When we get to the village, you may see what I have in my change purse. If you can count the coins correctly, they're yours. I hear that the Pickled Pig market has a marvelous display of Valentine's Day candy."

Jane glanced in the rearview mirror and saw a gleam appear in her sons' eyes.

"Speaking of Valentine's Day, are the preparations for Romancing the Reader complete?" Aunt Octavia asked.

"For the most part," Jane said. "Our guest of honor, Rosamund York, is being a bit of a nuisance."

Aunt Octavia didn't seem surprised. "She's a diva. Wants fresh roses in her suite each day. Will only drink a specific brand of spring water. Prefers not to mingle with her fans outside of her scheduled events. Her publicist sees to her every whim and handles all of Ms. York's communication. Am I getting warm?"

Approaching a sharp curve known as Broken Arm Bend, Jane reduced her speed. "You're spot on. How did you know?"

"Mrs. Pratt is a diehard Rosamund York fan. I had the misfortune of running into her at the bookshop. When I foolishly mentioned Romancing the Reader, she turned positively giddy. I've never seen a fiftysomething woman bounce in such a manner." She frowned. "It was rather disturbing."

Jane smiled. "Mrs. Eugenia Pratt is a devout fan of the entire romance genre. She reads three to four books a week, but I hadn't realized that she knew intimate details about her favorite authors as well."

"I'm sure she'd like to get *intimate* with the male cover models," Aunt Octavia said with a snort.

"What does 'intimate' mean?" Fitz asked.

"Being close to," Jane said as they entered the village. She pulled the car into the only vacant parking spot in front of the Pickled Pig and pivoted in her seat to address her sons. "Mr. Hogg is expecting you. Remember, he's providing you with lunch and will then introduce you to his new pet. You'll have a chance to enter the name-the-pet contest and afterward, you can fill a small bag with candy from the bulk bins." She held out a warning finger. "I expect you both to be on your best behavior. If I hear any unfavorable reports, I will hold your candy hostage until further notice."

The boys responded with the briefest of nods before Hem turned to Aunt Octavia. "Can we count your coins now?"

Aunt Octavia passed them her coin purse. "Just bring it into the market with you, my dears. I don't want to be any later for lunch than we already are."

Delighted, the boys jumped out of the car and ran into the market, nearly barreling into an older gentleman with a walker. Jane said a silent prayer that they wouldn't get into too much mischief and relocated the car to a spot in between Run for Cover, Eloise Alcott's bookstore, and Daily Bread, Edwin Alcott's new café.

Eloise must have been watching for them out the restaurant's window, because she whipped open the front door before Jane could reach for the handle. Jane's best friend was a lovely woman in her early thirties with chin-length dark hair that framed her heart-shaped face. Her gray eyes were kind and intelligent and she smiled often. She was devoted to Storyton Village, her customers, and the Cover Girls book club. One would expect her devotion to extend to her older brother, Edwin, as well, but Edwin and Eloise weren't exactly close. Edwin was a travel writer and had spent most of his adult life journeying around the globe. He could be impatient, blunt, and cryptic.

So naturally, Eloise was flabbergasted when her brother announced his intention to buy the failing café next door and completely transform the space in time for the Romancing the Reader week.

"You won't believe what Edwin's done," Eloise exclaimed as she ushered Jane and Aunt Octavia inside. "It's like entering another world. An exotic oasis right here in Storyton."

Eloise was right. When Jane entered the café, she gasped in wonder. Gone was the aging-diner look of the former establishment. The faded linoleum flooring had been replaced with dark rich hardwood and an assortment of kilim rugs. Chairs with wicker backs and plump ivory cushions were pulled up to hammered-copper tables. The walls were covered with antique maps and framed postcards. Potted palms stood like soldiers at regular intervals along the longest wall. At the back of the café, mosquito nets served as a divider between the main dining area and a lounge space. In this intimate alcove,

British Colonial chairs with animal print cushions were grouped around a black steamer trunk.

"Are we supposed to eat there?" Aunt Octavia gestured at the lounge area.

"It's a place for people to relax with a cup of tea or a smoothie. A conversation corner, so to speak," Edwin said, coming forward to greet his guests. He gave Aunt Octavia a deferential bow and then reached for Jane's hand. "I'm glad you could make it." He cast his gaze around the café, watching people take in little details that Jane had missed upon first glance, like the border of hand-painted tiles around the perimeter of the room, the antique birdcage, or the urn-shaped wall sconces. "What do you think?" he asked, turning back to Jane.

"It's wonderful," Jane said.

Edwin offered Aunt Octavia his arm. "May I escort you to the best seat in the house?"

Aunt Octavia inclined her head. After distributing menus to everyone, Edwin disappeared into the kitchen and a middle-aged man wearing a white linen shirt and linen trousers entered the dining room. He flashed them a bright smile from beneath a splendid moustache, introduced himself as Magnus, and declared that he'd be coming around with mango and cardamom smoothies for them to sip while they studied the menu.

Jane was delighted to find that all the sandwiches had been named after famous poets and were far more interesting than the dry roast beef and Swiss melts the previous owner had served. She found it difficult to decide which one to try first.

"I'm having the Rumi," Aunt Octavia declared. "You?"

"The Pablo Neruda."

The food was delicious. When Edwin came out of the kitchen to check on his customers, he was greeted by a burst of applause.

"You're going to be mobbed by all the romance fans next week!" Mrs. Pratt, another member of Jane's book club cried. The rest of the Cover Girls would have loved to be dining alongside Mrs. Pratt at this moment, but unfortunately, they had to work. "This setting is straight out of an

Elizabeth Peters novel. Are you a romantic, Mr. Alcott?"
Mrs. Pratt batted her lashes at Edwin.

"No," Edwin said. "That malady is for younger men."

"Come now," Mrs. Pratt pressed. "A man with such an
obvious appreciation for poetry must believe in romance."

"Lord Byron understood. He wrote, 'the heart will break,
but broken live on.'" Edwin smiled at Mrs. Pratt, but the
smile did not reach his eyes. "And now, if you'll excuse me,
I must see to the honey lavender crème brûlée."

As Edwin vanished into the kitchen, Jane wondered
who'd broken his heart. And when.

"Dark, brooding, and handsome. He's a modern-day
Heathcliff," Aunt Octavia said and then studied Jane. "You'd
do well to stay clear of that one. Heathcliffs don't make good
husbands or father figures for young and impressionable boys."

To her horror, Jane blushed. "What makes you think
Edwin Alcott ever crosses my mind?"

Aunt Octavia barked out a laugh. "I may be old, fat,
diabetic, and contrary, but I'm not blind. I've known men
like Edwin Alcott. Indeed, I have. They're trouble, Jane.
Trouble with a capital *T*."

"I had enough of that this past autumn," Jane said as the
server appeared with their dessert. "But Romancing the
Reader will be completely different than our Murder and
Mayhem week. We'll be hosting a company of ladies
devoted to happy endings. It'll be a lovely, festive, and har-
monious time. Not a single dead body in sight."

Daily Bread

SOUPS

The Robert Burns—cheddar and beer
The John Keats—chicken and wild rice
The Phillis Wheatley—sweet potato corn chowder

SALADS

The Robert Frost—tomato, watercress, and fennel
with lime vinaigrette
The Walt Whitman—fried green tomato with chipotle dressing
The Anna Akhmatova—roasted beet with mint and chèvre

SANDWICHES

The Homer—Greek salad on pita
The Dante Alighieri—prosciutto, smoked mozzarella,
and sun-dried tomatoes
The Pablo Neruda—Chilean beef or chicken, steamed
green beans, Muenster, hot peppers, and avocado
The Rumi—smoked turkey, sliced apple, and goat cheese
The Li-Po—shrimp and vegetable wrap, soy-laced mayo
The Emily Dickinson—egg salad with pickled celery
and Dijon mustard

DESSERT—CHEF'S CHOICE
(FOR THE ADVENTUROUS ONLY)

A selection of exotic teas or fruit smoothies can be enjoyed
in the main dining room or in the conversation area

TWO

Jane and the rest of the diners thanked Edwin for the excellent lunch and offered to pay for their meals, but he wouldn't hear of it, so the satisfied customers left generous tips for Magnus and filed out of the café. Jane knew word of Edwin's triumph would spread through the village before she and her family made it back to Storyton Hall.

Aunt Octavia, who'd savored every bite of her lunch, was wearing a self-satisfied smile. Jane suspected the expression had something to do with the two honey lavender crème brûlée desserts her great-aunt had polished off, but decided not to scold her for deviating from her diet. Mrs. Hubbard, Storyton's head chef, would have Aunt Octavia back on track by suppertime.

"Keep the motor running," Aunt Octavia said when Jane drove to the Pickled Pig to pick up the twins. "I don't feel like going inside just to see whatever bunny, bird, or rodent the Hogg brothers have adopted as their store mascot."

As it turned out, he was none of those animals. When Jane caught her first glimpse of the new pet sitting obediently in the center of a ring of children, his pink noise quivering in excitement and his curly tail wagging like a dog's, she laughed with pure delight.

"Mom!" Fitz cried when he saw her. "He's a pot-bellied pig! Isn't he awesome?"

Jane nodded. "He's splendid." She turned to her other son. "How was your lunch?"

"Fine." Hem only had eyes for the pig. "Mr. Hogg has been telling us all about his pet. He can take him on walks on a leash, and he says that pigs are super smart."

"Like Wilbur in *Charlotte's Web*," Fitz added.

At that moment, Tobias, the youngest of the three Hogg brothers, noticed Jane squatting next to her two sons.

"Hi, Ms. Steward. Feel free to get a little closer to our new pig. He's very fond of a good belly rub."

The children scooted out of the way and Jane knelt in front of the adorable animal. He grunted noisily as she scratched his pink skin, which was covered with strands of bristly hair. The pig nudged her palm with his trembling nose and rubbed up against her.

"The whole village is going to fall in love with this little guy," Jane said. "I look forward to hearing the winning name. Did all the kids enter the contest?"

"All the ones you see here and more." Tobias puffed out his chest with pride. Like his older brothers, he was a round man with fleshy cheeks and deep dimples. And though he resembled Rufus and Duncan Hogg in appearance, Tobias was as jolly as Saint Nick, while his brothers rarely cracked a smile.

No wonder they're bachelors, Jane thought, but she wished Tobias would find a nice woman. He was very fond of children and Jane judged he'd make a wonderful husband and father.

Suddenly, a matchmaking scheme popped into her head. "Have you heard about the Romancing the Reader event we're having at Storyton Hall?" she asked him. "It starts this Monday."

"That's why I took such care with the window display." Tobias gestured at the storefront. "I figured the ladies would be attracted to the heart-shaped boxes. I ordered all sorts of treats just for them, including some naughty conversation hearts." His cheeks reddened. "Of course, I wouldn't give those candies to my Valentine. I'd give her truffles. Homemade ones."

"I remember sampling yours at Christmas," Jane said. "How would you like to help Mrs. Hubbard with Tuesday's truffle workshop? We could use someone with your chocolate making skills, and it would be a great opportunity for you to tell the lovely ladies all about the Pickled Pig."

"Perhaps one of the single ladies will be looking for a man who'll treat her like a queen," Tobias spoke so softly that Jane was sure his hopeful words hadn't been meant for her ears. His eyes shining, he turned to her. "Count me in, Ms. Steward."

Jane told Tobias to check in with Mrs. Hubbard before Tuesday and then waved at the twins. "Come on, boys. Aunt Octavia's in the car and is probably annoyed that I've taken so long."

Hem held up the plastic baggie containing his selections from the bulk candy display. "Don't worry. If I give her a Tootsie Roll, she'll forgive us."

"But Mrs. Hubbard won't," Jane said and propelled her sons toward the exit.

With full bellies and several anecdotes to share with those back at Storyton Hall, the foursome drove home.

Jane let Butterworth escort Aunt Octavia into the lobby and then returned the Rolls to the garage. She told the boys they could take ten pieces of candy and whatever book they were currently reading to one of their hiding places. They had over a dozen scattered throughout the manor and outbuildings. Tapping the face of Hem's digital watch, she added, "You have an hour. After that, I *will* inspect your room, including the items you shoved in your closet."

Throwing promises over their shoulders, the twins dashed off to fetch their books. Jane headed into the kitchen, where she found Mrs. Hubbard decorating a cake.

"That looks heavenly. Is it for afternoon tea?"

Mrs. Hubbard finished forming a pale yellow rose and then straightened, surveying the beautiful confection with a critical eye. "This is a lemon layer cake with lemon curd and mascarpone. I thought it would complement the traditional sponge nicely."

"If I hadn't just had a smoothie, a sandwich, and dessert, I'd be drooling," Jane said. "And I'd better post a guard outside the Agatha Christie Tea Room or Aunt Octavia might try to sneak in and grab a slice of both cakes."

"No need to worry," Mrs. Hubbard assured her. "I made a low-sugar version of the Victoria sandwich for Ms. Octavia." She picked up another icing bag and began adding leaves to the roses. "Now, tell me all about Mr. Alcott's luncheon."

Jane knew she needed to ingratiate herself with Mrs. Hubbard before confessing that she'd invited Tobias Hogg to take part in the truffle workshop, so she shared every detail she could remember. While she was talking, one of the line cooks opened the back door for the UPS deliveryman.

Mrs. Hubbard, who'd been hanging on Jane's every word, suddenly held up a finger and frowned. "Again? I can scarcely believe it."

Setting the icing bag down, she wiped her hands on her apron and marched over to the delivery cart. Plucking a box from the top of the stack, she examined the label and shook her head. She then carried the box to her workspace and plunked it next to the cake.

"We have a mystery on our hands," she declared theatrically. "Our Mr. Lachlan has been receiving these unusual packages on a regular basis." She showed Jane the stamp on the top of the box. "They all come with the same warning: 'Perishable. Keep frozen,' and they're shipped by a company I've never heard of before."

Jane examined the address label. The box had come from a place called Indiana Trading, Incorporated. "These arrive often?"

"Regular as clockwork," Mrs. Hubbard said. "And Mr. Lachlan wants to be notified as soon as a package is delivered." She shrugged. "Mr. Lachlan is a charming man and I don't mean to imply that he's up to no good. I just can't help but wonder why the head of our recreation department needs perishable items in the dead of winter." She put a hand over her large, aproned bosom. "It's none of my business, but since you happened to be here . . ."

Mrs. Hubbard was clearly implying that while she was in no position to tear open other people's mail, the resort manager certainly had a right to do so. However, Jane had no intention of invading Mr. Lachlan's privacy. "I'll take a look at last month's expense report and see if this company has billed Storyton Hall. If so, I'm sure Mr. Lachlan can provide me with a reasonable explanation as to why he's ordering perishable goods."

She signaled to the line cook. "Roy, would you put this in the freezer, please?"

With the box gone, Mrs. Hubbard seemed to remember that she had yet to finish decorating the lemon cake. She glanced at the wall clock, blanched, and scooped up the icing tube. "Oh my! I've run my mouth and completely lost track of the time again!" Mrs. Hubbard hurriedly piped another green leaf and then began shouting frantic orders to her staff. They responded immediately, wearing knowing smiles and scurrying to obey.

Jane retreated from the kitchen, but not before snagging two chocolate madeleines from the cooling rack. She always helped herself to freshly baked treats to enjoy with her afternoon tea, but made a point of limiting them to a single scone, a thin slice of cake, or two cookies. Even with her new physical training schedule, which included martial arts, archery, and yoga, Jane didn't dare indulge in the afternoon tea bounty the way her guests did. After all, they were on vacation. She lived at Storyton Hall and needed to show restraint, especially when the weather turned warm and the Steward family took their tea on a table on the back terrace.

But spring seemed like a distant dream. The weather forecast had been warning of snow for days and the sky was tinged with the ghostly pink hue that often preceded a snowfall. Jane hoped the storm would come and go before Romancing the Reader began. As beautiful as Storyton's fleet of vintage Rolls-Royce sedans was, they weren't the best vehicles for navigating the icy mountains roads.

Fretting over the weather and a dozen other details concerning the forthcoming event, Jane headed to her cozy office.

She set her tea treat aside for later and focused on reading e-mails, reviewing next week's budget, and watching the radar map on her computer. According to the site, the snow would arrive that evening, dust the ground with half an inch of accumulation, and be gone by Sunday morning.

"I hope that's accurate," Jane said and then stared at the budget report. "If the ladies can't get to Storyton Hall on Monday, our bottom line will suffer a major blow."

Jane glanced at the corkboard hung on the wall opposite her desk. It featured orderly rows of construction paper in primary hues. Upon each piece of paper, Jane had written a long-term project goal. She referred to this display as her Hopes and Dreams Board and looked at it several times each day.

Gazing at the board, Jane wondered which project to pick first. "I doubt our guests would be overly impressed by roof repairs or the retiling of the Jules Verne pool." She moved her hand over the brown paper and the blue paper until it rested on the green paper. "They'd rather hear about the restoration of the orchard or the folly." She touched the purple piece next. "Or that we've opened a spa."

Silently vowing that she'd accomplish one of these major goals by the end of spring, Jane crossed a few more items off her to-do list. At three, she stopped for a tea break. As she sipped a cup of Earl Grey and ate her two madeleines as slowly as possible to prolong the pleasure, she called up the Romance Writers of America website and read the biographies of the authors who'd soon be coming to Storyton. When her teacup was empty, Jane went off in search of the twins.

She found Fitz and Hem exactly where she expected them to be: perched on stools in the kitchen. Judging by their chocolate moustaches and the clump of white stuff in Fitz's hair, Mrs. Hubbard had treated them to hot cocoa with mini marshmallows. Catching sight of their mother, the boys each gave Mrs. Hubbard a quick hug and then dashed outside.

"I think they just remembered that I'm about to inspect their room," Jane said.

Mrs. Hubbard laughed and took the kettle off the stove.

With the tea sandwiches, scones, cakes, and cookies safely arranged in the Agatha Christie Tea Room, Mrs. Hubbard could relax for a few moments until she began prepping for the dinner service. She always took her break between three and four o'clock so she could visit with the twins. Like Aunt Octavia, she doted on them terribly. While Aunt Octavia bought them books, puzzles, crafts, comics, and anything else that might spark their imaginations, Mrs. Hubbard spoiled them with food. It wasn't all unhealthy, and Jane had entered the kitchen many a time to see the boys snacking on ants on a log, grape caterpillars, cheese cube towers, coral fish made of shaved carrots and cucumbers, or palm trees with banana slice stems and kiwi leaves.

Jane glanced at the two smudges of chocolate on Mrs. Hubbard's apron and smiled. There was no one like Mrs. Hubbard, just like there was no one like Butterworth, Sterling, Sinclair, or the other people of Storyton Hall who'd become like family to Jane. Mrs. Hubbard poured water over her tea leaves and then smiled back, as though she understood exactly what Jane was feeling.

"Oh, I nearly forgot!" Mrs. Hubbard exclaimed. "Ms. Octavia mentioned that you were in charge of dessert for your book club tonight. I know how busy you've been trying to get everything ready for Monday, so I made it for you."

Jane gaped. "You shouldn't have! You have too much on your plate already. Excuse the cliché, but it's true."

"The cake's on the pantry shelf in a bakery box," Mrs. Hubbard said. "It's devil's food cake. It was Ned's idea, actually. He knows that your club is reading titles starting with the letter *D*, and last time he was babysitting the twins, he spotted a book called *The Devilish Duke* in your living room, so he suggested I make a devilish dessert." Mrs. Hubbard flashed Jane an impish grin over the rim of her teacup. "*The Devilish Duke* sounds like the type of novel that could produce a very lively discussion."

Jane recalled the scene she'd recently read and blushed. It had taken place in the duke's stagecoach after he'd carried off the chambermaid from the neighbor's estate and ravished her on the way back to his manor. The scene had been very, very descriptive.

After thanking Mrs. Hubbard again, Jane took her cake and hurried home.

That evening after supper, Fitz and Hem slung duffel bags over their shoulders and headed outside with a lantern. They were having a sleepover with Aunt Octavia and Uncle Aloysius and Jane knew they couldn't wait to play with the model train set Uncle Aloysius had set up on the floor in his office.

Jane walked her sons to the back terrace and kissed them good night before hurrying home to tidy the kitchen and living room.

She'd barely wiped an unidentifiable dried puddle of sticky stuff off the coffee table when the doorbell rang.

"Come in!' Jane called.

Three Cover Girls spilled into her house, trying to escape the bite of the February air. Because all the ladies lived in Storyton Village, they carpooled to their book club meetings. This way, most of them could enjoy whatever themed cocktail Anna Shaw had concocted.

Anna, who worked as an assistant pharmacist, was the first to come inside. She hung her parka on the coat rack by the front door and scooted out of the way to make room for Violet Osborne, the proprietor of Tresses Hair Salon.

"I washed my hair thirty minutes ago and I swear the damp parts froze on the car ride here," Violet said, carrying a covered dish into the kitchen.

Phoebe Doyle, who ran the Canvas Creamery, an art gallery combined with a frozen custard shop, touched the knit cap covering most of her head. "Our mothers always warned us not to go out in wintertime with wet hair."

"I'll just sit by the fire until the rest of our party gets here," Anna said after giving Jane a hug. "It won't take long to mix up our Devilish Duke cocktail."

"Did someone mention tonight's drink?" asked Betty Carmichael as she stepped into the house and beckoned for Eloise and Mrs. Pratt to hurry up and shut the door. "I could do with something to warm my bones."

Mrs. Pratt snorted and began unwinding a very long scarf from around her neck. "Why didn't you toss one back at the Cheshire Cat before we picked you up? After all, you own a pub."

Betty looked appalled. "Bob and I never imbibe during our shifts. It would be unseemly."

Phoebe shrugged. "I eat my own frozen custard all the time. And I have at least two espresso drinks a day."

"That's different," Betty said. "If I made a habit of sampling our wares, I'd end up serving Cosmos to Rufus Hogg and pints of dark ale to Pippa Pendleton."

Everyone laughed at the thought of the oldest Hogg brother sipping Cosmos.

"Let me near that oven, ladies!" cried Mabel Wimberly, who owned La Grande Dame Clothing Boutique and sewed all of Aunt Octavia's dresses. Though she specialized in clothing for plus-sized woman, she could create garments for people of any size or shape.

Jane followed Mabel to the oven. "What's in the casserole dish?"

"Beef and vegetable ragout," Mabel said. "It was the duke's favorite meal."

"We can sop up the extra gravy with my Bath buns." Phoebe touched the basket she'd set on the counter. "I made them with lots of butter and caraway seeds."

Mrs. Pratt leaned over, sniffed the basket, and moaned. "Smells delicious. I brought mashed turnips."

Violet, who wasn't overly fond of vegetables, grimaced. "I made a spiced pear compote."

"Becky and I thought a cheese board would go nicely with our cocktails," Eloise said, turning to Anna. "But that might depend on what mysterious concoction we're having. So far, all I know is that it's a lovely shade of pinkish red."

By this time, Anna had abandoned her seat by the fire to mix and pour drinks into the martini glasses Jane had purchased specifically for the book club meetings. "Fruit, cheese, and crackers will complement my Devilish Duke very nicely. This drink is two ounces of champagne, two ounces of Stoli Strasberi vodka, a few splashes of pineapple juice, and a thimbleful of daiquiri mix. I tried to create a cocktail that represented both the duke and the heroine, Venus Dares."

"This looks divine!" Mrs. Pratt exclaimed. "Do tonight's toast, Jane, so we can have a sip without further delay."

Jane raised her glass. "Mark Twain said, 'There is a charm about the forbidden that makes it unspeakably desirable.'" She picked up her copy of *The Devilish Duke* and smiled. "To forbidden love and rebellious women."

"Hear, hear!" her friends shouted and drank.

"And to saying farewell to the letter *D*," Phoebe added.

The Cover Girls, who'd been moving backward through the alphabet for the past two years, spent six to eight weeks on each letter. Voracious readers all, they'd already plowed through Bram Stoker's *Dracula*, Charles Dickens's *David Copperfield,* Veronica Roth's *Divergent*, Anne McCaffrey's *Dragonsinger*, and *Don Quixote* by Miguel de Cervantes. Rosamund York's *The Devilish Duke* was the last novel they'd discuss before setting their sights on books beginning with the letter *C*.

Unsurprisingly, the racy Regency romance had been Mrs. Pratt's pick.

"I adored *The Devilish Duke*," Mrs. Pratt said. "The duke was such a loveable scoundrel. And while it's hardly unusual to find a dark, brooding, and alluring man in a Regency romance, it *is* rare to encounter a female protagonist with as much pluck as Venus Dares."

Betty headed into the living room and took a seat on the sofa. "Out of curiosity, I did a little research on Ms. York's books." She ticked them off on her fingers. "In addition to *The Devilish Duke*, she's also written *The Bold Baron*, *The Cunning Count*, *The Naughty Knight*, *The Enticing Earl*, *The Mischievous Marquess*s, *The Rakish Royal*, and *The Lusty Lord*. Miss Dares appears in every novel and, according to the reviews I perused, readers genuinely love Venus. There are over twenty fan websites devoted to her."

"I don't think many 'well bred' women in the Regency era spoke their minds as freely as Venus," Violet said. "They were supposed to be demure—to sit with their ankles crossed, work on their embroidery, and keep their opinions to themselves."

Mabel rolled her eyes. "How boring. I'm with the rest of Ms. York's fans. I loved Venus. She has her own money, her own sizeable household, expresses radical ideas, and was given an education similar to a nobleman's."

"Even her name defies convention," Anna said.

Eloise nodded. "Miss Venus Dares. A surname that doubles as a verb. Venus *dares* to read subversive books, she *dares* to pursue equality for women, and she *dares* to speak her mind to any member of the nobility. And who could forget when she *dared* to enter the duke's bedroom unannounced and caught him in a rather compromising position with a lady from a nearby estate?"

"That was my favorite scene," Mrs. Pratt whispered, her eyes shining over the memory. "I felt like a voyeur. It was deliciously scandalous. I read that part just before turning in for the night and when I woke up at one in the morning, I couldn't tell if I was having hot flashes or had been dreaming of that scene."

"You're incorrigible." Mabel nudged Mrs. Pratt in the side. "Don't ever change."

Since her friends had drifted into the living room, Jane carried in the cheese board and set it on the coffee table. "I know we're meant to admire Venus, but I sensed a hollowness in her. I read an interesting article in *Romantic Times* about York's famous and much beloved heroine. According to the backstory provided in the first book in the series, *The Bold Baron*, Miss Dares is a specialized matchmaker. She's an upper-class spinster who once suffered a terrible heartbreak and vowed to never marry. Instead, she makes matches among the nobility. Her forte is "taming" the self-proclaimed bachelors. Often these men are gamblers, layabouts, and womanizers. But she finds the right woman—a strong, loving, good woman—to change their wicked and hedonistic ways. And by the end of each novel, the man has fallen in love with the woman Miss Dares has put in his path. There's a huge wedding, Miss Dares collects a big fee, and the story ends with Miss Dares setting out on an exotic vacation or returning to her estate. She never gets involved with anyone herself, and fiercely guards her independence."

"She's a romance heroine who doesn't yearn for romance," Eloise said, looking pensive. "I know we're discussing a work of fiction, but I can't help wonder about Rosamund York's love life."

"It has to be more exciting than mine!" Anna declared and all the women laughed.

Tantalizing aromas drifted in from the kitchen. Phoebe sniffed, checked her watch, and went to the other room. She placed her rolls on a cookie sheet, and slid the tray into the oven. The scent of buttery bread mingled with that of garlic and roasted meat.

Eloise turned to Mrs. Pratt. "You're our romance aficionado. I bet you know more about Rosamund York than the average reader."

Mrs. Pratt preened. "It so happens that I do. About five years ago, I attended a fan conference. Ms. York's third book had just been released to rave reviews and soared to the top of *every* bestseller list. She was in attendance at this particular conference to accept an award and disappeared well before the banquet was over. You see, Ms. York is an enigma. Very few details about her personal life are in circulation. Believe me, I've searched the farthest corners of cyberspace."

Jane could sense Mrs. Pratt's frustration. To a woman who lived for gossip, it must have been terribly irksome to not have access to scintillating rumors about one of her favorite authors. "Maybe her reclusive nature actually helps sell books."

Mrs. Pratt considered this possibility. "I think she's reclusive for a reason, and though I don't know what that reason is, I bet Georgia Dupree does."

Violet arched her brows, revealing the sparkly lilac shadow on her eyelids. She always wore a shade of purple somewhere on her person. Tonight, she was bundled up in a cozy lavender cardigan and had a scarf the color of amethysts wrapped around her neck. "Georgia Dupree's famous too. I see her books all over. Are she and Ms. York friends?"

"I should say not!" Mrs. Pratt nearly shouted. "I happened to share an elevator cab with those two. They didn't even look at each other until everyone else got out. It was only the three of us left, but I was way in the back and I don't think either lady knew I was there." She paused for dramatic effect.

Mabel nudged her again. "Don't leave us hanging! Get to the point before the meat in the oven turns into leather."

That was all the encouragement Mrs. Pratt required. "Ms. Dupree turned to Ms. York and said, 'I am going to show the world what a charlatan you are. And when I'm done, no one will ever buy a novel bearing the name Rosamund York again.'"

"How did Ms. York respond?" Betty asked breathlessly.

"She laughed. Quite derisively, I might add. It made Georgia Dupree furious," Mrs. Pratt said. "At that moment, we reached Ms. York's floor. The doors opened. And before Ms. Dupree disembarked, she got very close to Ms. York and, in a voice that sounded like an angry hiss, said, 'So help me, I will take my *rightful* place at the top—even if I have to kill you to do it.' And then, she got out and the doors closed."

Mrs. Pratt blinked, as though coming out of a daze.

Anna whistled softly. "Both of those writers are coming to Storyton for Romancing the Reader. They'll be under one roof for an entire week."

"It sounds like things could turn ugly. I hope you placed those two on separate floors," Phoebe said as Eloise gave Jane's arm a comforting squeeze.

"I gave Rosamund York the best room in the resort." Jane groaned unhappily. She put her face in her hands and mumbled, "The last thing I need is to stumble upon the dead body of a bestselling author in the Romance and Roses Suite."

Mrs. Pratt rubbed her hands together in undisguised glee. "This promises to be an exciting seven days. Oh, whoever thinks life in Storyton is uneventful has never attended one of your theme weeks, Jane!"

THREE

The snow began falling soon after the Cover Girls left.
When Jane woke the next morning to the sound of the boys squabbling over which cartoon to watch, the world outside her window was covered with a veil of shimmering white. The pristine snow, lit by the waking sunbeams, winked like polished glass, and since Storyton's guests had yet to venture outside, the lawns and curving paths were undisturbed. All was hushed, save for a few birds flitting among the tree branches. Jane took a long moment to savor the stillness and then went downstairs to restore peace between her sons.

Afterward, she made breakfast and then lounged around in her pajamas, drinking coffee and reading. Just before noon, she called Eloise and told her to wish Edwin luck with his official grand opening.

"Tell him yourself. He's pacing the floor like a caged panther. He looks like one too. His hair's wild and his eyes are dark and ferocious. Don't glare at me, Edwin. It's true."

There was a scuffling noise on the other end and then Edwin came on the line. "Hello, Jane."

The way he spoke her name gave Jane a little thrill. "I

just wanted to say break a leg or whatever is said to convey best wishes in the restaurant industry."

"I'm grateful for the support," he replied and then paused. "It's good to hear your voice . . . You have the ability to calm people, Jane."

There it was again. The sound of her name was like a breath of summer wind. Her cheeks growing warm, Jane smiled into the phone. "The café is already a success. I plan on being a regular."

"I hope so," Edwin said. "We didn't get the chance to talk much yesterday. I'd like to make that up to you by cooking you a meal after hours one night."

Jane's heart tripped. "That would be lovely."

Jane replayed her brief conversation with Edwin many times that day. Fitz and Hem, who caught her staring into space on several occasions, exchanged befuddled glances. Deciding their mother was coming down with something, the boys kept their distance. After a supper of beef stew and cornbread followed by several rounds of Chutes and Ladders—all of which Jane lost—Jane told the twins to get ready for bed and popped her beloved *Pride and Prejudice* DVD out of its case. Catching sight of the cover, which featured Colin Firth as Mr. Darcy, the boys groaned and hurried upstairs to read comic books.

When Sunday dawned, the snow was already reduced to semi-translucent patches tucked under bushes or shadowy eaves. The Stewards went to church and shared a large mid-day meal at Jane's house. That afternoon, Jane and the twins waited for Lachlan to take them to their archery lesson.

During the fall, Sterling had overseen their lessons, but with the onset of the cold weather, his chauffeur duties had kept him too busy. Jane missed chatting with him on the drive to the Robin Hood Range. Lachlan wasn't much on small talk.

"When spring comes and the guests start renting bicycles again, I'll take over for Mr. Lachlan," Sterling had told her in November. "That'll free Lachlan to focus on your survivalist training."

Recalling this conversation, Jane frowned. "I can't begin to imagine what that means. Will we have to eat bugs? I don't want to eat bugs. I don't want to practice archery today either. It's freezing. I'd much rather build a nice fire, curl up on the sofa, and read." Muttering crossly to herself, she pulled on her heaviest wool sweater.

Downstairs, Fitz and Hem were raring to go. The boys, who were never troubled by the cold, had turned their archery lessons into a competition. Hem carried a little note-book in his coat and was secretly keeping score of their shots. At this point, Fitz was more accurate at short distances while Hem had been able to hit a target at sixty meters. Jane was better than both of them, but felt that it was unnecessary to devote much time practicing seeing as she was unlikely to take down an intruder with a bow and arrow.

She'd just zipped up her parka when Lachlan knocked on the door. "Ready?" He smiled the shy smile that enchanted the majority of Storyton's female staff.

"I hope this activity is the stress reliever you promised it to be," Jane said while gesturing at the twins to hop into the cargo bed of the ATV. "With hundreds of guests descending on the resort tomorrow, my mind is all over the place."

"You'll have to focus so intently that everything else will fade away," Lachlan said. He waited for Jane to climb into the passenger seat and then handed her a thermos. "Very hot, very strong coffee. I wouldn't drink it now. You could burn yourself if we hit a bump."

Jane had no doubt of that. Unlike Sterling, who drove the Gator at a steady pace, Lachlan pushed the vehicle to its maximum speed. He seemed to revel in the bouncy ride. The twins did too. Channeling King Kong or Tarzan, they clung to the Gator's metal frame and howled wildly.

Lachlan rarely spoke during the trip to the range. His sea blue eyes stared straight ahead and a lock of his brown hair flapped over his knit cap like a sparrow's wing. Jane shot him a sidelong glance just as a ray of sun lit the lock, burnishing it reddish gold.

"Were you a redhead when you were little?" she asked, holding on for dear life as he accelerated around a bend in the path.

Lachlan nodded. "I was."

"Do you have brothers?" Fitz asked. "Did they have red hair too?"

Lachlan braked in front of the archery shed and turned to Fitz. "It's just me and my parents now. But when I was in the army, I had dozens of brothers." A shadow of pain appeared in his eyes and he quickly glanced away. "Let's get our gear. Today's lesson is going to be challenging."

For the first thirty minutes of the lesson, Lachlan had them each remove an arrow from their quiver, nock it as quickly as possible, and pull back their bowstrings as though they meant to fire. However, they weren't allowed to loose their missiles.

Using a stopwatch to monitor their progress, Lachlan made them repeat the loading maneuver over and over. Just when Jane felt like her left arm was about to snap in two from the strain of keeping the nocked arrow perfectly aligned with the center of the target, he told them to lower their weapons and rest for a moment.

"At this point, you're probably tired and sore," he said, and his pupils moaned in assent. "Good. Because danger rarely comes along when you're fully prepared to meet it— when you've had eight hours of sleep, a balanced meal, and are dressed in warm, comfortable clothes." A hard glint appeared in his eyes. "Take off your coats."

Jane, who could barely feel her fingertips, glared at Lachlan. "Excuse me?"

"Miss Jane," Lachlan said, addressing her as the other Fins did. "This drill is necessary."

Scowling at him, she unzipped her parka and dropped it on the brittle grass. The twins did the same.

"Your muscles hurt," Lachlan began. "You're cold. You're probably hungry. Soon, you'll start shivering. You'll begin to think of the things you'd rather be doing at this moment."

"Like drinking hot cocoa!" Hem yelled through chattering teeth.

Ignoring the outburst, Lachlan pointed across the range at their targets. "You're miserable, but that doesn't matter now. The bad guys are there! Look! They're coming for you. They're standing right in front of your targets. Load and fire! *Now!* Use every arrow in your quiver. Load again! Fire!" He ran behind them, shouting, "*Come on!* They're getting closer! *Fire! Fire!*"

Jane immediately responded to the urgency in Lachlan's voice. She no longer saw the hay-stuffed target, but a man in dark clothes. She pretended that the man wanted to hurt her family. He was a dangerous criminal bent on stealing treasures from Storyton's secret library.

I'll stop you, Jane thought. Reaching over her right shoulder, she loaded an arrow, whipped the bowstring backward until it grazed her cheek, and then released. Without waiting to see if the missile had struck its mark, she reached behind her and nocked another arrow. She repeated the movement until she was out of arrows. Only then did she lower her weapon. She stood, panting in exertion, and reminded herself that this was just an exercise. Her boys were safe. The library was safe.

She glanced over at Lachlan. Their eyes met and held. And then he nodded, as though he understood that she needed a few seconds to let go of the dark fantasy she'd conjured.

"I guess we'd be dead," Fitz murmured unhappily.

"Yeah," Hem agreed and directed an accusatory glare at Lachlan. "We can't hit anything when we're shooting that fast."

Lachlan strode over and placed a hand on Hem's shoulder. "This was your first try, Master Steward. You and your brother did very well."

"But we totally missed the target," Fitz argued.

"That's not as important as the fact that you both kept your cool. You stayed calm and kept loading and firing. You never lost focus." Still holding Hem's shoulder, he moved closer to Fitz and gave the frowning boy a pat on the back. "The accuracy will come with time and practice. You passed a hard test today and proved that you're made of tough stuff."

"What about Mom?" Hem asked. "Is she tough too?"

Lachlan pointed at Jane's target. "What do you think?"

Noticing the three arrows embedded in the hay, the boys gasped. "She got him!" they cried. "She got the bad guy!"

"I think she deserves some coffee, don't you, gentlemen?" Lachlan smiled at Jane, and she smiled back. It was the first time she felt a real connection to him.

Perhaps one can only get to know him bit by bit. A few words here. A smile there. I'll have to be patient, she thought.

The three archers were simultaneously weary and exhilarated. After they'd donned their coats again, Lachlan told Jane to sit in the Gator while he and the boys put the equipment away. By the time they were done, Jane was ready to go home and spend an hour reading in front of the fire.

When Lachlan pulled in front of their cottage, Jane thanked him for the lesson and asked if he'd like to come in for a cup of tea.

"Thanks, but I can't," he said. "I have things to see to before tomorrow."

He waited for the boys to leap out of the cargo area and then drove off without another word.

The next morning, Jane dressed in a blush-colored skirt suit, swept her strawberry blond hair into a loose chignon, and practically shoved the twins out the door and around the house to the garage where Sterling was waiting.

"Are you sure you have time to drop them at school?" she asked the head chauffeur.

"I can get them there before the bell rings and be at the train station with five minutes to spare," Sterling assured her. "I'll be making the forty-five minute drive over the mountain many times today." He tipped his cap. "We have a full house, Miss Jane."

"Music to my ears," she said.

As Jane walked up the path in the weak February sunshine, she pictured the steady stream of Rolls-Royce sedans carrying world-worn visitors to the resort. She could easily imagine the moment when the guests caught their first glimpse of Storyton Hall. She could almost hear them gasp as they took in the sprawling stone manor house. They'd stare, wide-eyed with wonder, at the mammoth clock tower rising into the sky against a backdrop of blue hills. They'd see how the manor's two wings stretched out like open arms—how the whole structure, from its large windows to the sweeping front staircase, appeared to be welcoming them.

Humming in contentment, Jane entered the hall and strode down the main corridor. She inhaled the scent of lavender beeswax and noted that the silver vases on every hall table were bursting with multicolored blooms. Jane paused outside the Agatha Christie Tea Room to examine a stunning arrangement of red French tulips, holly, and winterberry.

"Tom Green has been here," she said, looking around for the owner of the Potter's Shed. She found him in the lobby putting the finishing touches on the biggest arrangement in the entire resort. Butterworth stood nearby, a tray of crystal champagne flutes at the ready awaiting the arrival of the first guests.

"Good morning, gentlemen!" Jane called merrily.

Butterworth returned the greeting with a stiff bow. Tom, on the other hand, looped his thumbs under his suspenders and gave them a satisfied snap. "I can't thank you enough for suggesting that your lady guests order romantic bouquets for their rooms. I thought I'd be lucky to get ten orders of my Smoldering Rose or Cupid's Carnation arrangements, but I received dozens." His smile widened and dimples appeared in his round cheeks. "Dozens!"

"That's splendid, Tom." She gestured at the rolling cart of florist tools. "But how are you managing all the extra work?"

Tom adjusted a white lily before answering. "Valentine's week is my busiest time of the year, so I hire a few retirees to help run the shop and handle residential deliveries."

"Everything must be working out or you wouldn't look so jolly." Jane stepped back and admired the centerpiece.

Tom had filled a porcelain jardinière with roses, lady slipper orchids, parrot tulips, nerine lilies, and greenery. The effect was breathtaking.

"I poached a floral designer from a grocery store over the mountain. She's been such an asset that I might offer her a full-time job."

Jane smiled inwardly. People from Storyton referred to outsiders as being from "over the mountain." It was usually not meant as a compliment. Even though the locals frequented businesses and medical facilities in other towns, they only did so when absolutely necessary. They'd chosen to live and work in Storyton because it had no strip malls, neon signs, or cookie-cutter neighborhoods. In their little village, things moved slowly. For the most part, people walked or rode bicycles. They waved to one another. They had leisurely chats over garden gates and made chicken soup when a neighbor came down with a cold. Jane couldn't imagine living anywhere else.

Leaving Tom to his work, Jane headed to her office. She tried to focus on mundane tasks but was unable to concentrate. Again and again, her gaze traveled to her Hopes and Dreams board. When she couldn't sit still another second, she left her office and stepped into the room across the hall. The space was crammed with a massive copier, multiple fax machines, file cabinets, and a bank of monitors showing live feeds from spots all around the resort.

Jane peered at the screen showing the front entrance and smiled. Two Silver Shadows had pulled up to the curb and guests were exiting the vehicles. The first guest caught Jane's notice because she looked like a movie star arriving at a premier. A mane of platinum hair cascaded over the shoulders of her winter-white coat and her bright red lipstick matched the red dress peeking out from beneath the coat's hem. After gesturing languidly at a bellhop, she mounted the stairs. A second woman scrambled up the steps and grabbed the blonde's arm. Jane watched, intrigued, as the blonde lowered her enormous sunglasses and peered at the

Rolls-Royce in line behind their own. After a brief pause, she raised her arm and waved regally.

"Rosamund York has arrived." Jane allowed herself a small sigh of relief. Ms. York was the event's headliner. Without her, Romancing the Reader wouldn't have had the same appeal. Fans devoted to Regency romance novels had made the majority of the week's bookings. Many of these ladies were also coming to Storyton to see Rosamund York as well. Jane was eager to discover why Ms. York held such a powerful allure.

Rosamund and her fellow passenger disappeared from the screen and, half a minute later, another woman came into view. Jane assumed this was the woman Rosamund had been waving to.

"It's Georgia Dupree," Jane murmured.

Georgia's trademark red curls were unmistakable. Unlike Rosamund, who wore the self-satisfied expression of one who has achieved a notable measure of fame and fortune, Georgia's mouth was set in a deep frown and she stomped up the stairs as though she were marching to battle.

Perhaps she is, Jane thought and felt a momentary pang of sympathy for the romance writer. Although Georgia Dupree had achieved a great deal of success in her own right, Jane imagined it would be difficult to remain in another author's shadow year in and year out.

"If Rosamund York is the First Lady of Romance, then what does that make Georgia Dupree? A lady in waiting?"

Jane returned to her office and grabbed a compact from her desk drawer. Satisfied that her hair was still in place and that she didn't have lipstick on her teeth, she gave her suit jacket an officious tug and emerged behind the reception desk. She found Sue Ross, one of Storyton's best clerks, engaged in conversation with Ms. York.

Sue was always on duty whenever important guests checked in. Not only was she adept at remembering Storyton Hall's repeat customers but she also had a way of appeasing the prickliest guests. Her kind face and soothing voice put people at ease. She was also an excellent listener and held people's eyes while they were speaking, making it clear that she cared about what they had to say. Jane was thankful to have her manning the desk today.

"You must get comments like that all the time, but it's true," Sue was saying to Ms. York.

The romance writer smiled prettily. "I never tire of hearing how Venus has had a positive impact on women. She's touched people across the globe, even in this delightful little hamlet." Ms. York gestured at her companion. "This is Taylor Birch, my publicist. I believe she has a few items to review with you. Do you mind if I pop up to my room while she handles the sundry details? I was so inspired during the drive here that I want to jot down some ideas before they flit away like butterflies."

Jane stepped forward and introduced herself to Rosamund and Taylor. "I'll grab your key posthaste, Ms. York. I'm sure you'd like some time to yourself before your fans arrive."

"You understand me completely," Rosamund said gratefully.

She doesn't act like a diva, Jane thought as she removed the brass key to the Romance and Roses Suite from the key case. "Here you are. Room 402. This is one of our tower rooms. It commands breathtaking views of the mountains and will hopefully continue to inspire you. Billy will see to your bags. Please don't hesitate to call if you need anything."

"Thank you, but I doubt I'll have the chance," Rosamund replied. "Taylor always seems to know what I need before I do." She laughed gaily and then turned to find herself face-to-face with Georgia Dupree.

"Hello, Rosamund. It's lovely to see you again." Georgia's tone was cordial but noticeably cool.

"When I saw someone with flaming red hair getting out of the car behind us, I knew it had to be you!" Rosamund kissed the air next to Georgia's cheeks. The display was rather phony and Georgia didn't seem to know how to respond.

"It's been ages since we were at an event together. You'll have to catch me up on your recent, ah, career developments. I don't even know what you've published recently."

Jane wondered if Rosamund honestly didn't take note of what her competition was doing or if she was merely trying to belittle Georgia by pretending that she didn't pay attention to her work.

Judging by how quickly Georgia's forced grin faded, she'd taken Rosamund's comment as a slight.

"I'm just writing away. There's always a deadline looming." Georgia tried to sound breezy but failed. Her voice was low and husky and reminded Jane of Katharine Hepburn's. But the comparison ended there. The romance writer lacked Hepburn's natural poise and commanding bearing. She had a nervous energy about her that put Jane on edge.

"Yes. Deadlines." Rosamund was already looking over Georgia's head toward the center of the lobby where the elevator banks were located. "If you'd excuse—"

"Actually, I'm doing something exciting at *this* event," Georgia quickly added, flicking a lock of red hair off her shoulder. "I'm going to unveil the cover of the forthcoming Fitzroy Fortune novel, *The Lady and the Highwayman*. And during tonight's auction to benefit the Literacy Society, one lucky fan will win the chance to name the male lead."

A shadow of cruelty surfaced in Rosamund's green eyes like a leviathan rising from the depths of a dark sea. "That *is* exciting. I hope the fans will still have enough enthusiasm— and enough *cash*—left to bid on the item I'm offering. In exchange for a monetary donation to the literacy fund, each and every lady will receive an advanced reading copy of the first novel in my new series. If they thought Venus was groundbreaking, wait until they meet Eros, my sexy, domineering, too-much-to-handle hero. He's going to turn Regency's high society upside down!"

Georgia was gaping. "You brought that many ARCs to give away?"

Rosamund shrugged. "When you're one of your publisher's top sellers, you get perks. I bet if you asked your publisher . . .

well, never mind." She waved her hand dismissively. "I'm also debuting an *amazing* book trailer for *Eros Steals the Bride*—that's the title of my new contemporary romance—and handing out posters of the full-page ad that will run in *People*, *Vogue*, and *Romantic Times*." She tapped her chin pensively. "I wonder what I should wear for the *RT* cover shoot. Last year, I opted for a fabulous Oscar de la Renta dress, but I think I'll go for vintage Chanel this time. You can never go wrong with Chanel." She wiggled her fingers at Georgia. "See you at the auction!"

Georgia's eyes darkened with anger and her lips compressed into a tight line.

Jane didn't want to let it be known that she'd overheard the entire exchange, so she grabbed the clipboard sitting on Sue's desk and feigned great interest in the chauffeur schedule.

Luckily, no one else was around to witness Georgia's humiliation. Taylor, who'd been busy reviewing Rosamund's itinerary, circled something on a piece of paper and showed it to Sue. While the two women spoke, an elderly couple pulling carry-on bags got in line behind Georgia. As a rule, departing guests checked out by eleven in the morning and check-in began at three in the afternoon. However, Jane had e-mailed the most prominent Romancing the Reader attendees and invited them to check in early. These fortunate people included Rosamund and her publicist, Georgia, two other authors named Ciara Lovelace and Barbara Jewel, a journalist, and the woman nominated as the Regency Romance Fan of the Year.

The clerk next to Sue waved politely at Georgia. "Ma'am? May I be of service?"

Georgia didn't seem to hear him, and the elderly couple, taking advantage of her hesitation, hurried up to the desk. As for Georgia, she walked over to the nearest chair and dropped into it, still gazing across the lobby. Rosamund was nearly out of sight, but as she walked under a massive crystal chandelier, her hair caught the light and shone like a halo.

Jane moved behind Georgia with the intention of offering her a cup of tea. Because Georgia didn't hear Jane's approach, she didn't realize she was being overheard when she muttered, "I will take your place." She curled her hands into such tight fists that her knuckles went white. "I've been waiting for years to get rid of you." Her voice dropped to a menacing whisper. "The time has finally come for you to disappear. And I promise you this, Rosamund. Yours will *not* be a happy ending."

FOUR

Several minutes later, Andrew, the other front desk clerk, came out from behind the desk and cleared his throat to secure Georgia Dupree's attention.

"Sorry," she said, getting up from the chair and moving to the counter. "I lost myself for a moment. I can picture this manor house in the British countryside. It would make the perfect setting for a novel. And you, young man, are as handsome as any of my captivating characters."

Smiling politely, Andrew told Georgia how Storyton Hall was dismantled, stone by stone, and shipped across the Atlantic. "Walter Egerton Steward's English neighbors thought he'd gone off the deep end," the clerk added. "And yet, over a century later, Storyton Hall is still a reader's paradise."

Joining Andrew behind the desk, Jane introduced herself to Georgia. Smiling, she handed Georgia her key. "I hope you enjoy your stay."

"I plan to," Georgia said and Jane saw a flash of cold light in her eyes.

I'll have to tell the Fins about Ms. Dupree, Jane thought. *We need to watch her closely, in case what I overheard was a genuine threat.*

Taylor, who'd finished reviewing the itinerary with Sue, started taking photos of the lobby with her cell phone. Sue shot Jane a worried look and Jane mouthed, "I've got this."

"Are you all set, Ms. Birch?" Jane asked the publicist.

"I need to post pictures to Ms. York's Facebook page all week long. Tons of pictures." Taylor snapped photos in rapid-fire succession. "That way, the fans who couldn't make it to the event will feel like they're here. I'll take videos of the panels and demonstrations and lots of candid shots of Rosamund. They'll eat it up."

Jane frowned. "Did your chauffeur explain our technology policy, Ms. Birch?"

The publicist shrugged. "He said something about not using gadgets in public areas."

"Storyton Hall is a retreat from the modern world and all its demands. Cell phones, tablets, laptops—these types of devices are only permitted in the privacy of one's room," Jane said. "There is absolutely no video recording permitted during this week's events. I believe we stated that very clearly in the documents we sent well in advance of—"

Taylor shook her head in disbelief. "Surely those rules don't apply to Ms. York. The event wouldn't be sold out without her." She glanced slyly at Jane. "Don't you want Ms. York's fans to hear good things about Storyton Hall?"

Jane bristled. "Ms. Birch, we've had previous guests who refused to abide by our technology policy. After repeated warnings, we promptly drove those unfortunate people to the train station. They were asked to pay for the full length of their stay before departing." She smiled, but kept her voice firm. "If we must inconvenience the few to maintain an atmosphere conducive to reading, we will do so without regret. Am I making myself clear?"

Taylor stared at her phone in dismay. "What about my job? I'm here to promote Ms. York. How can I do that without technology? The publicist before me lasted less than three months. The one before that was fired after two weeks. I don't want to end up like those girls. If I can stick with Ms. York for a year, I can get my foot in the door of a major publishing house. It's such a competitive field and I need an advantage if I want to get hired. That's where I really want to be. Right now, I'm just a glorified servant." She chewed a nail. "Please don't tell anyone I said that."

Jane heard the anxiety in Taylor's voice and softened her tone. "Why not post a teaser chapter of Ms. York's new book online? The readers at Storyton are getting copies of the entire novel, but I bet the rest of her fans would do anything to feast their eyes on a sample of what's to come."

"That's a good idea, but I still need photos." Taylor folded her arms obstinately. "People want to see images."

"Tell you what. I'll let you come backstage before the Regency fashion show. You can photograph the models in their outfits." She raised a warning finger. "But that's the only time I'll allow you the use of technology."

Taylor looked crestfallen. "What about the male cover model contest? It's the most anticipated event of the week! I *have* to post a pic of Ms. York with the winner."

"Absolutely not." Jane fixed Taylor with the steely stare she used on the twins when they were misbehaving. "Heartfire, the publishing house sponsoring the contest, has expressly forbidden the use of photography or recordings. And they'll have an editor in attendance to present the winner with his contract, so it would be unwise to break the rules. If you want to be in the publishing business, offending an editor isn't the way to get noticed." She came around the desk and put a hand on Taylor's shoulder. "You can be creative without technology. Ms. York could send Storyton Hall postcards to some of her readers. I bet they'd love to receive a personalized card from her."

Taylor seemed confused by the concept. "Wouldn't I need stamps? Do you even have a post office around here?"

"We do. In the village." Jane continued smiling patiently, but she felt as though the muscles in her face were getting tired. "Why don't you talk it over with Ms. York? I'm sure she wouldn't mind signing a few postcards."

"I'm the one who signs everything," Taylor corrected her. "But I bet she'll really like this idea. People were always mailing stuff during the Regency era. Thanks. See you later."

Behind Jane, Sue was trying to suppress a giggle. "I hadn't realized that postcards belonged in a museum case."

"Right next to phone books, rolls of film, pay phones, paper maps, or—"

"I love maps!" Andrew interjected. "I used to go on road trips with my grandfather and we always used a map. I have a huge collection of them. Every time I unfold a map, I can picture my grandpa behind the wheel of his big Oldsmobile, singing along to the radio." His gaze was wistful. "Those old maps are full of memories. They smell like summer and asphalt and my grandpa's cologne."

"You *would* make a wonderful hero, Andrew." Sue gazed at her coworker with affection. "You'd better watch out. After the ladies see you in the fashion show, you could end up with all sorts of proposals."

"With Landon Lachlan and Edwin Alcott respectively channeling Mr. Bingley and Mr. Darcy, no one will notice me," Andrew replied amiably.

"I thought they both turned Mabel down," Jane said in surprise.

Sue threw out her hands in a show of helplessness. "How she convinced them is mystery."

"We seem to be surrounded by those," Jane murmured.

Throughout the day, the rooms of Storyton Hall became permeated with perfume, chatter, and the click of women's heels. There were women everywhere. They exchanged animated snippets of dialog in the elevator, lined up for afternoon tea, and explored the reading rooms with wide-eyed wonder. By the time the Romancing the Reader participants gathered for supper outside the Madame Bovary Dining Room, the resort's noise level had risen to a fever pitch.

"They're like a flock of twittering birds," Jane heard one of the bellhops say.

"Yeah, Alfred Hitchcock's birds," added a member of the maintenance staff who was industriously polishing the brass kickplate. "They've been searching all over for that famous lady author. They're practically stalking the poor woman."

The bellhop shrugged. "They're just really into romance novels. Personally, I'm glad they're here. These ladies are good tippers."

"That's because they're away from their husbands for the week. They can do whatever they want."

"Then let's hope they want to spend lots of money," the bellhop said. "Everyone knows about the board in Miss Jane's office. I'd like her to be able to put a check mark next to one of those projects."

The maintenance man nodded. "I would too. She's a good egg, our Miss Jane."

Jane felt a rush of affection for her employees, but she couldn't thank them for their kindness without revealing that she'd been eavesdropping, so she entered the dining room and offered to help the hostess seat the first wave of diners.

The women were frenzied with anticipation. As Jane walked among the tables, she heard the same questions and comments from the majority of the diners.

"Have you seen Rosamund York?"

"Someone said she's working on the next Venus Dares book. At this very hotel! Can you imagine?"

"I cannot wait for the auction!"

"Me either, but I also don't want to rush through this meal. This coq au vin is *divine*."

Eventually, the ladies finished their entrées and the wait-staff came around with coffee and dessert carts.

"After all those teatime treats, I shouldn't even look," declared one lady. But look she did. In fact, she ended up ordering a slice of chocolate and hazelnut cheesecake and a cup of decaf. "Wait!" she cried when the waiter turned to leave. "You'd better make that full octane. I don't want to fall asleep in the middle of the auction."

"I'll have the toffee cake with the nut brittle ice cream and an espresso," the woman sitting beside her told the waiter. She smiled at her tablemate. "I saved every dollar to win one of those name-a-character lots, so I want to be as alert as possible."

A third woman at the same table ordered a martini. Unlike her dinner companions, who wore colorful dresses and glitzy jewelry, this woman had opted for a plain white blouse and a black bead necklace. And while her tablemates were talkative and merry, this much younger woman didn't seem to be enjoying herself.

Worried that a guest was dissatisfied with her dining experience, Jane leaned close to the woman. "Hello, miss. I'm Jane Steward, the resort manager. I just wanted to make sure that everything's to your liking."

"I'm Maria Stone, and I prefer *Ms.* to *Miss*," the young woman said brusquely and then quickly modified her tone. "I'm very satisfied with everything, thank you. I'm just anxious for the auction to begin. I feel like I've been waiting my whole life for the chance to talk to Ms. York—to tell her what a wonderful character she created. Venus Dares is a model of female empowerment."

Maria's dining companions exchanged befuddled glances.

"Are you referring to her support of the emancipation movement?" the woman with the cheesecake asked.

"That and much, much more!" Maria's eyes gleamed and she leaned forward eagerly. Jane guessed that the younger woman had been waiting a long time to find people who shared in her devotion for Venus Dares. "Think of what a rare woman she was for that day and age! She did what she wanted, when she wanted, how she wanted. She was respected and admired. Even the men who believed they were superior to her in every way end up paying her homage. Not only that, but Venus always rescues other women from bad situations. In every novel, she saves a woman from an abusive relationship, servitude, slavery—all sorts of indignities. It's part of the subplot, but Ms. York never fails to raise awareness of a particular social injustice. We're still battling some of those issues. Like sex trafficking, for example."

At this, someone at the table seemed to choke on her cheesecake.

"Well, my dear, I sincerely hope you'll be able to meet Ms. York." A matronly woman seated across from Maria smiled warmly. "But don't be too disappointed if it doesn't happen. She's famously elusive at these events. According to one of her fan websites, she tends to hole up in her room. But if she's writing, that's good for us because that means more Venus Dares stories, correct?"

Maria grinned and Jane realized that she was the youngest fan in the room. Most of the diners were between forty and seventy, but Maria wasn't a day over twenty-five. Jane waited until the gong signaling the end of the dinner service sounded and then followed Maria into the lobby. "Ms. Stone," she whispered. "I know you're in a hurry to secure a seat for the auction, but I wanted to share some information with you. The authors have graciously agreed to stop by tomorrow's truffle-making workshop to sample the finished products, so if you haven't signed up for that yet, you might want to as soon as possible. Maybe, just maybe, you'll get a chance to speak with Ms. York."

Maria's face glowed. "This is going to be the best week of my life." And with that, she rushed off toward Shakespeare's Theater.

"Mine too," said a familiar voice. Jane turned to find Eloise pressed against the wall to avoid the stream of women. Hooking her arm through Jane's, Eloise led her down the hall to where the rest of the Cover Girls were gathered beneath a still life of irises.

"The best week of your life, eh?" Jane asked Eloise. "Are you expecting a record number of book sales?"

Eloise beamed. "I am! I can't believe how many customers I had today. I thought the ladies would spend all afternoon exploring Storyton Hall, but they visited Run for Cover in droves and left with armloads of books. Honestly, they were like locusts. Enthusiastic, credit-card-carrying locusts."

"The same thing happened to me," Mabel said. "It looks like a tornado hit La Grande Dame. However, *this* tornado left piles of money behind, so I'm not a bit troubled by the mess. It feels like we're having two Christmases this winter."

Anna rolled her eyes. "Though I'm thrilled for you both, *I* had to dash around the pharmacy in search of obscure lipstick shades, unusual herbal remedies, and lavender hand lotion while Randall lectured any customer foolish enough to go near him on how to avoid the flu."

Jane started to laugh, but the sound came out as a strangled squeak.

"What's wrong?" Violet asked.

"Don't look now or the guests might follow your gaze, but Muffet Cat is heading our way," Jane whispered. "And there's something in his mouth."

Naturally, the Cover Girls glanced down the corridor.

"I think he caught a mole," Phoebe said.

"If one of the guests spies him with that . . ." Violet began, but Jane was already moving to intercept the portly tuxedo before he could reach the doorway to the theater.

Fortunately, the women were so bent on securing seats near the front of the room that they failed to notice the approaching feline. However, the moment Muffet Cat spotted Jane, he dropped the small creature he'd been carrying, sat back on his haunches, and meowed. Knowing he expected to be praised, Jane bent over and stroked his head. "Good boy. Yes, you're an excellent hunter. Well done." She glanced over her shoulder and, to her horror, saw that one of Storyton's few male guests had also caught sight of Muffet Cat.

Damn it, Jane thought. Seeing no other recourse, she scooped up the dead mole and dropped it into the pocket of her suit jacket.

The Cover Girls released soft cries of horror and then ducked into the theater. At the same time, a tall man in his late forties made his way down the hall toward Jane. Squatting next to Muffet Cat, he held out his hand for the feline to sniff.

"He's a handsome fellow," the man said. "What's his name?"

"Muffet Cat," Jane replied and inwardly sighed in relief for having managed to remove the mole corpse in time. "When we found him, we thought 'he' was a 'she,' so my sons named him Miss Muffet. He went by that name for months before the vet explained that Miss Muffet was a male."

"How emasculating." The man laughed. He was attractive in a bookish sort of way and Jane found herself smiling at him. He scratched Muffet Cat under the chin and the tuxedo arched his back in delight and rubbed up against the man's pant leg. "I'm Nigel Poindexter," the man said after giving Muffet Cat a final pat. "I'm a freelance journalist and one of the few men attending Romancing the Reader. Lucky me, right? To be surrounded by all these lovely ladies?"

Jane moved to shake his hand but then remembered she'd just touched a dead mole with it. She pretended to sneeze. "I'm so sorry," she said, abashed. "Sometimes I sneeze around the cat."

It was a complete lie, but Nigel nodded in understanding. Holding up a notebook, he jerked his head in the direction of the theater. "I'd better go in. Rosamund York's publicist told me that her boss is making a major announcement tonight. If I miss the big news, then I won't have an article to sell tomorrow. It was nice to meet you both."

As soon as Nigel was gone, Jane cooed and snapped her fingers in hopes of coaxing Muffet Cat into following her to the kitchen. Instead, he sniffed the edge of the carpeted runner where he'd dropped his prize and then narrowed his yellow eyes. "How about some tuna?" Jane asked and the glare instantly vanished. The tip of Muffet Cat's tail curled like a question mark and he trotted alongside Jane as she entered the servant's passageway leading to the kitchen.

After thoroughly scrubbing her hands, Jane removed her jacket and held it upside down over the trashcan. She heard a thud as the mole dropped to the bottom.

"I won't be wearing that again this evening!"

Muffet Cat meowed impatiently and Jane gave him a scoop of canned tuna fish. He devoured it greedily. When he was finished, he licked his lips, blinked sleepily, and started to purr.

"I guess you're ready for bed," Jane said as he sauntered toward the exit. After accompanying him upstairs, Jane left the cat in the hall outside her aunt and uncle's apartment. She knew Muffet Cat would scratch on the door until someone let him in. He'd then spend the rest of the night sleeping on Aunt Octavia's pillow. He adored Aunt Octavia and she adored him right back. She kept the pockets of her housedresses stuffed with kitty treats and always gave him a small bowl of cream at teatime. To show his gratitude, he sat on her lap while she read, snuggled with her at night, and glowered at anyone she disliked.

With Muffet Cat's needs met, Jane returned to the theater in time to witness the arrival of the four female novelists. First in line was a stocky woman with mousy brown hair and pink glasses. She waved at the audience and sat on one of the chairs positioned in the center of the dais. Behind her came a tall, willowy woman with a heart-shaped face. To Jane, she looked like a fairy. Next, Rosamund and Georgia strode in. The crowd clapped wildly.

Sinclair, who was serving as auctioneer, turned on the microphone at the podium and introduced the authors. The stocky woman was Barbara Jewel and her willowy neighbor was Ciara Lovelace. Jane knew their names and recognized their faces from examining the books Eloise had been displaying at Run for Cover for the past month. Jane wished she'd had the chance to read at least one work by all four authors, but she'd only had time to get through Georgia Dupree's and Rosamund York's latest novels.

Sinclair cleared his throat officiously. "Please hold your numbered bidding cards high in the air. Our lovely authoresses have volunteered to exhibit tonight's items and they'll help me spot bids as well." He had to raise his voice to be heard over the animated whispers and excited mutterings coming from the crowd. "Ladies, are we ready to begin?"

The audience applauded raucously. Jane heard shouts and shrill whistles and smiled in amusement over the enthusiastic demonstration.

Eloise joined her by the doorway. "If this is what they're like at the auction, what can we expect at the male cover model contest? The only person who's keeping their cool is that man who was petting Muffet Cat. Do you think he'll bid on Regency-style trinkets?"

Jane noticed Nigel seated at the back of the room. "No, he's a journalist. He'll be here all week. Go ahead and sit with the Cover Girls. I'm going to hang out near the front in case Sinclair needs assistance. I see he's roped Lachlan into recording the winning bidder numbers."

Eloise glanced at the desk where Lachlan sat, his eyes fixed on Sinclair. "How can someone that good-looking be so dull?"

Jane followed her friend's gaze. "He's not dull. He's just reserved."

"But he's never been to the bookstore." Eloise shook her head in wonder. "Does he borrow books from your libraries?"

"I don't keep track of what my staff does with their free time," Jane said.

Eloise frowned. "Just remember what Lemony Snicket said: 'Never trust anyone who has not brought a book with them.'"

Jane smiled. "I trust Lachlan, but he could probably use a good story or two to help coax him out of his shell. Flaubert said that we should 'read in order to live.' Maybe Mr. Lachlan just hasn't found the right book to bring him to life. Maybe he needs the help of a professional bibliophile."

Eloise snapped her heels together and saluted. "I will make it my mission to find the perfect book. I'll have to ask him what he read as a boy. Remember that C.S. Lewis quote?"

"'No book is really worth reading at the age of ten which is not equally worth reading at the age of fifty and beyond,'" they spoke in unison.

"We sound like the twins." Jane laughed and then pointed at the dais. "You'd better sit down. Sinclair is waving his gavel."

Eloise nodded and hurried to her seat.

Sinclair opened the auction with a beautiful crushed velvet cape. Mabel had donated the item as a means of advertising La Grande Dame. Sinclair also took the opportunity to inform the attendees that there were still spaces available in Mabel's Make Your Own Reticle workshop, which would take place later in the week.

The bidding was surprisingly robust for a piece of clothing that wasn't exactly practical. And it continued to grow more aggressive over items like a ribbon and cameo choker necklace, a hair bandeau embellished with faux gems, kids gloves stitched with pearl buttons, a gold armlet, and a magnificent crimson shawl with a gold paisley border.

Following these lots was an assortment of baskets stuffed with candles and lotions, romantic comedy DVDs, handmade stationery, and signed novels by several notable historical romance authors who weren't able to make the event.

Finally, it was time for the four authors to present their items. Barbara Jewel offered to critique the first three chapters of a work-in-progress while Ciara Lovelace presented a special book club package.

"I'll send your group a list of discussion questions as well as a few fun prizes. I'll also use Skype to join in on the conversation," Ciara explained. "If your club is interested, I'll talk about some of the real men who inspired my fictional hunks."

This created quite a stir among the audience members and cards shot into the air all over the room.

When the bidding was done, Ciara graciously thanked everyone who'd participated and passed the microphone to Georgia Dupree.

Georgia gestured at the projector screen behind her and smiled. "Readers. Friends. You've been so loyal and devoted for all these years that I decided to save the cover reveal of the all-new Fitzroy Fortune novel until this evening." She waited for a wave of applause to die down before continuing. "Not only will you be the first to view this cover, but you can also bid on the honor of naming Lady Cecelia's love interest. The Fitzroy family is full of dramatic characters, but in this novel, the oldest daughter, Lady Cecelia, pulls out all the stops. She's become entangled with a dangerous man. A rogue. A scoundrel. A man who takes what he wants when he wants. Could this brigand become the hero Lady Cecelia secretly desires? Could there be more to him than avarice and villainy? Is he really a thief or is he a member of the nobility in disguise? That's for you to decide, dear readers. And now, I give you *The Lady and the Highwayman*!"

The image of a book cover filled the screen. Jane recognized

Lady Cecelia Fitzroy—a dark-haired beauty in a torn ivory gown—gazing up at a large and powerful-looking man with a close-cropped beard and stunning blue eyes. He was dressed in black breeches and a black coat and held a shiny dagger in his hand. The tip of its blade hovered seductively over the last scrap of fabric holding Lady Cecelia's gown in place. The audience responded with favorable gasps of delight, followed by cheers of approval.

"One of you will choose the highwayman's name," Georgia said, clearly pleased by the response to her cover. "As long as it fits the era, of course."

The bidding war was fast and furious. Jane was astounded by how much the women were willing to pay to name a fictional character, but was thrilled that the money would go to such a worthy cause.

After several minutes, the price escalated to a shockingly high amount. There were only a pair of bidders duking it out and one of them was Mrs. Pratt. Concerned that Mrs. Pratt was being reckless with her savings, Jane shot Eloise a worried glance, but Eloise responded with a thumbs-up. The rest of the Cover Girls were openly egging Mrs. Pratt on. Jane even heard them chanting, "Eugenia! Eugenia!"

Their rallying cries notwithstanding, Mrs. Pratt could not compete with the other bidder. The lady wore a diamond necklace that was probably worth more than the entire contents of Jane's house and simply refused to back down. In the end, Mrs. Pratt had to lower her bid card in defeat.

Jane felt sorry for her friend and fervently hoped that her dashed spirits would be restored by Rosamund York's announcement. Rosamund accepted the microphone from Georgia and wasted no time informing the crowd that she had advanced reader copies of *Eros Steals the Bride* to give to anyone willing to donate a minimum of twenty-five dollars to the literacy fund. The response from the audience was deafening. And when Rosamond's book cover, featuring a half-naked man with a chiseled torso and a wry grin appeared onscreen, the noise increased to the point where Jane feared that the theater's crystal chandeliers would shatter.

Sinclair reclaimed the microphone and tried to convince the women to settle down. When they'd finally stopped screaming and clapping, he said, "Please form an orderly line in front of the desk to my right, beginning with the first row. Mr. Lachlan will accept your donation and—"

Suddenly, a woman bolted from her chair in the middle of the room and started running up the center aisle.

"I want that book!" she cried. Jane recognized her as the passionate young woman from the dining room.

What are you doing, Maria? she thought and then gasped in alarm as more women leapt from their seats.

"Ladies!" Sinclair admonished from the dais, but they paid him no mind.

Chairs went skittering. Women shoved one another in their eagerness to reach Lachlan's desk and several ladies were pushed to the ground. No one stopped to help them up. The other women just jumped over them, such was their rush to get their hands on Rosamund York's new book.

Jane watched the pandemonium in horrified disbelief. But her shock was instantly replaced by a desire to act. If she didn't do something quickly, her guests could be seriously injured. An idea flashed in her mind and she ran to the bank of light switches and turned them all off, plunging the room into darkness.

Several women screamed, but the sounds of the crowd's chaotic scuffling ceased.

Jane counted to three and then turned the lights back on.

Throughout the room, women were frozen in place.

Taking advantage of the silence, Sinclair commanded everyone to return to their seats.

"There is no cause for such commotion," he reprimanded the group. "There are plenty of books for all. To prevent further chaos, I will now call you by row. If you cannot maintain order, then no one will receive a copy."

The women shuffled to their seats except for Maria Stone. "I have be the first person to get that book. I'm Ms. York's biggest fan! I deserve to be first!"

Sinclair's eyes narrowed. "You will return to your seat, young lady, or I'll have you escorted from the premises."

Maria glared at him, but eventually stomped back to her chair. She didn't sit, however. She stood with her arms folded, a murderous expression on her face.

Jane surveyed the crowd. Women examined angry, red scratches or fresh bruises on their arms or legs. Jane was appalled to see a trickle of blood on Mrs. Pratt's forehead. Luckily, Anna carried a small first-aid kit in her purse and was already applying a cotton pad to the laceration.

On the dais, Barbara, Ciara, and Georgia were huddled close together in fear. Rosamund York, however, was the picture of calm. She wore a smug smile and surveyed the room with a self-satisfied expression.

She's pleased because her fans are willing to trample one another—to draw blood, for crying out loud—to get their hands on her book.

"These aren't exactly the gentle readers I imagined," Jane muttered darkly. "If the rest of the week's events are like this, my martial arts skills are going to be put to the test."

FIVE

When Sterling returned from driving the twins to school, he called Jane into his office, which doubled as the video surveillance room.

"This needs to be a private meeting," He shut the door and locked it. "I've already shown this feed to the rest of the Fins, but you need to see it too."

Jane sat in a chair facing the bank of small television screens while Sterling lifted the framed map of Virginia off its wall hooks, revealing four more screens.

The screens showed a live, around-the-clock feed of the front driveway, back terrace, lobby, and the hallways leading to the guest rooms. Sterling's hidden screens focused on less visible areas of the resort.

At the moment, three of the four screens were active, but the action on the last screen had been frozen. Jane immediately recognized the door to the Romance and Roses Suite.

"I don't think I'm going to like this matinee, am I?" she asked, staring at the blurred shadow of a person standing outside the guest room.

"Probably not," Sterling said and hit the play button.

The figure came to life. A woman, Jane realized, paced

back and forth in a highly agitated state, like a person on the verge of making a serious mistake. "It's as though she's gathering her courage," Jane murmured.

"Butterworth would be impressed by your ability to read her body language," Sterling said. "Especially since you haven't had your first lesson with him on the subject yet."

Jane barely registered the compliment. She was too anxious to see what the pacing figure would do. "I recognize her clothes," she cried softly. "The white blouse, black skirt, and the bead necklace. It's Maria Stone, the woman who started the chaos at the end of last night's auction."

"That's correct. Keep watching. By the time the recording is finished, Sinclair will be here to review what he's learned about Ms. Stone."

Jane returned her attention to the screen where Maria Stone was raking her hands through her hair, destroying the sleek ponytail she'd worn earlier that night. Jane glanced at the time stamp in the corner of the screen. "It's just after midnight. What was she doing up so late?"

And then Jane remembered Maria's obsession with being the first to receive a copy of Rosamund York's new novel. "Of course. She stayed up reading *Eros Steals the Bride*." Jane noticed that Maria's lips were moving. "She certainly doesn't seem eager to heap praise on her favorite author. She's distraught. It's as though she were holding a one-sided conversation with Rosamund York. Hopefully, Ms. York is fast asleep and has no idea that a fan is coming to pieces outside her door."

Maria stopped pacing. She balled her hands into fists, shook them at the ceiling, and then abruptly deflated. Her shoulders sagged, her spine slumped, and her hair hung over her face like a dark curtain. Very slowly, she pulled an envelope from the pocket of her slacks. She gazed at it for a long time without moving and then bent down and slid it under Rosamund's door.

Mission accomplished, she straightened and turned her back to the door. She pushed her hair out of her face, squared her shoulders, and raised her chin defiantly. "It's like watching a break-up, only the other person in the relationship isn't present," Jane said.

"Ms. Rosamund's publicist delivered the note Ms. Stone slipped under the door to the front desk this morning. Ms. Birch is demanding to be given the identity of the letter writer and insists we post a guard by Ms. York's door."

Jane was taken aback. "A guard? This isn't Buckingham Palace. Is one of the bellhops supposed to stand in the hallway all night?" She shook her head. "Ned is so sweet that he'd probably volunteer, but unless Ms. Stone's note contains a serious threat . . ." She trailed off, realizing that the possibility was quite likely.

She glanced at the screen in time to see Maria Stone, looking tired and bereft, walk out the camera's field of view.

Sterling pressed the pause button and handed Jane a folded piece of paper. "I'll give you a few moments to absorb this bit of prose before I show you the second half of last night's footage."

Groaning, Jane unfolded the note and began to read.

To Ms. York,

There are no words to express how deeply offended I am by your new book. You've dealt our gender a crippling blow. How could someone who created Venus Dares, a character who openly encourages female equality, have reduced every female character in Eros Steals the Bride *to brainless chattel? Eros is just the sort of chauvinistic, self-serving, belittling, and abusive oppressor that women have fought against for centuries. You wrote a contemporary romance, but in Shamus Eros, the man who owns a matchmaking company for millionaire bachelors, you took women back in time by hundreds of years! No modern, independent, freethinking woman should be attracted to someone like Eros, and yet, he seduces the bride, a woman who owns her own law firm, the night before her wedding? I literally felt ill while reading this abomination of a novel.*

If you do not make major changes before the book is published, I promise that you'll regret it. I will devote my every waking hour to ruining you. I'll leave negative reviews all over cyberspace, write scathing comments on any blog mentioning your name, send letters to the publications promoting the book, and reach out to the women who host the Venus Dares fan websites. I will do everything in my power to prevent women from reading this piece of trash.

So think carefully before you publish something that could cause real harm. Don't you see how dangerous your message of subservience is? Eros reverses everything you've accomplished through Venus Dares. Why would you make our sex so weak? So stupid and desperate? You've betrayed us all!

Change it, before it's too late. Change it, or you'll be sorry. I won't stand aside and allow thousands of readers to be influenced by something that should never have been printed in the first place.

You've been warned.
A former *fan*

Jane folded the note and passed it back to Sterling. "This definitely sounds like a threat. The question is, will Ms. Stone act on it over the next few days? We have to assume that Ms. York will ignore Ms. Stone's over-the-top demands." She pursed her lips. "Though to be honest, *Eros Steals the Bride* sounds pretty unappealing."

"Do you think we can expect more of Ms. York's fans to become irate?" Sterling asked. "Those advanced reading copies are all over the resort. There are women in almost every chair and sofa with that book in hand. They're even reading over their breakfast plates." He flashed a wry grin. "It's a good thing Mrs. Hubbard can't see them. She'd be thoroughly insulted."

Jane pointed at the screen, the lines on her forehead deepening. "Show me the other footage, please."

Sterling fast-forwarded until the time stamp read 1:12 A.M. He then pushed play and sat back in his chair, hands folded on his lap.

Another figure appeared in front of the Romance and Roses Suite.

"A male visitor this time." Jane felt a knot form in her belly. "And he's carrying a liquor bottle."

"It's Scotch. The good stuff. Bowman Islay Single Malt, aged twenty-five-years. Costs nearly two hundred dollars a bottle," Sterling said. "It looks like our friend already guzzled one hundred and seventy-five dollars' worth."

Jane didn't like the sound of that. "Great. A drunken stalker. I'm sure Ms. York would be delighted to receive such a worthy admirer. Oh, brother. Now *he's* pacing." She could feel a headache coming on. "We'll have to replace the carpet in that hallway by the end of this event."

The man took swigs of Scotch as he lurched back and forth outside the Romance and Roses Suite. Finally, he stopped and raised his hand. He curled his fingers into a fist, preparing to knock on Rosamund's door, and then slowly lowered it again. He shook his head as though to dispel a foolish thought and then turned to leave. Jane only caught a glimpse of his face, but she recognized him immediately.

"That's Nigel Poindexter, a freelance journalist," Jane told Sterling. "He was friendly to Muffet Cat yesterday evening." She clucked her tongue. "And I thought Muffet Cat was such a good judge of character."

"We've already identified Mr. Poindexter," Sterling said. "Mr. Sinclair is digging deeper into his background as we speak. Ms. Stone's too."

Jane continued to massage her temples. "Do you have any aspirin?"

Sterling opened a desk drawer and fished out a bottle of Bayer. Smiling, he passed it to her. "Mr. Poindexter could probably use a few right about now."

"I doubt he's awake yet," Jane said sourly.

There was a tap on the door and Sterling leapt to his feet. "That's probably your great-uncle. He wanted to hear your thoughts on Ms. York's visitors."

To be on the safe side, Sterling replaced the map of Virginia before opening the door.

Uncle Aloysius appeared in the threshold, looking every inch the country gentlemen in his tweed suit, loafers, and fishing hat. He wore his beloved hat everywhere, only taking it off in church where he placed it reverently on the pew cushion. There was conjecture among Storyton Hall's staff that he slept in the hat, but Jane knew this was nonsense. There were several sharp hooks and hand-fashioned flies attached to the worn fabric.

"Good morning, my girl." Uncle Aloysius planted a kiss on Jane's forehead. Taking the chair next to hers, he pointed at the map of Virginia. "Such goings on last night, eh? What do you make of it all?"

"The man, a Mr. Nigel Poindexter, may be infatuated with Ms. York," Jane said. "Maybe he needed a large dose of liquid courage to approach her. Then again . . ." She frowned. "No man could be foolish enough to believe that showing up at a woman's door at one in the morning would produce a positive outcome."

Uncle Aloysius grunted. "I should say not."

There was a tap on the office door. Sinclair entered, said good morning to Jane, and distributed two sheets of paper to those present.

"As you know, we run basic background checks on every guest prior to their arrival," he said, addressing Jane. "We only probe deeper if someone strikes us as suspicious. On the first sheet, you'll find several red flags concerning Ms. Stone. The second sheet primarily focuses on Mr. Poindexter's financial woes."

Jane scanned the first paragraph on Maria's list, which painted a sad picture of her childhood.

"She spent half of her childhood in the foster-care system." Jane glanced at Sinclair. "What happened to her parents?"

"The mother died of a heroine overdose. The father is still alive, but Ms. Stone was removed from his custody shortly after her tenth birthday because he was physically abusive," Sinclair said solemnly. "He never tried to reconcile with her, and as far as I can tell, no contact was made after Ms. Stone became a ward of the state."

Jane imagined a small, dark-haired girl cowering in the

corner of a room as her father's long shadow fell over her. "That poor child," she whispered. "She must have felt scared and alone for so many years. No child should live like that."

"Keep reading," Sinclair prompted gently.

As a teenager, Maria had been arrested multiple times. "Vandalism, arson, breaking and entering." Jane whistled. "Why didn't these crimes come to light during your routine background check?"

"She was a minor at the time of each arrest. Juvenile records are sealed," Sinclair explained. "Mr. Sterling had to call in a favor to get this information."

Jane was about to ask another question when something on Maria's list caught her eye. "Its says here that she heads a group of millennial feminists called the Matildas. What's millennial feminism?"

Uncle Aloysius, who'd been silent up to this point, cleared his throat. "I can't speak to that precise term, but your aunt started her own feminist movement here in Storyton in the early seventies. She campaigned for equal pay for the women in the village, and when Storyton Hall became a resort, she made certain that our employees were given the same wages and benefits, regardless of gender." He smiled with pride. "We were both determined that none of our staff should be exposed to harassment. More than one fellow was tossed out on his ear for administering unwelcome pinches in the hallway or indecent whispers in the staff elevator."

Jane nodded in approval and then looked at the paper in her hands. "So what's the mission of the Matildas?"

Sinclair moved to the computer and pulled up a website. A graphic of Roald Dahl's child heroine, Matilda, the little girl with magical abilities, appeared onscreen. "Ms. Stone's group focuses on how the media portrays women. The Matildas oppose racism, objectification, unrealistic body image, harassment, and abuse against women in film, television, social networks, and print media.

"A worthy cause," Sterling said. "But why is Maria Stone attending this event? I don't picture the head of a feminist group as a diehard fan of Regency romance novels."

Jane shot him a censorious look. "That's just the type of stereotype Ms. Stone would find objectionable."

Sterling threw out his arms in a show of helplessness. "Am I out of line? Consider the book covers. The women are thin, gorgeous, and partially undressed. More often than not, a burly, half-naked guy has his hands all over her. Every cover implies that the couple is seconds away—"

"From having consensual sex?" Jane asked, amused to see Sterling redden. "Last time I checked, feminists were pro-sex. Their bodies, their choices, right? Besides, the romance genre is replete with strong female characters. Ms. York took that idea of a strong heroine and morphed it into something even more powerful. She created an unconventional protagonist in Venus Dares. A feminist heroine." She paused. "However, it seems like she penned the antithesis of Venus in Eros."

Sinclair rubbed his chin in thought. "Venus Dares is powerful because she's an independent woman of her own means. She still fits the romance formula because she creates happy endings, but she breaks the mold when it comes to Regency-era heroines. Considering Ms. Stone's childhood history of abuse, it's no surprise that she connected with this character on such an intimate level. And it's no wonder she's so upset by Ms. York's new book. If women are portrayed as weak and foolish, then I don't really blame her."

"The young lady feels betrayed. Betrayed by another woman." Uncle Aloysius picked up Maria's letter. "I wouldn't dismiss the seriousness of this threat."

Jane looked at him. "Should we ask her to leave Storyton? After all, she's definitely crossed a line."

"So she has," Uncle Aloysius agreed. "However, she's young. She let her passion overrule her good sense, and I believe she may already regret her actions. Speak with her, Jane. Make it clear that we know what she did and warn her that a second act of indiscretion will not be tolerated. If she seems contrite, let her stay. If not, send her packing."

With a nod, Jane turned to the second sheet of paper Sinclair had given her. Nigel Poindexter's list.

Nigel's red flags weren't as dramatic as Maria's. He lived

above his means and owed money to a dozen credit card companies. There was also a lien on his Florida home. For a man in his forties, he had no savings and very few possessions.

"And yet, he was drinking that expensive whiskey." Jane shook her head in dismay. "How can he afford a week at Storyton Hall?"

"His room was pre-paid several months ago," Sinclair said. "As far as any expenses he incurs this week, I don't know how he plans to pay for those."

Sterling pointed at the security camera, which showed a housekeeper pushing a supply cart down a carpeted corridor. "I had a quick word with the second-floor housekeeper and she informed me that Mr. Poindexter brought an entire case of whiskey with him."

Jane hated to think what his guest room looked like. She imagined empty liquor bottles, dirty tumblers, and spots of spilled whiskey on every surface. In her mind, clothes were tossed unceremoniously on the floor, pages of yesterday's newspaper were scattered across the carpet, and the bathroom towels were haphazardly draped over the reading lamp and chair.

Some people lose all sense of decorum when they don't have to clean up after themselves, Jane thought, and was then jerked back to the present by the sound of her name.

"Sorry. I wandered off for a minute." She glanced at her watch. "I'll speak with both Ms. Birch and Maria Stone after we're finished. Ms. Birch must be addressed first and I'll catch up with Ms. Stone as soon as I can. She'll need a stern warning about behavior, and I'll have to insist that she keep her distance from Ms. York for the rest of the week. Nigel Poindexter will also need to be cautioned. We can't have him pacing the hallway outside Ms. York's room again. Perhaps I can invite him to afternoon tea."

Uncle Aloysius shook his head. "I'm afraid Mr. Poindexter is booked this afternoon. He's covering the truffle demonstration for"—he turned to Sinclair—"which magazine was it?"

Sinclair pointed at the list of magazines, blog sites, and small newspapers Nigel worked as a freelancer for, but Jane was no longer listening.

"Heaven help me! I forgot to tell Mrs. Hubbard that I'd invited Tobias Hogg to help with the workshop. She's so seldom in the limelight that she covets these opportunities, but I thought, what with a room full of women, that Tobias—"

"Are you playing Cupid?" Uncle Aloysius asked, his eyes shining with amusement.

"I hope not," Sinclair said. "Cupid's Greek counterpart is Eros. And Eros is stirring up enough trouble as it is."

After Jane left the office, she couldn't stop thinking about Eros. Not the plump, winged, cherubic figure favored by Italian Renaissance painters and the designers of Valentine's Day greeting cards, but the older and less innocent version. The Eros who carried a bow and arrow or a flaming torch and could instill in his unsuspecting victims such an all-consuming desire that they thought of nothing but their obsession.

"Eros robs his victims of freedom of choice," Jane said to herself as she headed to the ballroom to catch the second half of the author panel, *Sugar or Spice: The Flavor of Regency Romance.*

Jane decided to watch the event from backstage. She was interested in how other readers would react to *Eros Steals the Bride* and hoped the moderator, the Fan Guest of Honor, would be able to keep the audience under control.

Apparently, she'd arrived during the short break because the room was filled with animated conversation. The authors had retreated backstage where they sipped ice water and glowered in the general direction of the podium.

"That woman should not be moderating this panel," Georgia complained to Jane the moment she saw her. "You need to take over. We're not supposed to field questions from the audience until the *end* of the panel, but they keep interrupting. Every time Rosamund opens her mouth, it's to dodge questions about her new book. There are three *other* authors on this panel and we'd like to discuss *our* works." She shot Rosamund a venomous glare and Jane noticed that Barbara Jewel and Ciara Lovelace seemed equally displeased.

At that opportune moment, Mrs. Pratt appeared at Jane's elbow. "I can help," she said brightly and turned to the authors.

"As a former high school principal, I can handle this crowd. They just need a firm reminder about conference etiquette. Last night's spectacle during the auction has allowed them to forget, but I'll be sure to remedy that."

Jane beamed at Mrs. Pratt. "I can vouch for this lady. Not only is Eugenia Pratt highly capable of the job, but she knows *all* of your books inside and out."

This seemed to mollify the authors and, having entrusted Mrs. Pratt with moderating the second half of the panel, they returned to their seats on the dais.

As soon as Mrs. Pratt took the podium, Taylor Birch strode up to Jane and hissed, "Did you find out who sent Ms. York that horrible letter?"

"Yes. We're handling the matter. I will speak with Ms. York about the subject after the panel."

Taylor shook her head. "That won't work. She's booked all day. She has a lunch interview followed by the truffle workshop. Tell me, and I'll pass the message along. That's why I'm here—to make things smoother for Ms. York."

"I'd still like to speak with Ms. York in person, but please assure her that she won't be disturbed by the letter writer again." Jane tried to infuse her tone with confidence.

"That letter was a threat," Taylor persisted. "Ms. York should press charges. To do that, I need the person's name."

Jane hadn't expected this. "Ms. York has every right to be upset by what happened, but I can assure you that my senior staff and I have things well in hand." Though Jane knew this wasn't entirely true, the last thing she wanted was for Taylor to retaliate against Maria or to publicize the entire affair on Facebook. Storyton Hall could lose thousands of potential guests if someone as influential as Rosamund York publically denounced the resort.

Jane scanned the audience in search of Maria Stone and found her sitting at the end of the third row. Jane was shocked by the young woman's appearance. Her skin was wan, her eyes were dull, and her hair hung in limp strands. Gone was the passion that seemed to light her from the inside out. Gone was the youthful vivacity and vigor. She didn't fidget or shift in her seat as she had during dinner the night before, but slumped in the chair as though she wanted to fold in on herself, to become so small that she might vanish altogether.

She looks like a mourner at the graveside, Jane thought and then realized that Maria *was* grieving. In reading *Eros Steals the Bride*, Maria had lost something precious. She felt betrayed by someone she admired and heartbroken on behalf of her entire gender.

Jane stared at her with a mixture of pity and wariness and then retreated a few steps into the shadowy backstage wing. Her mind shifted back to Eros. Eros had the power to create desire disguised as love, but Jane knew that spurned desire could deeply wound a person.

Suddenly, a snippet of poetry from a book Eloise had given her for Christmas entered her mind. Standing in the dark, watching Maria Stone, Jane whispered,

"'When love beckons to you follow him, Though his ways are hard and steep. And when his wings enfold you yield to him, Though the sword hidden among his pinions may wound you.'" Jane sighed. "I'm afraid you've been wounded, Ms. Stone. And not for the first time either."

All at once, she had the feeling that she was no longer alone.

"Are you reciting Khalil Gibran?" Landon Lachlan asked from behind her.

Though Jane couldn't see him clearly in the dim light, she knew Lachlan's voice well enough. "I'm impressed. I only know a handful of people who'd recognize those lines."

"I read some of his work during my second tour in Afghanistan," Lachlan said and then fell silent.

He was so close to Jane that she could feel his breath on her neck. Though puzzled by his sudden appearance, she was too interested in what he was saying to ask what he was doing backstage. She nodded to show that she was listening and waited for him to go on.

"There I was, in no man's land, reading Gibran," Lachlan spoke in a near whisper that increased the intimacy of the moment. He smelled pleasantly of wood smoke, fresh air, and apples. "Everything he wrote was the opposite of what I was living. One of our missions went wrong and . . . we lost people. My brothers." He swallowed hard. "That night, I read this in *The Prophet*: 'But if you love and must needs have desires, let these be your desires: To melt and be like a running brook that sings its melody to the night. To know the pain of too much tenderness. To be wounded by your own understanding of love; And to bleed willingly and joyfully.'"

"That's beautiful," Jane whispered over the sound of laughter from the audience. "But it's scary too. To deliberately surrender control like that." She gestured at the romance novelists. "That's a reoccurring theme in the books these lady authors write. Happiness is only possible when one of the main characters—male or female—surrenders to the other. Their willingness to be vulnerable makes them equals and binds them together."

When Lachlan didn't respond, Jane worried that he'd found her remark foolish.

"Ms. Jane." Grabbing her hand, he enfolded it within his larger one and started to raise it.

Is he going to kiss my hand? Jane thought, too stunned to move.

But Lachlan didn't kiss her. He lifted her entire arm and used it to direct her attention toward the side of the ballroom. "Look. Someone's breaking the rules."

Jane spotted Taylor Birch holding her cell phone in front of her face, her mouth curved into a smug smile.

"Damn it," Jane muttered angrily. "The girl isn't going to live to see Valentine's Day."

SIX

From her position behind the hostess podium in the
Madame Bovary Dining Room, Jane was able to keep a
close eye on Taylor Birch.

After Lachlan had pointed out the young woman's flagrant
disregard of Storyton Hall's restricted technology policy, Jane
had descended the stage stairs, marched over to the publicist,
and asked to speak with her in the hallway.

Taylor had tried to pretend that she'd just forgotten about
the policy and claimed that it was instinctual for her to capture
images and video during Ms. York's appearances. Unmoved,
Jane had given her a choice: Taylor could either surrender her
cell phone for the rest of the day or pack her bags.

"You can't do that!" Taylor had spluttered.

"You signed an agreement weeks before your arrival,"
Jane had patiently reminded her. "I will return your phone
after the truffle demonstration. Until then, I'll keep it locked
in my personal safe."

Taylor's shock had quickly turned to indignation. "But I
have to post these photos to Facebook."

"I'm sure that can wait until this evening." Jane had held
out her hand, her expression firm.

Her mouth contorting in anger, Taylor had slapped the phone against Jane's palm. "Do you realize Ms. York has thousands and thousand of fans? How do you think they'd react if I told them how the manager of Storyton Hall refused to let me document Ms. York's visit?" Taylor lowered her voice. "Don't you see what I can do for your resort? If I post photos of Ms. York eating cake in the Agatha Christie Tea Room, sipping a cocktail in the Ian Fleming Lounge, or dancing in the Great Gatsby Ballroom, your bookings would skyrocket. Why ruin such a golden opportunity for us both?"

Jane had bristled over the initial threat, but as she continued to listen to Taylor, she had to admit that the young publicist's argument had merit. Hesitating, she'd returned Taylor's phone. "All right. Post what you have so far, but do not take this out in public again. Do you understand?"

Flashing a wily smile, Taylor had nodded and returned to the panel.

Now, the publicist sat at a large table in the center of the dining room, feverishly taking notes. When Taylor glanced up to nod encouragingly at her dining companions, Jane noted the deep crease between her brows.

I wonder if Ms. Birch's dining companions are sharing how they feel about Ms. York's new book, Jane thought.

As for Rosamund York, she was having lunch with Nigel Poindexter in a secluded nook. Per Jane's request, the hostess had placed reserved signs on the two tables nearest the author, thereby creating a buffer between her and the rest of the diners.

"People are staring daggers at Ms. York," the hostess whispered, breaking into Jane's thoughts.

It was true. Jane saw several women raise their advanced reader's copies of *Eros Steals the Bride* in the air, give the book a violent shake, and cast hostile glances in Rosamund's direction. Luckily, she didn't seem to notice.

Gazing around the dining room, Jane saw the other three authors seated together at a table near the back. They were also shooting hateful looks at Rosamund. "I wish Ms. York hadn't insisted on being interviewed in such a public place.

Considering the uproar at this morning's panel, I thought a private luncheon in the William Faulkner Conference Room would have been preferable, but Ms. York was firm about being *seen* by her fans."

The hostess frowned. "She might be *seen* getting stabbed with a butter knife. Judging by the snippets of conversation I've overheard since the lunch service began, she's upset most of these women."

"Thank goodness for Mrs. Hubbard," Jane said. "It's as though she knew our guests would be in need of comfort food today. With specials like fried macaroni and cheese, double crust chicken pot pie, shrimp and grits, pecan-peach cobbler, and banana meringue pudding, who could be disgruntled for long?"

Jane's prediction turned out to be true. As soon as the food was served, the women's faces relaxed and their voices softened. The same could not be said of Rosamund, however. Jane was just about to leave the room to attend to several mundane tasks when Rosamund shoved her chair back from the table so roughly that both water goblets overturned. Nigel yelped and leapt to his feet, but not quickly enough. A dark patch spread across the crotch of his khaki pants where the water had soaked through his napkin.

"We're done, do you hear me?" he hissed at Rosamund. "It's over."

"You can't make it without me and you know it." Rosamund's mouth twisted into a triumphant snarl. And then, becoming aware of the sudden stillness around her, she turned to address the room at large. "I apologize for disturbing your lunch, ladies." To Jane's surprise, her eyes filled with tears. "I can't tell you how much your support has meant to me over the years, and it's my deepest hope that your loyalty won't waver now."

And with that, she fled the dining room.

After her dramatic exit, Jane hurried over to Nigel Poindexter. Grabbing a fresh napkin from one of the empty tables, she offered it to him. "I'm sorry about your lunch," she said. "Can I get you a fresh plate?"

Nigel shook his head. "No, thank you. I'm afraid I've lost my appetite."

Jane accompanied him to the lobby. "It looked like your interview was going quite well. Ms. York seemed downright jolly. I heard her laughing throughout most of your meal. It's a shame it ended the way it did. Can I do anything to smooth things over?"

"No. I just need to change my pants and take a break from all of these"—he made a sweeping gesture with his arm, incorporating all of Storyton Hall—"women!"

Jane let him go. The pressure of trying to keep this particular group of guests satisfied was very taxing. The painful truth was that all four of the celebrity guests, the publicist, and the visiting journalist had the power to damage the resort's reputation. And none of them seemed happy. The other authors and most of the fans were angry with Rosamund, and now she and Nigel had had a spat. But why?

"Did he press Rosamund about her fans' reaction to *Eros Steals the Bride*?" Jane wondered aloud. "Maybe she's genuinely fearful that she'll lose readers after the book is published."

Jane suddenly realized that Nigel hadn't taken any notes during his interview. He and Rosamund had spoken for over thirty minutes and he hadn't written a single line. Not only that, but their argument seemed personal, as though it wasn't the first time they'd had a disagreement.

Odd, Jane thought, remembering Nigel's late-night pacing session outside Rosamund's guest room door. She was about to share the lunchtime events with Sinclair when she caught sight of a familiar figure heading her way.

"Mrs. Pratt!" Jane hailed her friend. "Why, you're pretty as a picture. Have you come for lunch?"

Mrs. Pratt blushed and smoothed her cornflower blue blouse. "Gavin asked me to join him for a meal, and I wasn't about to pass up a chance to savor Mrs. Hubbard's cooking."

The previous head of the recreation department, Gavin had retired last fall at the age of sixty-five. After recommending his cousin, Landon Lachlan, for his former position, Gavin spent two months in Scotland visiting family. Not long before his departure, he'd admitted to Jane that he'd long harbored feelings for Eugenia Pratt. He vowed to woo her as soon as he returned from his trip.

"I hadn't realized he'd returned," Jane said.

"He arrived late last night and probably went straight to bed after phoning me." Mrs. Pratt did her best to sound nonchalant, but Jane saw the way her fingers drummed against her purse. She was a bundle of nerves.

Jane grabbed her friend by the hand and pulled her behind a potted fern. "I don't want to interfere with your lunch date, but would you be willing to extract some information from Gavin?"

The glimmer in Mrs. Pratt's eyes turned into a full-blown gleam. Her love of gossip was equal only to Mrs. Hubbard's. "What about?"

"See what you can learn about Mr. Lachlan. I have no *sense* of the man. Who are his friends? What are his habits? What is he *really* like?"

"Are you sweet on him?"

Jane shook her head. "Mr. Lachlan's been here for months, and I still feel like he's a stranger. As his employer, I should know him better than I do."

"And that's all there is to it?" Mrs. Pratt asked slyly. "It doesn't matter that he looks like he just stepped off the cover of a romance novel?"

Jane was saved from having to reply by Gavin's arrival.

"What are you ladies doing back there?" Gavin peered between the fronds in amusement. "Are you plotting and scheming?"

Jane threw her arms around Gavin. "It's wonderful to have you back. I've missed seeing lights on in your cottage." After examining his outfit, she smiled. "You look very handsome. These are your clan colors, right?"

"Aye," Gavin said, putting a fist on the plaid that crossed over his heart. "Our surname was originally McGavin and my family is kin to the clan MacIntosh. When you were a girl, you said that my kilt reminded you of Christmas because of its red and green."

"And you were as jolly as St. Nick himself," Jane said. "But forgive me for hogging your attention. I believe some-one else would like to admire your ensemble." Having heard Mrs. Pratt laud the merits of a man in a kilt, Jane winked at her friend, wished her a pleasant lunch, and strolled away.

Her step was much lighter than it had been before seeing Gavin and Mrs. Pratt. "Love is in the air," Jane declared en route to her office.

Inside, she immediately spied a strange object on her desk. It looked like a rose, but Jane could tell that it hadn't come from a garden or greenhouse.

Jane approached it slowly, cautiously. After all, she rarely received flowers. When the twins were younger, they used to pick them from Milton's gardens, but Jane explained that the flowers were more beautiful left intact because more people were able to enjoy them. From that point on, the boys made her tissue paper flowers. Jane half-expected the single stem on her desk to be one of their creations, but it wasn't. Black letters of uniform size marched across these paper petals.

"Book pages!" Jane exclaimed.

The stem, which was made of green leather, bore gilt letters from the book's spine or cover. Jane twisted the stem until she could make out the title. "Not the title. The author. Jane Austen. One of my very favorites."

Her curiosity piqued, Jane raised the petals closer to her face. A name leapt out at her. "Miss Bennet. These pages are from *Pride and Prejudice*."

As Jane pivoted the flower in search of familiar phrases, three petals fluttered onto her desk blotter.

"Oh!" Jane cried, fearing she'd handled the rose too roughly.

Scooping up one of the loose petals, she saw its letters had not been printed by a machine. They'd been written by hand in a delicate script by someone wielding a fountain pen. The message said:

I was promised a dance.

Jane picked up the second petal. It said:

The ballroom, immediately following the fashion show.

And the third said:

*To be fond of dancing was a certain step
towards . . .—E*

"Edwin," Jane whispered, tracing his initial with her index finger. She smiled, recalling the night of Storyton's previous costume ball. The guests had dressed as famous fictional detectives, and Edwin, looking dashing in his toga, had come as the Roman sleuth, Marcus Didius Falco. Edwin had approached Jane during the band's warm-up session when she'd thought she was alone in the room. He'd then bowed, taken her hand, and waltzed her across the empty dance floor.

As they danced, an electric warmth had spread through Jane's body. It was like having sunshine in her veins instead of blood. No one had held Jane the way Edwin had. Not even William, Jane's late husband.

From the first step on that dance floor, she and Edwin had become one entity—their hands locked, his arm around her waist, her chin resting on his shoulder. They'd moved with the fluid grace of water and Jane had lost all sense of place or time. There was only Edwin's face, so close to hers, and his hand on the small of her back. There was only the two of them, turning and swirling, like leaves on the wind.

Eventually, other guests had entered and the spell of being in Edwin's arms had been broken. But Edwin had made Jane promise to meet him in the ballroom one night in the future so that they might have a second dance. He also asked that they be the only dancers on the floor.

"He's ready for that dance," Jane murmured softly. "As am I."

Part of her—the part that was the manager of Storyton Hall and the mother of twin boys—worried that it was too much of a risk to get involved with Edwin Alcott, but the woman in her, the woman who hadn't been kissed in over six years, wanted to dance until dawn.

Jane pictured the dress Mabel had made for her to model

in the fashion show. It would be absolutely perfect for dancing. She need only speak with Butterworth about keeping the band playing for another hour or two and to ask Ned to watch the twins.

Picking up the third petal, Jane reread the line. "It sounds like an incomplete quote. I'll have to search for the rest before the fashion show. It may help me understand Edwin's intentions. After all, I'm a single mother. I can't enter into a frivolous dalliance."

I barely know him, Jane thought. *But I'd like to change that.*

And then she remembered Aunt Octavia saying that Edwin would never be a suitable husband or father. Jane shrugged. She wasn't thinking that far ahead. She was focused only on a vision of herself, looking ethereal in her Regency gown, leading Edwin to the back terrace to view the winter sky. She'd be cold, of course, and he'd pull her close to share in his warmth. Jane would tilt her face to his, their eyes would meet, and her lips would part in silent invitation.

"Miss Jane?" The front desk clerk knocked lightly on the open door and Jane's fantasy popped like a bubble. "Mrs. Hubbard has finished preparing for the truffle workshop and she's waiting for you in the Daphne du Maurier Morning Room.

"Did she say anything about Mr. Hogg being present?"

The desk clerk smiled. "She mentioned something about working with amateurs, but was her usual chipper self."

"I hope so. We have enough cranky people under this roof at the moment."

"Not you, Miss Jane. You're practically glowing."

Jane touched the paper rose petal in her pocket and grinned. "Who could blame me? I'm about to spend an hour watching not one, but two master chocolatiers at work. I'll bring back samples for you and the other clerks."

"This job definitely has its perks," the clerk said and handed Jane a clipboard with a sheet listing the names of the guests who'd signed up for the truffle workshop.

Feeling quite giddy, Jane made her way to the Morning Room.

Located at the eastern corner of Storyton Hall, the Daphne du Maurier Morning Room was filled with furniture and floral fabrics reminiscent of a 1930s British country house. Jane had always found the room calm and soothing. It was a sunny place with gold curtains, a white washed fireplace, and wallpaper featuring a pattern of white roses on a field of gold. Specially ordered from England, the pattern was actually called Manderley.

At the moment, there were no comfy sofas and chairs perched on the floral rug. They'd been removed to make room for rows of folding chairs and sturdy worktables. Mrs. Hubbard, who stood behind the longest table, was busy testing one of several portable gas burners while Tobias Hogg arranged a variety of chocolate, chopped nuts, fruit, and cordials into neat piles at the other end of the table.

"It already smells like heaven," Jane said to Mrs. Hubbard. "I hope you're both ready for a packed house."

"We most certainly are," Mrs. Hubbard said, her cheeks pink with exertion. She cast a glance at Tobias. "And I'm grateful for Mr. Hogg's assistance. Even with my staff on hand, helping so many ladies make their own truffles will be a challenge."

Jane looked around the room, wondering if they should have held the event in a different place, but the Morning Room was closer to the kitchen than the Ian Fleming Lounge or any of the conference rooms. And Shakespeare's Theater wasn't an option because a game of Regency Romance Charades would take place there in an hour's time. "What flavor truffles are you making?"

Mrs. Hubbard put her hands on her hips and surveyed the ingredients laid out before her. "Chocolate-covered raspberry, peanut butter pretzel, key lime, and mocha hazelnut."

"They sound delicious," Jane said. "And ambitious."

Tobias smiled. "Mrs. Hubbard wisely prepared the ganache ahead of time. The guests only need to concentrate on the filling."

Preening, Mrs. Hubbard said, "The ladies *will* have to add Chambord to the ganache for the chocolate-covered raspberry truffles. It just wouldn't be the same without that dash of liqueur. By contrast, the layers of flavor in the peanut butter pretzel truffle are all in the filling. Mr. Hogg created the recipe from scratch. For something relatively simple to make, it's most impressive."

"But not nearly as good as your key lime truffles. Rolling the finished truffle in coconut is pure genius. It adds texture to your perfect blend of lime and melted chocolate."

Clever Tobias, Jane thought. *It didn't take you long to figure out that Mrs. Hubbard is susceptible to flattery.*

Dimples appeared on Mrs. Hubbard's cheeks. "We have samples of each truffle for the ladies to nibble on while they're watching our demonstration. Would you like a few to enjoy with your tea?"

Jane thought of the front desk clerk. "Yes, please." And then, hearing the sound of voices in the hall, said, "I'll try some later. Your first attendees are arriving."

Moving into the hall, Jane raised her clipboard and greeted the first guest. "Are you here for the truffle workshop?"

"I am!" The woman grinned gleefully. "I've been looking forward to it for weeks."

"Your name, please?" Jane asked, made a check next to the women's name, and then turned to the next guest.

Anna, Betsy, and Mrs. Pratt were among the last to show up.

"We had to pry Mrs. Pratt away from her Scot," Anna teased.

"I wish all of the Cover Girls had been here to see them together," Betsy said. "They make a lovely couple."

Mrs. Pratt scowled. "We're hardly a couple. We shared a meal together. That's all."

Jane suspected her friends saw through Mrs. Pratt's protests as clearly as she did. "Well, there's no doubt in my mind that Gavin wanted to impress you. He only dons his kilt for special occasions."

"Just tic my name and let me get a seat, though the best ones are undoubtedly taken already," Mrs. Pratt grumbled.

The room filled quickly. Jane was just about to shut the door when Nigel Poindexter appeared in the threshold. "I didn't sign up for this event, but with your permission, I'd love to observe. I could take notes for a future article and then photograph the chefs and their finished products after the guests leave. I am well aware of the resort's technology restrictions and wouldn't dream of breaking the rules, which is why I'm seeking your consent first." He cleared his throat. "And while I have a moment of privacy, I'd like to apologize for what happened at lunch. I'm afraid I might have pushed a topic too far with Ms. York. I'll endeavor to make amends at the end of this event."

Relieved to hear that Nigel planned to smooth things over with Rosamund, Jane led the journalist into the room. "Why don't you take up position by the fireplace? If you're willing to stand, you should have an unobstructed view."

Jane then gave Mrs. Hubbard a little wave, signaling that the show was all hers.

For the next hour, Jane was as riveted by the demonstration as the rest of the audience. Watching Mrs. Hubbard and Tobias Hogg work their magic had a hypnotic effect. The scent of melted chocolate perfumed the room and Jane's stomach grumbled. She'd missed afternoon tea and was more than ready for a little refreshment.

When the demonstration portion of the event was over, Jane decided to sneak off to the kitchens to pilfer a treat from the cooling racks and to fix herself a cup of tea. She waited until Mrs. Hubbard had divided the guests into four groups and was guiding her eager pupils through the first steps of truffle making before slipping from the room.

In the noisy, warm kitchens, Jane put the kettle on and debated over whether to snack on a mango tartlet or a frosted butter cookie shaped like a teacup.

Touching the rose petal in her pocket, Jane felt a fresh flutter of excitement. "Why not one of each? I'll be training again tomorrow morning. I can burn off the extra calories then."

After devouring the sweets, Jane finished her tea and returned to the Daphne du Maurier Morning Room just in time to welcome the celebrity taste testers.

Georgia, Ciara, and Barbara walked closely together, keeping a noticeable distance between themselves and Rosamund. As for Rosamund, she seemed unperturbed by the snub. If she was upset by their aloofness, she showed no trace of it.

"Truffles are my weakness," she said to Jane in a conspiratorial whisper as Taylor preceded her into the room. "My fans know that I can't write a book without a box of truffles at the ready, and I plan to shower the ladies with compliments after I taste their handiwork. Despite the little hiccup we're experiencing with *Eros*, I don't want to disappoint a single reader."

With a toss of her blond mane, Rosamund strode into the room. Mrs. Hubbard rushed forward to meet her, smiling solicitously. Betsy, Anna, and Mrs. Pratt were the only women who seemed glad to see Rosamund. The rest of the women either glared at Rosamund or turned away in disgust.

"It seems as though her readers would rather poison her than fawn over her," Ciara said to Barbara in a low undertone.

Before Barbara could reply, a member of the waitstaff led Ciara to one of the fan tables while Tobias offered Barbara his arm. When she took it, he stared at her in open admiration. "Forgive me for being forward, but you're even prettier than the picture on your book jacket. My mother is one of your biggest fans."

"You can keep being forward as long as you like," Barbara said and squeezed Tobias's arm.

Cupid strikes again, Jane thought with a smile.

She watched the authors circulate around the tables, taking bites of truffles and extolling their virtues. Taylor trailed behind Rosamund, holding her water bottle and asking readers leading questions about Venus Dares. It was a shrewd move on Taylor's part and, for the moment, the ladies seemed to forget that they were angry with Rosamund.

Except for Maria Stone. Jane started when she caught sight of the young woman positioned between two matronly ladies by the table near the window. While Maria's dark eyes locked on Rosamund, Jane wondered how she'd missed seeing Maria enter the room. Jane could only assume that Maria had snuck in behind another group of women, but she was still furious with herself for failing to have remonstrated

Maria about the threatening note she'd slipped under Rosamund's door.

Oh no, Rosamund is heading right for her! And there's no time for me to run interference.

Jane looked on, her body taut with tension, as Maria offered Rosamund a truffle.

Jane waited for Maria to launch a barrage of disparaging remarks, but she did nothing of the sort. In a pleasant and completely conversational tone, she described the truffle—a mocha hazelnut—and watched Rosamund pop the confection into her mouth.

Rosamund chewed and chewed and then rolled her eyes and moaned. After taking a sip of water, she put a hand on Maria's shoulder. "I adore truffles made with nuts. The mocha hazelnut is my absolute favorite of the four flavors served today and yours had the richest mocha taste of all. Well done."

Rosamund praised the rest of the ladies at the table for their culinary skill and then moved on to the final group.

Spotting Nigel by the fireplace, Jane clenched her teeth. Maria might have refrained from confronting Rosamund, but would Rosamund illustrate the same restraint with Nigel or would there be another scene like the one in the dining room earlier that day?

However, Rosamund seemed to only have eyes for her fans. She sampled more truffles, enthusiastically praised the ladies, and accepted water from Taylor.

Her tasting duties done, Rosamund made to leave, but Nigel intercepted her before she could reach the door. He put his hand over his heart and bowed contritely. The pair exchanged a few words and then left the room together. Seeing them walk off, Jane released a pent-up breath.

High on chocolate, the rest of the women in the room chirped and twittered like songbirds. Jane glanced at her watch and decided to head for home. The twins would be ready for an afternoon snack and homework supervision. After that, it would be suppertime.

"Before I start cooking," she said to herself. "I must find the second half to Edwin's quote."

As it turned out, she couldn't look for the quote until after Fitz and Hem had gone to bed. Most of her evening was devoted to helping the boys finish their endangered species dioramas. Fitz, who'd picked a snow leopard, had managed to glue more cotton balls to the kitchen table than to his shoebox.

"Your leopard's habitat is spreading," Jane said while snatching a tube of blue glitter from Hem's hand. "Your water has enough sparkle."

"But, Mom," Hem protested. "Two people picked the North Atlantic Right Whale and I want my diorama to be the best!"

Jane patted his shoulder. "With all the green Laffy Taffy you used to make sea plants, yours is bound to be the sweetest project in the classroom."

To Fitz, she said, "And yours will be the fluffiest."

The boys finally finished their projects and spent a half hour watching cartoons and another forty-five minutes reading in bed before Jane finally switched off their lights.

When she was sure they were really asleep and not just faking it, Jane carried a glass of wine and Edwin's rose petal into the living room. Taking a well-worn copy of *Pride and Prejudice* down from the bookshelf, she curled up on the sofa and began to read the familiar passages. The words were like old friends, and it was a joy to reunite with them. The house was blissfully quiet. The only sounds were the snaps and crackles of the logs burning in the hearth, and Jane began to relax for the first time in days.

She read until she came to the novel's first dance scene and then sat bolt upright, nearly spilling her wine. Grabbing the rose petal, she read the complete quote aloud. "'To be fond of dancing was a certain step towards falling in love.'" She stared at the open page. "Falling in love? Oh my."

She sank back against the cushions again while her mouth curved into a secretive smile.

You barely know the man, the rational part of her brain chided.

Let's hope that changes very soon, the emotional side answered.

Later, Jane nestled deep under her covers and touched

Edwin's rose before she drifted off to sleep. She dreamed of dancing with a tall, dark-haired man in a toga.

The ringing of the telephone on her nightstand jarred her awake. Bleary-eyed, Jane reached for the handset while squinting at the clock. It was a few minutes past five in the morning.

"Miss Jane?" It was Butterworth. "Forgive me for waking you. I wouldn't have done so if the situation wasn't urgent."

"What situation?" Jane croaked, struggling to sit up.

"Mr. Sterling just found Ms. York in Milton's gardens."

Still groggy, Jane reached over and switched on the light. Wincing against the sudden brilliance, she asked, "What's she doing in the garden? It's freezing."

"I'm afraid she no longer feels the sting of the cold," Butterworth said gravely. "Ms. York is dead."

SEVEN

Jane sprang out of bed, pulled her warmest wool sweater over her pajama top, and slipped her bare feet into lined boots. Hurrying down the stairs as quietly as possible, she grabbed her coat and her sock monkey hat and then rushed outside.

The winter night was bitterly cold. High stars huddled around the moon and pale clouds scudded across the inky sky. Jane was too stunned to fully comprehend that she was jogging across the frost-covered grass toward a dead body.

She rounded the end of the hedge to find two figures near a weeping cherry tree. Whispers floated over the dormant plants and hard ground, and Jane's step faltered.

Suddenly, Butterworth directed a flashlight beam her way, creating a path of yellow light over the flagstones.

Follow the yellow brick road, Jane thought wildly as her gaze traced the light to its source. She recognized the other man by the tree. It was Sinclair.

Jane approached the men, rubbing her hands together against the cold and her own fear. She didn't want to be in this garden. She wanted to climb back into bed, snuggle beneath a pile of warm blankets, and not get out again until she heard the beep of the coffeemaker and smelled the aroma of her favorite dark roast wafting upstairs.

You are the Guardian of Storyton Hall, she reminded herself. *You must face this.*

Sinclair was the first to speak. "She's under the arbor."

Drawing strength and comfort from his familiar face, from his kind, intelligent eyes and the furrows of worry on his brow, Jane exhaled and said, "Take me to her."

Sinclair led her deeper into the garden while Butterworth followed close behind. He didn't say a word, but walked in a partial crouch, his body as tense and coiled as a cat preparing to leap.

Jane thought of how this path would look come spring-time. Rows of cheerful daffodils and tulips would grow at the feet of vibrant azalea bushes. The dogwood trees would unfold their bride-white petals and the sweet pea vines would climb up and over the wood arbor. The bench under the arbor was a highly coveted reading spot on mild spring days. And no wonder. To be surrounded by blooms and butterflies while sipping peach iced tea and reading was like spending a few hours in paradise.

At the moment, two more Fins blocked Jane's view of the bench: Sterling and Lachlan.

"Miss Jane has come," Sinclair said and the two men retreated, allowing the weak moonlight to wash over a figure in a white coat. Jane remembered how elegant Rosamund York had looked the day of her arrival. She'd worn the coat over a red dress and her lipstick shade had perfectly matched the dress. Jane's first impression had been that Rosamund possessed the glamour and grace of a movie star, but that glamour was gone now.

Death has diminished you, Jane thought, her gaze traveling from Rosamund's scuffed heels to her stained coat. She sniffed and recoiled involuntarily. Glancing at the ground in front of the bench, she asked, "Was she sick to her stomach?"

"Several times," Lachlan said. "I was able to track her

movements from the back terrace to the bench. She struggled to make it this far, Miss Jane. Her shoes are scraped, her coat is smudged with dirt, and she has leaves in her hair. I'd say she lost her footing more than once." His gloved hand hovered in the air above Rosamund's leg. "May I show you?"

Jane knew she'd have to call Sheriff Evans, but she and the Fins needed to investigate the scene first. Once the sheriff and his team were involved, all evidence would become his domain. Jane couldn't surrender control just yet. Storyton Hall, its occupants and treasures, were her responsibility.

"Yes," she answered and watched as Lachlan gently and respectfully pushed Rosamund's coat and skirt up to her mid-thigh, exposing raw, angry scrapes on both knees.

"Have you searched her pockets?" Jane asked, unable to quell the tremble in her voice. She was no forensic investigator, but she could tell that Rosamund's death had been terrible. The poor woman had vomited, fallen, and fought with the last of her strength to travel into the heart of the garden, and Jane wanted to know why.

"Not yet. We were waiting for you," Sterling said and gestured for Lachlan to step aside.

A chunk of matted hair covered most of Rosamund's face, and Jane knew they'd have to move it. They had to look at her, to stare at every inch of her face, to see if signs of how she'd met her death were written there.

Jane hesitated. She didn't want to gaze at a pair of unblinking eyes. She wasn't afraid of much, but she knew Rosamund's glassy stare would haunt her sleep. "Are her eyes closed?"

"Yes," Lachlan said. "It was the only kindness I could offer her."

"Thank you," Jane whispered.

Having already replaced his leather gloves with latex ones, Sterling carefully turned out the pockets of Rosamund's coat. Jane beckoned for Lachlan to move closer to Rosamund's head. "Would you push her hair back?" Jane asked. She was unwilling to touch the dead woman, as though making contact with her lifeless body would somehow contaminate her.

Lachlan had no such reservations. He carefully pried the hair off Rosamund's cheek and folded the stiff strand over her ear. Jane frowned at the dried spittle on Rosamund's smooth cheek and chin. "I wish I could clean you up," she whispered softly. "I know you'd hate being seen like this. I'm so sorry."

Sensing Lachlan's eyes on her, Jane shrugged as if to say, "I don't care what you think," but Lachlan said, "We can help her another way—by finding out what happened to her."

"She didn't die of natural causes." Sterling passed a crumpled note to Jane.

Sinclair and Butterworth, who'd taken up guard positions along the path, abandoned their posts and came to stand behind Jane, clearly eager to hear what the note said.

Smoothing the paper, Jane read the two lines aloud:

IF YOU WANT THE ANTIDOTE
BE AT THE ARBOR AT MIDNIGHT

"Antidote? She was *poisoned*." Jane studied Rosamund's face and tried to stay calm. Questions tripped over themselves in her brain, but Jane shut them out. She could only concentrate on one thought. One word.

"Poison," she repeatedly numbly. "That explains Rosamund's need to purge her stomach again and again. But who wrote this?" Jane held the note by its wrinkled edges, suddenly hating the sight of it. Its existence was perilous for Storyton Hall. Someone had murdered one of Storyton's guests. A famous guest. Soon, the chaos of scandal would descend upon them, giving the murderer the perfect opportunity to escape.

"Miss Jane." Sinclair touched her arm. She blinked and then nodded at him.

"We mustn't allow any of our guests to check out," she told the Fins. "I don't care if we have to pretend that all the trains have derailed and that every tire on every Rolls-Royce has a puncture. No one leaves the resort."

Sinclair pointed at the note. "Should we return that to Ms. York's pocket for the sheriff to find?"

Jane stared at Rosamund. With the moonlight falling upon her winter-white coat, pale hair, and waxen face, she looked like a marble woman. A tomb sculpture. Jane knew she could keep the note and the sheriff would be none the wiser, but the woman on the bench was not made of stone. Even though what had made her human was gone and all that remained was a hull, Rosamund York been alive a few hours ago. She'd been a guest of Storyton Hall. It was Jane's duty to see that Rosamund's killer was brought to justice, and that meant giving the sheriff their full cooperation.

"Mr. Butterworth? Would you place the call to Sheriff Evans?" Jane refolded the note. "Direct him here and beg him to be as discreet as possible. The twins won't stir for another hour, so I'll wake Uncle Aloysius and tell him what's happened. Lachlan, would you stay with Ms. York? While we wait for the sheriff, Sinclair, Sterling, Butterworth, and I will come up with a suspect list in my uncle's study."

"The kitchen staff will be arriving soon," Sterling said. "They're bound to see the sheriff and his deputies. And the coroner's van."

Jane considered what could be done to restrict the wild speculation that was sure to run rampant among the kitchen staff. Jane was desperate to keep the news of Rosamund's untimely death from reaching the guests' ears as long as possible.

"Allow me to deal with the staff," Butterworth said in a steely voice. "Anyone spreading rumors will answer to me. But what of the note, Miss Jane?"

Jane met the butler's eyes and then her gaze slid away, fixing once again on the ghostly form of the woman whose work was beloved by countless numbers of readers. Jane slid the note back into Rosamund's pocket, and then covered her bare legs with her coat as tenderly as a mother tucking a child into bed.

For a moment, Jane kept her gloved hand on Rosamund's arm. Within the hour, the moonlit arbor would be filled with noise and artificial light, and Jane felt that Rosamund, whose life was defined by the written word, deserved to have words spoken over her before she become known as a case number. As a murder victim.

Fingers of cold air snaked under Jane's collar. Shivering, she glanced up at the black, hulking trees and the memory of a short poem by Wordsworth came to her. The lines seemed fitting, there in the silent garden where a woman's last breath had been offered like a gift to the sleeping plants.

Jane whispered the poem over Rosamund.

A slumber did my spirit seal;
I had no human fears:
She seemed a thing that could not feel
The touch of earthly years.

No motion has she now, no force;
She neither hears nor sees;
Rolled round in earth's diurnal course,
With rocks, and stones, and trees.

Sinclair bowed his head as Jane spoke. One by one, the rest of the Fins did the same.

"We'll catch the person who did this," Butterworth said, and Jane knew he was addressing Rosamund's body. He then turned to her. "I'll call the sheriff's office and issue a warning to the kitchen staff. Mr. Lachlan, while you await the sheriff's arrival, would you retrace Ms. York's steps once more? I'm wondering if her assailant left any telltale signs along the path. According to Gavin, no one is your equal when it comes to tracking."

Lachlan immediately set to work. He moved at a deliberate pace, the beam of his flashlight casting shadows in his wake, his arm swinging from left to right like a pendulum.

"I'll download last night's camera footage onto a laptop and meet you in your uncle's study," Sterling said. "We must hurry if we're to make any progress before the cavalry arrives."

Together, they all turned away from the dead woman, leaving her alone in the dark.

* * *

"This had better be a matter of life and death," Uncle Aloysius croaked hoarsely as he fumbled with the deadbolt. The door swung inward and his octogenarian face, etched with sleep lines, appeared in the opening. "It's half past five, Jane. What the devil are you doing up and about?" And then, seeing Sinclair standing behind Jane, Uncle Aloysius's furry eyebrows knit together in consternation. "Come in, come in."

If the situation hadn't been so grave, her uncle's appearance might have amused Jane. He wore a shaggy green robe over flannel pajamas featuring a repeating pattern of fishing flies. His slippers were shaped like a pair of largemouth bass, and his white hair stuck out in all directions like a porcupine's quills.

"We should go to your office," Jane whispered. "I don't want to disturb Aunt Octavia."

"That would be most unwise," her uncle agreed.

Uncle Aloysius took a seat behind his massive oak desk while Sinclair approached a large landscape painting hanging between bookcases. "Would you lend me a hand, Miss Jane?"

Jane helped Sinclair take the painting off the wall. They turned it around, revealing a piece of slate, and propped the painting on the empty easel Uncle Aloysius kept in the corner of his office. Sinclair then took a tea caddy off the bookshelf and withdrew a piece of chalk from within.

"This doesn't bode well." Jane's uncle gestured at the blank slate, his expression solemn.

"There's been a murder," Jane said, feeling a surreal sense of detachment. "We need to make a list of suspects and figure out how to conduct our own investigation before Sheriff Evans arrives. Once he gets here, Storyton Hall will be thrown into chaos."

Uncle Aloysius crossed his arms across his chest as though bracing himself for impact. "Who was killed? And where?"

Jane told him. When she was finished, Butterworth entered bearing a tray laden with a coffee pot, mugs, and buttermilk biscuits. Steam rose from the golden crusts of the biscuits and Jane knew they'd just come from the oven. Her traitorous stomach growled and she reddened in embarrassment.

"We should all eat something," Butterworth said, catching sight of her blush. "This promises to be a trying morning. I phoned the sheriff's office, and Sheriff Evans will be here shortly."

Sinclair waved off the coffee and took up position next to the slate. He wrote the word POISON in the far corner, and in the center, the word, SUSPECTS. "I'll begin by writing Maria Stone's name unless anyone objects."

No one did.

"Add Georgia Dupree," Jane said. "She was tremendously envious of Rosamund York and envy has a way of rotting people on the inside." Jane went on to describe the threat she'd overheard Georgia mutter in the lobby upon her arrival.

Uncle Aloysius tented his fingers and studied Jane. "What of the other authors?"

Jane considered his question. "I didn't sense any animosity until Ms. York announced that she'd be giving away advanced reading copies of her new book. It caused a riot at the charity auction. After that, Ms. Lovelace and Ms. Jewel became noticeably unfriendly to Ms. York. In fact, Ms. Lovelace even made a comment about Ms. York being poisoned by a reader prior to the truffle sampling."

Sinclair wrote CIARA LOVELACE and BARBARA JEWEL on the slate.

"What about her fans?" Butterworth asked. "One of them could have poisoned Mrs. York—perhaps only with the intent to injure, not to kill. Point of fact, why *would* the poisoner offer an antidote unless he or she wanted something in return?"

"Like a complete rewrite of *Eros Steals the Bride*?" Jane puzzled.

Sinclair pursed his lips and then added DISGRUNTLED FAN below the names on the list.

"We have to put Nigel Poindexter up there too," Jane said.

"I heard about the incident in the Madame Bovary." Butterworth rubbed his chin thoughtfully. "If Mr. Poindexter hadn't been spotted pacing outside the Romance and Roses Suite, I wouldn't think much of a journalist pushing buttons during an interview, but between his drinking habits and his dire financial situation, we'll have to take a closer look at the man."

Jane watched Sinclair add Nigel's name to the list.

"My gut tells me that Nigel and Rosamund have met before," she said. "I can't explain why I believe that, but the way they interacted implied a sense of familiarity. My impression of their lunchtime spat was that of a married couple rehashing an old argument. If I remember correctly, Nigel was the one trying to sever whatever connection they had." Jane returned to that moment in the dining room. "It was Nigel who grew angry first. He glared at Rosamund and said, 'We're done. It's over.'"

"How did Ms. York respond?" Sinclair asked.

"She looked furious, but then her face cleared and she smiled what I can only describe as a triumphant smile." Jane paused to recall Rosamund's exact words. "Her reply to Nigel was, 'You can't make it without me and you know it.'" Jane glanced at Sinclair. "What do you suppose that means? Nigel doesn't rely on Rosamund for article material. According to your background check, he's a freelancer for a dozen different publications."

Butterworth filled a mug with coffee and pressed it into Sinclair's hands. "We'll have to dig deeper into Ms. York's past to see where her path might have crossed Mr. Poindexter's before. The conversation you overheard doesn't sound like the sort of dialog exchanged by strangers."

Jane bit into a biscuit and couldn't help but sigh. There was something profoundly soothing about the taste and texture of the soft, buttery dough. It was as though someone had wrapped a blanket around her shoulders and placed her feet in a basin of hot water. The feeling of comfort sank into Jane's bones and gave her strength.

"How did Ms. Stone react when you confronted her about her behavior?" Uncle Aloysius asked Jane. "Seeing as she slipped a threatening note under Ms. York's door and has a criminal past—albeit a mild one—the young lady is, regretfully, my primary suspect."

Jane's cheeks burned. "I missed my chance to speak with her at the truffle workshop. Prior to that, I saw her at a distance, looking deflated and forlorn, but had no luck contacting her directly. I called up to her room before yesterday's author panel and left several messages, but Maria didn't return my calls or stop by my office per my request. I also told the housekeeper on her floor to pass along my message, but she never saw Maria. The bellhops were keeping an eye out for her too, but there was no sign of her until the truffle demonstration."

Uncle Aloysius leaned forward, his shrewd eyes sparkling. "Which of our suspects was present at this event?"

Following her uncle's train of thought, Jane inhaled sharply. "Rosamund sampled truffles from each table. The truffles were prepared by the attendees." She stared at the names written in chalk. "Maria Stone personally handed Rosamund a truffle. So did several other readers."

"Where were the other authors?" Sinclair asked.

"They all sampled truffles, but they were never at the same table at the same time. They rotated."

Butterworth rubbed his chin, his expression pensive. "And Mr. Poindexter?"

"He stood by the fireplace. From his position, it would have been difficult for him to tamper with the truffles." As soon as the words were out of her mouth, Jane realized this wasn't strictly true. "However, I wasn't watching him every second. He could have swapped out the samples set aside for Rosamund. Apparently, her fondness for truffles, especially truffles with nuts, is widely known."

"Every suspect was at this event." Sinclair frowned at the slate. "We can't eliminate anyone. It was my hope that we could deliver the murderer directly into Sheriff Evan's hands, but now it looks like a full-blown investigation is unavoidable."

There was a light tap on the office door and Sterling let

himself in. Muffet Cat was close on his heels. The feline trotted straight to Jane, sniffed the air, and meowed loudly. Fearing he'd wake Aunt Octavia, Jane poured some cream into a saucer and placed it on the floor. Muffet Cat lowered his head, his white whiskers twitching, and set to lapping up the cream. "I know we don't have much time, but I've uploaded the footage from last night's guest floors, lobby, and outdoor cameras. I brought three laptops so we could divide the feeds among us."

While distributing the laptops, Sterling assigned each person a video file to review. "Mr. Butterworth, you and Mr. Sinclair have the lobby. Miss Jane, you and Master Steward have the view from the terrace. I'll take the guest hallways since there are multiple feeds to watch at once."

Jane pulled a chair up to her uncle's desk, put the laptop on the blotter, and clicked on the video file. She fast-forwarded the recording until the time stamp read 10:00 P.M. "We've been given the easiest feed," she whispered to her uncle. "No one in their right mind would be outside this late on a cold February night."

"Other than Ms. York," Uncle Aloysius said gravely.

"And her killer. Either this person wanted something from Rosamund, or they just wanted to see her suffer—to bear witness as she died a horrific death." On the laptop screen, the wind stirred the tree branches and made the bushes shiver. Jane stiffened at the tiniest movement, but none of the dark shadows were human.

Finished with his cream, Muffet Cat jumped onto Jane's lap. He rubbed his chin against her hand, purring softly, and began kneading her cotton pajama pants with his front claws. Jane was surprised by his behavior, for Muffet Cat usually reserved his affection for Aunt Octavia. Jane glanced down at the portly feline. "It's all right," she murmured to him as she stroked the shiny black fur. "It's going to be all right."

Suddenly, Butterworth bolted to his feet, gripping his cell phone. "The sheriff has arrived. Mr. Sinclair, would you join Mr. Lachlan in the garden while I arrange for coffee for his men?"

"And for Mr. Lachlan as well," Jane added. "He must be half-frozen by now." She turned to her uncle. "Would you continue watching this? I need to be home before the twins wake up. If they find themselves alone, they'll leave the house in search of me."

Sterling nodded. "I'll continue to review the feeds as well. Perhaps Master Steward and I will find something of import to share with the sheriff."

Jane carefully transferred Muffet Cat to her uncle's lap and stood. "Thank heavens the arbor isn't visible from the main house. I might just have time to figure out how to handle this tragedy before our guests discover what's happened."

Jane followed Sinclair and Butterworth through the apartment, down the hall, and into the staff stairwell. Emerging in the lobby, Jane was relieved to find that all was quiet. A few staff members were about, cleaning and polishing, but there wasn't a guest in sight.

Butterworth headed for the kitchens while Jane and Sinclair exited through the rear doors. Immediately assaulted by the frigid air, they hunched their shoulders and hurried across the lawn. Jane stopped at the entrance to Milton's gardens. "Please tell Sheriff Evans that I'll be available as soon as Fitz and Hem are dressed. I'll bring them to the kitchens for an early breakfast and ask one of the bellhops to run them to school when the times comes."

She and Sinclair parted company, and Jane didn't expect to encounter another soul. However, when she got close to her house, she saw a tall man dressed in a black coat and black cap standing in front of her door.

"Edwin? What are you doing here at this hour?"

He came forward to meet her, his gloved hands held out before him. For a moment, she thought he meant to pull her in against his chest, but he merely cupped her elbows with his large hands. "I've always been an early riser, and I ride Samson almost every morning about this time. We were trotting close to Broken Arm Bend when I saw the caravan of sheriff's cruisers racing for Storyton Hall, so I gave Samson his head and rode hard until we reached the archery range." His dark eyes roved over her face and then moved down her body. "I'm glad to see that you're unhurt."

Under his deliberate scrutiny, Jane felt her body temperature rise several degrees. "I'm well enough, but one of our guests has been murdered. She's a famous author and I have no idea how the resort can survive the scandal."

Edwin tightened his grip on her arms. "If anyone can maneuver Storyton Hall through treacherous waters, it's you."

"What makes you so confident? Eloise and I are as close as sisters, but you've only been in Storyton for a few months. You and I barely know each other."

"But I was here this past autumn, remember? I saw you fight for justice for another murder victim. You wouldn't back down, no matter what the cost to you and yours." He brushed a wayward curl from her cheek. "Besides, one can't help but be reassured by a woman wearing a sock monkey hat."

Blood rushed to Jane's cheeks. She couldn't begin to imagine how idiotic she looked in pajamas pants and a hand-knit monkey hat. "I should go in. The boys will need—"

"Let me take care of them," Edwin offered. "I took the liberty of putting Samson in the garage and I can ride him back to Hilltop Stables later. If you trust me with your sons and a set of car keys, I'll feed Fitz and Hem and drop them at school." The corners of his mouth twitched. "After all, you might want to change your clothes before joining the sheriff."

For the first time that morning, Jane smiled.

After inviting Edwin inside, she left him to examine the contents of her refrigerator while she went upstairs to rouse the twins.

Groaning, they finally got out of bed and Jane hurriedly showered, dressed, and wrangled her rebellious curls into a loose bun.

Downstairs, she found the twins sitting at the kitchen counter, riveted by whatever story Edwin was telling them. "And so, the only way to defeat the fearsome ogre for good was to *eat* his yellow eye. That eye held all his magic, you see."

"Awesome," Hem said. "And this is what it looked like?"

Edwin slid a plate in front of each boy. "Yes. Unlike you and your brother, the hero didn't have orange juice to help get it down his throat. But he was a brave lad and he ate every morsel without complaint."

"I bet I can do it faster than he did!" Fitz boasted, picked up his egg-in-the-hole, and took an enormous bite from one end.

Not to be shown up by his brother, Hem dug out his entire egg with his fork and popped it into his mouth.

"You'd both make excellent heroes," Edwin said with a grin. Seeing Jane, he quickly sobered. "Call me if our evening plans need to be postponed."

Tonight's the fashion show, Jane cried inwardly. *And my long awaited dance with Edwin.*

She held Edwin's eyes, thinking of how much she liked the sight of him in her kitchen. "I don't want to cancel. I was really looking forward to a waltz or two." She gazed at him for a long moment and then finally said, "Thank you for this."

Kissing the boys on the top of their heads, she pulled on her coat and opened the door. Her front stoop was wet. She raised her eyes to the sky.

The moon and stars were long gone, replaced by clots of gray clouds. A tentative rain had begun to fall, but as Jane looked to where the hills rose high above the tree line, she saw an ominous band of charcoal gray. This dark smudge was a portent of heavier precipitation. The rain would force Storyton's guests indoors, which was a boon because they might not see the sheriff's cruisers or the coroner's van. However, it also meant that Lachlan would be tied up with bowling and board game competitions and would be unable to help with the investigation. Worst of all, a violent downpour would wash away trace evidence.

Quickly stepping back inside the house, Jane grabbed an umbrella from the coat rack and then struck out for Milton's gardens.

She walked briskly until she noticed the yellow crime scene tape. Battered by wind and water, the tape writhed and quivered like a plastic snake, and Jane hesitated. Despite the chill, she stood in place for a moment, recalling a proverb she'd once heard from an elderly woman in the village.

"'The drowning man is not troubled by rain,'" she whispered.

And then, Jane reluctantly advanced toward the cluster of somber men, the sepulchral garden, and a body shrouded in white.

EIGHT

Catching sight of Jane, Sheriff Evans issued several quiet commands and then walked to her side. He touched the brim of his brown hat deferentially, and the water gathered around the brim streamed over his face.

"A sorry business." After wiping his brow with the back of his hand, he gestured first at the gurney and its burden, and then, at the expanse of grey sky.

"Yes," Jane agreed softly.

They stood in silence as the gurney was pushed down the garden path toward the loading dock. Jane glanced up at the high hedge and felt a tiny measure of relief that the only people who would witness Rosamund York's sad exit were the sheriff and his team, Lachlan, Butterworth, and herself.

Nearby, a deputy snapped an evidence collection kit shut. Issuing a nod to Sheriff Evans, the man strode off, a second deputy falling into step beside him. The moment they were gone, the rain intensified, as though it could no longer hold itself in check.

"I think we've gotten all we can hope to get for now," Sheriff Evans told the company at large. "Phelps, you're with me. You too, Emory," he added, crooking his finger at a young female deputy with clear blue eyes and auburn hair. To Jane, he said, "Shall we talk inside?"

"Please," Jane said, hugging herself for warmth. "Let's go to my office."

She and the sheriff headed for the manor house with Lachlan, Butterworth, and the two deputies followed behind.

Leaving her umbrella in a stand on the back terrace, Jane shook the water from her coat and dipped her chin in appreciation as Sheriff Evans did the same.

Except for two members of the housekeeping staff, the lobby was empty. One woman was polishing the wood tables while a second woman added water to a floral arrangement. They both stopped to stare at the dripping procession of lawmen and Storyton staff members.

Butterworth frowned in marked disapproval and the women immediately returned to their work.

At the front doors, Butterworth slowed. "I'll have a coffee tray sent to your office, Miss Jane," he said. "Mr. Lachlan and I had best return to our duties."

Jane knew he wasn't referring to his position as Storyton's butler, but his role as a Fin. After demanding discretion from the staff, he and Lachlan would rejoin Sterling, Sinclair, and Uncle Aloysius. Like Jane, they'd use the precious time remaining before the guests appeared for breakfast to discover the identity of Rosamund's killer.

"Good morning, Sue," Jane greeted the front desk clerk solemnly. "Sheriff Evans and I have some business to discuss. Could you see to it that we aren't disturbed? Other than to take delivery of a coffee tray, that is."

"Of course," Sue said and smiled politely at the sheriff and his deputies. Without the slightest hint of curiosity, she returned to examining the checklist of guest requests, which she'd placed next to the schedule of the day's events.

Struck by a thought, Jane told Sheriff Evans to go through to her office. When he and his deputies had moved away, Jane edged closer to Sue and asked, "Are any of our guests checking out today?"

Sue shook her head. "No. The rooms are all occupied by

Romancing the Reader attendees. I don't expect any of them to leave until Saturday."

Other than Rosamund York, who departed involuntarily, Jane thought glumly.

"Please inform me at once if any guest expresses a desire to check out this morning," Jane said and then entered her office.

Sheriff Evans sat in one of the guest chairs across from Jane's desk while the two deputies stood like bookends behind him.

"I'll grab another chair," Jane said. "I have a great deal to tell you."

After borrowing a chair from the surveillance room, Jane invited the deputies to sit. They only did so at the sheriff's urging and perched at the edge of their chairs like attentive schoolchildren. Sheriff Evans folded his hands over his slightly rounded belly and sighed. He was in his late fifties, but he looked older this morning. It was as though the early phone call and the time spent in the cold, gloomy garden had suddenly aged him.

"We collected as much evidence as we could before the rain started," Sheriff Evans began. "We took the necessary photographs as well as samples of the victim's vomit. And I'm sorry to say this, Ms. Steward, but I have no choice but to open an investigation into the murder of Rosamund York."

"Murder," Jane repeated woodenly.

"You don't seem surprised." The sheriff's gaze sharpened.

Jane shook her head. "I'm not. Unfortunately, Ms. York made enemies from the moment she entered Storyton Hall. Still, how can you be so certain? A murder has the potential to ruin us, Sheriff."

Reaching into his coat pocket, the sheriff removed a plastic evidence bag and laid it on Jane's desk blotter. He gave her half a minute to examine the note, not realizing that Jane had already read it, and then tapped the bag with his index finger. "Do you know who wrote this?"

At that moment, someone knocked on the office door and Jane called, "Come in."

Billy the bellhop opened the door and tipped his cap. "I'm sorry it took me so long to bring your coffee service, but Mr. Butterworth felt your guests might like a little something to eat." Having delivered the message, Billy wheeled in a cart bearing a silver coffee urn and several plates covered by shiny steel domes.

Butterworth must be trying to buy time, Jane thought. *I hope the Fins find something on those video feeds. And quickly.*

As soon as Billy left, Jane filled three mugs with piping hot coffee and added cream, sugar, or both based on the preference of her guests. After distributing the mugs, she waved at the evidence bag on her desk.

"I wish I could point the finger at a specific person and you'd close this case without delay, but I'm afraid things aren't that straightforward." Jane removed the domed lids to reveal platters of warm croissants, perfectly fried bacon, and a quartet of mini egg and cheese soufflés baked in white ramekins. She served the food, poured herself a cup of coffee, and then returned to her seat. "All I can do is give you the names of the guests you'll want to interview and my reasons for naming these particular individuals."

"I appreciate your cooperation," the sheriff said, staring at the food on his plate as though uncertain what to do with it.

Seeing his indecision, Jane motioned for her guests to eat. "You might as well get some food in you while I'm talking. I can put everything in writing after I've given you a brief rundown of the key players." She gave Sheriff Evans a pleading look. "I only ask that you and your deputies be as discreet as possible. The last thing I want is a resort full of hysterical guests."

"That won't help us either, ma'am," the sheriff said. "Considering the circumstances, I can't allow anyone to leave, but I don't need to drag people out through the front door in cuffs, either. We can find a way to work together, Ms. Steward. I'm only interested in seeing that justice is served."

Jane nodded. Sheriff Evans was courteous and competent and though Jane liked him well enough, she fervently wished there was no need for his presence at Storyton Hall. Unable to stall any longer, Jane ran through the names of the suspects Sinclair had written on the slate board in her uncle's office.

While she talked, Deputy Emory typed notes into a small laptop. The minutes ticked by and Jane felt like she was in a witness box providing testimony and that Deputy Emory was the court stenographer. Jane found it slightly unnerving that while the young woman's nimble fingers flew over the keys, her big blue eyes never left Jane's face.

When Jane finally finished and the deputy's hands fell still, Sheriff Evans stared into the middle distance and stroked the stubble on his chin.

"I'd like to conduct preliminary interviews on sight if that's all right with you," he said after a long moment of silence. "May I commandeer one of the smaller conference rooms?"

"Of course." Jane suppressed a sigh of relief. Allowing the sheriff the use of the William Faulkner Room had its advantages. First, the suspects would be more at ease there than in the stark interview room at the sheriff's station. The William Faulkner, with its wood paneling, lush carpet, oil paintings, and comfortable swivel chairs, was certainly less threatening. Secondly, Jane could listen in on every interview. Storyton Hall was filled with secret nooks, hidey-holes, and passageways, and it just so happened that a secret corridor had been constructed between two of the smaller conference rooms. Accessible through a hidden door in the back of a broom cupboard, Jane could tiptoe down the narrow aperture and squat down next to the air return panel. From this position, she could record the interviews and replay them later for the Fins.

Unless the sheriff is able to obtain a confession, Jane thought, but immediately dismissed the idea. After all, most of the suspects stood to gain from Rosamund's death. Georgia would probably become America's premier author of Regency romances. As for the Ciara and Barbara, their novels were likely to see a surge in sales after the media attention they'd receive once the news of Rosamund's untimely end spread. As for Maria Stone, she would no longer have to worry about a sequel to *Eros Steals the Bride*. The book that had so incensed her would be a standalone.

And quite possibly Rosamund's biggest seller, Jane mused to herself. *Everyone will buy it because it's Rosamund York's last novel.*

"I wonder if you could clarify something," Sheriff Evans said, breaking into Jane's thoughts. He'd scooted his chair back in order to view Deputy Emory's laptop screen. "You said that you were under the impression that Mr. Poindexter knew the victim—that the two had met before." Jane nodded and the sheriff continued. "You're far more knowledgeable about the publishing world than any of us, so what would be your best guess as to Mr. Poindexter's motive? Wouldn't Ms. York be more useful to him alive? He can hardly interview her now."

"If Mr. Poindexter were the last person to conduct an interview with Ms. York, he could sell that interview to the highest bidder," Jane said. "I don't know how much he could expect to make or even if he's capable of committing premeditated murder in exchange for a one-time payoff. This is purely supposition on my part, but I did get a strong feeling that he and Rosamund knew each other intimately."

"I appreciate your candor. We'll begin with the suspect list you provided." The sheriff got to his feet. "Deputy Emory, you and I will conduct the interviews while Deputy Phelps runs background checks." At the door, the sheriff turned back to Jane. "I wish your hotel wasn't filled with so many disgruntled fans. It sounds like any number of people would have gladly poisoned Ms. York."

Jane thought of how Rosamund had tried to reconnect with those fans during the truffle demonstration. It seemed to Jane that Rosamund had been succeeding. Could one of those women truly been angry enough to poison her? Wouldn't Rosamund or Taylor have noticed a cold light in their eyes? A tightening around the mouth? A trembling hand? Words punctuated with quiet fury?

"Taylor!" Jane cried softly. "I almost forgot about Taylor Birch, Ms. York's publicist. You'll want to speak with her as well. The young lady knows more about her employer than anyone in the hotel." Jane gave Sheriff Evans an imploring look. "Would it be all right if I tell her about Ms. York? I'm afraid she's going to take it very hard."

Sheriff Evans shot a glance at the wall clock. "I imagine your guests will be stirring by now. Do you have an event scheduled for this morning?"

"Two, actually. A Regency dance class and a Romantic Reads quiz show. After lunch, we're offering a Make-Your-Own-Reticule workshop."

The sheriff nodded. "As long as no one leaves the premises, I see no reason why you shouldn't carry on with these events. We'll send for Ms. Birch first and I'd welcome your presence during her interview. After that, we'll move down our suspect list. If I can't make an arrest after speaking with the individuals you've named, then we'll have to address the guests en masse."

Though Jane knew this was unavoidable, she cringed at the thought. At least she was somewhat involved in the sheriff's investigation and was therefore keeping her promise to find Rosamund's killer.

"I'll have Sue call up to Ms. Birch's room," Jane said. "I should also stop by the Ian Fleming Lounge, as I'd like to have something on hand to help Ms. Birch cope with the shock. William Faulkner said, 'There's no such thing as bad whiskey.'"

"On a day like today, I'd have to agree with Faulkner." Sheriff Evans gestured at the door. "After you, Ms. Steward."

In the Ian Fleming Lounge, Jane poured two fingers' worth of whiskey in a tumbler and then asked Sheriff Evans and Deputy Emory to meet her in the conference room.

"It's unlocked, so go in and make yourselves comfortable," she said. "I want to arrange for water and coffee to be delivered. Perhaps refreshments will make the interviewees less anxious."

The sheriff had used The William Faulkner Room on a previous occasion, so he and Deputy Emory headed down the lobby toward the west wing without delay.

As for Jane, she hurried to the Henry James library in search of Sinclair. The library was empty and Sinclair was in his cramped office, whispering into a cell phone. After ending the call, he turned to Jane with a grave expression.

"We've reviewed all the video feeds. The cameras picked up Ms. York's harrowing journey from her room, through the lobby, and out to the terrace. No one followed her."

"Could her poisoner have avoided the cameras if he or she knew where they were located?" Jane asked.

Sinclair frowned. "That is most unlikely. One would have to be aware of the existence of our secret cameras, and only your uncle and the Fins know where they are."

"Rosamund's killer wanted her to go to the arbor for a reason," Jane said. "Either he sent her there because he intended to blackmail her—to exchange the antidote for money or something else—or he wanted her to die in the garden. Is the place significant or was it chosen because it's secluded?"

"Another question: What type of poison would the promised antidote treat? Mr. Sterling is currently analyzing a sample of Ms. York's stomach contents as we speak. Identifying the poison is paramount. We also need to know if she ingested the poison during the truffle workshop or earlier. At lunch, for example."

Jane nodded. "I have to record the interviews between the suspects and Sheriff Evans. The sheriff has agreed to conduct them in the William Faulkner. I'm on my way there to break the news of Ms. York's death to Ms. Birch. May I borrow your phone? I need to place an order with a member of the kitchen staff."

While Jane called in her request, Sinclair unlocked a desk drawer, pulled out a state-of-the art digital voice recorder, and slipped it into the pocket of his tweed suit jacket. He then smoothed his charcoal grey wool vest and straightened his paisley bow tie. "Right. Let's be off."

In the lobby, every woman smiled or waved at Storyton's head librarian. Jane couldn't blame them. Sinclair was smart, kind, had impeccable manners, and could find the perfect book for the most discerning reader. He also had an unparalleled taste in men's fashion and was the only department head to eschew the livery, preferring tweed suits and colorful bowties. Jane thought he bore a close resemblance to Sean Connery and many of the guests did too.

Sinclair was the closest thing Jane had to a father, and she felt steadier in his presence. Her own parents had died when she was just a toddler, and though Aunt Octavia and Uncle Aloysius had lovingly raised her, Sinclair had always been the one she'd run to when she was injured or upset. And after her husband, William, had been killed in a car crash, Sinclair had been her crutch. He'd helped her manage Storyton Hall and had plied her with books about courage, strength, and fortitude. Eventually, the messages held within those stories had gotten through to Jane and she began to believe she could shoulder the double burdens of being a single parent and restoring Storyton Hall to its former splendor.

Until this morning, I thought I was doing a pretty good job, she thought morosely.

Pushing open the door leading to one of the many staff corridors, she and Sinclair strode down the dim hallway until they reached a metal storage cupboard. Jane paused to make sure they were alone and then whispered, "All clear."

Sinclair opened the cupboard and stepped inside. "Join me when you've finished with Ms. Birch." He pushed aside a group of brooms. "Remember not to speak when you're in the hidey hole. Sheriff Evans might hear you. At best, he'll think Storyton Hall is overrun with rats. At worst, he'll realize that you offered him the use of the William Faulkner Room in order to eavesdrop on his interviews."

"I'll be quiet," Jane promised and closed the cupboard door.

Returning to the lobby, she entered the conference room to find Taylor Birch seated at the polished table, her eyes wide with fright. Upon seeing Jane, she shoved back her chair and got to her feet. "What am I doing here?" Her voice was shrill. "And where's Ms. York? I rang her room twice and when she didn't pick up I went to her floor and knocked on her door. She didn't answer, and she always has me bring her a cup of coffee by now."

Jane set the tumbler of whiskey on the sideboard. She gently pressed Taylor back down into her chair and then sat beside her. "Ms. Birch, I'm afraid I have terrible news and the best way I know to tell you is to be as direct as possible." She took hold of Taylor's cold hand and spoke very softly. "Ms. York died early this morning."

Taylor's jaw went slack. She stared at Jane, her mouth working.

Jane saw that the young woman was struggling to speak. "It's hard to take in," she said. "Just give yourself a moment."

"No," Taylor finally whispered. She shook her head repeatedly, like a stubborn child refusing to listen. "No. It can't be true."

Jane glanced at Sheriff Evans and he held up his hand to indicate that he was ready to take over.

"When was the last time you saw Ms. York?" he asked Taylor.

Taylor didn't seem to have heard him. Her glassy-eyed stare, an eerie echo of the expression Rosamund had worn the night she died, fixed on Jane. She continued to shake her head and whisper, *"No no no no."*

Jane held out her free hand. "Deputy Emory? Would you pass me that tumbler?"

The deputy sprang to comply. She placed both the tumbler and a mug of hot coffee on the table.

"Drink this," Jane said, wrapping Taylor's fingers around the glass.

When Taylor didn't move, Jane put her palms under the tumbler and raised it to Taylor's mouth. "Drink this. Go on, you can do it," Jane said soothingly.

Taylor drained the tumbler and shuddered slightly.

"That's a girl." Jane took the glass away. "You're going to be okay. How about some coffee? It'll warm you up. You're cold to the touch."

Taylor reached for the steaming mug, but her hands shook so violently that coffee sloshed over the conference table.

Jane held the mug for her and Taylor took a tentative sip. "How will I be okay? She's gone. And so are my dreams."

"That's not true," Jane said. "I know how tirelessly you worked for Ms. York. And guess what? She still needs you. You've been her voice for months. Don't stop now."

This roused Taylor from her stupor. "I *am* her voice. Her readers depend on me."

"Then help the sheriff. Tell him what you know."

Sheriff Evans nodded gratefully at Jane and repeated his earlier question.

"I last saw Ms. York in her room. She'd sent me to the village for medicine because she had an upset stomach. I hired one of the drivers to take me to the pharmacy and by the time I came back, Ms. York was really sick." Taylor looked stricken. "Was she dying? Could something have been done to save her?"

Instead of answering, the sheriff jotted a quick note on his pad. "When did you return with the medicine?"

"Just after seven. I checked the time because we were supposed to be in the dining room by then, but after taking one glance at Ms. York, I knew she wouldn't be leaving her room." Taylor cradled her mug. "I asked if she wanted to have a bowl of broth sent up, but she said she couldn't stand the thought of food."

"Could you describe her appearance?"

Taylor's gaze shifted to the rain-splattered window. Her eyes grew unfocused and Jane guessed she was lost in her memories of the previous night. "She was sweating. Like she'd just finished a tough cardio workout. Her hair was sticking to her face and her skin was a funny color. She kept clutching her stomach and moaning. When I suggested she see a doctor, she told me that she just needed rest. She sent me away, saying that she didn't want to be disturbed and that she'd call me in the morning. That was the last time I saw her."

Taylor covered her mouth with her hand, as though trying

to keep a sob from escaping. Jane squeezed her arm. "You did your best to help her."

"Ms. Birch, we don't know how Ms. York died, and we won't have a definitive answer until the medical examiner shares his findings, but I'd like to hear your opinion of your employer's frame of mind. Before she became ill, was she content? Angry? Troubled?"

Taylor blinked in confusion. "Troubled?" Her eyes flitted wildly between Jane and the sheriff. "You didn't find her in the bathtub or anything like that, did you?"

"No," Sheriff Evans was quick to reply. "Forgive me. I didn't mean to imply that Ms. York's death was a suicide. However, I cannot say that it was accidental either. That's why I'd like you to tell me as much as you can about her time here. What was her frame of mind? Who did she associate with? Did she feel threatened? Any detail could prove helpful."

Taylor's mouth contorted in anger. She pointed at Jane and shouted, "I *told* you that letter was a real threat! You should have pressed charges against the crazy woman who wrote it! And it *had* to have been a woman—one of Ms. York's rabid fans gone off the deep end." Taylor face turned an alarming shade of red. "What did you do about the situation? Did you kick the woman out or let her stay? Because if she had anything to do with Rosamund York's death, I'll make sure the whole world knows that you're to blame!"

"Ms. Birch—" The sheriff tried to interject, but Taylor didn't even look at him. Her eyes glittered with fury.

"I'll tell everyone that it's *your* fault that one of the greatest romance writers of our age is gone! When I'm through, this place will be a tomb. A *tomb*!"

Droplets of spittle landed on Jane's cheek. She wiped them off with her palm and felt how flushed her own skin had become. It was difficult not to shrink in the face of Taylor's accusatory glare. After all, her outrage was completely justified. What if Maria Stone turned out to be the killer? Not only had Jane allowed Maria to remain in Storyton Hall, but she'd also failed to confront her about the note she slid under Rosamund's door.

"If you'd kindly excuse us, Ms. Steward," Sheriff Evans said, and Jane knew she was being given a command.

"Of course," Jane said, getting to her feet.

She opened her mouth to say that she was sorry, but then closed it again.

The person she should apologize to was no longer capable of offering her forgiveness, so she left the room without another word.

NINE

Jane didn't join Sinclair in the hidey-hole right away.
Instead, she headed for the front door where Butterworth
stood, as straight-backed and unblinking as a yeoman
warder. Jane considered the similarities between the elite
guardsmen and the Fins. The yeoman warders protected the
Crown Jewels, while the Fins guarded a priceless treasure:
Storyton's secret library.

*What will happen to the Eighth Wonder of the World if
Storyton Hall falls into ruin*? Jane wondered and then dismissed the defeatist thought.

"I'm going to listen to the rest of the interviews," Jane told
Butterworth quietly. "If the sheriff doesn't trim the suspect
list by the time the morning's events are over, I'll have to
make an announcement during luncheon. As of now, this
evening's Regency fashion show will proceed as planned. I'd
rather have all the guests in one place where we can keep an
eye on them."

Butterworth nodded. "I concur." He cleared his throat, a
sure sign of disapproval. "What of your plans with Mr. Alcott?
Though I am willing to offer my services as conductor—"

"*If* I decide to honor my commitment to Edwin, I'll ask

your backup to lead the band." Jane glanced at her watch. "I wanted to make sure the twins got off to school on time. Did you see them?"

Again, Butterworth made a soft noise in the back of his throat. "Indeed. Mr. Alcott drove past so that Hemingway and Fitzgerald could wave to me. They seemed quite merry and were undoubtedly thrilled to be running behind schedule."

Jane suppressed a grin. To Butterworth, tardiness was a serious transgression.

"Text Sinclair if you need me," she said.

Turning, she saw Maria Stone walking toward the west wing. Billy the bellhop was her escort, and though he seemed to be chatting with her in his usual friendly manner, Maria's lips were clamped together and her face was an unreadable mask.

"After all those years in foster care, she's probably adept at concealing her emotions," Jane murmured and then hurried back to the broom cupboard in the servant's corridor.

Having only entered the hidey-hole once before, Jane couldn't help but feel like one of the Pevensie children in *The Lion, the Witch and the Wardrobe* as she shoved the brooms aside, released the hidden catch, and pushed the door inward to reveal a dark cavity. Jane took two steps forward and then reached her hand out to the side. When her fingers came in contact with the wall, she closed the secret door behind her, and then shuffled along until she saw an illuminated pattern of overlapping octagons on the floor. The light slanting through the brass air intake vent made it possible to recognize Sinclair's silhouette. She sank down beside him without a sound.

Sinclair fumbled for her hand and gave it a squeeze. Jane knew that he was trying to reassure her, to negate Taylor's claim that Jane was responsible for Rosamund's death.

As Jane returned the gesture, she heard the sheriff say, "I should have arranged for a holding area for our persons of interest. Unless one of them decides to confess, we'll need to keep them sequestered while we conduct the rest of our interviews. Is Deputy Phelps still working on background checks?"

"Yes, sir," Deputy Emory answered. "He already e-mailed reports on every suspect except Ms. Dupree. I have the first report open on my screen."

"Good. Deputy Phelps will have to babysit our suspects while he continues his research. We'll have to ask Ms. Steward for a suitable space. I'll give the front desk a call and see what she can do for us."

Suddenly, Jane found herself holding Sinclair's phone. He'd typed a message into the text box:

I'LL OFFER THE JAMES HENRY LIBRARY. I CAN ASK DEPUTY PHELPS TO WATCH FROM MY OFFICE SO AS NOT TO ALERT THE OTHER GUESTS SHOULD THEY COME LOOKING FOR A BOOK. YOU STAY PUT.

Jane's fingers flew as she typed:

WHILE THE SUSPECTS ARE BEING INTERVIEWED, HAVE LACHLAN SEARCH THEIR ROOMS. IF THESE INTERVIEWS DON'T REVEAL ANYTHING, MAYBE THEIR ROOMS WILL. WE CAN'T WAIT FOR THE SHERIFF TO OBTAIN A WARRANT. WE MUST PROTECT THE HALL AND THE REST OF OUR GUESTS.

Sinclair patted her arm in wordless agreement and then pointed at the voice recorder, which was placed on the dusty floor directly below the air vent. Leaving his phone in her palm, Sinclair disappeared without a sound.

By this time, the sheriff had already left a message with the front desk clerk, and, judging from his next remark, was examining Maria's background check. "Ms. Stone has an arrest record."

"Yes, sir," Deputy Emory said. "If you look here, you'll see that most of the charges relate to trespassing and disturbing the peace. This part highlights her more recent activities."

A full minute of silence passed before the sheriff said, "It would appear that Ms. Stone is a woman with a strong opinion. If I run into a wall with her, I'll take a back seat and let you do the talking. She might respond more openly to a member of her own gender."

Smart man, Jane thought.

As it turned out, Maria was hostile from the get-go. Jane barely heard the sound of her shoes on the carpet before Maria shouted, "What is this? Why was I brought here?"

After introducing himself and Deputy Emory, the sheriff apologized for disturbing Maria's morning. "We'd like to ask you a few questions and would appreciate your cooperation. Would you care for coffee or water?"

"No!" Maria snapped. "Just get to the point. I know my rights and I don't have to tell you—"

"Sit down, Ms. Stone," the sheriff said in a soft, authoritative tone. "I have no intention of violating your constitutional rights, but I would like you to account for your actions between noon and midnight yesterday."

"My *actions* are none of your business," Maria retorted. "What's this about?"

Sherriff Evans paused for a moment and then said, "Rosamund York was found dead this morning.

Jane heard Maria's sharp intake of breath. "What?"

Her surprise sounded genuine, but Jane knew that people were capable of feigning surprise.

"I answered your question," the sheriff said. "Now it's time for you to answer mine. Take us through your movements yesterday, Ms. Stone."

Though Maria complied, she spoke in a sulky mumble. She gave a terse account of her activities, omitting any specific details or observations, and ended by saying that she'd had a pleasant dinner with a group of women who shared her beliefs, and then went to her room to post an update on her blog. "If you had my computer, you could check the timestamp," she said in a taunting voice that rankled Jane. "But since I'm not going to give it to you, you'll just have to take me at my word."

"What's your blog about?" Deputy Emory asked and Jane assumed Sheriff Evans had wordlessly signaled for his deputy to take over the interview.

"It's a group blog maintained by women interested in

protecting the rights, freedom, and equality of other women. We fight all kinds of social injustices like racism and gender discrimination."

"That's a worthy use of social media," Deputy Emory said. "Better than some of those beauty or fashion sites that seem to be all the rage."

Clever girl, Jane thought. *You knew just which button to push.*

"That kind of superficial focus is *exactly* what women don't need," Maria said, instantly animated. "I'm not saying we shouldn't care about our appearance, but as long as women are viewed as Barbie dolls, we won't be given an equal wage or the same benefits as men."

"Is there a term for your movement? And did you come to Romancing the Reader to gather material for your blog?"

"We're known by several terms and not all are flattering," Maria said. "But we're basically modern feminists. And no, I didn't come here with a political agenda. This trip was *supposed* to be my dream vacation." She paused. "I expected to meet lots of like-minded women because I assumed that anyone who was a fan of Venus Dares believed what I believed. Some of the attendees do, but others are hopelessly trapped in a 1950s mentality."

Deputy Emory made a noise to show that she was listening and then asked, "You mentioned Venus Dares. Who is she?"

In response, Maria launched into a lengthy monologue about Rosamund's celebrated heroine. Soon, she and Deputy Emory were chatting like old friends. "It sounds like you really admire Ms. York's work."

"I did." Maria's anger flared back into life. "That was *before* she penned an offensive piece of crap featuring a chauvinist hero. He's an oppressor of women. The *complete* opposite of everything Venus Dares represents. This Eros guy treats women like they're some kind of sub species. Like they're brainless. And they still like him despite how he acts. That's the worst part! How weak the female characters are. The whole book made my stomach turn!"

Deputy Emory whistled softly. "I don't like stories where

women are made to look inferior. That book would have upset me too. But nothing can be done about it, right? Isn't the novel already published?"

"No, we were given advanced reader copies." There was a glimmer of hope in Maria's voice. "There's still a chance to make changes, and if Ms. York's publisher doesn't want to offend thousands of readers, they'd better do some major revising. Honestly, they'd be better off canceling the project. There's nothing salvageable in that drivel."

"Were you able to talk to Ms. York about this? To tell her how you felt about her new book?"

Maria snorted. "It was pretty obvious how the majority of the women here felt about *Eros Steals the Bride*. Most of the ladies here aren't outspoken like the women in my Matilda group—that's the name of our organization—but they made it clear how much they disliked the book. Dozens of us tried to ask questions during yesterday's panel, but the moderator protected Ms. York from having to answer."

"So you hadn't expressed your concerns to Ms. York at all?" Deputy Emory pressed the issue and Jane sensed she was trying to get Maria to confess that she'd written Rosamund a threatening letter.

Maria didn't respond. Even from where Jane sat on the other side of the wall, she could feel a shift in the air. The silence was heavy with unspoken words. "Tell me why I'm really here, Sheriff Evans. I've had enough of the bad cop/ good cop routine."

A chair creaked on the far side of the table as the sheriff shifted his weight. Jane pictured him leaning forward and tenting his hands in an attempt to convey the gravity of the situation. "I don't think Ms. York's death was an accident, so if there's anything you'd like to tell me about your dealings with the victim, now would be the time."

"I have nothing to say," Maria said and Jane marveled at her stubbornness.

The sheriff gave her a long moment to change her mind and then used the radio attached to his uniform shirt to call Deputy Phelps. "Ms. Stone, you will join Ms. Birch in the library. You will not speak to her or to the other guests. Right now, you are a person of interest in this investigation. If, at any point, you'd like to come forward with any additional information, the deputy will escort you back to this room."

"You have no right—"

"I'm investigating a suspicious death," the sheriff interjected curtly. "You may want to reflect on my use of the term 'suspicious' while you're sequestered in the library. Deputy Emory, please show Ms. Stone out and return with Ms. Jewel."

Barbara Jewel was clearly shaken by the sheriff's presence and completely transparent in describing her movements of the previous day. She didn't even ask why she was being questioned until Sheriff Evans had all the information he needed. It was only when he thanked her for her time that she haltingly asked why he'd wanted to speak with her in the first place. After learning of Rosamund's death, Barbara burst into tears.

"I was unkind to her yesterday!" she wailed. "I was jealous of the attention she was getting. I've never cared much about bestseller lists or awards, but I do covet my connections to my readers and I felt threatened by Rosamund—as though she was out to steal every reader for herself." She stopped to blow her nose. "It was so childish of me. Readers aren't like that. They'll buy hundreds of books in the genre they love and they don't limit their support to one or two writers. I know that. And yet, I was still envious of Rosamund's popularity. I snubbed her. I was rude. Now I'll never have the chance to make amends!"

Eventually, Deputy Emory led the distraught novelist from the room.

Ciara Lovelace was next. Like Barbara, she was willing to provide the sheriff with a specific timeline and was equally upset when she heard about Rosamund's passing. Unlike Barbara, Ciara didn't cry. She fell quiet and didn't speak again until Deputy Emory asked if she had anything to add.

"I acted like a girl in a high school clique," Ciara said very softly. "Georgia kept whispering into my ear, pointing out ways that Rosamund stole our thunder at every conference. I was so swayed by her comments that I didn't stop to consider my own behavior. Is there anything I can do? Can I assist her family in some way?"

"Are you acquainted with Ms. York's family?" Sheriff Evans asked.

"No. I only knew Rosamund on a superficial level. We've attended many of the same conferences. She was friendly enough, but she always kept herself apart from the rest of the authors." Ciara sighed. "She and I never talked about anything beyond books or the publishing world at large."

As he had with Barbara, Sheriff Evans thanked Ciara for her frankness and cautioned her not to discuss the case with anyone.

The door opened, closed, and opened again five minutes later.

"Damn it!" Georgia Dupree cried. "That stupid cat nearly tripped me!"

Jane stiffened. Georgia could only be referring to one feline, but Jane couldn't imagine what would possess Muffet Cat to enter the conference room. At this time of the day, he was usually searching for a sunny place to take a long nap.

Muffet Cat released a low growl—a clear sign that he disliked someone.

"He's gone under the table," Deputy Emory said with a hint of a smile in her voice.

"Never mind about the cat," the sheriff said. "Ms. Dupree, please have a seat. Would you like a cup of coffee?"

Jane could see Georgia's leopard-print heels pause in front of the air vent. "I'd prefer an explanation. I'm at this event to be seen, not to be called away from an important activity to attend a clandestine meeting with members of local law enforcement." She sucked in a quick breath and continued. "I assume that a crime's been committed. A robbery, perhaps? I'm not missing anything if that's what you want to know."

"We're not investigating a theft, Ms. Dupree," the sheriff said and launched into his questions.

For that point on, Georgia behaved just like Maria Stone. She refused to account for her whereabouts until the sheriff told her that Rosamund was dead.

"Really?" Georgia failed to conceal her excitement. "How?"

The sheriff ignored her questions and repeated his own until Georgia reluctantly cooperated. In the midst of her recitation, Georgia seemed to suddenly realize that she was being asked to provide an alibi. Her smug demeanor vanished and she began to whine. "Wait a minute. Is some maniac targeting famous authors? Should I be worried? Could I be *next*?"

From somewhere under the table, Muffet Cat growled.

I'm with you, Muffet Cat, Jane thought. *Does Georgia really think the sheriff is going to buy her frightened female act? The woman is an egomaniac. Even now, she has to lump herself in with Rosamund.*

Jane suddenly realized that Sheriff Evans had asked Georgia another question.

"Naturally, there was a certain amount of competition between us, but we were both professionals," Georgia said. She'd dropped all pretense of fear and had adopted a haughty tone instead. "We didn't go around pulling each other's hair or exchanging insults in public."

Deputy Emory murmured something to the sheriff and then said, "I don't know much about romance novels—I'm a diehard mystery reader—but I did some research on your genre's most notable authors earlier this morning. Judging by the number of weeks Ms. York's novels remain on the major bestseller lists, she was not only a successful writer and a wealthy woman, but also a household name. Could the same be said of you?"

Jane smiled. She was growing fonder of Deputy Emory by the minute.

"We were nearly on par," Georgia muttered sourly. "I have no doubt that my next release would have been more successful than Rosamund's. Her fans were *very* disappointed by the advanced reader copies Rosamund gave away at the charity auction, so I was confident that I'd soon be outranking her on those bestseller lists."

"Perhaps you decided not to leave that up to chance," Sheriff Evans said.

"Are you implying that *I* killed Rosamund York?" Georgia's ire was rising. "That's absolutely preposterous. You heard my itinerary from yesterday. You must realize I hardly had time to sit down, let alone bump off my riv—" She halted abruptly and took a deep, steadying breath. "My novels might be filled with intrigue and violence, but I don't act out my plots. I'm not the sort of person who confuses fact with fiction, and I hope you aren't either, Sheriff. I hope you're not reenacting *The Crucible* or *The Witch of Blackbird Pond* just to make a name for yourself."

When the sheriff didn't reply, Georgia went on. "I can see that my literary references are lost on you. What I'm saying is that you'd better not be conducting a witch hunt."

"Actually, I am quite familiar with both Arthur Miller's play and the young adult novel by Elizabeth George Speare, and I can assure you that this is no witch hunt," the sheriff said. "This is a murder investigation. It's also your only chance to come clean, Ms. Dupree. Do you have anything else to share with us?"

One of the things Jane had told Sheriff Evans when they were back in her office was the threat Mrs. Pratt had overheard Georgia whisper to Rosamund in the elevator of another hotel. Georgia had called Rosamund a charlatan and vowed to take her rightful place "at the top." She'd repeated this notion shortly after arriving at Storyton Hall. Jane had recited her exact words to the sheriff. "The time has finally come for you to disappear," Georgia had said, "And I promise you this, Rosamund. Yours will *not* be a happy ending."

Making no mention of either of these occurrences, Georgia insisted she had nothing else to say. Jane heard the whoosh of wheels on the carpet as she pushed her chair away from the table.

"Before you go, Ms. Dupree, I was wondering if you could tell me why someone would call Ms. York a charlatan." The sheriff's tone was that of mild curiosity, but Jane wasn't fooled.

"I have no idea." Georgia sounded bored. "Maybe you should ask one of her fans."

"I believe *you* used the term to describe her," the sheriff continued in a low and dangerous voice. "I believe you also vowed to take Ms. York's place. How could you be so sure that hers would be an unhappy ending unless you had a hand it that ending?"

"How dare you!" Georgia shouted, shoving her chair backward until it struck the wall. Jane flinched and Muffet Cat meowed in alarm and raced over to the air vent. He pressed his face against the brass vent cover, his black nose quivering as he detected Jane's familiar scent. He meowed again. This time, it was a short, quick noise of inquiry, as though he were saying, *What are* you *doing back there?*

Luckily, Georgia was too incensed to pay attention to Muffet Cat. "Are you accusing me of killing Rosamund? Because if you are, I want a lawyer. If you're not, then I demand to be released. I will *not* be treated like a criminal. Not *everyone* in the world was a fan of the great and wonderful Rosamund York, you know. She angered dozens of people with that new book of hers. You have a hotel filled with potential suspects." She spoke so quickly and heatedly that she was nearly panting. "Well? Are you arresting me or not?"

Sheriff Evans sighed and explained that while he wasn't placing anyone under arrest, he would be sequestering certain individuals in the Henry James library. Hearing this, Georgia let loose a shriek of protest, claiming that it was her duty to interact with her fans. Her complaints fell on deaf ears.

At long last, Deputy Emory led Georgia from the room.

"What a piece of work," the sheriff mumbled and used his radio to send for his final suspect: Nigel Poindexter.

Jane prayed Nigel's interview would be brief. The three cups of coffee she'd consumed earlier had passed through her system and her bladder was uncomfortably full. Not only that, but her legs were cramped from being in the same position for nearly two hours on the cold, hard floor.

Muffet Cat peered between the octagons of the air intake cover again and when he mewled in frustration, Sheriff Evans snapped his fingers and make clicking noises with this tongue. "Would kitty like some cream?"

Muffet Cat vanished and Jane smiled as the sheriff fussed over the coddled feline.

"Sir?" The voice emitting from the sheriff's radio sounded

anxious. "The staff has been unable to locate Mr. Poindexter. They've searched the entire house and grounds, but there's no sign of him."

"Stay where you are, Phelps," the sheriff said. "I'll track down Ms. Steward. Deputy Emory and I had better look inside Mr. Poindexter's room."

I hope Lachlan already had the chance to search it, Jane thought. She was filled with a powerful sense of unease. Where could Nigel be? And how could he have disappeared without the Fins knowing?

Jane waited for the sheriff to leave the William Faulkner and then scrambled to her feet, grabbed the recorder, and, after peeking out through a crack in the broom cupboard door to be sure she was alone, hurried down the hall.

In the employee restroom, she glanced in the mirror and was startled by her appearance. Her skirt suit was covered with dust, her hair was unkempt, and her face was pale.

"You look like a ghost," she told her reflection, which frowned back at her.

Jane wiped the dust off her clothes with a damp paper towel, washed her hands, and then pinched her cheeks until two red spots bloomed on her skin.

"There. That's how the Guardian of Storyton Hall should look." She smoothed her jacket and squared her shoulders. "Like someone prepared to hunt down a killer."

TEN

Jane unlocked the door to one of Storyton's smaller guest rooms. Located in the front of the manor house, it had a view of the long driveway, the mist-covered blue hills, and the low, gray sky.

Out of habit, Jane knocked on the door before pushing it open, and then she, Sheriff Evans, and Deputy Emory entered.

Jane quickly scanned the room. Despite signs that Nigel had made himself at home—yesterday's paper was scattered over the desk, several paperbacks and a pair of reading glasses were on the bedside table, and half a dozen whiskey bottles were clustered on the dresser—the space felt curiously unoccupied.

"He didn't sleep here," Jane said. "The housekeeper performed her turndown service last night and this bed hasn't been touched since then. There isn't so much as a wrinkle in the coverlet."

"The treats on the pillows? What's inside the gold foil?" Deputy Emory asked.

Jane walked over to the bed. "Chocolate truffles. Homemade in Storyton's kitchens. The staff makes a different flavor each day. I believe yesterday's was caramelized white chocolate."

"I wouldn't leave those little gems behind, but it looks like Mr. Poindexter did," the deputy said.

Sheriff Evans wriggled his hands into a pair of blue latex gloves and looked at Jane. "With your permission?" he asked, and then opened the top dresser drawer. He rifled through a row of socks and folded undershirts before investigating the next drawer, which held a pair of pajama pants and a Florida Gators T-shirt.

"Deputy, would you check the bathroom?" the sheriff asked. Having finished with the dresser, he flipped on the closet light and examined the contents. Peering over his shoulder, Jane saw dress shirts, slacks, and a navy sports coat. Nigel's suitcase was propped on the luggage rack.

Without turning away from the clothes, Sheriff Evans said, "Nothing unusual here. If Mr. Poindexter left the premises, he didn't take much with him."

Jane edged past him and moved to the back of the walk-in closet. "His coat is gone. Was his wallet in the dresser?"

"No." The sheriff crossed the room, heading for the desk. "He's a writer, so—"

"Where's his computer?" Jane completed his thought. "Or his notes. Memo pads. Anything to show that he came to Romancing the Reader to write articles."

Sheriff Evans pointed at the phone. "It's time to mobilize the troops. If your people have already combed the house and grounds, we'll need to widen the search. I'll send men into the woods and have others canvas the village."

While the sheriff placed his call, Jane joined Deputy Emory in the bathroom.

"All the towels are folded," she said, looking from the sink to the shower and tub unit. "Have you found anything?"

The young deputy, who'd also donned a pair of latex gloves, was prodding the contents of a plastic bag with her fingertip. She didn't open the bag, but held it to the light and frowned.

"The bag was in the garbage can, buried under schedules from the recreation desk. These look like beans," Deputy Emory said. "Do you know what they are?"

The deputy laid the bag flat on her palm and Jane peered

down at the glossy brown beans. Each one was mottled by splotches of black and was about the size of a coffee bean. Very few of them were whole. Most had been split open and hollowed out. "They could be beans or a type of plant seed. I'm not sure."

Deputy Emory pulled an X-Acto knife from Nigel's medicine kit. "Unless he was scrapbooking in his spare time, he probably used this knife to cut open the beans."

"Tom Green should be arriving any minute now to deliver today's flower arrangements. I bet he can identify these for us," Jane said. "His knowledge of plants is boundless."

"We should definitely talk to him. Let me just show the sheriff first." The deputy left the bathroom and Jane seized the opportunity to look inside Nigel's medicine kit.

Staring at his comb, toothbrush, and bottle of aftershave without touching them, she thought, *Everything he left can be easily replaced.*

Jane glanced at her watch and, when she saw that it was nearly noon, the knot that had formed hours ago in the pit of her stomach tightened. Emerging from the bathroom, she caught the sheriff's eye. "I'll have to make an announcement to the guests. Most of them will be gathering in the lobby for the first lunch seating, but I can have them go into the theater where the trivia contest is still in progress and address them en masse. If they don't hear about Ms. York's death from me, I could be facing an angry mob by tea time."

Sheriff Evans nodded. "I'll stand with you. My presence will reinforce the directive that no one may leave the resort without permission. Shall we return to your office and draft a statement while Deputy Emory speaks with Mr. Green?"

As it turned out, Tom Green was waiting for Jane at the reception desk. He held a tall bouquet of red flowers in his arms as though he were cradling a newborn. "These are for you," he said, his face shining with impish delight. "From a *secret* admirer. He placed the order with my assistant, so I was unable to identify his voice, but he wanted to make sure that you were told the meaning behind the gladiolus flower."

"Which is?" Jane asked, feeling the curious gazes of both Sheriff Evans and Deputy Emory on her.

"Moral integrity and strength," Tom said and then shrugged. "It's not the most romantic sentiment, but maybe your suitor is saving that message for tomorrow, seeing as it's Valentine's Day."

Edwin, Jane thought, reaching for the flowers.

Though she wanted to rush into her office and bury her face in the fragrant blooms, Jane had no time to lose herself in girlish fantasies of a late-night dance or the hope of a moonlit kiss. "Tom, would you mind taking a look at the objects in Deputy Emory's bag? We're hoping you can identify them for us."

Deputy Emory placed the bag on the registration desk. "Please don't touch the bag, sir."

Tom raised his brows in surprise, but was too intrigued to question the deputy. Hands clasped obediently behind his back, he bent over the bag. "What do we have here?" Chewing thoughtfully on his lower lip, he murmured, "An excellent deer repellant. Fast growing. Lovely foliage. But dangerous." He straightened and looked from Jane to the sheriff. "I refuse to carry these at the Potter's Shed. Not in any form. Seeds, seedlings, or fully matured plant. They're too toxic and plenty of other plants can deter deer. Any plant or shrub with thorns, aromatic or sharp foliage, or fuzzy leaves. Deer are not fond of fuzzy leaves or—"

"Mr. Green." The sheriff cut him off. "Do these objects have a name?"

Tom looked at the bag again. "They're seeds from the castor plant. The entire plant is poisonous, but these seeds are where the real trouble lies. Inside these mottled casings are hulls so lethal that they make cyanide seem mild in comparison." He turned to Jane. "I don't sell the plant because a child or family pet, not knowing any better, might ingest one of the seeds. The plants produce beautiful, star-shaped leaves and are really quite lovely, but they're not worth the risk."

The sheriff exchanged a knowing glance with Deputy Emory and she scooped up the bag and dropped it in her pocket. "Thank you, Mr. Green," she said with a smile. "You were a big help."

"Glad to be of service," he replied and then touched Jane

on the arm. "I have to get moving. The van is loaded with arrangements for the guest rooms. Perhaps I'll be knocking on your office door tomorrow with another bouquet from your mystery man."

He bustled off while Jane led the sheriff and Deputy Emory through to her office. They drafted a quick announcement and then the sheriff asked to commandeer her space in order to check in with the station.

Jane took advantage of the respite to walk through the kitchens to the loading dock. She paused briefly at one of the prep sinks to drop the bouquet into a pitcher of water before heading out into the cold.

Coatless, Jane jogged across the lawn to the garage and knocked three times on a closed door marked with a *No Admittance* sign.

A shadow darkened the peephole and Jane could hear Sterling undoing a pair of dead bolts on the other side of the metal door. He opened it just wide enough for Jane to slip through and then quickly shut and locked it again.

Jane surveyed the head chauffeur's lab. She'd only been inside a few times and though she couldn't identify most of the aging pieces of equipment other than test tubes, beakers, or centrifuges, she was impressed that Sterling seemed able to conduct a number of basic experiments in the small space.

"There's a strong possibility that Nigel used castor seeds to poison Rosamund." Jane gestured at the test tubes. "Did you find a specific poison in the samples you collected from the garden?"

"Yes, and in copious amounts," Sterling said. "Mr. Lachlan brought me one of the seeds immediately after searching Mr. Poindexter's room. Not only was I able to identify the seed, but I also learned how easy they are to acquire. Despite their high level of toxicity, they're available online. Anyone with a credit card can buy them."

Jane stared at the microscope slide and wondered what a lethal poison looked like up close. "Why are castor seeds so dangerous?"

"Do you remember hearing accounts of letters containing

Ricin powder being sent to the White House and other government offices?" At Jane's nod, Sterling continued. "Ricin powder is the result of a chemical process. It's lethal when inhaled or injected. Ricin comes from the castor beans, which can be deadly in their raw form. However, if a healthy person were to swallow a handful of beans whole, they wouldn't die. A person needs to *chew* the beans for the poison to be released."

Jane gasped. "Someone who was fond of nuts in their dessert would certainly do that. Someone like Rosamund."

"Precisely. Our killer mixed the seed hulls into a chocolate truffle along with chopped walnuts. Ms. York didn't stand a chance. If she'd only had a seed or two, she might have survived. However, the lethal dose is eight seeds for a male of average height and weight. It wouldn't be a stretch to assume that Rosamund chewed that much poison simply by consuming two or three truffles."

"Then she was definitely killed during the truffle workshop." Jane moaned. "All of our suspects were present at that event."

"But only one has fled," Sterling reminded her.

Jane released an exasperated sigh. "How can he have evaded our cameras?"

"I've been asking myself the same question," Sterling said. "And the only answer I can come up with is that Mr. Poindexter hasn't left the house at all. We searched the public areas, Miss Jane, but not the private ones. Nor the secret ones."

"But that means . . ." Jane trailed off. "Could Rosamund's death have been a diversion? Something to keep us distracted while Nigel tried to find our hidden library?" She felt her panic rising. "I haven't spoken with Uncle Aloysius or Aunt Octavia all morning! What if—"

"I have, and they're both fine." Sterling patted Jane on the shoulder. "Actually, your aunt has a bit of a cold and has kept to her apartments since lunch time yesterday. Mrs. Pimpernel stopped by an hour ago to do some dusting and ended up fetching tea mixed with ginger and honey instead. She and Mrs. Hubbard have concocted a host of home remedies to treat your aunt's sniffles."

Jane knew Sterling was trying to make her feel better, so she nodded gratefully. "I wish I could check on her in person, but I have to make an announcement to our guests."

At this, Sterling picked up his cell phone and began to type. "Mr. Butterworth and I should be on hand for this. There's no telling how the guests will react."

"Isn't this more important?" Jane waved at the lab at large. "And if Nigel's our murderer, we should be examining his credit card statements from the months leading up to this event. If we can prove that he bought the seeds, then we'll know we're chasing the right person."

Sterling tapped the open laptop behind him. "I'm already on it." Glancing at his cell phone screen, he said, "We'd better go. Mr. Butterworth is already ushering the guests into Shakespeare's Theater."

Jane waited for Sterling to secure the lab and then stepped back outside.

"You should be wearing a coat, Miss Jane," Sterling chided, buttoning his own and pulling on a pair of leather gloves.

"Right now, I welcome the cold," Jane said. "It reminds me that I'm alive—that I have two amazing sons, a wonderful aunt and uncle, and the most incredible friends and colleagues. Today won't go down as one of the highlights of my career as Storyton's Guardian, but I will stand in front of our guests and promise them that, despite what's happened, they are perfectly safe." She stopped and fixed Sterling with a plaintive stare. "You have to help me keep that promise. For the sake of Storyton Hall, we must not fail another guest."

Jane tapped the microphone twice. After hearing the echoed "thump, thump," she said, "I apologize for delaying your lunch and for interrupting the trivia contest, but I have grave news to impart."

The subtle din of women whispering, fidgeting, or coughing abruptly stopped. All eyes were upon Jane and she felt the weight of their collective stares. Her palms were clammy and her fingers trembled, but she adjusted her grip on the microphone and reminded herself that the women gazing up at her with a mixture of curiosity and apprehension were her guests. They deserved honesty. They deserved to hear the unmitigated truth, or as much truth as Jane was able to provide.

"It is with a heavy heart that I must inform you that Ms. Rosamund York passed away late last night."

Jane waited for the crowd to respond. For a split second, no one reacted, but then, almost as a single entity, the women gasped. Throughout the room, women covered their mouths in shock. Several cried out. Others reached out to their neighbors, clasping hands or locking arms.

"At this point, we don't know what happened to Ms. York. She was unwell yesterday afternoon, and we believe that her illness intensified over the course of the evening." Jane gestured to her left. "This is Sheriff Evans of the Storyton Sheriff's Department. He's asking for your assistance in his investigation. If you have any helpful information about Ms. York—anything she might have said in passing or a remark she may have made during the truffle workshop, or at any other time, that you feel could be pertinent—please come forward after I'm finished."

Next, Jane turned her right. "If the sheriff is unavailable, Deputy Amelia Emory would be glad to speak with you."

A woman in the second row got to her feet. "You used the word investigation. Does that mean Ms. York's death is raising suspicion?"

A wave of anxious muttering swept over the room and Jane knew she must be the picture of composure if she wanted to prevent fear from spreading like a wildfire. "As I said, we don't know what brought on her sudden illness. I can assure you that it's not contagious, but the until the medical examiner completes his examination and reports his findings to the sheriff, we cannot say for certain what precipitated her passing."

"What happens now?" another woman asked timidly from an aisle seat in the ninth row. "Are you going to cancel Romancing the Reader?"

"Absolutely not," Jane said firmly. "I believe Ms. York would want you to enjoy the rest of the week's events. She came to Storyton Hall to interact with you, her readers, and to witness your delight as you learned Regency dances, created a reticule, or bid at the charity auction. I feel quite confident in saying that she would be disappointed if I canceled tonight's highly anticipated fashion show or tomorrow's male cover model search contest." Jane paused to give the women a chance to mull this over.

"I don't want to miss either of those things," a woman toward the front said.

Jane gave her a grateful smile. "Tomorrow is Valentine's Day. The national holiday of romance. Rosamund York was known as First Lady of Romance, so let's honor her memory by surrounding ourselves with flowers, music, food, candlelight, books, and handsome men. We have a trio of very talented authors in residence to help us continue celebrating the genre we all love. I say we go on. What do you say?"

Slowly, very slowly, a few women began to nod. And then, more and more ladies began bobbing their heads in agreement. This was followed by murmurs of assent from every corner of the room. Jane had swayed them, but she'd yet to tell her guests that they weren't free to leave.

"Today will be unpleasantly cold and rain will plague us until tomorrow. Please stay snug and dry inside and enjoy our afternoon activities followed by this evening's fashion show. If you have an urgent need to purchase something from Storyton Village, stop by the front desk and we'll be glad to assist you. I know that many of you are anxious to have your gowns fitted for tonight's fashion show, but you won't need to leave Storyton Hall to attend to this. Mabel Wimberly will be arriving shortly for the reticule workshop and has set aside several hours to make last-minute adjustments to your gowns." She smiled warmly at her audience. "Thank you for your patience and understanding. Before we adjourn, let's take a moment of silence in honor of Rosamund York."

Jane switched off the microphone and bowed her head. After a full minute, she descended the stage steps. Sheriff

Evans and Deputy Emory walked behind her and the women started quietly filing out of the theater. However, several ladies formed a queue by the theater door where they patiently waited to talk with the sheriff.

Jane hung back to listen to their accounts, hoping these women had valuable information to share. However, it soon became obvious that they were all only interested in engaging in wild speculation.

"I know exactly what happened. Ms. Rosamund took her own life because her new book was bound to be a failure," one woman theorized.

"That's ridiculous," a second woman said. "She could have changed the book. I'm sure her editor would have given her more time. *I* heard that she was suffering from depression. Maybe she popped too many pills by mistake. That would certainly make her feel ill, and celebrities seem to die from accidental overdoses all the time."

Sheriff Evans listened patiently, but after hearing a woman suggest that Rosamund might be faking her own death in order to make a dramatic appearance at the fashion show, Jane had had enough.

Back in the lobby, she spotted Eloise, Mabel, and Mrs. Pratt standing by the center table and felt a lump form in her throat. The sight of her friends, tugging at their gloves and mittens, made Jane acutely aware of the weight of her responsibilities. She wanted to lean on them. For just a moment, she longed to share her heavy burden with the women she thought of as sisters.

"Jane!" Eloise rushed forward and gave Jane a fortifying hug. "Your poor thing. Are you holding up okay?"

Jane blinked dumbly. "How did you—"

"Everyone in the village knows about Rosamund. Deputies are canvasing every house, shop, and eatery in search of"—she stopped, glanced around the busy lobby, and lowered her voice—"your missing guest. Edwin canceled lunch service at the restaurant to join in the hunt. He and Sam are now roaming the woods on horseback. Such cowboys," she said with a snort, but Jane saw pride in her eyes. Sam was the owner of Hilltop Stables and Edwin's oldest friend.

"That cowboy can throw me over his saddle any time," Mrs. Pratt declared fervently.

Mabel elbowed her in the side. "What would your Scotsman make of your infatuation with a younger man?"

Ignoring the remark, Mrs. Pratt fixed her attention on Jane. "Maybe we should we find a more private place to chat."

Recalling that she'd asked Mrs. Pratt to collect information on Lachlan, Jane nodded. "Let's go to the Jane Austen Parlor. It's bound to be empty, seeing as most of the guests are in the dining room. I'll order a tray of sandwiches and a pot of tea. We can have lunch while we talk."

Over Dijon chicken salad sandwiches, Jane told her friends most of what she knew. Normally, she would have held back dozens of details, but since Rosamund's murder didn't seem connected to Storyton's secret library, there was no need to omit much. She didn't mention Sterling's lab, the hidden passageway outside the conference room, or the surveillance footage, but she told them enough to have them gawking in shock.

"Nigel has to be the killer," Eloise said. "The poisonous seeds were found in his room and he's fled for the hills."

"He could also have been in collusion with another guest," Mrs. Pratt suggested.

Mabel raised a finger to stop anyone else from speaking. "But what's the man's motive? Jane, do you think Nigel and Rosamund were lovers?"

"All I can say is that they weren't strangers, even though that's exactly what they were pretending to be," Jane said.

Mrs. Pratt refilled her teacup with the day's featured blend, a fragrant and invigorating jasmine green tea. "Theirs must have been a case of unrequited love. It would take an intense depth of rage to plan such an agonizing death for a former flame. I only saw Nigel in passing, but he seemed like a friendly enough soul. I guess he fooled everyone." Frowning, she pulled a piece of paper from her handbag. "I've had no luck digging up anything on Rosamund's past. All I managed was a chronological list of her public appearances."

"That could be useful," Jane said. "If we cross reference

those appearances with Nigel's published articles, we'll discover if he and Rosamund attended the same events. That would help prove my theory that they knew each other."

"Where can Nigel be hiding?" Mabel puzzled. "Unless he packed foul-weather gear, he won't last long outdoors. He'd have to travel many miles to go over the mountain. Even with my natural padding, I need my heaviest wool sweater and my puffiest coat just to walk from one end of the village to the other." She shook her head. "Folks who think it doesn't get cold in this part of Virginia haven't visited in February."

"At least it's nice and toasty in here," Eloise said, smiling at Jane. "I'm glad you didn't cancel tonight's festivities. I'm sure Nigel will be found by then and everyone can focus on having fun. I don't know if I'm more excited about donning my Regency gown or seeing the men in their top hats and tails. Especially Sam and Edwin. I don't know how you convinced them to participate, Mabel."

Mabel winked. "I have my ways. Besides, what would a fashion show be without a bevy of attractive men on hand to escort the ladies down the catwalk? The male cover models don't arrive until tomorrow, so I had to make due with our local lads. Fortunately, we have plenty of lovely men to choose from." She took Mrs. Pratt by the hand. "You might just swoon tonight, my dear. Both Gavin and Lachlan will be attired in Regency-era Highland costumes. And they cut fine figures. *Very* fine figures."

"I'm surprised Mr. Lachlan volunteered to be a part of this spectacle," Mrs. Pratt said in a theatrical whisper. "I wouldn't think he'd be comfortable being in front of a crowd, seeing as he suffers from post-traumatic stress disorder."

Jane felt a rush of sympathy for the quiet and reserved Fin. "I got the feeling that not only had he seen action in the Middle East and in Afghanistan, but that he'd also lost some of the men in his unit. Men he was very close to. However, I didn't know about the PTSD. How awful for him."

Mrs. Pratt sipped her tea. "Yes, the men he fought beside were like brothers to him, but his deepest emotional wound occurred following his last tour of duty. Gavin told me that

Mr. Lachlan was present when his *real* brother, a DEA agent, was killed during a house raid. The back steps of the house had been booby-trapped, you see. The poor man never stood a chance. Lachlan, who'd been on a ride-along with his brother at the time, witnessed the terrible event."

The women fell silent. Jane was torn between regret and anger. On one hand, she was sorry that she'd asked Mrs. Pratt to gather information on Lachlan, but she was also upset to learn about Lachlan's issues months after he'd been hired. Gavin should have been more forthright with her concerning Lachlan's past. Knowing what she now knew, Jane wasn't sure that her newest employee was truly capable of protecting her family. Though he might be in dire need of professional help to cope with his PTSD, as far as Jane knew, Lachlan spent all his free time traipsing about in the woods.

"Mr. Lachlan might be among the walking wounded—a man whose injuries aren't visible to the naked eye—but thank goodness he found Storyton Hall. He definitely belongs here," Eloise said softly. "Storyton's books, beauty, and isolation are a balm to the saddest of souls."

"I agree. I've always felt that this house and our village were imbued with restorative powers," Mabel said.

"Oh, yes, they're very peaceful and soothing." Mrs. Pratt chuckled wryly. "As long as you discount the fact that somewhere in our bucolic utopia, a murderer is on the loose."

ELEVEN

Jane was perched on a stool reviewing Friday's menu when the twins burst into the kitchens.

"Mom, I made you something!" Fitz unzipped his backpack and dug around inside. He pulled out a pink construction paper heart with a white doily fringe. "I wrote a poem for you. Its says, 'Roses are red, cold lips are blue, and there's no cooler mom than you.'"

Jane examined the wobbly handwriting and felt her eyes grow moist with tears. "Oh, honey. I love it."

"I made one too," Hem said, stepping in front of his brother. His heart was purple and white. "It says, 'Roses are red, the summer sky is blue, and I will always love you.'"

Jane enfolded her sons in her arms. She inhaled their boyish scent of soap, rubber cement, and Rice Krispie Treats.

"Did you celebrate a birthday at school?" she asked. "I smell marshmallows. In someone's hair. Again."

Fitz and Hem pulled back and exchanged astonished glances.

"Good nose, Mom," Fitz said.

"It was Lacy's birthday and we had treats at recess, so we're already hungry," Hem said. "Can we have a snack?"

Jane nodded. "Go wash your hands. Mrs. Hubbard has been waiting to show you her work of art."

The boys jostled each other on the way to the sink. Just when Jane was about to scold them for squabbling, Mrs. Hubbard placed a pair of ruby-red dishes on the counter. "Take a seat, boys. I want to hear all about your day."

The twins hurriedly finished their ablutions and reached into their book bags for a second time.

"Surprise!" they shouted and presented Mrs. Hubbard with a handful of tissue paper flowers tied with a piece of yarn. The stems were creased and the flowers had been thoroughly squashed at the bottom of their bags, but Mrs. Hubbard didn't seem to notice.

"You darlings!" she cried, as though she'd been given a precious gem. After kissing each boy on the cheek, she said, "I'll put these in my best vase. Be right back."

Jane was continuously amazed by Mrs. Hubbard's creativity. She'd cut honeydew, cantaloupe, and strawberries into heart shapes and loaded them onto a bamboo skewer. The fruit shish kebabs were laid next to a bowl of homemade yogurt dip.

"I smell honey," Fitz said and plunged the top of his kebab into the dip.

Mrs. Hubbard returned with a remarkably improved bouquet. The tissue blossoms had been fluffed and the stems were now supported by green pipe cleaners and floral wire. "These are going to have pride of place in the kitchen," she declared, still beaming.

The twins devoured their snack, carried their plates to the sink, and slung their bags over their shoulders.

"Do you have homework?" Jane asked as the three of them struck out for their house.

"Just reading," Hem said.

"For twenty minutes," Fitz added. "That means we're free until bedtime because we always read before we go to sleep."

Jane shot her son a sideways glance. "Do comic books count as homework reading?"

Fitz sighed. "No. Miss Bedelia wants us to read books about *love*."

Hem made a gagging noise and Fitz stuck his finger in his mouth and rolled his eyes.

Suppressing a smile, Jane said, "Why don't we read together when we get home? I'll get the fire going and we can snuggle under blankets on the sofa and take turns doing the voices."

The twins brightened at this suggestion and immediately began speaking in high-pitched, singsong voices. The faster they talked, the faster they walked. Eventually, they broke into a run, racing to see who could touch the front door first.

Once inside their cozy house, Jane told the twins to prepare their reading space while she made herself a cup of coffee. She'd normally drink decaf at this hour, but she wanted to be wide-eyed and alert for both the fashion show and her waltz with Edwin.

When the coffee was ready, Jane carried it into the living room, lit a fire, and sank into the sofa cushions with a grateful sigh. Bookended by her sons, she asked, "What are we reading first?"

Hem handed her a thin paperback. "*Too Many Valentines.*"

Fitz placed his on top of Hem's. "Mine's better. It's called *Don't Be My Valentine.* It's a mystery, so someone might get killed. It would be better than reading about kissing and stuff."

Fitz's mention of murder whisked Jane from the snug, warm room and transported her to the gloomy early morning in Storyton's rain-soaked garden. She pictured the gurney and its shrouded burden and shuddered. The sight of Fitz and Hem playing tug-of-war with Miss Bedelia's book quickly dispelled the vision, however.

"Stop it," Jane said. "You can play rock, paper, scissors to see who goes first."

Fitz's paper covered Hem's rock, so Jane began to read *Don't Be My Valentine.* When she was done with the first page, Fitz read the next one, and then passed the book to Hem. They continued this rotation, pausing to laugh or comment on the story, until the book was finished. Jane took a break to gulp down the rest of her coffee before the trio read Hem's book.

"We can earn extra credit if we finish this book of Valentine's Day poems too," Fitz said.

"You two take turns with the poetry book," Jane said, standing up. "I need to start supper." She tucked the blanket under the boy's bums, tickling each of them as she did so. They squealed and squirmed until Jane was giggling too.

In the kitchen, Jane washed potatoes and carrots and took a roast out of the refrigerator. She wanted to get the meat in the oven before Ned and his girlfriend, Sarah, arrived.

She'd just set the oven timer when the doorbell rang.

"Come in, come in," Jane hastened Ned and Sarah inside. "You both look frozen. Would you like a cup of tea or coffee?"

Ned politely declined. "Actually, Sarah and I were planning to make a special V-Day hot chocolate with the twins after supper."

"It's strawberry hot chocolate served in mason jars," Sarah whispered so Fitz and Hem wouldn't overhear. Jane's gown was draped over her arms. Carefully laying it on the kitchen table, Sarah pulled a magazine photo from her coat pocket. "See? It has a strawberry ice cream base—which is why it's pink—whipped cream topping, and a melted chocolate rim."

"They'll love it." Jane smiled at the young couple. "Supper's in the oven. I expect to be rather late, so I'll just settle up with you now." She pressed an envelope of cash into Ned's hand. "I'd better go upstairs and change."

"We ran into Ms. Osborne in the lobby," Sarah said. "She wanted us to tell you that she'll be here in fifteen minutes to do your hair."

Jane paled. "That doesn't leave me much time. Okay, now I really have to hustle!"

With the twins in good hands, Jane showered as quickly as she could, rubbed lotion into her winter-dry skin, dabbed perfume on the inside of her wrists and behind her ears, and then reached for a palette of eye shadow in glittering rose and gold shades.

By the time Violet arrived, Jane was dressed in her gown. Her long, wavy hair hung down her back and she was brushing her strawberry blond locks when there was a light tap on her door.

"I hope you're decent because I'm coming in!" Violet called.

"I'm as decent as I'll ever be," Jane answered.

Violet entered the bedroom and gasped. "You're a vision! Seriously, Jane, you truly look like you just stepped from the pages of *Pride and Prejudice*. Edwin is a lucky man."

At the sound of Edwin's name, Jane started. She hadn't told anyone except Butterworth and the members of the Storyton band about her date, but if Eloise knew, chances were the other Cover Girls did as well. "It's just a dance," she said, trying to act cavalier.

"Just a dance, my foot. Except for the band, the two of you will be alone in the ballroom. Edwin will be in tails and you'll be a gilded angel in his arms." Violet touched the pale gold silk of Jane's gown. "Mabel really outdid herself, and I happen to have a matching gold ribbon to keep those curls in place." She clasped her hands together. "Any man would melt at the sight of you."

"Thank you," Jane said. She ran her fingers over one of the puff sleeves, touched the gathered bodice, and adjusted the edge of her swelling bust line. "I just hope everything stays in place. I couldn't reach all the buttons. Would you mind?"

"I'll get them after I finish with your hair. You might as well breathe freely for the moment." Violet shook her head. "It's no wonder women were always fainting back then. I'm glad Mabel asked me to model a day dress. Mine is a darling muslin number with lavender trim. It's quite flattering. Hides all my curves."

"Your curves are beautiful," Jane said. "Sam seemed to enjoy looking at them at our previous ball."

Violet waved this off, but Jane saw the glimmer in her friend's eyes. "Sit in the chair, lady. I need to get started."

Jane complied. While Violet brushed her hair and began to divide it into sections, Jane traced the vertical embroidery on the front of her dress. The floral design continued around the entire hem and Mabel had stitched tiny gemstones along the bust line. Violet piled Jane's hair on top of her head, exposing her long neck and shapely shoulders.

"The final touch," Violet said, winding a length of gold silk over Jane's curls. She stuck bobby pins here and there, finished buttoning Jane's gown, and then smiled in satisfaction. "Go look at yourself, milady."

With a swoosh of silk, Jane walked into the bathroom. She almost didn't recognize the regal-looking woman in the mirror. Most of her hair had been braided, pinned high on the top of her head, and secured by the twice-wrapped gold ribbon. Violet had allowed a fringe of curls to frame Jane's face. The effect was pure romance.

"You're a master of your craft." Jane kissed her friend on the cheek. "I've never felt this lovely or this confident. You and Mabel have done more for me than you realize."

"Just make sure Sam is my runway escort and we'll call it even." Violet quickly collected her supplies. "I have one more client to squeeze in before I get ready. See you backstage!"

After Violet left, Jane decided that she had just enough time to stop by her aunt and uncle's apartments before supervising the final arrangements in the Great Gatsby Ballroom.

Jane kissed her boys good night, slipped on her coat, and headed outside.

The rain had stopped, leaving behind a blue-black sky traversed with wispy clouds. The moon peeped in and out of the clouds, illuminating the frost-sparkled ground.

"I'm glad Regency ladies didn't wear stilettos," Jane said to herself. With her feet comfortably encased in ballet flats, she hurried into the manor house and ascended the staff staircase to the third floor.

"Jane, my girl!" Uncle Aloysius exclaimed upon opening his door. "It's a good thing you've come by. I just spotted something of great interest while reviewing this morning's video footage."

Shrugging out of her coat, Jane frowned. "But I thought you and Sterling went over that footage multiple times."

"We watched the feed from last night, yes, but not what

was recorded a few hours later. Consider this, my girl. Where were you at half past five this morning?"

"Standing in Milton's gardens with the Fins," Jane said. "Gazing down at Rosamund York's body."

Uncle Aloysius waved for her to follow him. "Indeed! While you were all preoccupied at the arbor, Nigel Poindexter was making his escape. A partial escape, at any rate."

"Aloysius!" Aunt Octavia barked from the doorway leading to the bedroom. "Have you nothing else to say to Jane before launching into investigative mode?"

Glancing from his wife to his great-niece, Uncle Aloysius looked confused. "Er . . ."

"You're resplendent, my dear!" Aunt Octavia bellowed and held out both hands. "Let me drink you in. Can you do a slow turn? I don't want to miss a single detail."

"Oh, er, yes," Uncle Aloysius mumbled. "You look lovely, Jane. Very lovely."

Scowling at him, Aunt Octavia put her hands on her hips. "Men."

"How are you feeling?" Jane asked her aunt. "I'm sorry that I haven't stopped by until now. Has your cold abated at all?"

Aunt Octavia patted the pocket of her housedress. "Never fear, I'm armed with tissues. And between cups of ginger-honey tea, several cat naps, and a hot bath scented with peppermint oil, I might live to see the morrow."

"You know I couldn't go on without you, my love," Uncle Aloysius said to his wife. "Would you like to join us in my office? I was just going to show Jane what our prime suspect was up to this morning."

"Only if you pour me a dram of whiskey when you're done. I need to keep my strength up."

In his office, Uncle Aloysius went straight to the laptop on his desk. Carrying it to the table by the window, he pulled out chairs for Jane and his wife.

"Note the time stamp, ladies. It's a quarter past five. At this hour, the only people unfortunate enough to be awake are outside in Milton's gardens. I suspect Mr. Poindexter was fully aware of this fact, for here he comes now."

Uncle Aloysius pressed the space bar and there was movement on the laptop screen. At first, it was just a shadow on the carpet in one of the guest room halls. But then, the shadow thickened and became more substantial. A dark figure, wearing a coat and hat, opened the door leading to the stairwell and disappeared inside.

After hitting the space bar again, Uncle Aloysius opened a new window and pointed at a second image. "This is the lobby feed. Our camera faces the elevator bank, but if you look closely, you can make out a change in the light on the right-hand side of the screen."

Uncle Aloysius started the footage. Jane peered intently at the screen and saw the ghost of a movement in the hall. A faint man-sized shadow fell across the floor and then, just as quickly as it had formed, it vanished again.

"So he turned right out of the stairwell," she said. "Were you able to pick him up again?"

"No," her uncle answered. "However, between this camera and the next, there would only be one place for Mr. Poindexter to go."

Jane's shoulders sagged. "The staff corridor. From there, he could have taken the servant's stairs up or down. He could have hidden in the boiler room, the attic, or in half a dozen closets. What I'd give for a trained bloodhound."

"Muffet Cat could sniff him out," Aunt Octavia said. "Though he'd probably get bored of the hunt after two rooms."

As though the mention of his name had conjured Muffet Cat, the portly tuxedo meowed from the doorway, his yellow eyes wide and inquisitive.

"Come here, my pet," Aunt Octavia cooed and Muffet Cat padded into the room and jumped onto her lap. His rumbling purr made Jane smile.

"If Nigel Poindexter smelled like tuna fish, Muffet Cat would find him in a flash. Instead, the Fins will have to conduct a second search. Somehow, Nigel evaded us today, though I can't imagine why he didn't just leave when he had the chance."

"I wondered the same thing," Uncle Aloysius said. "Take a look at what he was carrying." He reopened the first window and rewound the footage. Pausing when Nigel's figure was fully visible, Uncle Aloysius pointed at the messenger bag slung across Nigel's chest.

"His computer." Jane nodded in understanding. "It wouldn't have survived for long outside. Not with the cold and the rain. I suppose Nigel wouldn't have fared much better. He has a coat and hat, but those wouldn't protect him for more than an hour or two." She frowned, trying to predict Nigel's next move. "He might just be biding time—staying concealed until darkness and the hubbub of the fashion show gives him the necessary cover to sneak out."

"But where would he go?" Aunt Octavia asked. "He can hardly steal a bicycle and pedal to the train station."

"I don't know, but I'll have to pull some of the Fins out of the fashion show. I can't have them parading up and down the catwalk while Rosamund's killer escapes."

Uncle Aloysius gestured at the slate board containing the list of possible suspects. "*If* he's the killer. Lacking solid evidence, Sheriff Evans was forced to release the rest of the suspects late this afternoon. Any of those ladies could have been aiding and abetting Mr. Poindexter. We still have no idea what the killer's motive was, so we must continue to be suspicious of everyone on that list." He frowned. "How can we watch them all?"

Suddenly, Jane had an idea. "By putting them onstage." She jumped up, startling Muffet Cat, who bristled like a porcupine and dug his claws into Aunt Octavia's thighs.

"Hush, hush. It's all right," she said, trying to soothe the disgruntled feline. She then wagged a finger at Jane. "You won't be able to execute martial arts moves in that dress, so make sure you have a Fin nearby at all times."

"I will," Jane assured her aunt. *Except when I'm with Edwin.*

As Jane entered the staff stairway, she was torn between wanting the dance to take place as scheduled and hoping she'd be too busy turning Nigel Poindexter over to the sheriff to meet Edwin. After all, catching a murderer was more important than a date with a handsome and enigmatic man.

Touching the bodice of her gown, Jane thought of the

tattoo hidden beneath the gold silk. The owl with the scroll in its talons meant that she'd agreed to make sacrifices in exchange for being named the Guardian of Storyton Hall. She knew she should be more willing to sacrifice her time with Edwin, but she wasn't.

Jane laid a palm against the wall of the stairwell and wondered where Nigel was hiding. She wished she could put her ear to the wall and have the house whisper his location to her. All was silent, but the solidity of the cool stone gave her strength. Storyton Hall had withstood many trials. It would weather this one too.

When Jane entered the ballroom, she found Mabel gesticulating frantically to half a dozen staff members. Seeing Jane, she pointed at the runway. "I'm worried that people will trip. The candelabras are romantic, but I don't think there's enough light."

"Why don't I take a practice run?" Jane suggested.

Mabel hurried to the end of the runway and waved Jane forward. "Walk slowly and try not to look down. And pretend you have an escort."

Jane quickly declared that were too many shadows on the runway. "The crimson carpet is lovely, but it's hard to see the edge, and I can imagine someone plunging right off—especially if they're distracted by the crowd."

"Oh, dear!" Mabel fretted.

"There's only one thing for it," Jane said calmly. "We'll have to put duct tape along the edges."

Mabel shook her head. "That'll look horrible!"

"I don't think so. We have several rolls of white tape in the supply closet. The white on red will echo the Valentine colors. Aren't the men carrying red, pink, or white roses to toss to the ladies in the audience?"

"Yes. And you're right. I'd rather not have my models stage diving. I've worked too hard on their costumes to have them torn." She smiled at Jane. "I should thank you now in case I don't have the chance later. Not only are my coffers overflowing, but it was also a source of great joy to have created these clothes. It's been a true labor of love."

Jane swept her arm around the room, incorporating the rows of flickering candelabras, the balloon arch over the doorway, and the rose petals sprinkled on the seat of every folding chair. "This was your vision, Mabel—a delight for everyone involved. However, I might need you to work a little more magic, and I'm desperately hoping you have some extra dresses on hand."

Mabel grinned. "I might. What do you have in mind?"

"I need to add a few models to your show," Jane said. "They can wear nightgowns for all I care. I just want these ladies front and center where I can keep an eye on them."

As it turned out, Maria Stone had to model a nightgown. She scowled like a petulant child when she learned what Mabel wanted her to wear, but changed her tune the moment Mabel placed a gorgeous red paisley shawl around her shoulders.

"This shawl is for sale," Mabel said with a gleam in her eye. "And it really suits you. Tell you what, my dear. I'll give you first dibs if you model my nightgown with dignity. I'm hoping lots of ladies will place orders for nightgowns after seeing you in it."

Though Maria groused and grumbled and refused to be escorted by Billy the bellhop, who was dressed in Regency-era trousers, shirt, waistcoat, tailcoat, and a tall top hat, she managed to make it down the runway and back without incident.

Unlike Maria, Ciara Lovelace was delighted to participate in the fashion show. With her willowy frame and elfin face, she looked like a professional model as she strode down the runway in a Spencer jacket and a fern green dress with a matching parasol.

Barbara Jewel was also thrilled to have been included. The empire waist of her muslin day dress was very flattering and she glowed like a pearl when Tobias Hogg offered her his arm. Jane noticed that Tobias had two roses in his hand. One white and one red. When he and his companion reached the end of the runway, he tossed the white rose to a lady in the third row. He then presented Barbara with the red rose. Bowing low, he planted a delicate kiss on her hand. When Tobias straightened, Barbara rewarded his gallant demonstration by kissing him lightly on the lips.

The ladies in the crowd cheered at this display and Jane joined in. She'd enjoyed the sweet exchange so much that she nearly forgot that Barbara's name had yet to be crossed off their suspect list.

"She's no murderer," Jane murmured under her breath. "What does she have to gain from Rosamund's death? She seems content. I can't picture her deliberately hurting anyone."

The simple truth was that Jane didn't want Barbara to be a killer. She'd much rather imagine Barbara and Tobias walking down the church aisle and living happily ever after. And when Tobias escorted Barbara backstage, Jane could almost believe that an enchanted cherub called Cupid had indeed struck two people with his arrows.

Someone tapped Jane on the shoulder and she pivoted to find Taylor Birch standing behind her. Taylor was dressed in a magnificent gown of cobalt blue silk. Jane glanced down at her clipboard. Taylor wasn't listed as a model. This was the only time Jane had given the publicist permission to take photographs, and yet, here she was without her cell phone.

"This is Ms. York's dress," Taylor explained. "I decided to wear it in her honor." She jerked her thumb toward Mabel. "Ms. Wimberly said it was okay."

"You look stunning," Jane said. After a brief pause, she asked, "Did you take the gown from Ms. York's room?"

Taylor nodded. "Ms. York always gave me an extra room key so I could bring her coffee and organize her things." Touching the multicolored bandeau in her hair, which was embellished with false jewels, Taylor gave Jane a brave smile. "I know I don't cut the same figure she did, but it seemed like such a waste to leave this gown hanging in the closet."

"I couldn't agree with you more," Jane said kindly. "And here's your escort. Mr. Lachlan, may I present Ms. Taylor Birch?"

Lachlan bobbed his head and offered his arm. He held his body as stiff as the soldier he once was. Jane was suddenly tempted to apologize for making him go out onto the runway, but held her words in check. Now was not the time or the place.

Lachlan was the only Fin present. Butterworth, Sterling, and Sinclair were guarding Storyton's lesser-known exits. Gavin had been called in to watch the surveillance monitors, which would capture any movement around the front and rear doors. Jane suspected Uncle Aloysius would join Gavin after Aunt Octavia retired for the evening, as he was eager to play a part in the investigation.

Taylor returned from her runway walk, flushed and starry-eyed. "I guess that's my fifteen seconds of fame. What a rush," she whispered and politely thanked Lachlan for his company.

The rest of the ladies wearing evening gowns lined up. Andrew, the front desk clerk, escorted Georgia. She wore a canary yellow gown with a lace overlay and dawdled for a noticeably long time at the end of the runway, waving and blowing kisses to her fans.

"What a diva," Mabel murmured.

Jane frowned. "She's been waiting to stand alone in the spotlight for years. I wouldn't put it past her to shove Andrew right off the runway."

Sam, who'd taken a beaming Violet down the runway prior to Georgia's lengthy procession, now offered his arm to Anna.

"You look like a spring bride," Jane said, touching Anna's diaphanous white gown.

"Don't worry, my friend." Anna gave Sam a sisterly thump on the chest. "It's a short walk, not a lifelong commitment."

Sam was a big hit with the audience. After he and Anna completed their walk, he gathered up the extra roses and made his way around the room, presenting the flowers to the gratification of a dozen ladies.

Eloise took her place next to Jane and followed Sam with her eyes. "He's like a puppy. He reminds me of the dog in *Because of Winn-Dixie*."

"I love that book," Lachlan said, coming up to stand beside Eloise.

She swiveled and the skirts of her dress, a charming robin's egg blue, billowed around her ankles. The fabric brushed Lachlan's calves with a soft whisper. "Me too. The librarian is my favorite character. He fights off a bear with a book."

"*War and Peace*," Lachlan said and smiled.

Eloise gaped in surprise and then hooked her arm through Lachlan's. "You and I need to talk books some more."

"I'd like that," Lachlan answered and Jane saw him visibly relax. Eloise had that effect on people. With a word, a touch, or a smile, she could put them at ease.

Mabel gave Eloise a nudge on the back. "All right, my beauty, off you go. Work this finale for me."

Eloise and Lachlan strolled forward like a Regency-era couple promenading in Kensington Gardens. At the end of the runway, Lachlan tossed his rose to a lady in the middle of the room. At the same time, Eloise swiveled to wave to someone and her heel caught on a bubbled edge of duct tape. Jane watched in horror as Eloise wildly pinwheeled both arms as she fought to keep her balance, but it was clear that she was a breath away from pitching into the space between the runaway and the first row of chairs.

Lachlan reacted with lightning quickness. He lunged, caught Eloise by the hand, and, in a single, powerful motion, pulled her backward and out of danger with such force that she ended up barreling into his chest.

She sagged against him, her face creased with pain. It was obvious that Eloise couldn't put weight on her right foot. Masking her pain, Eloise produced a smile and put her hand on Lachlan's shoulder. She looked at him and nodded, as though to say that she could make it backstage despite her discomfort.

Lachlan shook his head. Without asking for permission, he scooped Eloise into his arms and carried her, as tenderly as a child, back down the runway.

The ladies cheered and Eloise, pink with embarrassment, hid her face in Lachlan's snowy neckcloth.

Cupid strikes again, Jane thought.

It was now time to close the event. Jane took a breath and prepared to step out onto the runway. She planned to walk to the end and then invite Mabel to join her in order to receive a round of well-deserved applause and a bouquet of roses the color of ripe peaches.

"Don't go anywhere," Jane told Mabel and started forward.

A hand on her elbow held her in check, and Jane turned to find Edwin at her side. He looked rakishly handsome in his striped waistcoat and dark tailcoat. His black top hat was tilted at a jaunty angle over his brow and a smile played at the corners of his mouth. He doffed the hat and inclined his head. "It would be my honor to escort you, Ms. Steward."

Jane's breath caught in her throat at the sight of him. Lacing her arm through his, she whispered, "I'm glad to see you."

"And I, you," he whispered back and then held out his other arm for Mabel. "Ms. Wimberly, may I have the pleasure of taking the most beautiful and talented woman in all of Storyton down the runway?"

Mabel winked. "Of course you can, you dashing devil."

Edwin flashed Mabel an impish smile and Jane's heart tripped over itself.

Damn you, Cupid, she thought. *I am the Guardian of Storyton Hall. I cannot afford to fall in love.*

Jane tightened her hold on Edwin's arm and stepped out into the flickering candlelight.

TWELVE

At long last, the ladies filed out of the ballroom. Some headed upstairs for bed, but the majority were bound for the Ian Fleming Lounge where the bartenders waited to serve the evening's specialty cocktail. Called Cherub's Cups, the drink was a blend of elderflower liqueur, vodka, and muddled strawberry topped by a splash of champagne.

Except for Eloise, the Cover Girls were too tired to imbibe. They hugged Jane, bid her good night, and left.

"Look at me. All dressed up with nowhere to go," Eloise said and flashed Jane a conspiratorial smile. She sat with her injured foot propped on a chair, watching the staff disassemble the runway. Lachlan, who'd fetched a bag of frozen peas from the kitchen and had used gauze to secure the bag to Eloise's ankle, was now dragging a large piece of wood backstage. "Perhaps your Mr. Lachlan would like to buy me a drink to ease my pain."

"I'm sure he would." Jane squeezed her friend's shoulder and murmured, "Just be careful, okay?"

"Don't worry. I just want to get to know him better, and I think the way to do that is to talk books with him. Since that's my favorite subject, I can't imagine a better way to round out what's already been a very exciting evening."

"Gavin is bringing you the crutches he used following his knee surgery." Jane gave Eloise an innocent look. "Unless you prefer to be carried all over Storyton, that is?"

"I don't want to overplay my Damsel in Distress card. Besides, *someone* will have to drive me home." She wiggled her brows until Jane had to laugh.

"Have fun, Eloise. You deserve it."

"So do you!" Eloise called as Jane crossed the room to where Lachlan stacked the last of the folding chairs onto a wheeled dolly.

"Thank you for participating in the fashion show," Jane said. "I hope it wasn't too awful for you."

Lachlan shrugged. "It was the best way for me to keep an eye on the guests while staying close to you. Should I take up a position by one of the exits now? Maybe Sinclair or Butterworth need a break."

Jane shook her head. "I'd rather you mingle with the guests for a bit—observe those of our suspects tossing back cocktails in the Ian Fleming Lounge. The alcohol may loosen their tongues." She raised her finger. "And if I could beg one more favor of you tonight? Eloise Alcott will need a ride home. I'd take care of it myself, but I'll be engaged for the next hour or so."

If Lachlan knew about her date with Edwin, he gave no sign of it. "I'd be glad to assist Ms. Alcott," he said and strode to where Eloise was sitting in a pool of candlelight.

With Lachlan and Eloise gone, Jane was alone in the ballroom. For a brief moment, she felt a stirring of alarm. The candles had burned low and dark shadows grew in the corners and along the perimeter of the vast space.

Just then, the members of the Storyton Band walked onstage, carrying chairs and music stands. After waving to Jane, they unpacked their instruments, opened their sheet music, and ran through some scales. Four men pushed a piano to stage left while a young woman followed behind with a stool. The conductor, Butterworth's understudy, was the last to appear. He bowed to Jane, turned to face his musicians, and then tapped his baton against the edge of his music stand.

"You were supposed to wear your silver dress," Edwin said from behind Jane, startling her.

"No lady can resist showing off a new gown. But if it's not to your liking, I could go home and change," she quipped.

"I wouldn't let you go now for all the world," he said, closing the space between them. "I've waited too long for this dance, Jane Steward, Mistress of Storyton Hall."

He whispered her name as though it were a line of poetry, and Jane longed to hear him say it over and over again. She raised her arms, holding one hand out for him to take while her other hand came to rest on his broad shoulder.

The band struck up the opening notes of "Waves of the Danube," and Edwin and Jane began to waltz inside the circle of candelabras.

Neither Jane nor Edwin spoke. For Jane, it was enough to hear the music fill the room. The melody was as delicate and joyful as a first snowfall or a shower of cherry blossoms in spring. Edwin's palm on her back felt warm and solid, but he cradled her hand in his as though it were made of glass. He led her with such confidence that she didn't have to think about where to step. They moved as one body.

The band swept them up in Chopin's "Grande Valse," Tchaikovsky's Serenade for Strings, and the airy strains of Strauss's "Tales from the Vienna Woods."

As they waltzed, Jane and Edwin exchanged snippets of conversation. Edwin told Jane about how he and Sam had searched for Nigel Poindexter without finding any trace of him in the woods.

"Considering the rain and the cold, that doesn't come as a surprise," Jane said, wishing Edwin hadn't brought up Nigel. She wanted to keep a bubble around this portion of the night, to prevent her real-life problems from infecting her fantasy. But then, she realized that she'd never get close to Edwin Alcott unless he and she talked about what shaped their lives, both past and present.

"The only person I've encountered as of late has been Mr. Lachlan," Edwin said, slowing his pace in time with the music. "Like me, he also keeps odd hours."

Jane smiled. "I guess you're both immune to winter mornings. Mr. Lachlan is a retired Army Ranger, so I'm sure he's braved harsher conditions than this. And you?" She stared into his eyes, which were dark pools in the dim light. "I get the feeling that your years of travel have taught you to survive without the creature comforts, but why do you choose to go out at such an hour?"

"I revel in the silence," Edwin said. "The world is so noisy. I always look for places where I can be alone, no matter where I go. A deep cave, a lake hemmed in by mountains, a primeval forest, an ocean of sand."

Jane, who also cherished her rare moments of quiet, nodded in understanding. "Whenever I can seize time to myself, I use it to read." She swept her arm out. "My whole world is here, so my travels occur in my imagination. My life must seem rather dull to you."

Edwin shook his head. "There's nothing dull about you, Jane. You are an extraordinary woman."

He spun her around until they were in the center of the room. Flushed from exertion and pleasure, Jane wished the night would never end. However, she couldn't help but notice how low the candles had burned. The room was so dark that the doorway had faded into black and the only thing Jane could see clearly was Edwin's face.

"One last song," Edwin whispered. He signaled to the conductor and the band began to play very quietly.

Edwin lowered his head so that his cheek rested against Jane's as they danced. His skin felt hot against hers and Jane was caught off guard by the rush of longing that flooded through her. She hadn't wanted another man since her husband's passing, but she wanted this man. She wanted Edwin Alcott.

Jane's hand strayed from his shoulder, her fingers plunging into his thick waves of hair. In response, he pressed her closer and closer, until the gap between their bodies was erased.

As though from a great distance, Jane heard the waltz from "Sleeping Beauty." While the notes tiptoed through the air, Edwin twirled her round and round and then dipped her toward the floor in a low, graceful arc. He leaned over at the same time, and Jane instinctively stiffened.

"Let go," Edwin murmured.

Closing her eyes, Jane went limp in his arms. She knew he was powerful enough to hold her and it was a thrill to put complete trust in his strength.

Edwin kissed her then. A long, slow kiss that was as soft and passionate as music. It made Jane's body sing. She wrapped her arms around his neck as he slowly raised her to her feet. That's when Jane felt a whisper of cool air on her décolletage. Far too low on her décolletage.

Jane's attention was divided. She wanted nothing more than to focus on the feel of Edwin's lips on her lips and the pressure of his hands on her back, but she was also acutely aware of her exposed skin.

Breaking off the kiss, Jane rested her cheek against Edwin's and cast a surreptitious glance down at her chest. The swell of her breasts was fuller than before and her owl tattoo was no longer concealed by the gown's bodice.

The song came to an end at this unfortunate moment and Edwin straightened. It was a slight movement, but enough to create a small space between them. Jane tugged the gathered silk up over her chest, but not before Edwin's eyes widened in surprise.

He quickly turned away and gave the band a deep bow of appreciation.

When Jane's gown was suitably repositioned, she applauded the musicians. They smiled, bowed in return, and put away their instruments. Jane wondered how long she and Edwin had been dancing. The candles were nothing but stubs and though Jane was tired, Edwin's kiss had lit a fire in her. She didn't think she'd ever be able to sleep.

Edwin took her by the hand. "Shall we blow out the candles?"

Jane's embarrassment over her dress mishap vanished. She and Edwin blew out all the candles save for one. Edwin plucked this taper from its holder and led Jane to the door.

Once bundled in their winter coats, they crossed the wide swath of lawn toward Jane's house. At her door, Jane blew out the stump of the candle.

"As Edna St. Vincent Millay said, 'My candle burns at both ends; It will not last the night; But ah, my foes, and oh, my friends—It gives a lovely light.'"

Edwin took one of the curls framing her face and gently wove it through his fingers. "Yes, it does."

"Now you know my secret," Jane whispered. "You saw my tattoo."

"We all have secrets." Edwin reached for her hand. He stroked the back of it and then turned it over and pressed a kiss in the center of her palm. A jolt of electricity coursed through Jane's arm. She was tempted to grab hold of him, to keep him from leaving, but Edwin released her hand and donned his top hat. "Thank you for an unforgettable evening. It was worth the wait."

"It was," Jane answered with a smile. "Good night."

As Edwin melted into the shadows, Jane couldn't help but wonder what secrets he kept.

By the next morning, Valentine's Day, it seemed to Jane that most of Storyton Hall's guests had forgotten about Rosamund York. The ladies rose late, undoubtedly needing to sleep off the effects of their late-night cocktails, and when they appeared in the lobby, it was plain to see they'd taken great pains over their appearance.

By eleven o'clock, every chair was occupied by women sipping coffee or tea. Though they all had books open on their laps, they couldn't keep their eyes on the page. As Jane moved through the lobby, stopping to ask how the women had enjoyed the fashion show, it became clear that her guests were all waiting for the male cover model contestants to appear.

"I should have gone to the silhouette workshop," a woman lamented to Jane. "Will the new guests arrive before or after lunch?"

"They'll start checking in this afternoon," Jane said.

The woman closed her book and got to her feet. "I'm going to attend the make-your-own dance card workshop. I hope every line of my card will be filled out by a smoldering hunk." She poked the woman next to her on the shoulder. "Are you coming, Lisa?"

"Go on, I'll catch up," Lisa said. Setting her teacup aside, she smiled at Jane. "I may be happily married, but I've been dreaming of the Ladies' Choice Valentine's dance for weeks. We can partner with any man in the room, right?"

Jane nodded. "You can choose from a wide range of men. Those from the village and Storyton Hall, and of course, the contestants from the cover model search as well."

Lisa shivered with delight. "Forgive my lack of tact, Ms. Steward, but if every author in this hotel dropped dead, I still wouldn't pack my bags and leave. Nothing's going to stop me from dancing with my own Fabio. Nothing!"

And with that, she pressed her romance novel to her chest and hurried after her friend.

Jane did her best to check items off her to-do list, but between Nigel's continued disappearance and memories of her date with Edwin, her plans to review the spring bookings went unfulfilled.

Ignoring the spreadsheet on her computer screen, she went across the hall where she found Sterling gazing at the bank of security monitors.

"Did you get any sleep?" she asked, taking note of the dark half-moons beneath his eyes.

"A few hours," he said. "I reviewed the footage of Mr. Poindexter entering the staircase a dozen times. No cameras pick him up from that point and we've searched the basements, attics, and servant's passageways. I can only come to one conclusion."

"Which is?"

"He exited through the loading dock door and made an escape in a delivery truck. If he crouched low enough to stay out of the camera's viewpoint, we'd have no way of knowing when he left the resort. We had a multitude of deliveries yesterday from the Potter's Shed, the Pickled Pig, and UPS."

Jane frowned. "But even if Nigel hid in the back of a truck, how would he get out of Storyton? Of those three deliveries, only the UPS truck goes over the mountain." She glanced at her watch. "We've had the same driver for over a year now. I'll ask him if he could have had a stowaway yesterday."

"Mr. Butterworth and I will speak with the local men," Sterling said.

Jane pointed at the screens. "And what of our female suspects? Have you observed their behavior?"

"They've been perfectly charming ladies, every one of them. Even Ms. Stone seems to have lost her ire following Ms. York's death."

Jane grew thoughtful. "Maybe her fury was spent killing Rosamund. As far as I'm concerned, none of them are in the clear." She put a hand on Sterling's shoulder. "You should get some rest. You have two hours before your first trip to the train station, and I'm sure my uncle would be more than happy to cover for you."

"I don't doubt that." Sterling smiled, but his smile faltered and then vanished altogether. "Actually, he and your aunt would like to speak with you. They're in their apartments." He turned back to the screens. "I believe Mr. Sinclair is also present. He found a definitive link between Mr. Poindexter and Ms. York."

Thrilled by the idea that they might have some insight into Nigel's reason for killing Rosamund, Jane rushed upstairs.

Her aunt was in the living room, an exquisite heart-shaped wreath made of paper roses resting on her lap.

"How lovely!" Jane cried. "Are the flowers made of book pages? And which novel?"

"You'd have to ask Mr. Alcott that question," Aunt Octavia answered testily. "He sent this on behalf of himself and his sister."

Ignoring her aunt's dour look, Jane reached for the wreath and examined its petals. "It's poetry. Examples of different poetry. This one's Elizabeth Barrett Browning, and I believe this line about spring's first rose was written by E. E. Cummings. And here's 'One Flower' by Jack Kerouac. Someone knows what makes good verse."

"*Someone* knows a great deal about books," Aunt Octavia said derisively.

"You're acting like that's a bad thing." Jane laid the wreath on the coffee table. "Are you upset that book pages were used to make this wreath or because I danced with Edwin last night?"

Even though Jane had spoken gently, Aunt Octavia's eyes darkened in anger. "I've told you before that Mr. Alcott isn't a suitable partner, but you refuse to listen."

"It was just a dance," Jane said, stunned by her aunt's reaction.

Aunt Octavia snorted. "You and Mr. Alcott were the only couple dancing in a candlelit ballroom. If that wasn't a scene set for romance, then I don't know what is."

Jane's ire rose. "And what of it? I've been alone for seven years! I need—".

Sinclair appeared from the direction of Uncle Aloysius's office and cleared his throat. Shooting an apologetic glance at Aunt Octavia, he said, "Pardon me, but before we're further sidetracked by the subject of waltzes, allow me to show this to Jane."

He proffered a sheet of paper. "Miss Jane, these are all the conferences Mr. Poindexter and Ms. York simultaneously attended. Note how many there are in the beginning."

As Jane studied the printout, her ill temper subsided. "This can't be coincidence."

Sinclair shook his head. "I don't think so either. I also looked up every article he wrote during this period—we're talking two years' worth of conferences—and Mr. Poindexter barely published a word. In fact, I'm not sure how he made a living as he didn't seem to have regular employment."

Jane sank into the sofa opposite Aunt Octavia and sighed. "A mystery within a mystery."

"There's more," Sinclair said, placing a second sheet of paper on top of the first. "Rosamund York must be a pseudonym because she doesn't exist in government databases. I've yet to discover her real name. I even placed a call to her editor and was met with stony silence. Rosamund York didn't come into existence until the year prior to the publication of her first book. Because Ms. York doesn't have a literary agent, only certain members of her publishing company know her legal name. Without that name, I cannot search for other places where she might have crossed paths with Mr. Poindexter."

"Her real name could be the key to solving this whole puzzle," Jane said. "She might have wronged Nigel—or someone else—before she became Rosamund York."

Sinclair nodded. "An assistant editor from Heartfire, Ms. York's publishing company, will be arriving later this afternoon. Perhaps she can be persuaded to help us."

"If she refuses, she can talk to Sheriff Evans instead." Jane's anger sparked into life again. "Once I see that she and the sheriff are comfortably settled in the William Faulkner, I'll creep behind the wall and listen to every word they say."

"It may come to that," Sinclair said. "In the meantime, Mr. Sterling and Mr. Butterworth will interview anyone who made deliveries to Storyton Hall on the day Mr. Poindexter disappeared. Someone must have seen *something*."

Sinclair moved to leave, but Jane held out her hand. "Would you stay for a moment? Please?"

Jane then called her uncle into the room. Facing the three people who'd been her mentors, advisors, and surrogate parents, she said, "It's time for all of you to tell me about Edwin Alcott. Why the stern warnings, Aunt Octavia? Why the sideways glances from you and the other Fins, Sinclair? Whenever Edwin enters Storyton Hall, there's a noticeable chill. What do the three of you know about him that I don't?"

Aunt Octavia looked at Uncle Aloysius and said, "We have no choice. Tell her."

When her uncle's kind eyes filled with sorrow, Jane was suddenly afraid of what he had to say.

"We didn't think he'd stay in Storyton, my girl," her uncle said solemnly. "And we never imagined he'd try to win your heart. If we'd seen that coming, we would have spoken sooner. I see that we were foolish to have waited this long."

"What has he done?" Jane's voice was thin with anxiety.

Aunt Octavia held out her hands in supplication. "Because he's your best friend's brother, we decided not to elaborate on his nature when he first returned. We didn't want the knowledge to taint your friendship with Eloise. You two have been like sisters since you came back to Storyton all those years ago." She pulled a handkerchief from the pocket of her mauve velvet housedress and wound it through her fingers. "You're falling for him, Jane, and the man isn't worthy of licking your boots."

Jane growled in exasperation. "Stop dancing around the subject. What sins has he committed?"

"The most deplorable kind," her uncle muttered.

"He is the worst of men," Aunt Octavia said, her mouth pursed in disgust. "A book thief."

Picturing Edwin hoarding a stack of overdue library books, Jane nearly laughed. "What are you saying—that he steals books from shops and libraries? I find that hard to believe when his sister owns a bookstore."

"We're not talking about a boy filching a comic book," Sinclair said gravely. "Mr. Alcott is a notorious and highly-skilled thief. He steals extremely rare books. Irreplaceable books. Invaluable books. Books worth more than gold and jewels."

Jane stared at Sinclair in astonishment. "Books like . . ." She pointed at the ceiling. "Like ours?"

"Yes," Sinclair said.

"I thought he was a travel writer!" Jane spluttered.

Aunt Octavia smirked. "One cannot own properties around the world on a travel writer's salary. Free and clear, I might add. Mr. Alcott also bought his new café outright. He's a wealthy man, Jane."

Unable to sit still a moment longer, Jane began to pace the floor. "I can't believe this. A book thief? Who does he work for?"

"He's a freelancer," Uncle Aloysius said. "Or perhaps, I should use the term mercenary. In short, he's paid by the job. Very handsomely too. He goes by the name the Templar. I believe this is a nod to the Knights Templar, though why he choose that moniker is beyond me." He turned his gaze to the hearth, where a crackling fire created an atmosphere of somnolent warmth that was, to Jane, completely incongruent with their conversation. Her heart felt as cold and heavy as a dropped anchor.

Her uncle continued his narrative. "It can take months for the Templar to steal one book. First, he must establish himself in the region of the world where the book is located by finding employment and befriending the locals. Next, he studies, observes, and plans. Once he's arranged for a suitable distraction to take place, he strikes. He's as silent as a shadow and as patient as water wearing down stone."

"Has he ever been caught?" Jane asked. She desperately wanted the image her uncle was painting to be untrue, but even as she fought against it, she could picture Edwin creeping through a museum at night with the stealth of a panther. How many times had she compared him to a feline on the prowl? "Does he have an arrest record?"

Sinclair straightened his paisley bow tie. "He does."

"I'd like to see it," Jane said, pressing her hands to her throbbing temple. "But not now. I need to be alone. I'm going upstairs."

The lever that would release the secret door leading to Storyton's hidden library was hidden behind an air return vent at the back of Aunt Octavia's walk-in closet. Without saying another word, Jane rushed into her aunt's room, shoved aside the colorful dresses, and pushed a metal shoe rack out of the way. Using the penknife tucked inside one of her aunt's slippers, Jane unscrewed the vent panel, tossed it on the carpet, and then removed the key she wore on a long chain around her neck. The key stayed hidden under her shirt and she only took it off when she showered or slept.

Jane slid the key in the keyhole with one hand and turned it clockwise while moving the lever handle next to the keyhole counterclockwise. She heard gears spinning deep inside the wall.

She returned to the living room, where the china cabinet had swung away from the wall to reveal a vertical slash of darkness. Feeling the eyes of her aunt, uncle, and Sinclair on her, Jane plunged into the void.

There was a battery-powered lantern on the floor just inside the opening and Jane's fingers closed over the handle. Switching it on, she began to climb the narrow, spiral stairs leading to the turret room.

She hurried upward, swatting impatiently at cobwebs. She'd never felt such an acute need for solitude, for a silent sanctuary.

At the top of the stairs, she pushed open the metal door, shut it behind her, and sagged against it. Her chest was tight with anger and something that felt like grief. She'd been falling for Edwin Alcott, but he was not the man she believed him to be. The man who'd volunteered to hunt for Nigel Poindexter. The man who'd made breakfast for her sons. The man who'd kissed her in the center of a ring of candlelight. He was not Jane's Mr. Darcy. He was a rogue and a liar. Worst of all, he was a book thief.

As tears burned down Jane's cheeks, she set the lantern on the table in the center of the room, pulled on a pair of white cotton gloves, and moved to the wall of drawers. Though the space looked like a bank's safety deposit vault, Jane could sense the presence of many books. Just thinking of all the stories tucked safely away in this fireproof, temperature-controlled room made Jane's world less imbalanced.

Wiping away her tears with the back of her glove, she opened a random drawer and reached inside.

The treasure she pulled out was a hand printed copy of T.S. Eliot's poems. Jane drank in the beautiful engravings in the margins, replaced the book, and thumbed through a diary belonging to Ralph Waldo Emerson next. The words of the long dead writers spun a cocoon of warmth and safety around her, softening the raw edge of her pain.

After spending another thirty minutes studying the contents of the drawer, which included a fragment of Latin script encased in Plexiglas and bearing the label: ENNIUS (c. 239 BC–c. 169 BC, *Father of Roman Poetry),* Jane's fingers backtracked to a slim volume of George Eliot's poems. A laminated bookmark tucked inside the front cover read, AKA MARY ANN EVANS. Jane remembered that George Eliot was the male pseudonym for the female writer, Mary Ann Evans.

Jane sat down at the table and gently leafed through the book. "You used a man's name so that you'd be taken seriously. Has a man ever used a woman's name? I wonder . . ."

Replacing the poetry book, Jane closed the drawer and removed her gloves. She picked up the lantern, moved to the door, and turned to face the room again.

"As long as I live and breathe, Edwin Alcott will never step foot in this library," she vowed to the silent space. "I will not let my guard down again. I swear it."

She closed the heavy door, descended the staircase, and reentered the living room.

"Are you all right, my girl?" Uncle Aloysius asked, his eyes filled with concern.

"I will be," Jane said firmly. "If you'll excuse me, there's a lead I'd like to pursue before our next round of guests arrive."

Aunt Octavia arched her brows. "What of Mr. Alcott?"

Jane drew herself up to her full height. "Mr. Alcott will learn to keep his distance from Storyton Hall. If he doesn't, he may end up with an arrow sticking out of his chest. And I'm not talking about Cupid's arrow, but one bearing Storyton's gold-and-blue fletching. Like that cursed little cherub, I've become a damned good shot."

THIRTEEN

Jane went straight to her office, shut the door, and unlocked the desk drawer where she'd placed the biographical sketches on Maria Stone and Nigel Poindexter.

Skipping over the details on Nigel's journalism career, Jane went farther back in time to when he taught English and creative writing classes at a small Florida college.

"If only I could get my hands on a yearbook," Jane murmured and then recalled an ad she'd seen online. The ad, which featured a smiling high school girl with a mane of hair teased to the high heavens, promised to replace missing yearbooks.

Wondering if the same service was available for college yearbooks, Jane did a Google search and was pleased to discover that not only were the yearbooks from Sarasota College available, but they'd also been uploaded for anyone to view. Every yearbook from the mid eighties to the present was listed. After glancing back at Nigel's timeline, Jane opened the virtual yearbook from 1999.

Clicking until she reached the faculty pages, Jane zoomed in on the photos of the English Department. "There you are. Nigel Poindexter, adjunct professor."

Jane studied Nigel's face. She'd found him bookishly handsome when they'd first met, but there was something even more attractive about his younger self. He had a kind, honest face and his smile was playful. "You must have been carefree then—before all the debts began piling up," Jane addressed Young Nigel. "Your students must have loved you. I wonder how many coeds had a crush on you."

Jane continued clicking on yearbook pages until she found a section called "Clubs & Activities," where she spotted a photograph of Nigel flanked by several students—mostly female—who formed the Creative Writing Club.

Zooming in again, Jane examined every face, but none of the young women resembled Rosamund York. Just in case, she looked over the entire graduating class, but none of the girls were Rosamund.

Foiled, Jane began to search through other yearbooks. As the years passed, Nigel continued to teach the same classes and run the same club, but none of his students included a pretty young woman who would one day become a successful romance writer named Rosamund York. That is, until Jane saw the photograph of the Creative Writing Club from 2004.

"Gotcha!" she cried.

No names were listed below the image, but Jane was positive that she recognized the college student perched on the edge of Nigel's desk. At twenty-two, this woman had yet to possess the sophisticated style she'd later cultivate, but she was a natural beauty. In the photograph, she wore tight jeans with holes in the knees, a striped tank top, and ankle boots. Her blond hair was pulled back in a messy ponytail and she wore too much eye makeup, but her skin glowed with good health and her big, bright eyes gazed at Nigel Poindexter in adoration.

For some reason, the naked expression of desire on Rosamund's face made Jane think of Edwin. Shaking her head dismissively, she searched the online yearbook until she found Rosamund's senior portrait. Jane stared at the familiar face and the halo of blond hair and murmured, "It's nice to meet you, Rosie Yates."

Jane thought of the promising career awaiting this young

woman and of how her life would come to an abrupt and violent end in a cold, dark garden.

"You didn't deserve such an ending," Jane whispered.

For the next thirty minutes, she tried to find information on Rosie Yates. Her efforts bore no fruit until Rosie's name popped up in conjunction with a writing contest sponsored by *Writer's Digest*. Rosie hadn't won the grand prize, but she'd snagged first place, which entitled her to a cash prize as well as the publication of her story in the magazine.

"Is this where your writing career began?"

The contest had occurred in 2004, the same year Rosie had been a student of Nigel Poindexter's.

Rosie won two more contests that year. She received another cash award for a contemporary short story, but the second contest was a major coup. The Golden Palm Contest was for novel-length historical romance and included the privilege of having one's manuscript critiqued by the editor of a well-known publishing house. The Florida Chapter of Romance Writers of America printed a short piece featuring quotes from the winners, including Rosie.

"I couldn't have succeeded without the help of my mentor," Rosie had said during the interview. "He might be a man, but he taught me more about writing romance than any of my female teachers. I guess he's my muse."

"Was he more than that, Rosie?" Jane asked. "I think he was. I think you and Nigel were partners."

Jane printed out the Sarasota College yearbook photos, and the details about the writing contests Rosamund York had won as Rosie Yates, and left her office.

She didn't make it very far because Sue stopped her to point out an arrangement of red poppies sitting on the reception desk. "These are for you. Mr. Green is delivering the rest of the Valentine's flowers to the guest rooms. Mrs. Pimpernel is assisting him."

"Good," Jane said, her mind still fixed on what she'd learned back in her office.

"Aren't you going to read the card?" Sue asked in surprise.

Jane would have liked to tear the card into shreds, but

she smiled and shook her head. "Not at the moment. I have too much to do."

In the Henry James library, she found Sinclair presenting a thick tome to an elderly woman. "This should keep you occupied until tonight's festivities, ma'am."

"Are you sure?" The woman squinted at him through a pair of reading glasses with hot pink frames. "I can polish off most books in a single sitting."

"It's over eight hundred pages and I believe there's enough historical detail to slow your pace."

The woman frowned. "I still say that time travel belongs in science fiction novels, but I'll give this"—she paused to read the title—"*Outlander* a try."

Sinclair smiled warmly. "That's all any author, or librarian for that matter, can ask."

"I'm glad we own the rest of Diana Gabaldon's novels," Jane said to Sinclair after the woman had gone. "I have a feeling that guest will be back for more."

"One can only hope," Sinclair said. His eyes moved to the papers in her hand. "Did you find something?"

Jane glanced around to make sure she wouldn't be overheard, but all of the library's occupants had their noses buried in books. "A crazy thought came to me when I was in our *special* library. I was looking at a poem written by George Eliot."

"The pseudonym for a very talented lady writer," Sinclair said.

"Yes. A woman writing as a man. Thinking about gender roles led me to wonder why Nigel Poindexter attended so many conferences for authors and readers of romance novels. Even if he'd been madly in love with Rosamund, would he really travel to every conference just to be near her? She would have been preoccupied with panels, lectures, banquets, etcetera."

"When Mr. Poindexter showed up with a bottle of Scotch and began to pace outside Ms. York's guest room, you suggested the possibility that he was either in love with her or obsessed with her."

Jane moved to a bookshelf and ran her fingers along the

spines. She breathed in the scent of leather, old paper, and dust. To her, there was no sweeter perfume in the world. Tracing the gilt letters on an edition of *Wuthering Heights*, she said, "The most celebrated romance stories have mostly been written by women. The Brontë sisters, Jane Austen, Margaret Mitchell, M. M. Kaye, and so on. But if you take romantic poetry or plays into account, writers like Shakespeare, Blake, Neruda, Rumi, Keats, and Byron balance out the genders. So let me ask you this: Can a man pen a bestselling romance novel?"

"Certainly," Sinclair answered. "I can think of several. *The French Lieutenant's Woman* by John Knowles, D. H. Lawrence's *Women in Love*, E. M. Forster's *Room With a View*, and who could forget Boris Pasternak's *Doctor Zhivago*?"

Jane nodded in agreement. "Do you see what I'm trying to say? What if Rosamund and Nigel were more than lovers? What if they were partners?" Beckoning for Sinclair to follow her to the closest table, she spread the printouts across its polished surface and pointed at Rosie's senior photograph. "What if this young woman fell in love with her writing teacher? What if she had the ideas, the look, and the charisma, but lacked the talent to become a popular romance novelist?"

"Rosie Yates." Sinclair stared at the image. "You found her. Well done."

Jane tapped the photograph of Nigel posing with the Creative Writing Club. "What if *he* had the talent, but wasn't the right gender? After all, how many bestselling *contemporary* romance novels are written by men?"

Sinclair studied the printouts. "If Mr. Poindexter truly possessed the ability, he could have written under a female pseudonym."

"For a little while, maybe, but today's writer is expected to have a website and a social media presence. Eventually, Nigel would be pressured into making appearances— attending book signings, conferences, library talks. He wouldn't be able to hide behind a female name forever."

"You make a valid point," Sinclair said.

Jane looked at her printouts and sighed. As interesting as her research was, it wouldn't help them locate Nigel.

"What if he's still near Storyton Hall? He might be entertaining a wild hope of speaking with the Heartfire editor? Of convincing her that he's the real author of the Venus Dares books."

"That would be rather foolhardy," Sinclair pointed out. "Unless he aspires to write from behind bars. And this is all conjecture, Miss Jane. We have no proof that Mr. Poindexter could pen a romance novel, though I admit his articles are very well written. I read as many as I could over the past forty-eight hours."

At that moment, Ned entered the library. Spotting Jane, he hurried over to her and whispered, "The UPS truck just pulled up to the loading dock. Mr. Butterworth told me to fetch you as soon as we saw it coming down the driveway."

"Thank you, Ned."

"We'll keep chipping away at this," Sinclair said to Jane before turning to assist a guest. She nodded and followed Ned out of the library.

As usual, the kitchen was a scene of organized chaos. Mrs. Hubbard was wielding a wooden spoon and barking commands like a five-star general. When the UPS driver appeared up in the doorway, she waved at him.

"I have a tin of cookies for you, Grant. They'll keep you warm on this cold Valentine's Day. Would you like milk or coffee to go with them?"

The man in brown glanced at his watch. "I'd love a coffee, but I don't want to trouble you in the middle of your lunch rush."

Mrs. Hubbard beamed at him. "Oh, Jane will see to it, won't you, dear?"

Jane led Grant to a counter near the walk-in refrigerator. "It's wise to keep a safe distance. Mrs. Hubbard has been known to throw things." She gave Grant a conspiratorial wink and then fetched a takeout cup and carried it to the commercial coffeemaker. "I'll brew you a fresh pot. It'll only take a minute."

Grant checked his watch again and Jane quickly pulled on an oven mitt and slid a steaming triple berry tart from the cooling racks onto a dessert plate. Setting the plate as well as a napkin and fork on the counter, Jane said, "Have a treat while we wait on the coffee."

"Twist my arm." Smiling, Grant cut into the tart and waved at a plume of steam.

"I wanted to ask you a hypothetical question," Jane said as she put her signature on Grant's handheld device. "Could a person hide in the back of your truck?"

Grant considered the question. "I guess someone could squeeze in between boxes, but I'd probably find them at the next stop."

"Where do you go from here?"

Pausing to load his fork, Grant said, "To the village. I start at the Cheshire Cat and work my way down Main Street." He ate half of his tart in two bites. "Does this have anything to do with your missing guest?"

Jane stared at him. "How did—?"

"My wife shops at the Pickled Pig. While she was in line at the deli counter, she heard some other customers talking about it." He polished off his tart, wiped his mouth with his napkin, and put down his fork. "I'm sure that I've never had a stowaway, ma'am, but I parked right next to the florist's van. Maybe his van was unlocked."

Though Jane felt leaden with disappointment, she thanked Grant, gave him his coffee, and wished him a good day.

"I nearly forgot," Grant said on his way to the door. "The box on top of today's stack is a little worse for the wear. It was like that when I loaded it at the warehouse, but I wanted to let you know, especially since the contents need to be kept frozen."

Seeing that the damaged box was addressed to Landon Lachlan, Jane took it off the pile and carried it to the counter. There was a deep gash in one side and the tape securing the flaps closed was partially torn. Jane lifted one of the flaps and tried to peek inside, but a layer of air pillows blocked her view of the contents.

Jane glared at the box. She knew she had no business opening it, but when she recalled how Eloise had gazed at

Lachlan with the same look of adoration a student named Rosie had bestowed on her teacher, one Nigel Poindexter, Jane felt a rush of anger.

"I need to make sure Lachlan is worthy of Eloise's affection. Clearly, Nigel didn't deserve Rosie's, just as Edwin doesn't deserve mine." Jane removed a serrated knife from the knife block and severed the remaining strip of tape.

"Are you all right, my dear?" Mrs. Hubbard was suddenly at Jane's side. She placed a bowl of soup on the counter and frowned. "You look a bit peaked. Sit down and warm your belly with my chicken and wild rice soup." She pointed at the box. "I hope that's the crème fraîche I ordered ages ago."

Jane started to warn Mrs. Hubbard that the box was Landon's, but Mrs. Hubbard yanked out the air pillows before she had the chance.

"Lord have mercy!" Mrs. Hubbard shrieked and pressed both hands over her chest. "Never in my life!"

Putting a reassuring hand on Mrs. Hubbard's back, Jane looked inside the box, gasped, and instantly closed the flaps. "What would a normal person do with those?"

Mrs. Hubbard, white-faced and shaken, began to fan herself with her hand. "I don't want to know. I *really* don't!"

By this time, the staff member who'd been tasked with putting away the deliveries stepped out of the freezer and walked over to where Lachlan's box sat on the counter. "Does this need to be unpacked too?"

"Not unless baby chicks are on tonight's menu," Jane said.

Mrs. Hubbard moaned. "I'm willing to serve exotic foods, but there's a limit to what I consider exotic. Let's just stick the box in the freezer and forget we ever saw it. I have too much to do to spend time wondering why Mr. Lachlan has been receiving regular shipments of . . ." With a shiver of repulsion, she walked away.

Jane glanced down at the bowl of soup and felt her stomach turn.

"Can this Valentine's Day get any worse?" she muttered to herself and then, catching sight of the paper flowers the twins had made for Mrs. Hubbard, she realized that it could.

She'd forgotten to pick up the special valentines she'd ordered from the Pickled Pig. If she didn't borrow one of the Rolls-Royce sedans right now, she wouldn't have the car back in time for the next pickup at the train station.

"I officially hate this holiday," Jane grumbled on her way to the garage.

"Miss Jane!" Tobias Hogg hailed her from behind the bakery counter at the Pickled Pig. After handing a loaf of honey-wheat bread to a customer, he gestured for Jane to meet him at the far end of the counter.

"I was wondering when you'd come for the boys' treats," Tobias said. "I was planning to deliver them to Storyton Hall if I didn't see you within the hour."

"You're far too busy for that." Jane waved her hand to incorporate the whole market. The aisles were crammed and customers were lined up at both checkouts, their carts full of Valentine's-themed goodies like wine, bread, cheese, and chocolate. Tobias's display case of homemade truffles was nearly empty and the candy section was thoroughly picked over.

Tobias grinned. "I love the hustle and bustle. It's like Christmas all over again." He reached behind the counter and pulled out a white shopping bag. "I have your items ready to go. Would you like to see how they came out?"

Jane nodded and Tobias pulled out a plastic tube filled with red, pink, and white gumballs. At the top of the tube was a single chocolate kiss and a little tag reading, "Blow me a kiss."

"You should get plenty of hugs and kisses for these," Tobias said.

Jane smiled. "I hope so. And what about you? If I had to hazard a guess, I'd say that you put your very best truffles aside for a certain lady."

Tobias nodded enthusiastically. "Yes, I did. I want Barbara to pick me for every dance tonight. Those cover models might be hunky, but would they cook gourmet meals for her? Would they rub her sore back after she'd been typing all day? Would they listen to her read chapters out loud?" He folded his arms across his chest. "*I* would. And I'm going to do whatever it takes to convince her that what I feel for her isn't some passing fancy. I'll follow her over the mountain if need be, but only to convince her to return to Storyton one day. As my wife."

"But you barely know each other." Jane felt like a cad for diminishing Tobias's fantasy, but she was too hurt and angry over Edwin to stop herself.

Unperturbed, Tobias shrugged. "I'm letting my heart lead me. It's never steered me wrong before." He smiled dreamily. "I'm going to spend every spare minute with Barbara until the week comes to an end. After that, I'd like to offer to pay for her to stay at Storyton Hall for another week so I can court her. If she agrees, I know I stand a chance at winning her hand."

"In that case, I hope you succeed," Jane said and meant it. Just because she'd been taken for a fool didn't mean everyone else would suffer the same fate. She accepted the shopping bag and turned to go, but then remembered that Tobias had made a delivery at Storyton Hall the morning Nigel had vanished. "Tobias, have you spoken with Mr. Butterworth or Mr. Sinclair today?"

He nodded. "I can assure you that no one was in my van except for—" His hand flew to his mouth and he chuckled. "I almost told you our pig's name and ruined the surprise!" He clapped his hands gleefully. "Anyway, our piggy mascot would have snorted and grunted if someone had been in the back with him. He's *very* social and incredibly talkative. Storyton Hall was my only delivery that day because I had to take our pig over the mountain for his vet appointment. So unless your missing guest was clinging to the undercarriage, there's no way he hitched a ride with me."

Jane thanked Tobias, paid for her purchases, and hurried down the street to Geppetto's Toy Shop. She pushed open the front gate and stopped at the Pinocchio statue to the right of the flagstone path to touch the wood puppet's nose. All the locals did this before entering Barnaby Nicholas's shop. No one knew how the tradition had started, but it had become a collective habit. Now, people were afraid not to touch the puppet's nose, as though passing the puppet by was unlucky.

Inside Geppetto's, Barnaby was manipulating a ballerina marionette for a customer.

"I'll take it!" the woman exclaimed. "Mr. Nicholas, what would we do without you? You've made holidays magical for Isabella since she was a baby."

"Mine is the business of quickening imaginations and sparking smiles, Mrs. Rowe." Barnaby grinned. "Let me wrap her for you."

Several minutes later, Barnaby bid the woman good-bye and turned to greet Jane. "When I was a tyke, kids were lucky to get a card on Valentine's Day. Now, every holiday is a big deal." He shrugged. "I'm not complaining. Holidays keep me afloat, but times have certainly changed."

"Maybe parents like me buy things to make up for how many hours we end up having to work instead of spending quality time with our kids." Jane let loose a dry laugh. "Isn't that I'm doing right now? Ever since I started planning Storyton Hall's latest event, I feel like I've neglected my boys."

"Stuff and nonsense," Barnaby said. "You're a very attentive mother." He presented her with a shopping bag. "Besides, you're giving them the gift of mystery. What could be better than that?"

"Mysteries are only satisfying when one can find the solution," Jane said and left a befuddled Barnaby to tend to his next customer.

Jane made it back to Storyton Hall in time to turn the Rolls over to Sterling. "I'm off to collect the first Fabio," he said, saluted her, and drove away.

Jane expected the lobby to be filled with women waiting for the cover model contestants to arrive, but after glancing at the grandfather clock, she realized that it was almost teatime. The guests would be lining the hall outside the Agatha Christie Tea Room.

Jane thought of the special Valentine's Day treats Mrs. Hubbard was about to serve. She could almost taste the sandwiches: sun-dried tomato and cucumber cream cheese, smoked salmon mousse, roast beef with cherry chutney, and goat cheese with honey and walnuts. And the desserts! Jane's step quickened at the very idea of raspberry scones with lemon curd, triple chocolate brownie tarts, red velvet cake, chocolate dipped strawberries, heart-shaped Linzer cookies, and multi-colored cupcakes decorated to resemble conversation heart candies.

When Jane entered the kitchens, her stomach rumbling in anticipation, she was met with a chorus of "Surprise!" from Fitz and Hem.

Jane pretended to swoon. "Be still, my beating heart," she cried, hiding her shopping bags behind her back.

"Hem and I would like to invite you to tea," Fitz said in his best British accent.

Adopting the same accent, Hem said, "Close your eyes, please."

Putting the bags down, Jane complied. Her sons took hold of her hands and led her down the quiet staff corridor to the public hallway and into what Jane guessed, judging by the distance from the kitchens, was the Jane Austen Parlor. The room was commonly referred to as the Paperback Parlor due to the number of paperbacks stuffed into the bookcases lining both walls. Over the years, readers had begun leaving a copy of their favorite Jane Austen title with their name, date, and often, a short message inscribed on the inside of the front cover, in the room. Both guests and staff members enjoyed plucking a random paperback from the shelf to see what a former visitor had to say about Ms. Austen's work. The most popular quote, which came from the pages of *Pride and Prejudice*, was, "I declare after all there is no enjoyment like reading! How much sooner one tires of any thing than of a book!"

"You can open your eyes now," Fitz whispered.

"Okay." Jane gasped in delight when she saw the small table and three chairs set up in the middle of the room. The boys—assisted by Mrs. Pimpernel and Mrs. Hubbard, no doubt—had draped the table with a rose-colored cloth. Paper doilies decorated with crayon drawings served as placemats. A bouquet of pink and purple flowers bloomed from the teapot and the teatime treats included peanut butter and jelly sandwiches, heart-shaped strawberries, and shortbread cookies covered with a raspberry drizzle.

"You two did this?" Jane asked, her heart swelling.

"We had a little help," Hem admitted. "But we made the sandwiches and put the flowers in the teapot. You can take them out when you're ready for tea. See? They're in a jam jar."

Jane ruffled his hair. "My brilliant boys."

Fitz pointed at the table. "And we drew hearts on the placemats so they'd look fancy."

Hem pulled out a chair for Jane and Fitz placed a napkin on her lap.

"Happy Valentine's Day to the best mom ever!" they said and gave her a hug and a kiss. While the boys served themselves, Jane furtively dabbed at her wet eyes.

"How do you like your tea?" Hem asked after Jane had finished her sandwich and was devouring her fifth strawberry.

"It was the best I've ever had," she said. "And I have treats for you too. Be right back."

She hurried to the kitchen, grabbed the gifts, and returned to the parlor.

The boys dug through the bags, shouted with glee when they saw the tubes of gum and frowned in confusion after shaking the wooden boxes from Geppetto's Toy Shop.

"Sounds like a puzzle," Fitz said.

Jane nodded. "It is. And when you put it together, you'll discover a special message from me."

Hem's eyes widened. "Like a secret code?" He nudged his brother. "Let's go home and work on it."

"Can we, Mom?"

"Sure. I'll be there soon."

The boys gave her one more hug and dashed from the room.

While savoring a shortbread cookie, Jane studied the crayon hearts the twins had drawn on her placemat. She smiled, feeling content for the first time in what felt like ages. She didn't need Edwin's red poppies or his promises. She didn't need to dance with him or feel his arms around her. She had all the love she needed.

Jane got up and walked to the back door so she could watch

her boys race across the lawn. "I know what Mark Twain meant when he said, 'To get the full value of a joy you must have someone to divide it with.'"

She pressed her hand against the glass. "I divide my joy with you, Fitz and Hem. My sweet, impish, maddening, darling boys."

And then she blew against the pane so that her breath fogged up the glass. She traced a heart in the clouded glass and watched her sons through the opaque outline until they disappeared from view.

FOURTEEN

Jane made sure she was at the registration desk to welcome the Heartfire editor in person.

"Ms. Jamison. I'm sorry that we aren't meeting under happier circumstances," Jane said to a petite woman with glasses, a lovely smile, and sky blue eyes.

The woman took Jane's outstretched hand. "Call me Lily. All of us at Heartfire are devastated by Rosamund's passing, but we're also glad that you decided not to cancel the rest of the week's events. Rosamund wouldn't have wanted that. She was very devoted to her readers."

A burly young man with shoulder-length hair and sun-kissed skin strode up to Lily and handed her a book. "You left this in the car." He pointed at her wheeled suitcase. "Would you like me carry that to your room?"

Lily shook her head. "Thank you, Alex, but I think I can manage."

After Alex rejoined the other cover models lined up to check in, Lily whispered, "The man flirted with me the whole way here. I guess he was trying to get an edge in tonight's competition, but it didn't work."

Jane glanced at the group of men. They all had chiseled

jawlines, powerful builds, shiny hair, and bronzed skin. When they smiled, they flashed bright white teeth.

"I'm glad I'm not a judge," she told Lily. "It can't be an easy task, though I know my friends will enjoy every second of deliberation."

Jane had asked Phoebe and Mrs. Pratt to serve as judges. Phoebe was Storyton's resident artist and Mrs. Pratt was their romance novel expert. If anyone could decide which hunk deserved to grace the cover of a future Heartfire novel, it was Eugenia Pratt.

"May I show you to your room?" Jane asked Lily.

"If you don't mind, I'd like to pay my respects to Rosamund first. Could you take me to the place where . . . ?" She trailed off, looking uncomfortable.

"Of course," Jane said. After grabbing her coat from her office and calling for a bellhop to see to Lily's bag, Jane led her through the house and out into Milton's gardens.

"It's hard for me to imagine Rosamund here. She hated the cold. She said her Florida blood got thinner by the year."

Jane glanced at the editor. "How did Rosamund end up signing with Heartfire?"

"Francine Bloom, a senior editor at Heartfire, read a partial manuscript Rosamund submitted for a contest. Francine loved her writing and asked to see the rest of the novel. That novel was the first Venus Dares book."

Jane nodded. "How does the editing process work? Once you have the complete manuscript, what comes next? Do you talk with the author on the phone?"

"Not anymore," Lily said. "Everything is electronic. We type our suggestions or questions in comment bubbles in the manuscript's margin. The author addresses them and sends the corrected manuscript back to us."

"How can you be sure the author is doing the editing and not someone else?" Jane asked.

Lily laughed. "Not many authors could find someone who knew their books well enough to take over the edits. Every author's voice is unique." She smiled a sad smile. "Rosamund's books were usually very clean. Francine often remarked how little needed to be done to improve them." Her eyes lifted to the high hedge to her right. "Rosamund could behave like a diva at events such as this, but she was a delight to work with. She never missed a deadline and her communication was always polite and professional."

If everything was done electronically, then Nigel could have easily written the Venus Dares novels, Jane thought. *He and Rosamund could have argued about all kinds of things: plotlines, the events Rosamund should attend, how the money would be divided.*

Jane felt a quickening of her pulse. What if Nigel asked for more money to cover his debts and Rosamund refused to comply? That would definitely give him a motive to commit murder. Then again, by killing Rosamund, he'd never see another dime from the Venus Dares novels. Jane darted a quick look at Lily. If Nigel told the assistant editor that he was the talent behind Rosamund York, would Heartfire hire him to continue the bestselling series?

"What did you think of her new novel?" Jane deliberately slowed her pace as they approached the arbor.

Lily shrugged. "It's not my favorite, but it'll sell because Rosamund's name is on the cover." Her face took on a closed expression and Jane decided to stop hammering Lily with questions. Lily wanted to say farewell to someone she'd known for years and deserved a little privacy.

Jane came to a halt. "I'll wait for you here. As soon as you round this bend, you'll see the arbor. That's where she was found."

"I was told she died at night," Lily whispered. "It must have been freezing."

Jane touched the other woman's arm. "I like to think that the last thing she saw were the moon and stars. All those lights shining down on her."

Lily's eyes filled with tears. She nodded wordlessly and then walked away.

Once Lily was out of sight, Jane paced in a slow circle. The movement kept her blood flowing and helped her process what Lily had told her. Five minutes had passed when Jane heard raised voices coming from the direction of the arbor. The voices turned to shouts.

Jane broke into a run, and the second she rounded the curve in the path, she saw Maria Stone gripping Lily by the collar of her coat.

"Let go of me!" Lily cried angrily.

"Not until you swear not to publish that filth." Maria's mouth twisted in rage.

"Ms. Stone!" Jane infused her voice with authority. "You will release Ms. Jamison this instant."

Maria shot her a scathing glance. "Not until she gives me her word."

Jane took another step forward. "You will release her immediately or I will force you to release her. Do I make myself clear?"

"I'm fighting for our gender!" Maria shouted and tightened her grip on Lily's collar. Lily gave a little squeak of pain. "Just swear to me—"

Maria's speech was cut off by the force of Jane's roundhouse kick. Jane's right foot slammed into the back of Maria's knees. Her legs buckled and she went down. Taking advantage of Maria's fall, Jane pressed her knee into the younger woman's back and pulled out her cell phone.

"Come to the arbor immediately," she told Butterworth. "And bring restraints."

"You're crazy!" Lily, who'd retreated to a safe distance, was holding her throat and staring at Maria in horror. "It's just a book."

"Books have power," Maria murmured from the ground.

Though Jane agreed with her, she had no intention of saying so. "Don't move. I'd rather not kick someone who's already down." She glanced at Lily. "Are you all right?"

Lily nodded. "A bit shaken, but yeah, I'm okay."

"You won't be troubled·by this young woman again," Jane promised. She eased her knee off Maria's back. "Shame on you, Ms. Stone. Rosamund York is dead. A *woman* lost her life this week. There are appropriate ways to further one's cause, but you don't seem to understand that. You've crossed the line again, Ms. Stone. This time, there will be repercussions."

Butterworth appeared, breathing heavily. "Madame?" He bowed to Lily. "Are you injured?"

Lily managed a weak grin. "Thanks to Ms. Steward's well-aimed kick, I'm fine." She pointed at Maria. "I've seen my share of rabid fans, but this one takes the cake."

"She will be removed from the premises without delay," Butterworth said. "In the meantime, you've suffered a shock. May I send something to your room to help you recover?"

Lily waved him off. "All I need is a hot bath and a cup of tea."

"Ah, here's our Ned. He'll escort you to your suite." Butterworth turned to Ned. "Please get Ms. Jamison whatever she'd like from the room service menu."

"This way, ma'am." Ned smiled at Lily. "While we walk, why don't I tell you about today's tea menu? I could bring you a plate of the choicest treats."

"Was anything made of chocolate?" Jane heard Lily say as she and Ned headed back to the manor house.

"Absolutely! We love chocolate around here," Ned said, and when Lily laughed, Jane relaxed. A bath, a pot of tea, and Mrs. Hubbard's sweets might help Lily put the unfortunate episode behind her.

Meanwhile, Butterworth had hauled Maria to her feet and secured her hands behind her back using plastic wrist ties.

Maria twisted her shoulders left and right and bellowed, "You can't do this to me!"

"I'm merely restraining you until Sheriff Evans arrives," Butterworth said. "Where would you have me take her, Miss Jane?"

"To the garage," Jane said. "And tell the sheriff that Ms. Jamison is not to be disturbed. I'll press charges on her behalf. Ms. Stone could use an evening or two in lock-up to reflect on her behavior."

Maria glowered at Jane. "The sheriff can't hold me."

"You assaulted a woman without provocation. In these parts, that's a crime, Ms. Stone."

"What about you?" Maria retorted. "You kicked me!"

Jane grinned. "I most certainly did."

With that, she turned and walked away. As she hurried up the path, she thought of how pleased Sinclair would be to learn that his pupil had used her martial arts skills to protect an innocent guest from harm.

With thirty minutes prior to the start of the male cover model contest, the Cover Girls convened in Jane's kitchen. Other than Eloise, who was perched on a stool to avoid putting strain on her tender ankle, the women stood around the center island and waited for Jane to fill their glasses with a fruity red wine.

When everyone was served, Jane showed her friends the Sarasota College yearbook photographs and shared her theory about Nigel Poindexter being the talent behind the Venus Dares novels.

"Impossible," Mrs. Pratt spluttered. "No man could write a woman that well."

Eloise arched her brows. "I'd have to disagree. I can think of a dozen male writers who created complex female characters. Roth, Updike, Steinbeck. And what about Tolstoy's heroine, Anna Karenina? She's more complex than this wine. No offense, Jane."

Mrs. Pratt shrugged. "I don't have your expertise when it comes to classic literature, but I know my contemporary romance novels. If we were talking about a man writing two hundred years ago, then I might believe it. But now? Modern romances aren't written by men."

"That we know of," said Phoebe and winked at Mrs. Pratt.

Violet looked pensive. "Technology has made it easy for people to invent personas. In cyberspace, we can decide what version of ourselves we want people to view, and it's usually a rose-colored version, if not a downright fictitious one."

"That's true." Mabel said. "And despite the warning not to judge a book by its cover, folks do make judgments based on what they see."

"Lots of programs can alter how you look too. Like Photoshop." Anna said. "I could turn myself into a twenty-year-old bikini babe."

Violet, who was bent over the yearbook photographs, glanced up at Anna. "You can't improve on that gorgeous hair."

Anna touched her newly layered locks and grinned. "I want to look my best tonight. I'm wearing control top pantyhose that practically stretch from my toes to my neck, so one of those sizzling hot men had better hold me close."

Eloise looked at Jane, and Jane feared that her best friend might raise the subject of her date with Edwin, but before anyone else could speak, Mrs. Pratt said, "You'll have to be aggressive, girls. The seasoned women in this room aren't shy. Isn't that right? Betsy? Mabel?"

Mabel laughed. "Right you are!"

"What about Gavin?" Betsy asked Mrs. Pratt. "Won't he be jealous if you dance with other men?"

"Ours is not an exclusive relationship," Mrs. Pratt said firmly. "I am free to dance with whomever I please. Would Bob object?"

Betsy snorted. "Not in the least. He hates dancing and hopes I'll get my fill tonight. Besides, he has to run the Cheshire Cat. Valentine's Day isn't a happy holiday for everyone. Some people feel terribly lonely on this day, and my Bob will do his best to make them feel less blue."

"I hope you all have the time of your lives tonight," Jane said. "But don't let your guard down. Nigel Poindexter is still at large." She swirled wine around the base of her glass. "At least one of our suspects is out of the picture."

"Who?" Mrs. Pratt demanded eagerly.

Jane told them about Maria Stone.

"I can't help but feel sorry for the young lady," Mabel said. "It sounds like she's scratched and clawed her way through life. No child should be raised without love."

"Speaking of children, where are yours, Jane?" Eloise asked.

Jane smiled. "After volunteering to clean up the kitchen, they packed their overnight bags and left. They're having a sleepover with Uncle Aloysius and Aunt Octavia and are dying to give them the cards they made at school. Apparently, the boys invented their own Valentine's Day knock-knock jokes and riddles."

"Those two are so creative," Phoebe said. "Maybe they'll grow up to be artists or writers."

"Speaking of writers, are Georgia, Ciara, and Barbara in the clear?" Violet asked, smoothing the skirt of her lavender dress.

Jane frowned. "Unfortunately, no. Ciara and Barbara seem like genuinely nice people, but they could be putting on an act. And Georgia? Watch her if you can. She looks extremely self-satisfied."

"How could a person take pleasure from another's death?" Eloise said.

No one responded, and eventually, Jane tapped her watch face and said, "We'd better get going. If my hunch about Nigel is correct, he'll risk being seen in order to speak with Lily Jamison, the Heartfire editor."

Mrs. Pratt put her wineglass in the sink. "Since we're both judges, Phoebe and I will be sitting on either side of Ms. Jamison. We promise to keep a close eye on *all* the men she talks to after the contest."

Chuckling, the women buttoned up their coats and pulled on gloves while Eloise remained on her kitchen stool.

"I'm worried about you," Eloise whispered as Jane rinsed the wineglasses. "If you really believe Nigel could pop up in the middle of tonight's ball, how will you respond? Do you plan to tackle him in a dress and heels? Edwin should be here to help. Sam too. Of all the nights for them to have committed to a poker game."

Jane handed Eloise her crutches. "It's fine. I have plenty of security."

"Well, I suppose Nigel could be halfway to Mexico—or wherever people run to—by now, "Eloise said. "Maybe he killed Rosamund because she didn't return his affections and then bolted."

"There has to be more to it than that," Jane argued. "Remember what Mrs. Pratt told us during our last book club meeting? Two years ago, she overheard Georgia threaten to expose Rosamund as a charlatan. What if Georgia knew that Nigel was writing Rosamund's books?"

"She'd have exposed her ages ago. Unless . . ."

"Unless she was waiting for a chance to obtain proof." Jane helped Eloise to her feet. "What if the only person who could provide her with that proof was Nigel Poindexter? What if, for whatever reason, Nigel gave it to her?"

"Too many questions without answers." Eloise gazed at Jane with concern. "Just be careful, okay? Don't chase a bad guy down an empty corridor by yourself. Come get me first."

Jane gave her friend a bemused smile. "And what will you do to protect me?"

Eloise shrugged. "Pummel the louse with books? I'd use big ones—like a collection of Shakespeare's plays. That tome could inflict serious damage."

Laughing, Jane joined the rest of her friends by the coat tree. Bundled up to the chins, they ventured outside. The melody of their voices and the scent of their perfume drifted into the night air, and for just a moment, Jane could pretend that she was just an ordinary girl going to a dance with her friends. But when the dark shadow of a bird taking wing startled her, her smile slipped. Once again, the secret side of her, the Guardian, moved to the forefront.

As she lifted her eyes to the glowing windows of Storyton Hall, Jane suddenly felt very alone.

Mrs. Pratt and Phoebe sat in chairs in the front row of Shakespeare's Theater. Eloise had volunteered to serve as an alternate judge in case of a tie, so she also had one of the most coveted seats in the room. Georgia, Ciara, and Barbara filled out the rest of the row while Jane opted to stand in the rear. She wanted to have a clear view of the entire space, especially the exits.

Sinclair, looking very dapper in his tux, took the stage and tapped the microphone. "Good evening," he said in his rich, deep voice. "The moment you've all been waiting for has arrived. The Heartfire Male Cover Model Search will start in a few minutes."

The ladies in the audience clapped and whistled in zealous anticipation.

"The contestants will begin their promenade onstage," Sinclair continued once the noise died down. "When they have finished, they will proceed down the stairs to my left, walk up the aisle, and then cross to the right aisle and return to the stage. Please do not hinder the gentlemen's progress in any manner." Sinclair stared at the crowd. His expression was stern. "Individuals who fail to comply with this rule will be asked to leave."

Twitters of dismay followed this declaration. Satisfied that his warning had been received, Sinclair continued. "Once the contestant has returned to the stage, his portfolio highlights will appear on this projector screen." Right on cue, the, crimson curtains parted to reveal an enormous white screen. "We have thirty finalists, so if you're ready, I will introduce our first contestant. Let's give a warm welcome to Roberto Caballero from Las Vegas, Nevada."

Roberto strutted onstage in a Phantom of the Opera costume. After waving his cape around, he untied it and tossed it to an audience member. His white linen shirt was open to the navel and he ran a hand down his chiseled chest, smiling roguishly all the while. The ladies responded with gratified moans. And when he tore his shirt down the middle and let it fall to the floor, they shrieked and applauded boisterously. As the theme song from the famous musical floated out of the theater's speakers, Roberto played the air organ. With every movement of his fingers, the muscles in his arms tensed and rippled.

Just when Jane started to wonder how much longer this scene would go on, Roberto finally descended the stairs. After making a big show of removing his mask, he sauntered up the aisle. By the time he returned to the stage, his four portfolio shots had appeared on the projector screen. In every pose, Roberto held a beautiful woman in his arms. The full-length images accented his bare chest and emphasized how his muscular legs looked in tight breeches, leather pants, jeans, and a very short kilt.

As the evening progressed, it became clear that the contestants favored particular costumes. Jane watched a steady parade of bare-chested vampires, cowboys, buccaneers, centurions, and Highlanders, while also scanning the room for signs of suspicious activity.

After all the models had taken their turn in the spotlight, the first round of voting took place and three finalists were chosen. Roberto made the cut, as did Wyatt from Dallas and Griffin from Tennessee. Onstage, the men struck poses while Phoebe, Mrs. Pratt, and Lily Jamison exchanged a flurry of whispered remarks.

The audience members, who'd been silent for the majority of the deliberations, began shouting the names of their favorite contestant. Listening to their enthusiastic cheering, Jane smiled. She had no doubt that her guests were having the time of their lives and fully expected the gaiety to continue at the Ladies' Choice Ball.

In the end, Griffin was declared the winner. Lily ascended the stage steps and presented him with a mock contract tied with a silk ribbon. She extended her hand for him to shake, but he swept her up in his arms and spun her in a circle instead.

Looking relieved that the contest was finally over, Sinclair asked the ladies to make their way to the Great Gatsby Ballroom.

"I'm ready to add names to my dance card," a woman told her friend as they filed out. "If Roberto dances with me, I'll go to my grave happy."

Jane heard similar remarks as she joined the flow of bodies moving through the lobby. It was like being in a river of glittering, colorful, perfumed fish. Caught among swishes of satin and taffeta and excited chatter, Jane found the sensation of being swept along with her guests extremely agreeable.

The Great Gatsby Ballroom was resplendent. The women were dazzled by the sight of flickering candles and rose

topiaries strung with fairy lights. The local men and Storyton Hall staff members who'd volunteered to serve as dance
partners stood in two columns. Straight backed and smiling,
they bowed as the women streamed in. The ladies wasted
no time presenting their dance cards, giggling and blushing
all the while.

When the cover model contestants entered the room several minutes later, they were instantly mobbed. Luckily, the
Storyton Band struck up the first chords of a tango and many
of the women scurried off to find the partners already pen-
ciled in on their dance cards.

By the second song, all the men were on the dance floor.
Jane wandered over to the refreshment station, which featured
punch bowls filled with Love's First Blush—a blend of champagne, lime, and raspberries. There was also a selection of
heart-shaped cookies, cheeses, and finger sandwiches.

For the most part, the guests remained in the ballroom,
but both gentlemen and ladies occasionally stepped outside
for a breath of fresh air or to use the restroom. Jane did her
best to stay alert and vigilant, but as the night wore on, she
began to tire. And while she enjoyed seeing Tobias Hogg
lead Barbara Jewel in dance after dance, she was less pleased
by the way Lachlan stuck to Eloise's side like a metal shav-
ing captured by a magnet. Though he fulfilled his duty by
dancing with other guests, he always returned to the empty
chair next to Eloise's. He examined her ankle, fetched punch
for her, and gave her his undivided attention whenever she
murmured in his ear.

At least Edwin's not here, Jane thought and wondered why
he hadn't volunteered to be one of the dancers.

"He was willing to dress up like Mr. Rochester and dance
with me," she mumbled to herself. "But if he thought he
could seduce me in order to gain access to the private
reaches of Storyton Hall, then he was sadly mistaken."

"Are you having a conversation with the candelabra?"
Sterling asked, having noiselessly appeared at Jane's side.

"I'm trying to avoid falling asleep on my feet," she answered.

At that moment, a group of dancers shifted and Jane saw

Lily near the front of the room. A tall, thin man with the beginnings of a dark beard led her in a waltz. Jane only caught a fleeting glance of the couple before other dancers obscured them, but she stiffened so abruptly that Sterling was instantly on alert.

"What is it? Did you see something suspicious?"

Jane stood on tiptoe and tried to locate Lily again. "I'm not sure."

The waltz ended and half of the dancers cleared the floor. Some headed for the refreshment table while others sank into one of the many chairs surrounding the dance floor. Several exited the room altogether, and Jane spotted the man again just before he disappeared into the lobby. Like most of the men, he wore a black tux. That in itself didn't cause her alarm, but the memory of the contents in Nigel Poindexter's closet did.

"We need to look at our laundry records for the week," Jane told Sterling. "Now."

Sterling followed Jane to the front desk where she asked the clerk on duty to pull all transactions involving the pressing of garments.

"What are we searching for?" Sterling wanted to know.

"An order for a man's suit or tuxedo. I saw someone who looked like Nigel on the dance floor. It was just a flash, but this man was wearing a tuxedo and there was no tux in Nigel's closet. The suit I saw hanging there was too casual for this event, so if he meant to attend tonight's dance, even if only as an observer—a reporter—what did he plan to wear?"

Sterling understood immediately. "He obviously didn't have a formal suit on his person the morning he fled. We saw the video feed. He had a messenger bag, which was just large enough to hold a laptop."

"It could just be wild imagining on my part," Jane said. "But you know what Aunt Octavia always says about imagination."

"That it's more important than knowledge." Sterling's gaze was fixed on the computer screen. "Einstein also said that 'Logic will get you from A to B. Imagination will take you everywhere.'" He pointed at a laundry order. "I'd say that logic and imagination just came together with a big bang."

Jane's stared in astonishment. "Nigel's tux was pressed and delivered to Georgia Dupree's room! Could she have been hiding him this whole time? Sterling, take a master key and search Ms. Dupree's room. I'll alert the rest of the Fins. I believe Nigel was the man I saw dancing with Lily. He's not clean-shaven, but I think it's him. Lily may have been waltzing with a murderer. And an unsuspecting cover model or Storyton staff member could be holding Nigel's accomplice, aka Georgia Dupree, in his arms this very moment!"

Sterling sprinted down the deserted lobby to the servant's stairs. At the same time, Jane sent a group message to the Fins and then hurried toward the ballroom.

She stopped in the hallway to read a text from Sinclair saying that Georgia was not in the ballroom.

"Where are you?" Jane asked aloud.

Suddenly, she heard a whisper of silk. Glancing up from her phone, Jane saw Georgia rush from a room at the other end of the hall. Clad only in a slip of a dress with a plunging neckline, she burst through the doorway leading to the back terrace, completely ignoring Jane's shouts for her to stop.

Jane used speed dial to reach Sinclair. "Georgia just left the house!" she cried. "She's heading for Milton's gardens. I'm going after her."

"Do not go alone," Sinclair commanded. "Mr. Lachlan will join you directly."

Jane knew it would be foolish to chase after Georgia alone in the dark, so she decided to meet Lachlan at the end of the hall. She was desperate to find out what Georgia had been doing in the Jane Austen Parlor.

She hustled down the empty corridor and came to a halt in the doorway. Her heart hammering, she looked inside the dimly lit room and saw Nigel Poindexter on the fainting couch. His shoulders were slumped and his was head bowed. He didn't look up at the sound of Jane's approach.

Jane was about to speak, to warn Nigel to stay where he was, but the words died on her lips.

The man who Jane suspected of poisoning Rosamund York wasn't going anywhere. Jane knew this to be true because of the unnatural stillness of Nigel's body.

And because she saw blood soaking into the back of the sofa's velvet upholstery.

She stood in the doorway, transfixed with horror, and stared as ruby-red droplets gathered on the underside of the couch and fell onto the rug in muted thuds. Their slow, steady rhythm was more frightening than a scream.

She couldn't tear her gaze away from the red stain. She stood, immobile, until Lachlan squeezed her shoulder. "Miss Jane? Are you all right?"

Turning to grip Lachlan's arms, Jane spoke in a harsh whisper. "Do not let that woman get away. Do you hear me? *Get her.*"

Lachlan darted through the exit doors. The cold air swept over Jane's bare skin and she shivered. And then, she drew in a deep breath and entered the Jane Austen Parlor. There was nothing to do now but wait.

She must wait, and keep vigil with the dead.

FIFTEEN

Jane shut the parlor door and, keeping clear of the rug, walked behind the fainting couch. Knowing better than to taint a crime scene, she touched nothing. It only took her a second to identify the murder weapon.

One of the gilt and bronze candlesticks had been taken from the fireplace mantel and brought down hard on the back of Nigel's skull. The candlesticks, which belonged to Jane's ancestor, Walter Egerton Steward, were very heavy. With a square base rising to a bronze column, each candlestick was capped by the figure of a naked child cradling a golden horn. Jane stared at the bloodied antique and grimaced. The plump, dimpled child reminded her of a cherub. Or of Cupid.

The only light in the room came from a floor lamp in the corner by the hearth. In the dimness, shadows loomed. The longer Jane stared at the bronze child, whose body was slick with Nigel's blood, the more sinister it looked.

Eventually, her gaze shifted from the candlestick to the dead man's ruined head. There was a large depression at the base of his skull and the sight of fractured bone made bile rise in Jane's throat. Still, she could not look away. She saw how blood had leaked from the wound and stained the collar of Nigel's white shirt a dark shade of red before soaking into the black jacket of his tuxedo.

"Miss Jane?" The door opened and Sterling peered inside.

"Stay there," Jane whispered. "I'm coming out."

Joining Sterling, Jane leaned against the wall and accepted the bottle of water he proffered.

"Nigel Poindexter is dead. Georgia Dupree struck him with a candlestick. She must have been incredibly angry to inflict such a terrible wound. His skull . . ." She stopped to take a tentative sip of water.

"Mr. Lachlan has her," Sterling said, taking in the parlor's grim tableau. "He and Mr. Butterworth are holding her in the garage. Mr. Sinclair sent me back to get you. We called Sheriff Evans and informed him that we have a second criminal for him to take into custody. I hope Ms. Dupree will be more cooperative than Ms. Stone. The latter tried to bite one of the deputies when they loaded her in the cruiser."

Jane hadn't registered anything beyond the line, "Mr. Lachlan has her." After asking Sterling to lock the Jane Austen Parlor and stand guard outside the door, she took off at a clipped pace for her office.

Grabbing her coat and scarf, she left Storyton Hall through the kitchens.

Outside, the night wind whistled through the bare trees and stung Jane's eyes. She breathed deeply, inviting the air into her lungs. She hoped its sharpness would help clear her mind of the image of Nigel's horrible wound and the bloodied candlestick.

In the garage, Sinclair, Butterworth, and Lachlan stood in a loose circle around Georgia Dupree. They'd given her a chair and had yet to restrain her, and she was taking advantage of her freedom to wave her arms around and shout, "I didn't kill him! I'm telling you, you stupid oafs, that he was already dead when I went into that pink and red monstrosity of a room."

Georgia's eyes blazed and her cheeks were flushed with indignation. Upon seeing Jane, she attempted to rise, but Butterworth put a restrictive hand on her shoulder and pushed her down again.

"Don't touch me!" Georgia spat. "I'll sue you. *All* of you!"

Butterworth removed a handkerchief from his pocket and dabbed at his coat. "Madame, please remain in your seat until the authorities arrive. If you cannot comply with this simple request, I shall be forced to tie your hands behind your back."

"You wouldn't dare," Georgia hissed and then turned to glare at Jane. "I'm not some housewife on a dream getaway. I'm a well-known and highly respected author. You can't treat me this way."

Jane grabbed the chair near the workbench and dragged it to the center of the room. She dropped into it with a sigh. "It's been a long day, Ms. Dupree. In an hour or two, I'll be able to sleep. Not you. Your night will be filled with questions and more questions. When Sheriff Evans is finally satisfied that you have nothing left to say, you'll be escorted to a holding cell. I doubt you'll find the cot as cushy as the bed in your Storyton guest room. The wool blanket will hardly compare to our soft comforter either." Jane shrugged. "Still, it's better than being laid out on a metal table. That's the harsh fate awaiting Mr. Poindexter."

"But I—"

"If you want my help, Ms. Dupree—and I'm offering you help because you're a guest of Storyton Hall—then you must start by explaining why you allowed Mr. Poindexter to hide in your room. You knew full well that he was wanted by the authorities."

Georgia crossed her arms over her chest and pressed her lips together in a display of stubborn silence.

Jane rubbed her hands together, shivered theatrically, and glanced up at Lachlan. "Do you have any spirits in your cottage? Something that might coax the feeling back into my fingertips?"

"I have just the thing," Lachlan said and hustled out. He returned a moment later carrying a bottle of whiskey and a battered tin cup. "I don't have any proper glasses," he said apologetically.

"This will do nicely, thank you." Jane poured a splash of whiskey into the cup and took a tiny swallow. She then added more whiskey and put the cup in Georgia's hand. "You must be freezing. Mr. Lachlan? Lend Ms. Dupree your coat, would you?"

Lachlan removed his tuxedo jacket and draped it over Georgia's shoulders. She clutched the lapels and shot Jane a suspicious glance. "There's no sense trying to butter me up. The harm's already been done. I plan to bankrupt you."

"Then I might as well drink up," Jane said breezily and reached for the cup.

Her ploy worked. Georgia snatched the cup away, raised it to her lips, and gulped down the contents.

Jane smiled indulgently. "That'll get your blood flowing again." She offered to refill the cup and Georgia grudgingly accepted. "Why were in you in the Jane Austen Parlor in the first place?" Jane asked in a gentle tone.

"Why should I tell you?" Georgia curled her lip. "The only person I plan to speak to is my attorney."

"Because if someone else is responsible for Mr. Poindexter's death, then apprehending him or her would prove your innocence. Otherwise, you could spend a great deal of time in that holding cell. You won't be able to work on your next novel or interact with your fans. If people hear you're being held as a murder suspect, you could lose hundreds of loyal readers."

Georgia's face went ashen. "I was supposed to meet Nigel in the parlor at eleven o'clock. We made a deal. In exchange for keeping him hidden in my room—not to mention bringing him food and making sure his tuxedo was ready for tonight's ball—he was supposed to give me something." She put the cup on the floor and burrowed deeper inside Lachlan's jacket.

"So you had an arrangement," Jane said. "What were you promised in return for your assistance?"

"I can tell you this much; what I was promised was *not* in the parlor. Either Nigel lied to me or his killer took it."

Watching Georgia closely, Jane asked, "Were you and Mr. Poindexter in collusion? Did you help him poison Ms. York?"

"No, I did not." Though her eyes were still dark with

anger, Georgia had grown calmer since she'd been given whiskey and a coat. "I had no idea he was going to do that." She shrugged. "Not that I would have gotten in his way had I known, but I didn't. I write romance novels, not mysteries. I don't know a damned thing about poison."

"But you had a compelling motive. With Rosamund York gone, you could take your rightful place at the top." Jane cocked her head inquisitively. "Isn't that a direct quote? Haven't you always felt that the title of First Lady of Romance should have been yours? Even though Ms. York consistently outsold you, you act as though she was unworthy of her accolades, of her awards, of her legion of devoted—"

Georgia bolted upright in her chair. "She didn't write the books! She was just a pretty face! A cardboard cutout. *Nigel* wrote every single Venus Dares novel. Rosamund couldn't pen a grocery list. I'd been on enough panels with her to know that something was amiss. She had to consult notes about her *own* characters. She couldn't answer instinctively. She avoided questions about the writing process. And I always saw her having clandestine meetings with Nigel. A few years ago, just before Rosamund and I were about to get on an elevator, a fan questioned Rosamund about a scene in her first novel. Instead of answering, Rosamund pretended to feel ill and shut the door in the woman's face. She couldn't answer, you see, because she didn't remember the scene. It's one thing to read a book and *quite another* to write one."

"Is that what you wanted from Mr. Poindexter?" Jane asked calmly. "Proof that Ms. York was a fake? A charlatan?" When Georgia didn't answer, Jane changed tack. "Did you really think you could trust him? The man murdered his partner. She died a horrible, agonizing death."

"I wasn't afraid of Nigel because he could only get what he wanted through me," Georgia said flatly. "He told me about the castor seeds. He swore up and down that he meant to use them to convince Rosamund to pay him what he was owed. It was his intention to give her the worst stomachache of her life. Nothing more. While she was suffering, he was going to tell her that the discomfort he'd caused was only the beginning of what he'd do unless she agreed to immediately transfer money into his bank account. Nigel's debts made him . . . rash. He was desperate for money, but after he found Rosamund's body, he became a frightened little boy." Georgia's voice held a hint of sympathy. "He knocked on my door the next morning."

To Jane, Georgia's tale sounded more than a little fictitious. "Why did you let Mr. Poindexter in?"

"I didn't realize he was a suspect when he came to me. I figured he showed up because he had something to offer. I was more than willing to listen because I had a proposition of my own," Georgia said airily.

"I assume that you're not going to tell me what you were after, but what did Mr. Poindexter want?" Jane asked.

Georgia shrugged. "For me to get his tuxedo and to keep him out of sight until tonight's ball. Simple enough."

Jane was positive that Georgia would go to any length to secure her place in the limelight, but she had no idea how helping Nigel would advance Georgia's career. "Not only have you broken the law, but you also put yourself at great risk. Once you knew he was a murder suspect, why didn't you turn him in?"

As though bored, Georgia yawned loudly, and Jane was tempted to shake her until her teeth rattled. Instead she continued with her questions. "By the time he came to you, Mr. Poindexter had already eliminated your competition. So why would you put yourself in harm's way to help him?" Jane sat back in her chair and studied Rosamund. "Your story doesn't make sense. You've built a career on fabrication and I think you're doing it again now."

Georgia smiled wryly. "I don't care what you think. Nigel Poindexter gave me the most exciting week of my life. Rosamund was an idiot to have mistreated him. Not only was he a master wordsmith, but he was excellent company as well, if you get my meaning." She flashed Jane a enigmatic smile. "I'm sorry that he's dead. He and I could have made history together."

Jane adopted a dubious expression. "The two people responsible for the Venus Dares novels have been killed, and you still claim to be innocent of any wrongdoing. Are you saying that it's just a matter of good fortune that you'll reap the benefits of two murders?"

"The cream always rises to the top," Georgia replied smugly. "And since *Nigel's* new Eros book is sure to be reviled by most of Rosamund's fans, I believe I'm going to have a very successful year." Her eyes danced with a zealous light. "Even though I didn't get what Nigel promised me, there was no need for me to kill him. With or without it, I'm moving up the food chain."

At the sound of approaching sirens, Jane instructed Butterworth to hail the sheriff and lead him into the garage. Georgia watched the butler leave and then flicked a lock of red hair over her shoulder. "You should worry less about me and more about yourself, Ms. Steward. There's a murderer on the loose in your hotel."

Jane got to her feet. "Yours is a hollow victory, Ms. Dupree. Mark Twain once said, 'Man will do many things to get himself loved; he will do all things to get himself envied.'" Though she heard voices behind her, Jane continued to stare intently at Georgia. "I don't know what things you've done, but there will be a reckoning."

Georgia responded with a dismissive flick of her wrist.

Jane smiled coldly at her. "Cream does rise to the top, Ms. Dupree. But guess what? So does scum."

As soon as Georgia was Mirandized and escorted to a cruiser by Deputy Emory, Sheriff Evans turned to Jane. "Did you witness the murder?"

"No. I was at the other end of the hall when I saw Ms. Dupree leaving the parlor. I shouted for her to stop, but she exited Storyton Hall through the doorway leading to the terrace. I hurried after her, but stopped to look in the parlor. That's when I saw Mr. Poindexter. I spoke to him and he didn't respond, so I entered the room." Jane recalled the sight of the bloodied candlestick and suppressed a shudder. "I only had to glance at the back of Mr. Poindexter's head to see that he was dead, so I quickly left the room without touching anything. Mr. Sterling is standing guard."

The sheriff nodded. "We'll take it from here, Ms. Steward. If one of your staff could direct me to the scene . . ."

Jane signaled to Butterworth, who immediately gestured for Sheriff Evans and his deputies to follow him to the Jane Austen Parlor.

"The ball will be ending soon and I hope our guests will go straight to bed," Jane said to Sinclair and Lachlan when the sheriff was gone. "If so, they won't hear about the murder until tomorrow morning. In the meantime, how can we dissuade people from wandering toward the parlor?"

"We can make it look like there's a maintenance issue," Lachlan suggested. "I'll roll two housekeeping carts into the center of the hall and hang a *Work Zone, No Admittance* sign from the carts. That should do the trick."

Jane liked the idea. "Will you see to that immediately? Mr. Sinclair needs to review the footage from our security cameras and I have to return to the ball."

Lachlan nodded and hurried off.

"What do you think of Ms. Dupree's story?" Sinclair asked as they hustled back to the manor.

"Georgia Dupree has wanted to upstage Rosamund York for years, and I believe she'd cross several lines to achieve that goal. The fact that she sheltered Nigel has me thinking that she's either deranged or totally blinded by her desires."

Sinclair grunted. "Perhaps she was seduced. Mr. Poindexter clearly had a way with words."

"I'd like to know what words he spoke to Lily Jamison. I saw the two of them dancing together just before Nigel left the room." Jane felt a chill race up her spine. "He was murdered minutes later. If I'd followed him instead of going to the front desk to examine the laundry orders, he might still be alive."

Sinclair took her hand. "You've come a long way in the short time since you were named Guardian, but you will never know the intentions of every soul passing through Storyton Hall's gates." He released her hand and swept his own in the direction of the manor house. "Think of all the books in the library that have plain brown leather covers. They look utterly unremarkable. Now, consider what happens when the cover is opened—how a cornucopia of images sweeps the reader along on an unpredictable journey. Your guests are all like books you've never read before."

"Then I need to become better at reading people." Jane's voice was heavy with self-recrimination. "Two people have died this week, Sinclair."

"This story isn't finished." Sinclair opened the back door. "You haven't had much control over the plot thus far, but you *can* influence how this tale will end."

Jane responded with a determined nod. "I have to do everything in my power to make sure Sheriff Evans has what he needs to make this arrest stick." She hesitated, her hand on the door. "But what if Georgia is telling us the truth? What if she didn't kill Nigel and the real murderer is roaming free? I must consider all possibilities. Call me the moment you've finished reviewing the video footage, okay?"

"I shall," Sinclair said.

The two parted in the lobby, and Jane hastened to the ballroom, where she spotted Lily seated in a chair by the punch bowl.

At this late hour, the dance floor was considerably less crowded, and the only Cover Girls still at the ball were Eloise, Anna, and Violet. Anna and Violet were dancing with models while Eloise chatted with Billy the bellhop. Jane knew Billy was a devoted reader of fantasy novels and was undoubtedly sharing his views on the latest work by George R.R. Martin or Neil Gaiman.

Jane saw Eloise enthusiastically gesticulate as she spoke with Billy. Eloise's passion for all the literary genres was contagious and Jane wished she could join the conversation. She'd like nothing better than to help herself to some punch, pull up a chair, and forget about the dead body in the parlor. Instead, she asked Lily Jamison to follow her into the lobby.

"Gladly. I'm exhausted," Lily said. "Not many women are paid to travel to a beautiful resort or are given the happy assignment of dancing with a dozen gorgeous guys, but I'm not much of a night owl. I usually fall asleep with a book in my hands by ten."

Jane offered to walk Lily to her room. In the elevator, Jane said, "I saw you dancing with a tall, thin man in a tuxedo. He wasn't a model or a staff member. His name was Nigel. Do you remember him?"

"I know this sounds terrible, but the names started blurring together after my fifth or sixth dance partner," Lily said.

"He may have discussed romance novels. Possibly those written by Ms. York."

The elevator doors opened and Lily stepped out of the cab. "I did have an unusual exchange with a man. He never mentioned his name and he was strangely eager to talk about the Venus Dares series. He also wanted to know if I'd read her Eros novel and was very keen to hear what I thought of it. At the end of the song, he asked me such an odd question."

"Which was?"

Lily stopped in front of the door to her suite. "He wanted to know if Heartfire would continue to publish Venus Dares novels if someone were to produce previously unseen Venus Dares manuscripts. Isn't that a bizarre thing for a complete stranger to say?"

If Jane wanted to tell Lily about Nigel's death, this would be the moment to do so, but she decided that it would be prudent to distrust everyone. She didn't dare confide in Lily Jamison, as much as she would have liked to be honest with her. "And you've never seen this man before?"

Lily shook her head. "I don't think so."

"What do you tell him?"

"The truth—that Heartfire would be interested in anything by Rosamund York," Lily said. "I planned to follow that statement with a question of my own, but when the song ended, my partner thanked me for the dance and left the room."

Jane nodded encouragingly. "What would you have asked him, given the chance?"

Lily let out a dry chuckle. "I'd obviously had too much punch, because there was something about the way he looked at me when he mentioned those manuscripts that made me believe they might actually exist. It's ridiculous, but I was going to ask if he had proof. I wanted to ask if he knew Rosamund." Staring down at her brass room key, Lily traced the design of the open book on the fob. "I wasn't even Rosamund's editor, but I'd love to get my hands on those manuscripts. I'd be the heroine of Heartfire." She laughed. "See? This is why I shouldn't stay up this late. I'm clearly functioning on half a brain. But why are you interested in this man? Did he tantalize all his dance partners with questions about undiscovered manuscripts, or was I the only one?"

"He might have mentioned them to another person," Jane said. "If I discover more, I'll let you know. But for now, I've delayed you long enough. Have a restful night."

"After all that dancing," Lily said as she unlocked her door, "I'm going to sleep like the dead."

Moments later, Jane joined Sinclair in the security office.

"Someone entered Storyton Hall through the rear entrance." Sinclair pointed at a monitor. "Watch."

He played the feed and a figure wearing opera gloves and a floor-length hooded cloak ascended the stairs from the back terrace and crept into the manor house. Her movements were slow and stealthy, as though she were trying to be especially quiet.

"Her face is turned away from the camera," Jane said. "Does she reappear on the lobby footage?"

"No." Sinclair hit the fast-forward button and kept his gaze fixed on the time stamp. He then paused the feed. "Less than ten minutes later, she leaves the way she came in."

The dark figure moved more quickly and her gait was somewhat ungainly. She took the steps two at a time, her shoulders hunched.

"She looks like Quasimodo," Jane said, and asked Sinclair to replay the footage again, this time in slow motion, but there were no distinguishing characteristics about the figure. Again, she kept her face turned away from the camera.

Jane sank into a chair. "What about Georgia? When does she show up?"

"Seven minutes later." Sinclair sped up the footage until Georgia, coatless and wide-eyed with shock, bolted through the doorway and onto the terrace. Her hair streamed out behind her as she ran and her mouth was open, forming a dark oval.

"Good Lord," Jane whispered. "That's hardly the expression of someone who just committed murder. I probably looked just like her after I saw Nigel."

Sinclair picked up the phone. "I'm ordering a pot of strong coffee. I don't think we'll see our beds tonight—not unless we find the woman in the cloak."

Jane pointed at the screen showing The Great Gatsby Ballroom. "The Ladies' Choice Ball is over. Everyone's either retired to their guest rooms or returned to their homes in Storyton Village. So where is the woman who bludgeoned Nigel Poindexter with a candlestick?"

"We should also ask ourselves why she killed Mr. Poindexter," Sinclair said. "Did she need to silence him?"

"Or did she want what he promised Georgia Dupree?" Jane was suddenly energized. She jumped out of the chair and pointed at the television displaying the back terrace feed. "After Rosamund's body was discovered, Nigel went into hiding. He took his laptop case with him. Where is his laptop now? It might contain drafts of every Venus Dares novel. Ideas for future books. Unpublished manuscripts. That computer could be worth its weight in gold."

Brows furrowed, Sinclair quickly rewound the footage and replayed the scene of the woman's exit from Storyton Hall. "Ah," he said. "If she's hiding a laptop case under that cloak, it would explain her ungraceful posture."

As Jane replayed the footage once more, she caught a flash a familiar label sewn into the side front lining of the cloak.

"I need to call Mabel," Jane said. "We're looking at one of her Regency cloaks. When I'm done with that call, we'll have to speak with every woman who ordered a cloak from La Grande Dame. The guests won't thank me for disturbing them, but I have no choice."

Sinclair understood at once. "By process of elimination, the lady who doesn't answer her phone or respond to the knock on her door is our prime suspect."

"Yes." Jane's eyes were locked on the monitor. "Dante Alighieri claimed that pride, envy, and avarice were the sparks that set a fire in the hearts of all men. I believe that such a fire fueled Georgia Dupree's actions. But what of this woman?" Jane touched the image of the hooded figure. "What sparked the fire in her heart? And who else does she mean to burn?"

SIXTEEN

"Hello?" Mabel's sleepy voice was a soft rasp.

"I'm sorry to call you at this hour," Jane said. "But it's urgent."

There was a rustle at the other end of the line and Mabel whispered, "What's wrong?"

"Nigel Poindexter has been murdered."

"Good Lord!" Mabel was now fully awake. "What can I do to help?"

Jane was touched. How many people would respond to news of a murder by instantly offering assistance? "The killer's face was hidden by the hood of one of your Regency cloaks, so I need the name of every woman who bought a cloak from you."

"I'll have to look in my record book. It's downstairs," Mabel said. "I'll get right back to you."

Jane begged her to hurry and then hung up. She paced behind her desk for several minutes, feeling a fresh pang of regret over having disturbed Mabel's sleep. Between the dress fittings, the fashion show, and the reticule workshop, Mabel had to be exhausted.

We can all rest after I catch the killer, Jane thought.

The phone rang and Jane lunged for it.

There were fourteen names in all, but Jane only recognized two of them. After thanking Mabel, Jane hurried out to the reception desk. Andrew was on duty and Jane quickly explained what she needed from him. Within seconds, he'd pulled up the room number of the first name on the list and was dialing the extension.

Moving to the other computer, Jane looked up Barbara Jewel's room. As she reached for the receiver, Jane recalled how happy Tobias and Barbara had been on the dance floor. The pair had stared at each other as though no one else existed, as though the music was playing for them alone.

Jane swallowed a lump in her throat. She'd felt that way two nights ago when Edwin had taken her in his arms and led her in waltz after waltz.

"For your sake, Tobias, I hope Ms. Jewel answers her phone," Jane said as she pressed the number keys.

Barbara Jewel didn't pick up.

Jane called Butterworth next and told him to knock on Ms. Jewel's door. She then returned to the security room. Sinclair was studying a still frame of the hooded figure. He was concentrating so intently that his bushy brows were nearly touching.

"Do you remember seeing Barbara Jewel in tonight's footage?" Jane asked.

Sinclair reached for the controls. "Yes. I spotted her leaving just before eleven."

Jane was confused. "Leaving? To go where?"

"You'll see." Sinclair pointed at the screen displaying footage of the front entrance. Sure enough, there was Barbara Jewel. Draped in her Regency cloak, she and Tobias Hogg descended the stairs to a Pickled Pig Market van. Tobias opened the passenger door for Barbara, held her elbow as she climbed inside, and then kissed her hand.

When the van pulled away, Jane felt a wave of relief. "I didn't expect her to leave with Tobias, but I'm glad to see that she wasn't involved in Nigel Poindexter's murder. I like her."

"Apparently, Mr. Hogg does as well," Sinclair said with a

hint of reproach. He clearly disapproved of Barbara going home with a man she barely knew. "Who else is on your list?"

"Andrew is calling the other ladies as we speak. I told him to get me if a guest fails to pick up her phone. The only names I recognized were Barbara Jewel and Rosamund York."

Sinclair shot her a questioning look. "Ms. York ordered a cloak?"

"No, Mabel made one for her in hopes of getting some free publicity," Jane said. "If someone gained access to Ms. York's room—" She inhaled sharply.

"What is it?" Sinclair asked.

"Rosamund's publicist." Jane clapped her palms against her cheeks. "Taylor Birch had access to Rosamund's room! Taylor, who wore Rosamund's dress the night of the fashion show. Taylor, who'd do anything to break into publishing. *Anything* at all!"

Sinclair headed for the door. "I'll look up her room number," he called over his shoulder.

Jane contacted Butterworth and was unsurprised when, several minutes later, the butler reported that Taylor hadn't responded to repeated knocking on her door.

"Use the master key and let yourself in," Jane said. "Sinclair and I will join you shortly."

As Jane hurried through the lobby, she tried to organize her thoughts by sharing them with Sinclair. "I think Ms. Birch discovered that Nigel wrote Rosamund's books. Maybe she overheard them arguing over money or something that hinted at their secret partnership."

Sinclair pushed open the door to the staff stairwell. "Judging by the manner in which she blatantly disregarded our technology policy, she's a strong-willed young lady."

"A young lady who'd grown tired of being a lackey," Jane added. "Taylor told me that she dreamed of a career in publishing. She said that it's a highly competitive field and that she'd need an advantage to get her foot in the door." Jane jogged down the third floor hallway. "What if she stumbled upon the perfect advantage?"

"An unpublished Venus Dares manuscript on Mr. Poindexter's laptop, for example?" Sinclair said.

"I'm not sure." Jane lowered her voice so as not to disturb the other guests. "Nigel would surely have multiple copies of each file. You and I have met dozens of writers. They all keep backup files. And while I can't say why Nigel's laptop is such a prized possession, I think Taylor killed him to get it."

When the pair reached Taylor's room, they found the door slightly ajar. Inside, all the lights were on and Butterworth was carefully poking through the young woman's drawers. Jane noticed that he'd donned a pair of gloves.

"Ms. Birch's toiletries are missing. As is her phone," Butterworth said. "I haven't finished with my search, but nothing appears to be out of the ordinary."

Jane nodded. "Sinclair, can you see if Taylor left any notes or clues in the trash?"

While Sinclair rifled though the bathroom bin, Jane examined the contents of the writing desk. She found nothing in the top drawer other than a Storyton Hall pen and notepad. However, the pen looked strange. An object was lodged beneath its metal clip and when Jane held the pen under the direct light of the desk lamp, she knew at once what it was.

She showed the castor bean to Butterworth.

Sinclair stepped out of the bathroom, peered at the pen, and pulled out his phone. "Mr. Sterling, we need to locate Ms. York's publicist, Taylor Birch. We believe she took Ms. York's cloak, entered Storyton Hall through the terrace entrance, and waited for Mr. Poindexter in the parlor. After striking him with the candlestick, she fled, undoubtedly to hide Mr. Poindexter's laptop." He paused to listen. "Yes, you and Mr. Lachlan should search the outbuildings."

"I bet Taylor believes she's gotten away with murder. Literally." Jane stared at the castor bean. "She knew where our cameras were in position and avoided facing them. Because she wore gloves, her prints won't be on the murder weapon. If we don't recover that laptop, all we'll have on her is this castor bean. It's enough for the sheriff to take her in for questioning, but it doesn't prove that she killed Nigel. And possibly Rosamund." Jane shook her head. "At this point, I have no idea who murdered whom."

"Let's focus on what we do know," Butterworth said. "Ms. York was poisoned with castor beans. The fact that Ms. Birch has one of these beans in her room suggests that she could have been involved in the first murder. Nigel also had beans in his possession, so nothing is clear about Ms. York's death. If Ms. Birch took Ms. York's cloak, however, then it's likely she committed the second murder. That means Ms. Dupree didn't kill Mr. Poindexter, though we can still use her arrest to our advantage. If Ms. Birch thinks she's gotten away with murder, she might do something foolish."

Jane fell silent while she weighed their options. "Perhaps we can entrap Ms. Birch with a little help from Lily Jamison." A plan took shape in her mind. "I'll speak with Lily in the morning. Until then, we must find that laptop."

"As well as the cloak we believe Ms. Birch wore tonight," Sinclair said. "The cuffs or sleeves are probably stained with Mr. Poindexter's blood. One cannot inflict that kind of damage without . . ." he trailed off. "You saw the wound, Miss Jane."

"Yes," she said absently, her eyes scanning the room. "Where are you, Taylor? If killing Nigel was a premeditated act, then you'd want an alibi for tonight. Your toiletries are missing. So where are you sleeping? And with whom?"

Butterworth and Sinclair exchanged a brief, whispered conversation, and Jane raised her brows in question. "What are you talking about?"

"We think you should grab a few hours' rest. Tomorrow will be a trying day and you need to be sharp, especially if we're going to act like we know nothing of Ms. Birch's involvement."

Jane nodded. "We'll have to inform the guests that there's been another tragic death at Storyton Hall, and before they have a chance to panic, assure them that Sheriff Evans has already made an arrest."

"Precisely," Sinclair said.

"I don't like deceiving our guests." Jane put the pen back in the desk drawer.

"Romancing the Reader is nearly over," Butterworth reminded her. "If Ms. Birch committed murder, we must find proof before time runs out."

Jane ran her hand over the Storyton Hall notepad. "I'll compose a letter to slip under every guest room door. Once the announcement's been made and the guests realize Georgia Dupree is missing, they'll assume she's the killer. This might destroy her reputation."

"She risked her reputation the moment she decided to harbor Mr. Poindexter," Sinclair pointed out.

"That's true," Jane agreed. "While I write the statement, I'd like the two of you to review all the video footage from an hour prior to when Nigel was killed until now. We need to know where Taylor spent the night if we want to poke holes in her alibi. To do that, the person she's sleeping with will have to admit that she wasn't in his room until after Nigel was killed."

After making sure that Taylor's room was exactly how they'd found it, Jane turned off the lights. In the hallway, she sighed heavily. "How will I break the news to Uncle Aloysius and Aunt Octavia? And what about the twins? They're bound to hear that something awful happened at Storyton Hall. It was one thing to keep Rosamund's murder from them, but there's no way I can prevent them from learning about a second death." She rubbed her temples. "I can't have them hearing about it from someone at school."

"Take time to speak with your sons in the morning," Butterworth said. "Mr. Sinclair and I will handle things during your absence."

Jane gave him a grateful smile. "All right. Thank you."

"And I wouldn't worry about your aunt and uncle," Sinclair said as they emerged from the stairwell into the lobby. "They come from tough stock. As do you, Miss Jane."

The trio parted ways and Jane headed home. She managed to shrug off her coat and shoes before collapsing on the living room sofa. "I'll just close my eyes for second," she mumbled drowsily.

She fell asleep almost instantly, and her dreams were haunted by frightful images of bloodstained cherubs. Dozens of them surrounded her as she stood in the middle of the Jane Austen Parlor. Their plump arms stretched out, reaching for her, their chubby fingers grasping hungrily. Jane turned to flee, but Nigel Poindexter blocked the doorway. She looked at his misshapen skull and the trickle of blood dripping onto his shirt collar and tried to scream, but she couldn't utter a sound. Something was obstructing her airway.

Jane shoved her fingers down her throat and pulled out a thin, metal object. It was the pen Jane had found in Taylor's room. The pen with the tiny castor seed wedged beneath its metal clip.

Only the seed was gone.

The next morning, Jane wheeled a cart into her aunt and uncle's apartment. "Who's ready for breakfast?" She smiled, hoping her makeup hid the fatigue etched into her face. "I have scrambled eggs, bacon, and fresh fruit."

Muffet Cat trotted into the room and meowed. Jane gave him a tiny piece of bacon. He gulped it down, licked his lips, and stared at her with expectant eyes.

"You're up early," Aunt Octavia said. The twins were dressed in sweaters and corduroy slacks, but Aunt Octavia was still in her terry cloth bathrobe and fuzzy striped socks. Uncle Aloysius wore plaid pajamas and his favorite pair of fish-shaped slippers.

Jane fixed plates for her sons and then poured coffee for her aunt and uncle.

Fitz and Hem carried their plates to Aunt Octavia's small library table while Jane conversed with her aunt and uncle in hushed tones. After a time, she joined her sons.

"There's something I need to tell you," she said, looking from Fitz to Hem. "One of our guests passed away last night."

Hem stopped chewing. "We had a Rip Van Winkle?"

Jane hesitated. Rip Van Winkle was a code the staff used to describe a guest who'd expired in their room or on the grounds. Prior to the Murder and Mayhem event, there had only been one Rip Van Winkle in the history of Storyton Hall. But after Jane discovered the body of a guest in the Mystery Suite last autumn, Fitz and Hem had learned about the code name and its meaning.

However, Nigel hadn't died peacefully in his sleep or suffered a heart attack on the tennis court, as had Storyton Hall's first Rip Van Winkle. He'd been brutally murdered.

They don't need to know that, Jane thought.

"Sheriff Evans has already taken care of everything," she continued, being deliberately vague. "I don't want you to talk about this at school. It is our duty to protect the privacy of all our guests—even a Rip Van Winkle. Do you understand?"

The boys nodded and said, "Yes, ma'am."

"Do you have any questions?" Jane studied her sons. She wanted to dissuade them from gossiping about the latest death, but she also needed to make sure the news hadn't upset them.

Hem looked thoughtful. "Was it a man or a lady?"

"A man," Jane said.

Fitz laid his fork down and reached for his orange juice. "Was he old?"

"He was about forty." Jane knew that the twins viewed anyone over thirty as being old.

Hem twisted his napkin in his hands. "Are *you* old, Mom?"

Jane knew what Fitz meant. "This man died because of an injury, not because he was forty. Okay? You don't need to worry about the same thing happening to me or to Aunt Octavia and Uncle Aloysius. We're all safe." She hugged both of her sons. "Come on, I'll drive you to school. We can sing the Broken Arm Bend song all the way there."

Fitz and Hem thanked Aunt Octavia and Uncle Aloysius for letting them spend the night, gave Muffet Cat a quick scratch behind the ears, and then grabbed their coats and book bags.

"Last one to the car is a rotten egg!" Hem shouted.

"And the first one has to eat it!" Fitz retorted.

Following the boys to the apartment door, Jane cast an exasperated glance over her shoulder. Her aunt and uncle were smiling.

"Longfellow once said, 'Youth comes but once in a life-time,' but those two keep me young." Uncle Aloysius wriggled his toes, making the red mouth of his fish-shaped slippers open and close.

Aunt Octavia swatted her husband. "Quickly, Aloysius. We don't have a moment to lose. You and I need to get dressed and take up positions at the reception desk. As soon as the guests read Jane's letter, they'll want a more detailed explanation. Or worse, a refund. Jane needs to focus on catching a murderer, so you and I must handle the rest."

Uncle Aloysius grabbed his wife's cane and pointed it in the air. "To battle!"

Muffet Cat, startled by the movement, dashed out from under the sofa and into the hall. He padded to the door leading to the staff stairwell, where he sat on his haunches and meowed.

"Let's go, Muffet Cat." Jane opened the door. "It's hunting time."

After dropping the boys at school, Jane parked in front of the sheriff's department.

She entered the squat stone building, which looked more like an English cottage than a law enforcement hub, carrying a hamper in each hand. The larger basket was for the sheriff and his deputies and the smaller one was for Georgia Dupree. It was Jane's plan to offer food from Storyton Hall's kitchen in exchange for a visit with Georgia.

"Is that a bribe?" Sheriff Evans asked when Jane stepped into his office. "Because if you have buttermilk biscuits in that hamper, I'll probably say yes to anything."

"I do have biscuits," Jane said. "And I'd like to spend a few minutes with Ms. Dupree. She's still a guest of Storyton Hall, so I feel responsible for her."

The sheriff accepted the basket and called to Deputy Emory.

"Show Ms. Dupree to an interview room, but leave the door open a crack and stand outside," Sheriff Evans told his deputy. "You never know what you might hear." To Jane, he said, "Ms. Dupree was not very cooperative last night. Other than insisting she had nothing to do with Mr. Poindexter's death, she refused to talk."

"She might be telling the truth." Jane quickly explained her theory that Taylor Birch was the real murderer. "But I have no proof. Yet," she added. "With Ms. Dupree's help, I might be able to get something more concrete. *If* she's willing to speak with me, that is."

The sheriff opened the hamper. "She turned her nose up at our breakfast, so if she's hungry enough, she might be willing to chat. See if you can find out why she wrote Mr. Poindexter a check for five thousand dollars. It was found in his tux jacket."

Filing the detail away for later, Jane said, "I'll do my best."

A night in the sheriff's holding cell hadn't improved Georgia's prickly disposition, but when Jane offered her an egg and cheese biscuit, Georgia managed to grumble a soft, "Thank you."

"I also have hot, strong coffee," Jane said, placing the thermos and a container of cream on the table. She waited while Georgia served herself.

"Why are you being so nice to me?" Georgia cast a suspicious glance at Jane.

Jane leaned in. "Because I don't think you killed Nigel. However, the rest of the story you told me last night was made up of partial truths. To catch the real murderer, I need to know everything."

Instead of replying, Georgia unwrapped her biscuit and placed a paper napkin on her lap. Jane decided to let her eat while she continued to talk.

"Nigel was supposed to meet you, but when you showed up in the parlor, he was dead and his laptop was gone." Jane dug into the hamper and came out with a Tupperware container filled with cut strawberries. "I'm not sure why his computer mattered to you. Nigel undoubtedly kept backups of every file he created, so the only conclusion I can draw is that you wanted a current file—something that was generated during the Romancing the Reader event. Am I getting warm?"

Georgia, who'd devoured the biscuit as though she hadn't

eaten in days, wiped her mouth with her napkin and sat back in her chair. "Nigel and I were going to work together. He spent many hours in my room, and whenever I was free, he and I would add to the outline we were creating for the next Eros book. Nigel's an incredible writer, but he got it all wrong with Eros. He was sick of writing Venus Dares and wanted to use a male voice for a change, but his protagonist was a pig. I told him exactly how to rework the first book and shared my ideas for the second. He loved them." Georgia's eyes shone. "We were both really excited about the future. The plan was for me to continue writing my Regency novels while Nigel and I penned the Eros series together."

"How?" Jane asked. "*Eros Steals the Bride* will be published under Rosamund's name."

"And mine." Georgia's predatory smile surfaced. "As soon as I heard about Rosamund's death, I called my agent, and *she* talked with Rosamund's editor later that same day. My agent told Rosamund's editor that not only had *Eros Steals the Bride* been poorly received by the readers at Storyton Hall, but that I could fix it and continue writing the series for them. It was practically a done deal. All I had to do was e-mail a proposal to Heartfire. Nigel and I wrote one that afternoon, and Rosamund's editor loved it."

Jane was repulsed by how quickly Georgia had taken advantage of Rosamund's demise. "How could you trust a man who poisoned his current partner?"

"Because I had the upper hand. He needed me," Georgia explained reasonably. "Nigel was going to end up facing consequences for what he'd done to Rosamund eventually. And while he could continue to write from the comfort of his jail cell, he was going to need me to handle everything else for us when it came to the Eros series. So I agreed to help him in the short term in order to reap the benefits in the long run. It was worth the risk. If Rosamund's editor hadn't fallen in love with our proposal, I would have simply called the sheriff and told him Nigel was in my room. But she did love it, so I decided to keep him hidden."

"Nigel obviously needed his tuxedo so he could blend in

with the other men at the ball, but what were his plans after that? Was he going to flee Storyton?"

"He said that he'd arranged for transportation," Georgia said. "I didn't want to hear the details, so I didn't ask. Hiding him in my room was enough of a risk."

"Did you know that Nigel danced with Lily Jamison, the assistant editor from Heartfire?" Jane asked casually. "I saw them toward the end of the song and, from what I could see, he had a great deal to say to her."

Georgia's eyes darkened with anger. "He was *dancing*? He was supposed to sneak out of my room once the ball was underway and meet me in the parlor with his computer. That's what we agreed on."

"I think Nigel Poindexter deceived you from the get-go." Jane opened the Tupperware lid and inhaled the perfume of ripe strawberries. "Maybe killing Rosamund wasn't an accident. Maybe that was just one of the many lies he told you."

When Georgia didn't answer, Jane popped one of the strawberries in her mouth and chewed. "Hm," she moaned softly.

Georgia made a "give me" gesture and Jane slid the strawberries across the table. "Rosamund wasn't poisoned during the truffle workshop," Georgia said after eating three strawberries. "Nigel gave her a small box of truffles when they met for lunch. He bought them at the village market that morning. Nigel knew Rosamund tended to eat sweets when she was upset, so he made sure she was plenty upset during their meal. By the time she got to the truffle workshop, she'd already ingested all four truffles."

"How many castor seeds did he use?"

"Two. He chopped them up in his bathroom and pushed the pieces inside using a pair of tweezers. Then, he dipped his finger in hot water, smoothed over the chocolate layer, and put them back in the box. It was a clever plan."

Jane couldn't contain her surprise. "Two seeds? That's all it took?"

"Don't you get it? He only wanted to make her suffer. Why else would he tell me exactly what he did? He never set out to kill her." Georgia licked strawberry juice from the tip of her thumb.

Jane suppressed a grimace. She was almost done with Georgia Dupree, but she had one more question to ask before she left. "Who else would want Nigel's computer?"

Georgia was about to shrug again. She lifted her shoulders halfway, her mouth set in an obstinate line, but then her eyes flew open wide. "Rosamund's publicist! What's her name? *She* must have discovered that Rosamund was a fake too. Boy, I bet that made her really mad. There she is, taking care of Rosamund's e-mails and social media sites, as well as fetching lattes and polishing shoes, only to discover that her boss is nothing but a pretty face." She barked out a laugh. "Oh, that must have stung! All these publicists want the same thing, you know—to *be* the woman they're working for. So how could what's-her-name *be* Rosamund? By getting her hands on Nigel's computer. Just because Rosamund was dead didn't mean her writing had to die with her. If the publicist claimed that she had access to unpublished Venus Dares manuscripts, she could pass them off to Heartfire as the work of Rosamund York. She'd gain the attention of all the right people."

"But Taylor could only succeed if she silenced Nigel," Jane said under her breath.

"You need to find that girl!" Georgia shouted imperiously. "I want that computer!"

Jane got to her feet and picked up the hamper. "Why weren't you this forthright last night? You could have saved us a heap of trouble."

"I didn't think you could help me, but I've since changed my mind. You and your staff are my best shot at getting copies of the material Nigel and I created together. Find that girl so I can get out of here."

At that moment, Sheriff Evans entered the room. "That won't be happening anytime soon, Ms. Dupree. You harbored a fugitive."

"A minor crime compared to murder," Georgia scoffed. "I should be given a stern warning and released."

Sheriff Evan sat down at the table and waved at Deputy Emory to take the chair in the corner of the room. "Now that you've breakfasted, you can provide me with a complete statement."

Seeing that her visit was over, Jane thanked the sheriff and left the station.

Outside, her steps faltered. At the end of the path, a man was leaning against the garden gate. He had his arms crossed over his chest and seemed to be waiting for someone.

It was Edwin Alcott.

And Jane knew that he was waiting for her.

SEVENTEEN

"I was heading to the Pickled Pig when I saw you go into the station," Edwin said when Jane reached the end of the path. "Has Mr. Poindexter been found?"

Jane was assaulted by such a tumult of emotions that she could barely speak. Outrage battled with humiliation and she found that she was unable to look Edwin in the face. She experienced another sensation as well—a knife-twist ache deep in her chest. She was familiar with the pain and recognized it for what it was. Grief. She was mourning the loss of something that wasn't even real. The thought of Edwin's deception allowed her simmering anger to take control, but she masked her feelings and met his gaze straight on.

Looking into his dark eyes, she tightened her grip on the hampers and said, "Mr. Poindexter is no longer missing. I discovered his body late last night. The news will sweep through the village by lunchtime, so there's no harm in telling you." Glancing down Main Street, which was just starting to show signs of activity, she started forward. "I'd better go. Storyton Hall is probably in a state of chaos."

Edwin grabbed her arm. "Let me help you."

Jane wanted to slap his hand away. Instead, she shook her

head. "You can't. My plan to entrap the murderer will only succeed if the killer feels safe. Any unusual component, such as your presence, could jeopardize my chance of bringing an end to a week tainted by violence and deceit."

Jane wondered if the latter word would elicit a reaction from Edwin, but he merely stared at her with a worried expression. Brushing a strand of hair off her cheek, he let his fingertips linger on her cold skin. And then, he dropped his hand and something in his expression shifted. "Just know that I'd do anything for you," he said. "Call, and I'll come running."

So you can poke around Storyton Hall when I'm too busy dealing with a murderer to notice? Jane thought, her ire rising.

"I have to go," she repeated and twisted free of his grasp. As she hurried to the Rolls, she could feel his gaze on her back. Once, the thought of him watching her would have flooded her body with warmth. But no longer. Gooseflesh erupted on her arms and neck.

"Tell me one thing," Edwin called after her. "The card that came with your Valentine's Day flowers. Did you open it?"

Jane thought of the bouquet of red poppies she'd left at the reception desk. She'd never bothered to read the card.

After opening the car door, she turned to face him. "Not yet. I've been too preoccupied with murder to concentrate on romance." And with that, she slid into the driver's seat and started the engine.

As she drove off, Jane glanced at her rearview mirror. Edwin stood alone on the sidewalk, staring at the Rolls. Even when he was no longer visible, Jane could feel him thinking about her.

Approaching Broken Arm Bend, she recalled a line from a German poet named Heinrich Heine. "'Oh, what lies lurk in kisses,'" she quoted angrily and then sighed. "I'll miss Edwin Alcott's kiss. We only shared one, but it was unforgettable."

Back at Storyton Hall, Sterling was waiting for her in the garage. His face was drawn with fatigue.

"Did you get any sleep?" Jane asked him.

He shrugged. "I'm fine. More importantly, I know where Ms. Birch spent the night. Seeing as the man is one of my drivers, I thought I should tell you myself."

"Ms. Birch was with a *staff member*?" Jane couldn't hide her astonishment. She assumed that Taylor, an attractive young woman in a hotel filled with older matrons, would try to seduce one of the male cover models. Not only that, but Storyton Hall employees knew that fraternizing with a guest would lead to immediate dismissal. With the exception of the housekeepers or members of the waitstaff delivering room service, employees were not permitted to enter a guest's room. And they were strictly forbidden to invite guests back to one of the tiny staff cottages spread across Storyton's grounds.

"Who is this person and where is he now?" Jane demanded.

"Glenn. He's our newest driver and has been an excellent addition to our team. Until now." Sterling frowned. "He's in the staff kitchen. It's best that you speak with him there. If you make an appearance in any of our public areas, you'll be swarmed by hysterical guests."

Jane shut her eyes for a moment. "Is it that bad?"

"Your aunt and uncle are managing the situation, but a number of guests have expressed their desire to check out."

The sense of urgency Jane felt last night returned full force. "While I'm speaking with Glenn, please find Lily Jamison and bring her to the kitchens."

As they walked from the garage to the main house, Jane shared her plan. It was met with Sterling's approval and he promised to pass along the details to the rest of the Fins.

In the staff kitchen, Jane found Glenn sitting at the scrubbed wood table. His shoulders were slumped and his gaze was fixed on his folded hands.

When Jane entered, he bolted to his feet. "Ma'am, I'm so sorry! I had no idea—"

"Sit," Jane commanded tersely. "When did Ms. Birch first make overtures toward you?"

Glenn blinked. "Overtures?" And then, comprehension dawned on his face. "No, no, it wasn't like that. I drove her into the village yesterday. On the way, she told me she was scared of being alone in Storyton Hall. She believed that the man who'd gone missing, Mr. Poindexter, would come after her the first chance he could. She was headed to the hardware store to buy a can of pepper spray. We'd just crossed the bridge when I explained that none of our shops sold pepper spray. That's when she started to cry."

Jane studied Glenn. He was reed-thin with a kind, homely face and couldn't be a day over twenty-five.

No wonder he was moved by Taylor's performance, Jane thought with a touch of sympathy.

"What happened next?" she asked.

"I didn't know what to do, so I pulled into the Cheshire Cat lot to see if Ms. Birch needed some fresh air. When she tried to get out of the car, she fainted. Luckily, I was able to catch her." Glenn's eyes went glassy as he was swept up by the memory.

Jane nodded. "Lucky indeed. Go on."

"When she came to, she begged me to sit with her until she felt better. I would never have done that except I was worried she might faint again. She didn't look right, ma'am. She was awfully pale." He raised his hands in a show of helplessness. "She talked for a long time and I listened. She said she was desperate for a place to sleep that night—a place where Mr. Poindexter couldn't find her. I told her to speak with the sheriff, but she said she had to stay silent to protect an innocent person."

What a load of crap, Jane thought, but made an encouraging noise.

"I told her she could stay at my place," Glenn said and then hurriedly added, "alone. I'd bunk with another staff member." He looked at Jane with a plaintive expression. "I didn't think I was doing anything bad, so I promised to show Ms. Birch to my cottage before the ball ended. I'd let her in, and she'd leave the key under the mat the next morning."

Jane's gears were turning swiftly. "What time did you escort her to your cottage?"

"Ten thirty or so. We used a staff corridor so no one would see us together." Glenn's cheeks reddened. "I thought I was doing the right thing, even though I was breaking the rules."

Jane made a noncommittal noise. "Do you remember what she was wearing?"

"Her dress was dark blue. And she wore long gloves."

"Did she have a cloak?"

"Yes, ma'am. She wore a dark cloak with a hood. I thought she'd freeze to death walking to my place. I unlocked my door and she went inside. She put one of our plastic laundry bags on the sofa—I guess she brought a change of clothes—and said good night. When I went back this morning, she was gone. No note or anything." Jane heard the disappointment in Glenn's voice. He'd rescued the damsel in distress and had nothing to show for it. In fact, he expected to lose his job as a result.

Jane put a hand on Glenn's shoulder. "You made several poor decisions, but you did so out of kindness. I'd like to give you another chance to prove that you're worthy of wearing Storyton's blue and gold."

"I'll do anything, ma'am!"

"Good," Jane said. "Listen closely."

After making sure that Glenn was primed for his minor role in her plan, Jane invited Lily Jamison into the staff kitchen. Over cups of rooibos tea, she told Lily why they needed to take Taylor Birch down. And then she explained how this could be accomplished. As Jane spoke, Lily's expression went from shock to horror to indignation.

Jane finished by saying, "Her fate is in your hands, Ms. Jamison. Are you willing to sit next to a murderer, lie to her, and trick her into incriminating herself?"

Lily was silent for a long moment. "Yes. I want her to be punished for what she did. Not only did she commit murder to get ahead, but she also robbed the world of a talented storyteller. Even if Rosamund York was a partnership between Nigel and a woman named Rosie Yates, the books they created gave people hours and hours of reading pleasure. The sudden end of those stories is a great loss." She raised her cup. "Count me in."

She and Jane clinked rims, finished their tea, and then parted ways.

Jane took the staff passageway to the Isak Dinesen Safari Room, where she found Sinclair and Lachlan rearranging furniture.

"I believe this will work," Sinclair told Jane with a twinkle of pride.

He and Lachlan unfolded a black lacquered screen painted to resemble a scene from an Ancient Egyptian tomb. A pharaoh stood in the bow of a skiff, ready to spear one of the fish or waterfowl clustered around his boat. The screen, which was nine feet tall, completely obscured a side table and two chairs when unfolded.

To complete the tableau, Lachlan moved a large potted fern from the other corner of the room and placed it in front of the screen. Sinclair positioned a tilt-top table next to the plant and stacked a pile of Egyptian-themed books on its surface. Both men were satisfied with the results.

"Sheriff Evans has arrived," Sinclair said after glancing at his phone. "Mr. Butterworth is bringing him in through the staff entrance. He'll be in the public hallway for a few minutes, but Glenn has already pulled Ms. Birch aside. He's playing his part by promising to get her out of Storyton Hall after lunch."

"Mr. Sterling is searching Glenn's cottage for traces of Ms. Birch's cloak and gloves, and I thought I'd offer my assistance," Lachlan said to Jane. "Unless you need me here."

Jane shook her head. "Sinclair and Butterworth will be more than happy to intercede should Ms. Birch made a run for it. The sheriff's deputies will also be in cruisers out back, waiting on the sheriff's orders. Finding that cloak is crucial, so search as quickly and meticulously as you can."

Lachlan made to leave, but Jane stepped in front of him. "Later, after Ms. Birch is safely in the sheriff's custody, I'd like to know why you're receiving shipments of frozen chicks."

Though Lachlan's composure never faltered, a shadow flitted across his handsome face. "Fair enough, Miss Jane," he murmured deferentially and left.

At that moment, Sheriff Evans entered the Safari Room. He glanced at the African tribal masks, Aboriginal shields, mounted animal heads, and primitive weaponry decorating the walls. His gaze traveled over the zebra-print chairs and leather sofas to the massive fireplace.

"Now, *this* is my kind of room," he declared appreciatively. "A place where a man might read the sports page in peace."

Despite her nervousness, Jane smiled. The room certainly had a masculine appeal. It smelled pleasantly of aftershave and wood smoke as countless men had visited the space to play cards or savor glasses of brandy after dinner. Few women chose to read in the Safari Room. Like Jane, most of them felt uncomfortable around hunting trophies.

"Our stakeout location." Jane gestured at the lacquer screen.

Sheriff Evans peered behind the screen and nodded in approval. "Clever."

He and Jane took their seats. The sheriff sat closest to the gap between the screen and the bookcase, ready to spring into action should Taylor threaten Lily's person. Sinclair closed the gap by repositioning the screen and left the room.

Sheriff Evans placed a recording device on the table. He pressed the record button and gave Jane a thumbs-up sign.

Jane managed a nervous nod and laced her clammy hands together. In a few minutes, Lily and Taylor would enter the room. If all went well, Sheriff Evans would leave Storyton Hall with a murderer in custody. But theirs was a game of chance. Anything could go wrong.

The room filled with the steady ticking of the grandfather clock on the opposite wall and, much more faintly, the noise of guests moving up and down the hallway. Amid these soft sounds, Jane wouldn't be surprised if Sheriff Evans could hear the pounding of her anxious heart.

Someone entered the room and sat in one of the zebra-print chairs on the other side of the screen. Lily Jamison cleared her throat and whispered, "Are you ready?"

"Yes," Jane whispered back.

There was a distinct rustle of a newspaper and Jane imagined Lily doing her best to appear captivated by an article on the skyrocketing costs of snow removal or highlights of the week's basketball games.

"Ms. Jamison?" Taylor's voice floated across the room from the threshold.

Lily's chair creaked softly as she shifted her weight. "Yes. Come join me."

Jane held her breath as Taylor crossed the hemp rug.

"It's *such* a pleasure to meet you," Taylor said. "Ms. York spoke so highly of everyone at Heartfire, and since I handled a great deal of her communication, I feel like I already know you."

"Heartfire is a great place to work," Lily said brightly. "I love my job. I get to read some of the best books in the business, travel to incredible places, and spend evenings dancing with male cover models. My coworkers are like family and I never get tired of calling an author to congratulate her on a new publication, for winning an award, or making a bestseller list." She paused for breath. "As you said, you handled much of Ms. York's communication. You probably knew her better than any of us, so forgive me for asking, but I have to know if Rosamund had any work in progress saved on her computer or in a desk drawer at home. Outlines, unfinished manuscripts, ideas for future series. Anything."

"I think she did," Taylor said carefully.

Lily shifted in her seat again. "I realize it seems terribly insensitive of me to be asking, but my job is to help produce fabulous novels and to get those novels into the hands of hungry readers. It's very rewarding when a Heartfire author acquires a large following. And Rosamund's following is huge, as you well know. I imagine you served as Rosamund's voice and were responsible for managing her fan mail and social media presence. Am I right?"

"I actually did much more than that. I also helped Ms. York with plot ideas and served as a beta reader. She valued my feedback and used all of my recommendations."

"Is that so?" Lily sounded impressed. "That's great to hear. This might be premature, because I don't even know if you're interested in a career in publishing, but do you think you could complete any of Rosamund's unfinished projects? You've already been her voice in many ways."

Jane expected Taylor to leap at the chance, but the young woman was wily. "Would I be considered an author-for-hire or an employee of Heartfire? Because I'd prefer to join the team. My skill set could be useful to a publishing house. Having worked for Ms. York, I already have editing and marketing experience."

"Hm." Lily fell silent and Jane pictured her furrowing her brows in mock consideration. "I'm afraid I can't offer you a position without proof that you have something to bring to the table. Heartfire has over a hundred applicants for the opening on our editorial staff. The only way you could rise above the more experienced candidates would be to net us a sure winner. A Rosamund York novel."

Now it was Taylor's turn for silent contemplation. "I could e-mail you when I get home. Ms. York had a number of projects going, and I have several on my desktop. We were, well, I guess I don't have to keep it a secret anymore, but Rosamund and I were collaborating on the next Venus Dares book."

"How marvelous!" Lily clapped her hands in excitement. "The fate of that novel is in your hands, Ms. Birch. I expect the next Heartfire team member will be hired by the end of today. That someone could be you. If you could give me something concrete, I'd make a call to the powers-that-be. You could be in New York by Monday, starting a whole new chapter in your life." She laughed. "I know that phrase is a cliché, but I think it's fair to use book-related clichés in our line of work, don't you?"

Brilliant, Jane thought. *You're already making Taylor feel included.*

"I . . ." Taylor trailed off. "So let me get this straight. If I show you Rosamund's files, you'll guarantee me a job at Heartfire?"

"In a word, yes. I can change your life today, Ms. Birch."

Taylor exhaled slowly, as though she suddenly realized that her wildest dreams were about to come true. "I could go to New York. I could be in publishing." Jane could hear the lift in Taylor's voice. She'd fallen for Lily's ruse. However, she still had to fetch Nigel's computer in order for

Jane's plan to succeed. "I have just what you're looking for on my laptop," Taylor said after another a painful hesitation. "I forgot that I had copies of Ms. York's files with me. Do you mind waiting while I get my computer?"

"Not at all. It'll give me the chance to finish this article about Rosamund." Lily shook the paper. "They're saying she ingested castor seeds, which are poisonous, but I'm not buying it. A person would have to eat dozens for them to be fatal."

"Actually, it would only take four. They're extremely potent if chewed," Taylor said in a confident tone.

"Really? I had no idea." There was a smile in Lily's voice as she said, "Smart and talented. I'm going to like working with you."

Jane listened to the sound of Taylor's hurried steps and met the sheriff's eyes. He put his fingers to his lips, but Jane saw a smile playing about the corners of his mouth. He was clearly pleased with Lily's work thus far.

No one spoke for a full minute. Finally, Lily whispered, "How am I doing?"

"You'd make an excellent spy, Ms. Jamison." The sheriff leaned over his recording device and, satisfied that it was functioning properly, patted his gun holster. "Just don't push Ms. Birch too far. If she killed Mr. Poindexter in a fit of rage, she's just as likely to strike out at you if she sees through this charade."

"I feel like the heroine in a Linda Howard or Sandra Brown novel," Lily said. "But I'd better get back to my fake reading. She could walk in at any second."

They didn't have to wait long. When Taylor returned, she was breathing hard. She practically ran to the chair she'd recently occupied.

"I can show you the outline for the next Venus Dares book," Taylor said, sounding like a young girl in her excitement. "I came up with the title. What do you think of *The Shameless Sovereign*? In this installment, Venus Dares tangles with a king."

"Splendid!" Lily exclaimed and Jane didn't think her enthusiasm was feigned. "Readers will love it. Can you show me the file?"

Hearing the soft clicks of Taylor's nails striking computer keys, Jane wanted to jump up and cheer. Nigel's missing laptop was in the room. Taylor *had* taken it from Nigel after hitting him on the back of the head. Her possession of the computer, along with the castor seed in her room, gave Sheriff Evans cause to arrest her on suspicion of murder.

Jane wished she could see Taylor's face when the sheriff appeared from behind the screen. After all, the young woman had murdered at least one person in the name of ambition. Not only that, but she'd done her best to ruin Storyton Hall's first romance convention. Jane had never been so eager to see a person apprehended.

Suddenly, Lily gasped and Jane focused on the conversation on the other side of the screen again. "This is a complete outline for *The Shameless Sovereign*. Did Rosamund start the manuscript? Please tell me that she wrote a few chapters."

"The book is two-thirds done," Taylor said. "I can have the novel completely finished by the end of June."

"If not, we can always hire another author. You'll still get the credit for acquiring the next Venus Dares novel," Lily assured Taylor. "Are there more outlines?"

"Two. *The Playful Prince* and *The Reckless Regent*."

"You have a treasure trove on your laptop. May I?" Lily asked and then let out a little cry. "It's cold to the touch. Where were you keeping it?"

"I had to hide it. After what happened to Mr. Poindexter, I didn't want to take any chances. People would kill to get their hands on these files."

Lily murmured in agreement. "When we're finished here, I should help you get Rosamund's things together. Though she and her mother weren't close, her mother should have her effects. Especially any jewelry or custom-made dresses. Did Rosamund order one of those stunning hooded cloaks?"

"I . . . I don't remember."

"Well, I'll ask Ms. Steward for a key to the Romance and Roses suite. Of course, the sheriff might not let me in. Do you have a key?"

"Yes, but . . ."

Lily didn't give her a chance to finish. "Oh, here's a synopsis for the next Eros book. And what's this? A list of proposed changes for *Eros Steals the Bride*." There was a short silence before Lily said, "I don't understand. This was written *after* Rosamund's death."

"I wrote that," Taylor lied. "I'm sorry to say this, but when I saw how badly the advanced reader copy was received by the fans, I decided to make suggestions on how to fix the book."

"I admire your initiative," Lily said. "What's this file?"

"Please don't open anything else!" Taylor cried sharply. "I have copies of some of Ms. York's personal files and I wouldn't feel right letting others see them. She wouldn't have liked that. She was a very private person."

Lily was quick to apologize. "I didn't mean to intrude. May I take a moment to read through the recommendations you made concerning *Eros Steals the Bride*?"

Taylor must have given some kind of wordless permission because the room was slowly enveloped in a gentle silence— the kind that surrounds an intent reader.

As the minutes passed, Jane focused on keeping still, but when she heard the rustle of the newspaper again, she abruptly stiffened. If Taylor scanned that paper, she wouldn't find an article mentioning castor beans and she'd know that Lily had been lying to her.

Across the table, Sheriff Evans shot Jane an alarmed glance. Clearly, he'd been thinking the same thing.

"This is excellent, Taylor. I can't wait to show this to the Heartfire team," Lily said. "If you don't mind, I'm going to use your e-mail program to forward this to my . . ." she trailed off. "Why are all the e-mails in this Inbox addressed to Nigel Poindexter?"

"Give me that!" Taylor snapped and Jane assumed she'd made a grab for the laptop. What followed were the grunts and scuffles indicating a struggle and Sheriff Evans leapt to his feet, his gun drawn.

He left his hiding place behind the screen just as a woman's terrified shriek pierced the air.

"Don't move, Sheriff," Taylor said in a near-growl. "I'll cut her, I swear it. She *tricked* me. She *lied* to my face!"

There was another whimper and Jane could imagine the tip of a blade digging into the tender flesh of Lily's throat.

"Put the knife down, Ms. Birch. It's over." The sheriff sounded remarkably calm. "If you hurt a hair on Ms. Jamison's head, you'll only make things harder for yourself."

Taylor laughed a shrill, maniacal laugh. "*Harder?* What do I have to lose? Everything I've done this week—all the risks I've taken—it's all for nothing!"

"It sounds like you were a strong candidate to enter the publishing field because of your experience working with Ms. York," Sheriff Evans said. "Why did you feel it was necessary to break the law?"

"Because I didn't want to wait anymore. I spent months being treated like a servant by that woman and she didn't even write the books!" Taylor shouted. "Do you know how I found out? I was supposed to be doing one of my millions of menial tasks—this time, it was unpacking Rosamund's bags—when I heard her cell phone buzz. Her highness was in the bathroom, so I read all the texts Nigel had sent over the past few days. I couldn't believe what I was seeing, but it sank in quickly enough."

"And you decided to act on your discovery," Sheriff Evans said.

Taylor grunted. "That's for damned sure. I took Nigel aside soon after he arrived at Storyton and threatened to expose him if he didn't pay me. The loser didn't have any money, but he told me how he planned to get it from Rosamund."

There was a soft "Please" from Lily and Taylor muttered a low, angry reply that Jane couldn't hear.

"I demanded to see the castor beans, so he brought some to my room. Since I knew how he added them into the truffles, it was no trouble for me to squeeze in a few more. Rosamund predictably threw a tantrum after her lunch with Nigel, so I suggested she rest while I got her a soothing cup of tea. I went back to my room, chopped up the extra castor seeds Nigel had given me, and added them to the truffles.

They didn't look that great, but I pretended that I'd put them too close to the hot teapot. Rosamund didn't care. She ate every piece, gorging on that poisoned chocolate like the spoiled brat she was."

Nigel told the truth, Jane thought, aghast. *He used just enough castor seeds to make Rosamund sick. Taylor added the lethal dose.*

"Showing mercy to Ms. Jamison could go a long way when it comes time for your sentencing," the sheriff said. His heavy tread on the carpet indicated that he'd moved forward by several paces.

"Stop right there!" Taylor's voice was a dangerous snarl. "Look at me, Sheriff. I *will* cut her. See?" A whimper of pain echoed across the room. Jane longed to lash out at Taylor, but there was little she could do from behind the screen.

"Put your gun down or I'll do it again," Taylor said.

There was a soft thud as the sheriff laid his gun on the rug.

Jane surveyed her little corner of the room. She needed a weapon. Fortunately, the bookcase behind her was full of them. Unfortunately, most were African antiques. Jane didn't think the Boa sword or curved Ngala knife would be of much use. And even if she could wriggle the Ngbandi spear out of its case without alerting Taylor, she'd never used one before. She had no experience with the throwing blades either. Feeling frantic, her gaze fell on a plaque reading, "Bow and Arrow of the Chokwe."

Jane opened the cabinet door as carefully and quietly as possible and removed the bow and solitary arrow from the display. She froze when the bow scraped against the glass cabinet door, but Taylor starting shouting something at Lily and Jane feared that Taylor was heading for the hall.

Jane tested the tension of the bowstring. It felt nothing like the bow she used on the Robin Hood Range, but when she nocked the arrow and pulled back on the string, she believed there was enough resistance to release the arrow with force.

She had one arrow. One chance to stop Taylor Birch. If Taylor left Storyton Hall with Lily Jamison as her hostage, there was no telling what would happen. Jane wouldn't stand for that. She needed to rescue Lily and ensure that Taylor was brought to justice.

With the bowstring grazing her right cheek and her left arm stretched straight, Jane stepped out from behind the screen and quickly took in the scene.

Sheriff Evans stood off to her right, his hands raised in surrender. Taylor was nearly at the door. She held a steak knife against the side of Lily's neck, and a thin trickle of blood ran down from a wound beneath Lily's ear. Lily's eyes were glassy with terror.

Jane quieted her mind. She focused her energy on the bow in her left hand and the nocked arrow in her right. She inhaled once, fixing her gaze on her target. All sound faded. She didn't hear Taylor speak or notice Sheriff Evans motioning at her. She exhaled through parted lips and let the arrow fly.

Time crawled. The seconds stretched out like yarn on a loom, and the arrow seemed to be traveling underwater. Suddenly, its point punctured the soft flesh just above Taylor's armpit. She jerked and dropped the knife. Lily broke free from Taylor's grasp, grabbed the knife, and ducked behind the closest sofa.

Jane lowered the bow and looked at Sheriff Evans. He'd scooped his gun off the floor and was pointing it at Taylor.

As for Taylor, she couldn't stop staring at the arrow protruding from her shoulder. Finally, she groaned like a wounded animal and slid to the floor, landing on her rear with a thud.

While the sheriff called for backup, Jane rushed to where Lily was huddled.

Jane grabbed a wad of tissues from the box on a nearby table and gently wiped the blood off Lily's neck. Thankfully, it was a shallow cut and would heal cleanly.

"Are you all right?" Jane asked softly.

Lily nodded. Her wan face was starting to regain some color.

"You were incredible," Jane said.

"Me?" Lily shook her head in disbelief. "*You* were incredible. You were just like Venus Dares in *The Bold Baron*. There's a scene where she shoots the baron's uncle with an arrow because he's about to push a scullery maid off the roof." Lily managed a wobbly smile. "I never met a heroine like the ones I encounter in Heartfire novels. Until now. You did it, Jane. You saved the day."

"*We* saved the day," Jane said. She stood up and offered Lily her hand.

After Lily rose unsteadily to her feet, she and Jane embraced. They wept and laughed, relieved that the ordeal was over. And then they hugged once more, clinging to each other like long lost friends.

EIGHTEEN

"I don't know about you, ladies, but I found this book club meeting particularly cathartic," Mabel said.

"I agree." Anna sighed in contentment. "I never thought these words would pass my lips, but I can't eat another bite of chocolate."

The other Cover Girls laughed.

"I'm with you, sister." Phoebe tapped a nail against her martini glass. "Our menu was pretty decadent. Cocktails mixed with Godiva liqueur, fresh greens with chocolate-balsamic vinaigrette, and pork medallions with a dark-chocolate chipotle sauce. And then, we topped it all off with two-bite chocolate cream pies and chocolate mousse cups. It's a good thing it's sweater season."

Jane, who'd gone into the kitchen to start the coffeemaker, returned to the living room and sank down on the sofa. "I'm glad you had us read *Chocolat*, Betty. I don't think I could have handled anything too heavy after Romancing the Reader."

"This has certainly been the most exciting February on record," Mrs. Pratt said. "And you're a media sensation, Jane. I've read a dozen accounts comparing you to Katniss Everdeen."

Jane rolled her eyes. "Unlike the Hunger Games heroine, my survival doesn't depend on a bow and arrow."

"Archery has become really popular thanks to those novels. Maybe I should take it up. Do you think they make purple arm guards?" Violet twirled the end of her lavender scarf and then nudged Mabel in the side. "You could design a line of feminine archery gear."

Mabel groaned. "Honey, I am officially on vacation. I have stitched, hemmed, trimmed, and basted until my fingers burned. This gal is *tired*." She winked at Jane. "But my piggy bank is stuffed."

Eloise gave Jane's hand a squeeze. "Can you take a page from Mabel's notebook and hang a closed sign on your office door for a few days? Taylor's been transferred to a women's correctional facility and the news vans have finally left. Even the villagers are starting to talk about other things. You should take time to recover."

The rest of the women murmured in agreement.

"We can't begin to understand what it's like to strive for normalcy after two murders," Anna said. "But if you want to trade places for a day or two, let me know. Ever since Randall got his copy of *Journal of Infectious Diseases*, he's been pouncing on any customer over fifty. He corners these hapless individuals in the vitamin aisle in order to educate them on the signs and symptoms of whatever new strain of virus is attacking the elderly."

"I hardly consider fifty to be *elderly*," Betty said, sounding affronted.

Anna threw her hands in the air. "I tried to tell him that he was insulting people, but Randall is incapable of listening. One can't hold a conversation with the man. Whenever I speak, he talks right over me."

"I like a man who knows when to be quiet," Violet said. She turned to Mrs. Pratt. "Does Gavin hang on your every word?"

Mrs. Pratt looked unhappy. "He does, but I wish he wouldn't. I'm feeling a bit . . . suffocated."

Jane was stunned. "When we discuss the romantic scenes in our book club novels, you always say how lovely it would be to have a man wine and dine you, give you flowers, and treat you like a queen. Isn't that exactly what Gavin's been doing?"

"Yes," Mrs. Pratt said. "He's a darling man, and I'm very fond of him. However, he's asked me to move to Florida with him."

The Cover Girls stared at her in collective astonishment.

"Did he propose?" Eloise asked breathlessly.

"He might have if I hadn't told him that I wouldn't leave Storyton. Not now. Not ever." Mrs. Pratt's eyes grew moist. "This is my home. I can't see myself anywhere else." She sniffled. "I don't want Gavin to stay for my sake either. If I loved him, it would be different. I enjoy his company very much, but is what I feel love? I'm not certain."

Phoebe glanced around at her friends. "When can a person ever be sure? I think it takes a long time before we really know. Then again, I don't believe in love at first sight."

Eloise blushed prettily. "I do. Not in the way it's depicted in novels, but I believe that a moment occurs when a person shows you a glimpse of their true self, and in that moment, you can fall in love with them."

"Are you speaking from personal experience?" Mabel wanted to know.

Before Eloise could reply, Mrs. Pratt said, "Too many relationships start off like a romance novel and end up like a horror story. Take a young coed named Rosie Yates, for example. From what I read in the papers, she was smitten with Nigel Poindexter the second she entered his classroom. Her infatuation wore off over time and she wanted him out of her life, but she couldn't be Rosamund York without him."

"Hers was a gilded cage," Betty said. "And Nigel didn't fare much better. He invested his future partnering with a much younger woman and began to live above his means. He was as naïve as Rosie. She grew to resent him and he grew to envy her. Their relationship was bound to implode sooner or later."

Phoebe twisted a corkscrew curl around her finger. "And along comes Taylor Birch, the catalyst. Seeing a chance to advance her career, she decided to exploit their situation. She'll spend years behind bars because of that decision."

"We can't mention exploitation without including Georgia Dupree," Anna said. "I'd wager a year's supply of antibacterial lotion that she gets a book deal out of this."

Jane smiled at Anna. "Not with Heartfire. After Georgia pled guilty to several criminal charges, she tried to convince Lily Jamison that she was still worthy of continuing the Venus Dares novels, but Lily turned her down flat."

"No matter who writes them, the books will never be as good as Nigel's." Mrs. Pratt raised her face skyward and sighed forlornly. "I can't believe I was duped. All these years and I never guessed that a *man* was writing some of my favorite Regency romance novels."

Mabel slung an arm around Mrs. Pratt's shoulders. "People can surprise us, can't they?"

"Maria Stone certainly did." Jane beckoned for her friends to follow her into the kitchen where the coffeemaker had finished gurgling. After pouring coffee into an assortment of book-themed mugs, she continued her narrative. "When the sheriff brought Maria back to Storyton Hall, she was hissing like a feral cat. She couldn't wait to tell the press how she'd been mistreated. Nothing I said had any effect on her. Eventually, I gave her up as a lost cause, but Aunt Octavia didn't."

Eloise grinned expectantly. "Did she give that girl a tongue lashing?"

Jane shook her head. "I think Ms. Stone has experienced more than her fair share of those. On the other hand, she's received little in the way of kindness or respect. Sensing this, Aunt Octavia invited Maria to her apartment for tea. She sat across from that angry young woman and listened to her talk. For *three* hours."

"What did they talk about?" Anna asked while dabbing at her eyes with a paper towel.

"I don't know," Jane said. "All I can say is that Maria left Storyton Hall with a quiet confidence she hadn't possessed before. Not only has Aunt Octavia pledged to be Maria's pen pal, but she's also the newest member of the Matildas."

"Maria's feminist group?" Eloise giggled. "Look out, world! Aunt Octavia's taken up a cause. Maybe Storyton Hall will be the setting for an activist conference in the near future."

Jane groaned. "It'll be a long time before I'm ready to host *any* special events. Though I've already had several requests . . ."

"From which groups?" Mrs. Pratt asked.

"The most memorable was from The Medieval Herbalists."

Mabel took a sip of coffee. "They sound harmless enough."

"That's what I thought about the romance writers and fans," Jane muttered. "Still, we might have something very unique to offer these nature-lovers." She put her coffee mug down and smiled at her friends. "I want to show you something amazing. We'll have to walk to Lachlan's cottage to see it, so bundle up."

The Cover Girls didn't hesitate. They pulled on coats and gloves, wrapped scarves around their necks, and donned knit hats.

On the way to Lachlan's, Jane told them about the mysterious deliveries of the frozen chicks.

Eloise looked concerned. "Please tell me that he's not a psycho."

Instead of answering, Jane hooked her arm through her friend's and walked even more briskly to Lachlan's little cottage.

One of Lachlan's curtains twitched and a moment later, he was standing in the doorway, a shy smile on his face. His eyes met Eloise's and his smile grew brighter. Then, he turned to Jane. "It's best if we don't make too much noise."

As soon as all the Cover Girls were inside Lachlan's, Jane put her fingers to her lips. "We need to be quiet. We don't want to startle Lachlan's ward."

Eloise gave Lachlan a puzzled glance, but he disappeared into his bedroom without a word and returned a moment later wearing a leather glove on his right arm. The glove reached to his elbow and was clearly necessary, for the bird perched on Lachlan's forearm gripped the thick leather with dagger-sharp talons.

The Cover Girls were struck dumb with awe.

"This is a saker falcon," Lachlan said. "A drug dealer with a penchant for collecting exotic animals purchased her. Unfortunately, she was injured during a shootout between the dealer and the DEA."

Eloise gaped at Lachlan. "How did you end up with her?"

A flicker of sorrow passed over Lachlan's face. "My older brother was a DEA agent. I was on a ride-along with him when he got the call to apprehend this dealer. I'll skip the raid details. All I can say is that bullets flew and one of them struck this falcon's wing. She was going to be euthanized, so I took her. I have some experience with falcons because I use to volunteer at a raptor rescue facility, but I wasn't sure how Ms. Steward would feel about a bird of prey living in my cottage, so I kept her hidden."

"And you feed her frozen chicks?" Phoebe shuddered in revulsion.

"Until she can hunt on her own, yes." Lachlan was completely animated. "She's doing really well. I've taken her out for some short flights and I think she'll be bringing down squirrels and small rodents come springtime."

Eloise took a tentative step forward. "She's beautiful. May I touch her?"

Lachlan nodded in approval. He held his arm out and, using his other hand, pointed at the back of the falcon's neck. "She's used to having her feathers stroked here."

Watching Lachlan and Eloise, Jane felt the cold sting of jealousy. Lachlan's secret was hardly nefarious. It was nothing like Edwin's. In fact, Jane completely understood Lachlan's desire to save the magnificent raptor. In order to explain why he needed frozen chicks, Lachlan had introduced Jane to the saker falcon. And when he'd seen how positively she'd reacted to the bird, he proposed they start a falconry program at Storyton Hall.

"The man who built this house was a world-class falconer," Jane had told Lachlan. "Show me a detailed budget and I'll consider the idea."

Lachlan had immediately handed her a thin stack of paper. "Done. Also, there's a Harris's hawk for sale in North Carolina.

If we can get our licenses and permits approved in time, I think he'd made a great addition to our fledgling program."

Jane grinned at the pun and promised to look over the proposal that evening.

Now, Lachlan was murmuring something to Eloise and she was bobbing her head up and down in assent.

"We go out pretty early. Wear plenty of layers."

Eloise smiled. "I will. See you then."

The Cover Girls wished Lachlan and his falcon good night and then headed back to Jane's house. The women only popped in long enough to collect their handbags, dishes, and copies of *Chocolat*. It was late and they were all ready to go home, change into flannel pajamas, and nestle under warm blankets and quilts.

As was her custom, Eloise lingered behind. She and Jane stood side-by-side at the kitchen sink, washing and drying the martini glasses in companionable silence.

"It sounds like you and Lachlan have a date," Jane said when they were halfway done.

Eloise's smile was hesitant. "Is that okay? I don't want to create an awkward situation, seeing as he works for you."

"The only thing I care about is your happiness, Eloise. You and Lachlan obviously like each other and there's no reason why you shouldn't date." Jane raised a warning finger. "But if he hurts you, he'll be bunking in the mew with his falcon."

Eloise laughed. "Listen to you with your 'bunking in the mew.' How many falconry books have you read since confronting him about his creepy deliveries?"

"Three." Jane handed Eloise the last glass. "It's been a pleasant diversion. I went to the meadow the other evening to watch the bird exercise, and her short flight lifted my spirits. I feel like I've been shot through the wing too. I know that sounds melodramatic, but with all that occurred during the Romancing the Reader week, I feel . . . wounded."

Eloise shot Jane a sideways look. "It wasn't just the murders, wasn't it? Something, or *someone*, added to your pain. Was it Edwin?"

Jane released a pent-up sigh. "I didn't know how to raise

the subject with you, Eloise. You're my best friend and Edwin's your brother, so I kept it to myself."

Tossing the dish towel aside, Eloise turned to Jane. "First of all, you and I are more like sisters than friends. Secondly, I know my brother. He has his good points. He's loyal, generous, and brilliant, but he's not an easy man to be around. He's distrustful, moody, and secretive. I could tell that he had feelings for you, and I neither encouraged nor discouraged him. So if you two aren't getting along, you might be relieved to hear that he's left the country." She shrugged. "He's off to Damascus or Syria or someplace."

Jane knew she should greet this news with relief, but she experienced a stab of bitter disappointment instead. "Is he going back to travel writing? What about Daily Bread?"

Eloise began to put the glasses in the cupboard. "He left Magnus in charge. It all happened overnight. That's how things always are with Edwin. He stopped by my house long enough to say good-bye and to assure me that he wouldn't be gone long. He also asked me to look after you, like I wouldn't have done that anyway."

Jane couldn't tell Eloise what she'd learned about Edwin without revealing her own secrets, but she owed her friend a partial explanation. "I was falling for Edwin too, but I had to pull back. I can't take chances as though I were young and single. My boys come first."

"So *that's* why Edwin said that he had to prove himself to you." Eloise brightened. "What he thinks he'll find in Lebanon or wherever to win you over is beyond me, but he mentioned something about showing you his true character. No matter how much I pried, he wouldn't elaborate." Eloise frowned. "He can be maddening, Jane, and I don't know whether you should run in the opposite direction when you see him coming or give him the benefit of the doubt. I really don't. But nothing you do will alter our friendship. Not ever."

Jane switched off the kitchen lights and the two women moved to the living room. Eloise buttoned her coat and held her copy of *Chocolat* against her chest. "I want to read you a few lines that spoke to me." She opened to a bookmarked page.

"'I could do with a bit more excess. From now on I'm going to be immoderate—and volatile—I shall enjoy loud music and lurid poetry.'"

"Are you going to follow in the heroine's footsteps?" Jane teased. "Because I'd fully support your decision to sell chocolate at Run for Cover."

Eloise wasn't smiling when she put her hands on Jane's shoulders. "You could do with a bit more excess, my friend. It's time for you to stop thinking of yourself as a widow and a single mom. You're a woman in the prime of her life. A smart, funny, and beautiful woman. You also have excellent taste in books and in best friends."

Jane laughed. "Message received. You'd better get to bed. A certain falconer rises very early. See you at the Pickled Pig tomorrow."

Eloise opened the door and stepped outside. "Let's not end up like J. Alfred Prufrock," she said, hugging herself against the cold. "Let's take a vow not to measure out our lives in coffee spoons."

Jane, who'd memorized the T.S. Eliot poem in college, offered Eloise her hand. "'Do I dare disturb the universe?'" she quoted.

"Yes, we do!" Eloise vigorously shook Jane's hand. With a final smile, she darted off into the darkness.

As for Jane, she went upstairs to her bedroom and opened the lid of the jewelry box on her dresser. Withdrawing the card that had accompanied Edwin's Valentine's bouquet, she pressed it between her fingers, squeezing gently. She'd repeated the same examination every night since she'd run into Edwin on the street outside the sheriff's station, and though she knew there was an object sealed inside the envelope, she'd yet to look at it.

"Do I dare?" she whispered.

She thought of how she'd watched Lachlan and the falcon during their evening exercise. When Lachlan had removed the bird's hood, her piercing yellow eyes had darted everywhere, taking in the meadow, the trees, and the expanse of grey sky. She'd stretched her mighty wings, and then, Lachlan had thrust his arm up and out and the falcon had leapt off her human perch. She'd let loose a cry of wild abandon as she hit the air. A cry of unadulterated joy. The sound had echoed inside Jane's heart. It came back to her now as she sat on the edge of her bed with Edwin's card in her hand.

"I dare."

Jane ripped open the envelope and pulled out a notecard. When she unfolded it, a small object wrapped in a thin sheaf of tissue paper dropped into her palm. Ignoring it for the moment, she read the words Edwin had written in his calligraphic script.

I waltzed with you once upon a dream.

I know you.

Edwin had switched the order of the lyrics of the song from Disney's *Sleeping Beauty*, but the melody immediately began playing in Jane's mind. She returned to the night she and Edwin had danced alone in the ballroom and the memory was so strong that she could almost feel his hand pressing against her lower back.

Jane closed her eyes and lost herself in images of that unforgettable evening. If only she could return to that state of blissful ignorance, back to when she hadn't known the truth about Edwin Alcott.

"I know you too, book thief," she whispered. Opening her eyes, she peeled the tissue away from the object nestled in her palm to reveal a gold owl pin. Its eyes were tiny pearls and the scroll in its talons looked like ivory. It was an exact duplicate of the tattoo on her left breast.

Jane could see the piece of jewelry was delicately made and probably quite old. She was less certain of Edwin's reason for giving it to her, however. Was it supposed to be a token of affection? Edwin's way of saying that he knew she was the Guardian of Storyton Hall? Or was it a warning? A portent of his plans to locate the secret library and steal one of its precious treasures?

Jane had no idea what the gift meant, so she put the card and the owl pin in her jewelry box and shut the lid.

She glanced out the window, seeking the dark bulk of Storyton Hall across the lawn. Jane lifted her gaze to the side of the house where her sons were curled like commas in their beds in her aunt and uncle's guest room. She blew them a kiss, thinking of the special pancake breakfast she'd make for them in the morning, and then got ready for bed.

Pulling back the covers, she reached for the book on her nightstand, but didn't open it. She placed the hardcover on the spare pillow and stared at the spine until her lids became heavy.

Even after switching off the lamp, she could still see the bold letters of the title, *The Art of War*, in her mind.

There would be time to read and to prepare for the future tomorrow. As for tonight, Jane wanted to dream of pleasant things. The gardens in springtime. A falcon taking wing. Against her will, however, she drifted off to the distant strains of Tchaikovsky's *Sleeping Beauty* and the glimmering, incandescent memory of a candlelit waltz.

EPILOGUE

The next day, after church services and a hearty lunch of roast chicken, mashed potatoes, and Brussels sprouts, Jane drove the boys into the village. Uncle Aloysius and Aunt Octavia followed behind in a second Rolls.

The Steward clan entered the market and glanced around at the pig-themed decorations. Pig cutouts hung from the ceiling, pig balloons were attached to the cash registers, and every employee wore pink pig ears.

"Welcome! Welcome!" Tobias Hogg rushed forward to meet them. In addition to the pig ears, he also wore a rubber pig snout over his nose. With his beady eyes, the effect made him look more like a two-legged swine than ever.

A woman wearing a matching rubber snout rounded the corner of the snack and soda aisle and waved at Jane. "Surprise!"

"Ms. Jewel! How nice to see you," Jane said.

Barbara smiled. "Call me Barbara. After all, we're neighbors now. I'm renting a cottage across the street from the bank."

Jane glanced at Tobias and saw pure joy in his eyes. "That's wonderful news," she said sincerely. "How's the writing going?"

"I'm working on two projects. Finishing my current manuscript is one. Trying to win Mrs. Hogg over is the second." Barbara nudged Tobias in the side. "This boy is her baby, and no one's quite good enough for him. But I have a plan." She leaned closer to Jane. "I'm making Mrs. Hogg a character in my book. A resourceful and devoted mother revered by both her children and the townsfolk. What do you think?"

"It's brilliant," Jane said.

Barbara shot a meaningful glance at Tobias and then touched Jane's arm. "Could I share something with you in private?"

Jane followed Barbara over to the bulk candy bins.

"I wanted to tell you something about the night Mr. Poindexter was killed." Barbara pulled off her pig snout and lowered her voice. "I understand that I was seen leaving Storyton Hall with Tobias. It was quite late and I, ah, didn't return to the resort until the next day."

Taking note of Barbara's discomfort, Jane said, "Please, it's none of my business—"

"I want everyone, especially Mrs. Hogg, to know that we weren't sneaking off like a pair of teenagers looking for a place to park. I'm not that kind of woman." Barbara's cheeks grew bright pink. "We left because Tobias wanted me to meet his mother. She's an insomniac who takes long afternoon naps and is usually wide-awake at midnight. Apparently, Tobias thought his mother would be thrilled to meet the object of his affection. He expected her to welcome me with open arms even though she was in her nightgown and robe."

Having met the formidable Mrs. Hogg, Jane thought it more likely that Barbara was received with glowers and grumbles.

"Mrs. Hogg aside, Tobias and I shared a magical evening. The moon was shining over Storyton Village as we drove through Main Street. And I've never seen so many stars! It was that sight, as well as the presence of the kind and attentive man beside me, that convinced me to rent a house here. Tobias and I are taking things slowly, though I'm very tempted to jump in with both feet! I've been waiting my whole life to be romanced."

Jane smiled at Barbara. "I'm thrilled to call you neighbor. And I firmly believe that you and Tobias will live happily ever after."

Just then, the store's intercom crackled and a tinny voice asked all customers to congregate in the bakery section.

Half of the village seemed to be gathered around a small platform featuring a ten-speed bicycle with a red frame and white-wall tires. A blue ribbon hung from the handlebars and a generous gift certificate to the Pickled Pig was taped to the seat.

Wide-eyed children surrounded the bike. They whispered to one another and bounced on the balls of their feet. They elbowed and jostled and chattered like squirrels. With one exception. Jane spotted a little girl from the twins' class. The girl, whose name was Abigail, tugged at the end of her long braid and stared at the bike with a mixture of hope and despondency.

She must want that bike very badly, Jane thought.

Tobias led his spotted pig through the crowd. "Thanks for coming to our naming ceremony today, folks! We had so many wonderful suggestions that it was really tough to pick just one. I have runner-up prizes for two lucky kids. Congratulations to Marcy Pruitt and Robbie Carson for winning gift certificates to Geppetto's Toy Shop. The names they chose, Hamlet and Francis Bacon, were great. Let's give our runners-up a round of applause."

Rufus and Duncan Hogg, who were as stony-faced as usual, passed out the certificates. Tobias clasped his hands over his round, aproned belly and grinned like a proud parent. "And now, without further ado, I'd like to congratulate Hemingway of Storyton Hall for submitting the winning name, Pig Newton. Master Hem, you're our grand prize winner!"

Hem hooted in triumph and exchanged high-fives with his brother and a dozen other children. He paused in the midst of accepting congratulations when he caught sight of Abigail's face. It had crumpled in disappointment and her eyes had filled with unshed tears. Hem looked at her for a long moment and then whispered in Fitz's ear.

Fitz drew back in surprise, but Hem grabbed his shirt and pulled him in close for another furious bout of whispering.

Finally, Fitz nodded and the two boys asked to speak with Tobias in private.

The trio ducked behind the bakery counter, held a quick conference, and then resumed their places. "All right, folks, we're going to have a short parade around the store. Hem Steward will have the honor of holding Pig Newton's leash. Lead on, son!"

Music blared through the speakers and Hem marched forward. The rest of the children immediately mimicked his high-knee walk, giggling over the silliness of parading down the frozen food aisle behind a boy and a small pig. As for Pig Newtown, he appeared to be enjoying himself immensely. He grunted and trotted at Hem's side like an obedient puppy.

Jane was about to follow along when she noticed Tobias beckon Abigail to come closer. He waited until the other children were gone before squatting down and speaking to her in low tones. He then pointed at the bike, clapped her on the back, and moved away.

The girl covered her mouth with her hands in astonishment. Her eyes shone with such delight that Jane could guess what had had happened. She suddenly remembered that Abigail's father had lost his over-the-mountain factory job several months ago. It had probably been a lean winter for Abigail's family.

Abigail's mother detached herself from the crowd and took her daughter's hand. The little girl whispered excitedly and then threw her arms around her mother's neck. Abigail's mother glanced at the bike and the gift certificate taped to its seat. She then scanned the surrounding faces until she found Jane's. She mouthed a big "Thank you."

Jane felt a hand on her shoulder. "You should be proud, my girl," Uncle Aloysius said.

Swallowing the lump in her throat, Jane turned to her uncle and said, "Those boys never fail to surprise me. They've always been generous, but what they just did was inspiring. I think we should follow their lead."

Aunt Octavia harrumphed. "I am *not* marching around a grocery store. I might trip an unruly child with my cane. Purely by accident, of course," she added with an impish gleam in her eye.

"I don't mean *literally* follow their lead," Jane said. "I'm talking about breaking with a centuries-old tradition. I want to share our treasure, Uncle Aloysius. Not all of it. Just a few items. Think of the gift we'd be giving the world and of how Storyton Hall would benefit in return. You both know about my Board of Dreams. Well, there's no more room left on that board. It's full, but our savings account isn't."

Uncle Aloysius was already shaking his head. "Impossible. We'd be opening ourselves up to incredible danger. We might as well send formal invitations to every book thief on the planet. We gave our word, Jane. Not directly, but every time one of our predecessors accepted an item, they pledged to keep it safe. Safe means hidden. It's your duty as Guardian to keep that pledge. For the rest of your days."

"I understand that, but not all of the materials are dangerous. Times have changed so drastically that the players in this drama—the authors, subjects, donors, and Steward guardians—are long dead. We're treading a fine line between protection and censorship. Can we try blowing the dust off of a few treasures? To bring them out into the light where they were meant to be? Stories belong to the world. Should a single story, poem, play, essay, or missive be under lock and key? I think not."

"We've been over this, my dear, and—"

Aunt Octavia put her hand on her husband's arm. "I agree with Jane, my love. We could find a way. We could try it. Just this once."

"We tried it forty years ago. Don't you remember what happened when we sold that poetry book?" Uncle Aloysius looked pained. "How many unwelcome visitors came to Storyton Hall afterward? And what of the fire in the east wing?"

Nodding gravely, Aunt Octavia clamped her lips together.

Jane hadn't heard about the fire. "We can talk about this over tea tomorrow afternoon. I'd like to know what went wrong all those years ago and see if we might have more options open to us today. Will you at least agree to a discussion?"

Uncle Aloysius gave her an indulgent smile. "Of course. I am willing to talk this over with you, my girl."

The parade was returning to its starting place. Hem had given the leash to Fitz and the twins had their arms slung around each other's shoulders. They came to a halt in front of the red bike and Fitz passed the leash to Tobias. Tobias shook hands with both boys, gave them a brief salute, and then scooped Pig Newton off the floor.

As the crowd dispersed to sample pig-shaped sugar cookies and cups of pink lemonade, Aunt Octavia called the twins to her side.

"I have never been so proud of you boys." Beaming at them, she pointed at the bulk candy bins. "You can fill a bag to the tippy top. My treat."

"Awesome!" Hem shouted while Fitz cried, "Sweet!"

Grinning, the boys raced off, nearly barreling into an elderly woman with a walker. They swerved at the last second and Jane expelled a long sigh. "Angels, they are not."

"Thank heavens for that," Aunt Octavia said. "Living with a bunch of angels would be tedious, don't you think?"

"No." Uncle Aloysius bent down to plant a kiss on his wife's cheek. "I've been married to one for decades."

Aunt Octavia pretended to push him away, but she didn't try very hard. "Stop it, Aloysius. Valentine's Day is over."

"For me, every day is Valentine's Day."

Jane watched her aunt and uncle move slowly toward the exit. Uncle Aloysius took his wife's arm and Aunt Octavia leaned into him. They talked softly as they walked, their heads tilted toward each other, their gaits evenly matched. Jane wondered if she'd ever find someone to grow old with, if she'd experience the happiness that came from a lifetime of shared memories.

"Mom?" Hem interrupted her maudlin thoughts. "Can we get truffles? Or do they cost extra?"

Seeing the bulging bag of candy in her son's hand, Jane

frowned. "Absolutely not. If I never see another truffle for the rest of my life, that'll be just fine with me."

Two days later, Jane sat in her office reviewing the blueprints for the falcon mews. She'd agreed to go ahead with the project even though it would take most of the Romancing the Reader profits to cover the cost of construction, adopt a second raptor, and train another handler. Jane decided that the program should be purely educational at first.

"To think this all started with a mysterious package." Jane shook her head in wonder.

Lachlan placed a brown box on her desk. "Looks like you've received one of your own."

Catching sight of the handwriting on the label, Jane forgot to breathe. She glanced up to ask Lachlan when the package had arrived, but he was already gone.

With trembling hands, Jane moved her teacup to the bookcase and the blueprints and budget spreadsheets aside. Settling herself in her chair, she stared at the stamps on the top corner of the box.

There were multiple paper stamps as well as U.S. Customs labels. Jane was most fascinated by the Damascus stamps with their Arabic script, colorful background, and images of monuments with tall minarets. Jane had only traveled to exotic places in her mind. All of her life, she'd relied on books to transport her through time and space. And now, something from a distant and mysterious land had been sent to her.

Reaching for the scissors, Jane severed the tape and pulled back the flaps to reveal a smaller box. This one was long and thin and made of wood, not cardboard. When Jane peeled away a layer of bubble wrap, a white notecard drifted onto her desk blotter. Jane scooped it up and read:

I find what has been lost, restore what has been damaged, and retrieve what has been stolen. This belongs to Storyton Hall. It was taken from your library many years ago. When I return, I'd like to tell you the whole story. I can only hope that you'll be willing to listen.—E

"Who do you think you are? The Robin Hood of book thieves?" Jane scoffed. She was about to ball up his note when she remembered what Edwin had told Eloise. He'd said that he left the country on a mission to prove his character.

"What have you done, Edwin?" Jane whispered.

Easing the lid off the wooden box, she discovered a manuscript page captured in Plexiglas. The paper was yellow and brown-spotted with age. Most of the Latin text was printed in black, but one line was comprised entirely of red letters. The next line began with an oversized capital *O*. The letter was painted red and blue.

Jane examined the page for several minutes, noting the twin columns of text, the red lettering on the top margin, and the red embellishments on every capital letter.

"This looks like . . . No, it couldn't be." But the more Jane stared at the page in its Plexiglas coffin, the more she believed she knew what was sitting on her desk.

Doing her best to keep calm, Jane called Sinclair and asked him to come to her office.

At the sound of his knock, she ushered him in, locked the door, and pointed at her desk. Sinclair's eyes went right to the manuscript page.

"If I didn't know better, I'd say that was a page from a Gutenberg Bible," he said.

Jane nodded. "Edwin sent it."

Sinclair couldn't conceal his surprise. Tugging his bow tie, he read Edwin's note. His gaze then returned to the manuscript.

Jane told Sinclair why Edwin had supposedly left Storyton. "If Edwin set off on this so-called mission, then he must have realized I'd discovered that he was a book thief. I *was* rather cold to him when we last met . . ." Jane looked at Sinclair. "I wonder he if went abroad to retrieve this page. Do we even have a Gutenberg Bible? And if so, is ours incomplete?"

"Many of them are," Sinclair said. "Throughout history, pages have been cut from the bound books and sold for over a hundred thousand dollars apiece on the black market. The more illumination, the greater the value. There are twenty-two known copies of this forty-two line Bible. It was printed using movable type by Johannes Gutenberg in the 1450s. It marked the true birth of books. Books for the masses, not just the few. Knowledge could be shared. Stories that had been purely word-of-mouth would be captured for posterity. It was a golden moment in time. And yes, we have a copy."

"Is ours missing pages?"

Sinclair nodded. "Several."

"Shall we go up and see if this is one of them?" Jane touched the corner of the Plexiglas. "Because if this came from our Bible, then Edwin Alcott knows more about our holdings than I do. It also means that we may have misjudged him."

Sinclair put the Plexiglas back in the wood box. "Let's find out."

Minutes later, after providing Uncle Aloysius and Aunt Octavia with a brief explanation, Jane and Sinclair ascended the narrow spiral staircase to the tower room. They both pulled on white gloves and then Jane impatiently waited for Sinclair to retrieve the Bible from a deep drawer.

The book was kept in a custom cradle, and Sinclair placed it on the table and began to gingerly turn the ancient pages. After what felt like eons to Jane, he said, "The sheaf Edwin sent is from Song of Solomon. It's one of my favorite books of Scripture."

Jane didn't reply. Her mind was a whirlwind of questions. How had Edwin known about their Bible? How had he retrieved this page? What story would he tell her when he returned to Storyton?

Sinclair closed his eyes and sighed. The sound brought Jane back to the present. "'Arise, my love, my fair one, and come thy way,'" Sinclair quoted, his voice melodious and serene. "'For behold, winter is past: the rain is changed, and is gone away.'"

"Does the page belong to this Bible?" Jane whispered.

Sinclair opened his eyes and smiled. "Yes, Miss Jane. To

paraphrase Mr. Alcott, what was damaged can be restored. We're still missing pages, but the Song of Solomon is now complete. I don't know how he came to be in possession of this page, but he has done us a great service."

Jane glanced at all the airtight drawers and decided that it was high time for her to review the conditions accompanying each acquisition. Surely, some of these priceless treasures could be shared. There had to be a statue of limitations to the promises made by previous Guardians.

"Their stories are our stories," she quietly spoke the motto branded on every guest room key fob and carved into both sides of the massive gates at the end of Storyton Hall's driveway.

Sinclair nodded. "Mr. Gutenberg would agree." Touching the Bible with reverence, he added, "I'm going to share this unexpected windfall with your aunt and uncle. I believe it might improve their opinion of Mr. Alcott. At the very least, it might raise doubts about this particular book thief's reasons for doing what he does."

Jane left Sinclair with her aunt and uncle. She wanted to be alone to process what had just happened, so she grabbed her coat from her office and headed outside to Milton's gardens. She was so absorbed in thoughts, images, and memories of Edwin, which swirled around in her mind like glitter in a snow globe, that she didn't pay attention to where her feet were taking her.

Rounding a bend in the path, she came to the arbor where Rosamund York's life had ebbed away. Jane sat on the far end of the bench. Her eyes scanned the colorless garden until they settled on a cluster of snowdrops growing at the base of the arbor.

The bell-shaped flowers filled Jane with a sudden rush of joy. The afternoon was mild and the late-winter sun felt glorious on her skin. She sat quietly and dreamed of spring. Of cerulean skies, of guests strolling down garden paths, of the whoosh of falcon wings.

After several peaceful minutes, Jane plucked one of the tiny snowdrops and placed it on the bench where Rosamund's head had rested. Jane remembered standing in the rain on that early morning. She remembered watching the paramedics wheel Rosamund's body away. She remembered feeling that all was lost.

"'Winter is past,'" she whispered, repeating the Song of Solomon verse Sinclair had spoken earlier. "'The rain is changed, and is gone away.'"

As if responding to the words, more sunlight washed over the garden, brightening the darkest of shadows. The white snowdrops glowed like brides.

Jane smiled. She knew the warmth seeping into the nooks and crevices of her heart didn't come from the sun alone. It was the warmth of hope. Hope for the future of Storyton Hall. And the hope, as lovely and fragile as the fragile blossoms at her feet, that she would dance again.

Next time, Jane decided, there would be no music. There would be no candlelight. There would be no witnesses. There would be an exchange of truths. The secrets that she and Edwin kept must be shared. Only then could Jane step into Edwin's embrace and trust him to lead her in a slow waltz beneath the stars.

Jane took one last look at the snowdrops and thought of a line of poetry by Rainer Maria Rilke. "Spring has returned. The Earth is like a child that knows poems."

Glancing up at Storyton Hall, Jane saw poetry in every brick, in every winking window. She raised her eyes to the attic turret and silently recited their motto—*Their Stories Are Our Stories*—as though she were making a solemn oath. Which, of course, she was. She would share the stories that had been secreted away for far too long.

Finally, she turned and headed for home. She planned to fix herself a cup of lemon-ginger tea and pick a book from the stack on her coffee table. It didn't matter which title she chose, every book had something unique to offer. They were memories she'd yet to make. Worlds she'd yet to discover. Friends she'd yet to meet. And she was looking forward to making their acquaintance.

Dear Reader,

Thank you for spending time with Jane Steward, her family, the quirky merchants of Storyton Village, and the devoted staff of Storyton Hall. Jane and company will return in the summer of 2016 with the next installment in the Book Retreat Mysteries.

Until you're able to visit Storyton Hall again, I'd like to recommend another book-loving, mystery-solving ensemble. Olivia Limoges and her friends, the Bayside Book Writers, live in the quaint coastal town of Oyster Bay, North Carolina, and are deeply devoted to the written word.

In the next installment of the Books by the Bay Mysteries, Writing All Wrongs, Olivia Limoges and Sawyer Rawlings head to Palmetto Island to enjoy a brief honeymoon. The rest of the Bayside Book Writers, who arrive on the mysterious island to attend the Coastal Crime Festival, soon join them. The five friends expect to engage in crime-related events but when someone starts bringing famous local ghost stories to life, the writers soon realize that someone on the island is bent on murder, and if they don't catch the killer, they could be writing their last words.

For a taste of what's in store for Olivia and the Bayside Book Writers in Writing All Wrongs, coming November 2015 from Berkley Prime Crime, please turn the page for a special preview.

As always, thank you for supporting traditional mysteries.

Yours,
Ellery Adams

Marriage—a book of which the first chapter is written in poetry and the remaining chapters in prose.
                                        —BEVERLEY NICHOLS

"No one ever told me that marriage was murder," Olivia Limoges complained while pouring cream into her coffee.

Dixie Weaver, Olivia's longtime friend and proprietor of Grumpy's Diner, put her hand on her hip and smirked. "You haven't been married long enough to be comparin' the holy state of matrimony to a capital offense." She pursed her lips, which glistened with frosted pink gloss. "It's only been three months. What could be wrong?"

"Me. I'm what's wrong." Olivia stirred her spoon around and around, creating little whirlpools in the mug. "I've lived by myself all my life, Dixie. And though the chief and I spent a great deal of time together before we were married, he often slept at his house so he'd be close to the station. He kept things at my house—clothes and toiletries—but now his stuff is *everywhere*. It multiplies when I'm not watching, I swear."

Dixie shot a quick glance around the dining room. Her customers were either eating or chatting amiably over cups of coffee and no one appeared to need her. "What did you think would happen? That he'd go on livin' out of a drawer? The man's your husband now, 'Livia."

Olivia shook her head in exasperation. "That's not the problem. It's not about his things or the way he leaves globs of toothpaste in the sink. It's not about how he snores like a freight train when he sleeps on his back or how he'll finish the milk, but won't add it to the shopping list. I can handle that stuff. It's having him around all the time that's hard. I'm not used to having someone around *all* the time. Only Haviland." She looked down at her standard poodle with affection and he gazed up at her, his caramel brown eyes smiling.

Dixie gave the poodle's neck a fond pat. "You can't hold the chief up to Captain Haviland's standards. The poor guy is only human. And a damned fine human at that."

"I know." Olivia's voice crackled with anger. "He's a far better person than I am. He has no idea why I've been so moody. I'd just love to have my house to myself for a few days. Is that so strange?"

Dixie frowned. "Do you want your house to yourself? Or your life to yourself? 'Cause that's how this works. You're either together or you're not. You need to figure this out, hon. Aren't you headin' out on your delayed honeymoon in two days?"

Olivia nodded.

Dixie pointed at the television set mounted high behind the counter. Permanently tuned to The Weather Channel, the television's volume was muted, but the screen was visible from most of the Andrew Lloyd Webber–themed booths. The locals were always interested in the forecast. This was especially true for the fishermen, dockhands, and day laborers who filled the diner before the sun had risen. They'd order Grumpy's early-bird special—a hearty breakfast of eggs, sausage, toast, and hash browns—and drink cups of black coffee while watching the forecast. The tourists liked to keep tabs on the weather too. They'd plan their days based on what they saw while savoring Grumpy's maple pecan pancakes or three-cheese omelets.

"You're still leavin' on Tuesday?" Dixie asked. "Even though the tropical storm will hit Palmetto Island tonight?"

Olivia shrugged. "Rose is a category-two storm. I'm not

discounting its potential for making a mess, but even if Palmetto Island loses power, which is quite likely, we'll be fine. We'll do jigsaw puzzles, read by lantern light, and sit out on the deck with glasses of wine. If we want to have a honeymoon before the rest of the Bayside Book Writers join us, then we need to check into our rental house as scheduled."

A customer in the *Evita* booth signaled Dixie. She nodded in acknowledgment and then wagged her finger in warning at Olivia. "If there's trouble in paradise before the honeymoon, then this trip could make things worse. You'd best not pack your problems in your suitcase."

Having delivered her advice, Dixie skated across the linoleum floor. When she reached the *Evita* booth, she executed a graceful one-hundred-and-eighty-degree turn, causing her diaphanous tutu to float around her legs like a surfacing jellyfish, and handed her bemused customer the check.

After that, Dixie cruised around the dining room refilling coffee cups, clearing dirty plates, and collecting credit cards. Olivia watched her pensively. Even with the extra height lent by her roller skates and her blond hair, which had been sprayed into place until it resembled a shellacked soft-serve cone, Dixie was barely five feet tall. For someone with diminutive stature, her personality was large and loud. She spoke her mind without fear of consequence, and Olivia had always found that to be one of Dixie's most admirable qualities.

"She's right, Haviland. I need to deal with my issues before we leave. If not, our honeymoon will feel like a prison sentence."

"Have you seen the storm footage?" Rawlings asked Olivia later that night. "Rose is raging up the Cape Fear River. How do you think our rental house weathered the high winds?"

Olivia speared a piece of flounder and swirled it around the puddle of butter, lemon juice, and fresh dill on her plate. "It's probably seen worse. Hurricanes Floyd and Isabel, for example. Still, I can get by without electricity for a day or two."

Rawlings laughed. "I can't picture you eating pork and beans out of a can."

"As long as we can heat up grits in the morning and soup or pasta for lunch and supper, we won't suffer." She examined the food on her plate. "I guess it wouldn't hurt to ask one of the sous chefs at the Boot Top Bistro to pack us a hamper."

"There you go again." Rawlings made a clicking noise with his tongue. "Abusing your power."

"Me?" Olivia poked Rawlings with her fork. "What about you? Taking a vacation week before the season's officially over."

Rawlings studied the back of his hand with exaggerated concern. "It's September. Things are calm now that the season's over. Sure, they'll be a few more drunk and disorderlies and a scattering of reckless driving citations, but in another two weeks, things will be quiet, verging on dull."

Maybe that's my problem, Olivia thought. *I've been involved in so many of Rawlings's cases—the serious and scary ones. Maybe I don't know how to be with him when things are peaceful.*

"Where did you go just now?" Rawlings asked, calling Olivia back to the moment.

"I'm afraid I've been analyzing us," Olivia confessed. "I've been wondering why I've been restless since we exchanged vows. After all, you're the anchor I was looking for—the person I needed to save me from drifting. So why do I feel like cutting the mooring line? Just for a day or two?"

Such candor would have rankled other men, but not Rawlings. He gave Olivia a warm smile and covered her hand with his. "You're not the only one having trouble adjusting. I haven't put my house on the market, have I? I like to go over there and putter around. I only like to paint in that garage. The lighting's crap, the floors are hard, and it's cold as a meat locker. But it's my space. I've used every tool on the pegboard, built furniture on that workbench, and spent endless hours trying to turn a blank canvas into art. I can block out the world there."

"I guess this whole house has been my garage," Olivia said.

Rawlings nodded. "And now, I'm here. Every night. Every morning. You've lost your garage moments—that time when no one's watching. That's when you spill coffee all over your shirt and don't bother changing. Or sing along to some cheesy rock ballad at the top of your lungs. Or eat junk food like a varsity football player. Garage time."

Olivia grinned. "You haven't had much of that lately either."

"I know. I felt like I was supposed to be here. With you." He gave her hand a squeeze. "But we're both accustomed to time to ourselves, so let's take it when we need it. When we get back from our trip, we'll figure out how to do that."

"Okay," Olivia said, feeling lighter than she had in weeks. "Have you thought about what you want to pack?"

"A little. The whole station thinks we're nuts to combine a honeymoon with the Coastal Crime Fest, but what do they know? Stories, the seaside, and crime? They're the constants of my life." After pouring more white wine into Olivia's glass, he added a splash to his own. "The guys hassled me most about our spending part of the week with the Bayside Book Writers."

Olivia arched a brow. "What's wrong with that?"

"They think it's weird that we're not planning on spending the week in bed."

"That's because most of them are twenty years younger than us." Olivia scoffed. "Did you mention that we're bringing a thousand-piece jigsaw puzzle along?"

Rawlings wiped his mouth with his napkin. "I omitted that detail. In order to maintain my manly man status, I focused on pirate reenactments and the fact that Silas Black would be on the island scouting locations for his hit TV series. When they heard Mr. Black was the headliner at the crime festival, they stopped giving me grief and begged me to get paraphernalia from his show—preferably autographed."

"Harris is ecstatic over the idea of rubbing shoulders with Silas Black. He's read all of his novels and is a huge fan of his show. What's it called again?"

"*No Quarter*," Rawlings said. "You and I might be the only people in Oyster Bay who aren't parked in front of the television from nine to ten every Sunday night. It's all anyone talks about at the station on Monday mornings."

Olivia cleared their dishes and began to rinse them in the sink. "I'm not surprised. After all, the series was partially filmed in New Bern and Ocracoke. Personally, I'm for it because the film industry stimulates the local economy." She paused in the act of loading a plate into the dishwasher. "However, I read something in the *Gazette* several months ago about the liberties Mr. Black has taken with our region's history." She tried to remember the details. "Something about how vicious he made the pirates. And there was criticism about his use of violence—that he crossed a line with his graphic rape and torture scenes."

"Sounds like the majority of the programs on the premium cable channels."

"That's why I stick to *Masterpiece Theatre*," Olivia said.

Rawlings took Olivia's place at the sink. This was a nightly ritual. Olivia handled the dishes while Rawlings cleaned the pots and pans. "According to water-cooler gossip, Mr. Black is attempting to ingratiate himself with the inhabitants of Palmetto Island by financing the recovery of a shipwreck near Frying Pan Shoals. Apparently, the tropical storm preceding Rose carried the ship into shallower waters. Mr. Black hoped it would be a schooner from North Carolina's golden years of piracy, but it's a Civil War blockade-runner."

Olivia passed the dishtowel to Rawlings. "So let me get this straight. Not only are we attending the Coastal Crime Fest, but we're also going to be sharing an island with television people, underwater archaeologists, pirate reenactors, novelists, fans of the crime genre, and our friends?"

"Don't forget the conservationists. The Society for the Protection of the Loggerhead Turtle has been protesting a land development proposal for weeks. To raise money for their cause, they're hosting a moonlight march around the island. I think the walk takes place the same night the crime festival starts. The pirates sail in the following day."

Olivia picked up both wineglasses and pointed her chin toward the back deck. Rawlings opened the door and Haviland shot outside, barking in anticipation. He raced down the stairs and over the rise of dunes, the sea oats parting as he ran. Olivia drew in a deep breath of salt-laced air, and a breeze tinged with a metallic scent lifted her hair off her forehead.

"I can smell the storm," she said.

Rawlings stared out over the water, his gaze fixed to the south, where they'd soon be traveling. Eventually, he turned to look at the lighthouse, standing proudly on its bluff. "Not too long from now, we'll be seeing another lighthouse. The oldest in North Carolina." He smiled wistfully. "I climbed to the top dozens of times when I was a boy. It's what I remember most about the island. That, and the spit of land called Cape Fear. I always thought it was a strange name for a place of such incredible beauty. A place, for those not navigating the dangerous waters surrounding it, that was anything but fearful."

"Leona showed me some old maps of the island when I stopped by the library last week," Olivia said. Overhead, a scattering of stars tried unsuccessfully to burn through the cloud cover. Their soft, gauzy light made them look more like pearls than stars.

Not a helpful light. No good for a sailor navigating at night, Olivia thought. Aloud, she said, "Cape Fear used to be a sharper point. It jutted out into the ocean like a stingray tail. If you stood on its tip, you could see a virtual highway of ships in motion. Leona also showed me the area's shipwreck map. There are tons of wrecks around the island, Sawyer. Schooners, steamers, blockade-runners, fishing trawlers, pleasure boats. The Graveyard of the Atlantic, indeed."

Olivia watched the waves, which curled onto the shore with a languid murmur, but she knew that within the next twenty-four hours, they would change. The water would surge forward in jagged peaks; sand roiling under its surface; white froth, like the mouths of a thousand rabid animals, crashing against the beach.

"With all those wrecks, it's no wonder our coast has been the source of so many ghost stories," Rawlings said. "I'm sure we'll hear some choice tales this weekend."

"I like ghost stories," Olivia said, her gaze sliding to the lighthouse keeper's cottage. Once, its rooms were haunted by Olivia's child self. A quiet, lonely girl with long legs, freckles, and sun-bleached hair.

I'm not alone anymore, Olivia thought and smiled at Rawlings.

Haviland returned and sat on his haunches next to Olivia. His eyes seemed tuned to the shimmering path on the water created by the lighthouse beacon. Rawlings looked at it too. As if to himself, he whispered,

> *So from the world of spirits there descends*
> *A bridge of light, connecting it with this,*
> *O'er whose unsteady floor, that sways and bends,*
> *Wander our thoughts above the dark abyss.*

Olivia squeezed his hand until he turned away from the sea and met her gaze. "We can save both the ghost stories and unsettling poetry for our trip," she said, feeling a sudden chill. "Let's go in."

"All right. No more Longfellow." Rawlings stood up, collected the wineglasses, and went into the house. After casting a final glance at the water, Olivia called for Haviland and then shut the door. The sound of the waves was diminished, but not gone.

As Olivia lay in bed, they lulled her to sleep. She dreamed of shipwrecks. Of wooden carcasses. Large black smudges in a black sea. In her dreams, the sails were raised. And they rippled as if still being filled by a ghostly wind.

Two days later, Olivia parked her Range Rover in the ferry terminal lot.

Rawlings jerked his thumb at the back of the car. "I'm going to track down a luggage cart. There's no way we can haul all of this gear onboard by ourselves."

Olivia shot him a wry grin. "It's just a few staples."

"A pair of suitcases, grocery bags, a packed cooler, and a waterproof bin filled with books, flashlights, and jigsaw puzzles. Staples, eh?"

Olivia shrugged. "The electricity's out across the island. Just because we're without modern conveniences, doesn't mean we can't be comfortable. And well fed. Michel packed us a special honeymoon hamper." She shook her head in distaste. "I feel stupid using that word. It should be relegated to greeting cards or travel brochures."

Rawlings laughed. "From henceforth, I shall refer to this time together as a marital retreat. Better?"

Olivia tossed a balled-up napkin at him. "No! We'd better hurry. Our ride leaves in fifteen minutes."

Later, Olivia stood on the ferry's lower deck, holding the end of Haviland's leash tightly as the crew cast off. Rawlings was nowhere in sight. He'd left to explore the rest of the boat the moment the ferry eased away from the dock, his eyes gleaming like a boy's.

When the ferry entered the channel, Olivia noticed a concrete platform sitting squarely in the busy waterway. The potentially dangerous obstacle seemed overtly out of place. Curious, Olivia approached a deckhand and pointed at the platform. "Excuse me. What is that?"

"Quarantine pad, ma'am," the man answered. "From the old days. Ships had to dock at the quarantine station before they could continue to any port. Folks were terrified of catchin' diseases like yellow fever or smallpox. They had no way to fight 'em, so they did their best to keep 'em out. That platform has been there since the late 1800s and probably saved thousands of lives. There were buildings at the station too, but they burned. Every one. All that's left is the pad."

"Isn't that hunk of concrete a hazard for ships? Especially at night?"

The man issued a noncommittal grunt. "It's on all the nautical charts. Has a light on it now too. The Coast Guard added it after a lady was killed in a boating accident. Sad business, that." He swept his arm in a wide arc, incorporating the surrounding waters. "There's all kinds of hazards here, ma'am. Everywhere you look. Shallows, sandbars, shoals. Hidden bits of reef that'll tear your hull in two—you don't take to these waters without a healthy dose of fear. Even the most seasoned captains say a prayer before they head out for Cape Fear."

"I grew up with fishermen and learned that it's unwise not to respect the ocean." Olivia glanced around the ferry deck. She guessed there were fewer occupants on board than usual. "Did Rose make a big mess?"

The man followed her gaze. "Nothin' serious. Trees down. Power outages. Some of the roads flooded, but in a day or two, we'll have forgotten about Rose." He grinned, displaying a row of tobacco-stained teeth. "A storm has to work much harder than that to impress us." He lifted his chin to indicate a fellow crewmember coiling a length of rope on the port side. The man's face was weathered by years of working outdoors and his thick hands and forearms were scarred by rope burns.

"What brings you to Palmetto Island?" the crewman asked. "The crime festival?"

Olivia nodded. "Yes. My husband grew up hearing tales of buried treasure from his grandfather and he's trying to turn those stories into a book."

"Silas Black sure made a bundle off our history," the crewman grumbled and then instantly brightened. "But they say he might film episodes of his show on the island. Even hire some local folks as extras. I'd sure get the ladies' attention if I was on TV. They're not real impressed when I say that I work on the ferry, but if I said I was a pirate on Black's show? I'd be like a rooster in the hen house."

He laughed and Olivia joined in. Raising her head, she saw Rawlings leaning over the rail of the upper deck, waiting to catch her eye. He waved for her to join him.

"I think you'd make a fine pirate. Good luck," Olivia told the friendly crewman and whistled at Haviland to heel.

On the top deck, Olivia and Rawlings watched brown pelicans dive bomb into the water. A particular swift bird off the port side captured a fish, and it glinted like a silver coin in his bill, and then, in a flash, it was gone, disappearing down the bird's throat. Out in the open, Olivia shivered. The air had a crisp edge to it. It was ocean air. Air that swirled around the humped backs of whales. Air sliced by freighter bows and shark fins. It spoke of the end of tourists and the beginning of gray skies and deserted beaches.

Another ten minutes passed before Olivia spotted the island's lighthouse. It wasn't as tall as Oyster Bay's, but there was something profoundly comforting about the solid pillar of white standing guard over the harbor. Olivia kept her eyes on the old structure until the ferry docked.

As she, Rawlings, and Haviland disembarked, Olivia noticed that signs advertising the crime fest had been stapled to every pylon. Each poster featured a skull and crossbones motif and a list of festival highlights. At the end of the dock, a black banner flapped in the wind.

"Has the arrival area changed much since you were here last?" Olivia asked Rawlings.

"That was a million years ago, so yes." He pointed at a large building at the end of the pier. "This marina wasn't here. That hotel had a different name, and the houses surrounding the docks were small and modest. The boats were mostly fishing vessels or skiffs, not these luxury powerboats or yachts. And there were no slips. Just a long dock for loading and unloading." He shrugged. "It's the same as Oyster Bay, I guess. When you and I were young, our town was as yet still undiscovered. Palmetto Island was meant to attract tourists from much earlier on than Oyster Bay, but it wasn't nearly as developed as it is now." He gestured at the hotel. "It's all marshland behind there. No good for building, but the perfect habitat for alligators. If I didn't see at least one gator while visiting my grandparents, I was crushed."

Olivia glanced down at Haviland. "Did you hear that, Captain? Alligators. You have to wear this collar all the time."

Haviland sniffed the air, his black nose quivering. His eyes darted wildly around and he pranced on the pads of his feet in anticipation.

"I think he's picked up a scent coming from that seafood restaurant," Rawlings said.

Olivia gave the poodle's head an affectionate pat. "We'll check out the eateries later, Captain. We need to rent a golf cart first."

Rawlings told Olivia to join the queue in front of the rental shack while he tracked down their luggage.

Just as Olivia and Haviland got in line behind a couple in their early twenties, the young woman let out a dramatic gasp and tugged on her boyfriend's arm. "OMG, there's Leigh Whitlow! See? She's in that golf cart behind the hotel. I can't believe she's really *here*!"

The boyfriend cast a disinterested glance at a slim woman with tanning-bed skin and glossy brown hair. "Who?"

"Seriously? Do you live under a rock?" The woman nudged her boyfriend. "That's Silas Black's girlfriend. *Everyone* knows who she is."

The boyfriend shrugged. "If she was a tavern wench on *No Quarter*, then I'd recognize her. That woman looks kind of used up. You sure Black is banging *her*?"

What a gem, Olivia thought, glaring daggers at the back of the young man's skull.

"Hello? I know my celebrities." The woman pretended to be offended, but she was too fascinated by Leigh Whitlow to maintain the act. "She is *so* thin. I think she looks great for someone in her forties. Shoot, she might even be *fifty*."

The boyfriend pushed his sunglasses onto his forehead and focused on the dark-haired woman in the golf cart. "She has to work hard to hold on to her man," he said. "He could probably have his pick of a hundred babes, so keeping him interested must be a full-time job."

Olivia would have loved nothing more than to push the jackass boyfriend right off the dock, but she knew she'd be stuck listening to him for at least another ten minutes. The line was moving at a snail's pace and there was no sign of Rawlings.

"There are rumors that Black is fooling around behind Leigh's back," the young woman said. "Some woman on his staff. A history geek. Can you imagine? Cheating on Leigh Whitlow with a nerd? Everyone knows that Leigh is one hundred percent psych-ward crazy. That's why Silas won't leave her. She'd kill any woman who dared to get between them. Oh, man, I am *so* glad we decided to come to this festival for extra credit, aren't you?"

The boyfriend was no longer listening. A trio of giggling high school girls had caught his attention and he was eying them appreciatively.

"If that nerd girl is on the island, there's going to be a bloodbath," the young woman gleefully predicted as the line finally moved forward. Having turned to the right in order to keep the large man standing in front of her from blocking her view of Leigh Whitlow, the young woman was completely unaware of the flirtatious glances being exchanged between her boyfriend and the three girls. "I mean it, Rob. If you came here hoping to learn about crime and violence for your creative writing paper, you might just get your wish. Leigh Whitlow's thrown jealous rages before. She drove Silas's convertible car into a lake this summer and threatened a cute fan who got too cozy with him at some book event in Chicago."

The line moved again, but the young woman didn't budge. Leigh Whitlow's slightest movement had her riveted. By every impatient flick of the famous woman's dark brown tresses, how she splayed her nails or adjusted the rings on her fingers, and by the way she stared straight ahead, her jaw set in a hard line.

"When will you finally lose it?" the young woman murmured, clearly reveling in Leigh's discontent. "When will your jealousy finally push you over the edge?"

At that moment, Rawlings came up alongside Olivia. Noticing her pinched expression, he whispered, "Is anything wrong?"

Before she could answer, a man hopped into Leigh's golf cart and shooed her into the passenger seat. Scowling fiercely, Leigh complied, and the pair drove off in a cloud of sand-colored dust.

"Not yet," Olivia said in answer to Rawlings's question. "But the day is still young."